2023

Dearest
MAMKA —

ENJOY
my
JOURNEY.!

Joan

# The Red Velvet Diary

Joan Isaacson

authorHOUSE®

AuthorHouse™
1663 Liberty Drive
Bloomington, IN 47403
www.authorhouse.com
Phone: 833-262-8899

Published by AuthorHouse  01/25/2021

ISBN: 978-1-6655-1488-0 (sc)
ISBN: 978-1-6655-1494-1 (e)

Print information available on the last page.

This book is printed on acid-free paper.

# Dedication

To the memory of my parents, Clorindo and
Lula, you raised five awesome people.
To my daughters, Cassie, Mica, and Rachel,
you taught me unconditional love.
To my grandchildren, Rocco, Lula, Carina,
AJ, Gia, and Adam. You fill my heart to
overflowing, and I wrote this for you.
To my husband Sheldon, you are my eternal soulmate.

# Acknowledgements

A few years ago, I started writing a journal for my grandchildren to tell them where they came from and introduce them to their ancestors. As I recounted tales of my youth and characters came to life, and the spirits of my mother and grandmother sat at my table and insisted on sharing their own stories. I found myself walking in their stockings and feeling their heartbeats.

My siblings were patient with my calls, texts, and e-mails. "Do you remember the time.....?" Or "What was that story Mom used to tell....?" So, I thank you all, Mike, Madeline, John, and Maria, for helping me remember and for your unwavering support along the way. Maria, my baby sister, thank you for letting me bother you day or night and for your insight and intelligence.

My first cousins in both Italy and Greece were generous with their time and research. When I visited them the year I started writing, I came home with a folder full of treasure in documents and dates invaluable to the story's timeline.

Lynn Dolynchuk at The Write Strategy, my editor and now friend, made me feel assured and confident and I knew I could turn to her for guidance and honesty. Thank you, Lynn.

To the team at Author House Publishing, thanks for your support and patience with this first-time novelist.

Sage Osa, my beautiful spiritual friend, I will never forget that you told me a very long time ago that I had to write it all down. You repeated it over and over until I listened, and it has been one of my most incredible journeys.

My grandchildren, Adam, Gia, Carina, Lula, AJ, and Rocco, you inspire me every day with your beautiful innocence, love, and joy. You are like a bouquet of hand-picked flowers chosen just for me.

Mike and Anibal, my handsome sons-in-law, thank you for your love and support and for not reminding me daily that I am a complete technological mess.!

Cassie, Mica, and Rachel, I suppose I can take a little credit for raising you into the amazing women you became. But, you have more than repaid me with your love and strength. Thanks for holding me up when I could barely stand.

Sheldon, you are my rock and my forever love. Thank you for encouraging me to find my voice. I'm glad I didn't listen to my mother when she said I shouldn't marry you. You are the best decision of my life.

# Contents

JOAN - New Haven, Connecticut - 2011......................................1

VANNA (Joan) - Chianchetelle, Italy - 1954 .........................14

JOAN - New York, New York - 1968...................................34

JOAN - New Haven, Connecticut - 2011................................47

ARGHIRULA - Athens, Greece - 1939 ...............................51

JOAN - New Haven, Connecticut - 2011................................60

MIRIAM (Maria) - Smyrna, Turkey - 1901...........................65

ARGHIRULA - Athens, Greece - 1939 ...............................73

JOAN - New Haven, Connecticut - 2011................................82

JOAN - Weehawken, New Jersey - 1968 ...............................90

JOAN - Weehawken, New Jersey - Summer, 1968 ..................99

MARIA - Athens, Greece - 1903.........................................105

ARGHIRULA - Athens, Greece - 1940..............................110

JOAN - New Haven, Connecticut - 2011..............................118

JOAN - Weehawken, New Jersey - 1968 ..............................122

MARIA - Athens, Greece - 1905.........................................130

MARIA - Athens, Greece - 1906.........................................135

ARGHIRULA - Athens, Greece - 1942................................141

ARGHIRULA - Athens, Greece - 1942................................149

ARGHIRULA - Athens, Greece - 1942................................155

MARIA - Athens, Greece - 1906............................................ 165

ARGHIRULA - Athens, Greece - 1942................................. 176

MARIA - Athens Greece - 1906............................................ 182

ARGHIRULA - Athens, Greece - 1942................................. 187

JOAN - New york, New York/ Weehawken, New
Jersey - 1968 .......................................................................... 193

MARIA - Athens, Greece - 1906............................................ 197

ARGHIRULA - Athens, Greece - 1942.................................205

ARGHIRULA - Athens, Greece - Christmas 1942............... 213

MARIA - Athens, Greece - 1906............................................ 216

ARGHIRULA - Athens, Greece - 1943................................. 221

MARIA - Athens, Greece - 1906............................................225

JOAN - Westport, Connecticut - 2011 ................................230

ARGHIRULA - Athens, Greece - 1943................................236

MARIA - Athens, Greece - 1906............................................250

ARGHIRULA - Athens, Greece - 1943................................256

MARIA - Athens, Greece/Odessa, Russia - 1906................ 276

JOAN - New york, New York/ Weehawken, New
Jersey - 1968 ..........................................................................289

ARGHIRULA - Athens, Greece - 1943................................298

MARIA - Odessa, Russia - 1906............................................ 312

LULA (ARGHIRULA) - Athens, Greece - 1943-44.............. 321

MARIA - Odessa, Russia - 1906............................................346

LULA - Athens, Greece - 1944 ............................................. 351

JOAN - Weehawken, New Jersey - 1969 .............................. 355

MARIA - Odessa, Russia - 1906............................................ 358

LULA - Athens, Greece/Chianchetelle, Italy - 1945............. 362

JOAN - Westport, Connecticut/New Haven,
Connecticut - 2011................................................................. 376

Epilogue ................................................................................381

# JOAN - New Haven, Connecticut - 2011

"It's NOT cancer!" I repeat.

I feel the color rush back to my cheeks. Still shaky, but standing more solidly than I had in months, I desperately try to make sense of recent events. It may not be cancer, but the fact remains that my husband of forty-two years is lying in a hospital bed unable to breathe without the help of a ventilator.

"What's wrong with him?" I feel less hopeful than I sound, although I am relieved that we are here at Yale-New Haven Hospital. *Can they fix him?* I'm not sure of anything. I hang onto each word as Dr. Takyar addresses us, glancing from one to the other.

"We don't know exactly. We'll prepare you tonight for a VATS in the morning." I must look confused because he explains, "We will perform a video-assisted thoracic surgery and take some samples from his lungs." I search for confidence but see only concern as he continues. "Mr. Isaacson, you will be intubated and placed in a medically induced coma before we perform the procedure." He turns to me. "Dr. Kim is the thoracic surgeon, and he will contact you after we take the samples."

I'm not sure what I expected, but in my confused and exhausted state, I hoped that they would have a quick fix, and we could go home based on the past few days' events. When the doctor leaves, Sheldon and I sit quietly, concerned, yet unable to speak. He falls asleep while I sit back in the big green chair and close my eyes.

My mind goes back to the early visits to Dr. Renser, Sheldon's doctor of 15 years. "I don't understand!" I complain, "This is his third time here, and he's still having trouble breathing."

Renser shuffles through the thick pile of loose sheets and notes in the paper folder marked *Sheldon Isaacson* as if it is the first time he's seen it. Without responding, he gets up holding his stupid stethoscope, places the diaphragm against Sheldon's chest, closes his eyes to listen, and proceeds to do the same in the back. "There's no problem, and everything sounds clear." He says without making eye contact.

Thoroughly exasperated, knowing all too well how my husband has been feeling, I refuse to be dismissed. "Can we request an X-ray?" I ask. *Really? Why do I have to ask for this? I can't stand this guy!*

"We can take one, but it all sounds clear!"

*Is he just arrogant or a true ass?* A dozen unkind words pop into my mind.

Although it is minimal, the X-ray shows a dark spot, which is possibly pneumonia. It is barely visible, but it is there, nonetheless. "I am going to prescribe an antibiotic...

all should be clear within a few days," the good doctor informs us. Sheldon is relieved, but I am angry!

"We are scheduled to go on vacation this Saturday. Do you think it's OK?" asks Sheldon.

My brain is screaming, "Shel, you're worried about vacation?"

They continue their discussion, "Where are you going?" asks the marvelous medic.

"St. Martin," Sheldon responds.

"The sunshine will be beneficial!" says the sage, with authority. "You should go! I'm going on vacation too!"

*Asshole!*

What starts as a simple discussion turns into a fight. "Let's cancel the trip, Shel!"

"No!" he is emphatic. "I'll be better in a few days, and honestly, the thought of warm weather sounds great! You heard the doctor, and the sunshine will do me good!" As if to emphasize, he pulls the scarf closer to his neck.

Over the next two days, he feels tired, and his normal breathing has yet to return.

"Let's cancel the trip!" I must have said this ten times in the last forty-eight hours, but he does not want to discuss it.

"I'm feeling better!" he insists. "I think the antibiotics are working, and I'm looking forward to laying in the sun." So we pack our bags and go.

Mike picks us up at the airport, and since they have already been here a week, he tells us the plans for the next few days. Because Linda's sister is the ultimate planner, this vacation requires very little thinking on my part. However, since the flight has taken its toll on Sheldon, and his breathing is more challenged than it had been at home, we bow out of tonight's dinner plans.

Sheldon sleeps all afternoon while I sit at the pool and read my new book, *Fifty Shades of Grey*. I order dinner from The Hideaway Restaurant, which is on the premises, and I take it back to the room. Sheldon tells me he feels much better and eats most of the mango mozzarella salad and Caribbean chicken that I brought to share.

"You look better!" I'm happy to tell him.

Nodding in agreement, he suggests, "Let's go out to the pool and have a drink at the bar."

I am thrilled that he is proposing this, and I believe that the medication is beginning to kick in. He orders an unsweetened iced tea, and I have two BBC's, and tonight feels like a vacation as I am warm from the day in the sun and happy in my sandals and sundress.

Back in our unit, we turn on the TV and he is asleep and snoring within five minutes. I return to reading my book, which is by no means literary genius and just short of soft pornography. Bored and a little buzzed, I am compelled to keep reading even though I know there will be no romance tonight. The realization sucks as this book is making me horny.

We awaken to a perfectly sunny day and temperature near 80 degrees, and I admire the beautiful blue of the St. Martin sky. My cell phone rings and Linda asks, "Do you want to have breakfast with us?" Sheldon says he feels well, so he agrees. A half hour later, we meet the others at Turtle Pier.

John and Joan and Jimmy and Joanne are already seated

at a large table, so we join them and catch up from the last time we were together in New Jersey. Having known each other since high school, we repeat old stories and share great memories. Breakfast is delicious, and the conversation turns to which of the many spectacular beaches we should visit today.

Joan says, "We'll go to Simpson Bay and enjoy the further away beaches later in the week when Sheldon will be feeling better." I'm grateful and know that she and Linda have already figured it out. So after breakfast, we head to Simpson Bay and reserve our chairs for the day.

Few places in the world offer spots that look and feel like St. Martin's Caribbean beaches. The color of the water is almost turquoise, and the sand is perfectly textured. Sheldon ambles from the car to the cushioned lounge chair and, once seated, stays in it most of the day. Our usual beach walks are out of the question.

My family and friends are so rightly concerned about the situation, and we collectively try to guess and project without really coming up with anything concrete. I spend the day chatting and sunning and reading my book, while in the back of my mind is a nagging feeling of doom. But, we are here where he wants to be, and in all our years together, Sheldon has always had the right gut instincts.

We pass on going to dinner again tonight, and although Sheldon and the others try to convince me to join the crowd, I won't leave him. I resolve myself to another evening of reading.

The remainder of the week, we have two failed beach attempts, three pool visits, one restaurant meal and for Sheldon, sleep, sleep, and more sleep.

The tremors start on Wednesday night, and the first one is an absolute surprise.

"You don't look well," I say, watching him covering up with a blanket.

"Yea, I don't feel great..." he responds. "I have the worst chills!"

I touch his head. "You are burning up!" I gasp, surprised at how hot his head feels. Within fifteen minutes, his body is shivering, and he gets progressively worse, with his body shaking and teeth chattering. The episode passes reasonably quickly, but it terrifies me.

The second episode comes the next morning as I am making coffee in the kitchenette. I put a sweatshirt on him and then a blanket, thinking that he needs to be warmed up, but I soon understand it has nothing to do with heat.

"Do you think you should go to the hospital?"

"No!" He is emphatic about not going to see a doctor. "When the chills stop, I feel fine!"

When his body has been calm for an hour, he suggests that we go to the pool and, surprised that he is up for it, I take it as a good sign. We stay at the pool for a few hours after the breakfast that he barely touched, but the sun is shining, and he is a trooper. As he naps, I read my book.

By Friday night, the tremors are more frequent, and the shaking is often uncontrollable. I feel helpless as I wrap my arms around him and lean my full body weight on him. I'd like to believe that this slows down the shaking, but I know I am fooling myself into thinking that this helps.

I call Mica, "Can you get a recommendation for a pulmonologist and get us the earliest appointment possible? We'll be home tomorrow night."

I chastise myself over and over for not seeing a specialist before we came here. But, I can't change what has already happened, and I'm trying to deal as best I can under the weight of this surreal situation. I feel helpless in the face of my reality, and I admonish myself that we are here, in a foreign country when I should have followed my instincts to stay home.

Jimmy holds Sheldon's arm to help him manage the steps, and I see that he has pulled the car half-way up the narrow walking path and as far as it could go without touching the wall. I murmur a grateful "thank you" as we guide Sheldon into the front seat. When we reach the airport, Jimmy handles the check-in, arranges for a wheelchair, and takes Sheldon to a remote corner just as one of the tremors starts. We hope that no one notices that he is sick or tries to stop us from boarding.

I take the middle spot, and we help Sheldon occupy the aisle. The minute he sits, he puts his forehead against the back of the seat in front of him and does not move. Fortunately, the young woman at the window alternates between sleep and reading for the entire four-hour flight, and Sheldon stays motionless until we land in Newark.

With Sheldon safely in the back seat of a limo, I say good-bye to our friends, "I couldn't have done this without you! Thank you!" Holding back tears, I climb into the car next to my husband. The ride is uneventful, although it feels eternal. Sheldon remains in and out of sleep as he continues his struggle to breathe, and I say a heartfelt prayer as I thank God that I am home.

Sunday is our anxious waiting day, and no doubt, he is slipping. Dr. Cochran sees us at 9:00 a.m. on Monday, and although Rachel and I are early for the appointment, it is a brief examination, and the doctor has a good poker face.

"Take him to Norwalk Hospital emergency. It's the best way to get him admitted quickly, and I will go see him as soon as they settle him."

It all feels strangely calm and well organized, and I am grateful that we are back in Connecticut and that the wheels are back on. Rachel takes us to the emergency room, and there is barely a wait before they accept Sheldon in one of the pods. He is given a bed within an hour, and Dr. Cochran, true to his word, shows up to examine him and confer with the hospital staff.

After two days, other than establishing that they have an extremely sick man on their hands, the doctors at Norwalk Hospital seem bewildered by Sheldon's condition. They have found that it is not pneumonia, but his lungs are solidifying, and there is no explanation nor an immediate plan of action. In my desperate state of mind and old school belief that doctors will always cure, it takes a bit of time to realize that nobody here has any idea of what to do next. I see only questioning looks and actual head-scratching as a team of doctors circles Sheldon's bed.

Nothing changes in the next two days, other than that they give him enough oxygen to keep him breathing. Dr. David Lorenz, Sheldon's cardiologist, arrives to examine his heart, and I am comforted that we can speak as friends. He sits with me and patiently listens as I tell him what has happened since Sheldon first felt ill. I tell him the whole story, including the fact that we were in Egypt in October, a few months before it all started. "I have more than once wondered if there is some connection!" When I finish, I am drained and afraid, but mostly grateful for his emotional support. Finally, wiping my tears, I ask him, "What would you do if this were your dad?"

Without skipping a beat, he responds, "I would take him out of here!"

By eleven p.m., Dr. Cochran signs the necessary transfer papers. Sheldon is admitted to Yale-New Haven Hospital and not a moment too soon. During his first night here, and in the few short hours when I am home catching up on desperately needed sleep, he suffers a coughing attack of monumental proportions.

Since I was not there, Dr. Takyar explains what happened, and I am selfishly glad that I did not have to witness the incident. He explains that they treated him for the cough and stabilized his breathing. I think of what the outcome could have been if he were not herc, and I thank the universe for creating the proper path. Although there is no real improvement, I feel somewhat reassured by the efficiency of these doctors and nurses and the strength of my daughters, who barely leave my side.

As I gaze mindlessly outside, my eyes rest on the windows two floors down and across, where the building creates a U shape. I realize that I am looking at Smilow's Children's Cancer Center. The lineup of stuffed toys on the window sills transfixes me. My heart is gripped by pain for the parents sitting with their children in these rooms. How do they do it? Tears well from deep inside, and a tear falls down my cheek as I try to calm my tangled mind.

I hear their voices and turn to see the girls speaking softly to their dad. As I wipe my eyes, I take in the heart-wrenching scene. They lean in and take turns, holding his hands as they tease him. I can barely hear him as he engages, but the girls laugh. He dozes and awakens with the air they give him, and eventually, he falls into a deep sleep.

"Hey, Mom, how are you doing?" Rachel moves closer to me. My baby girl, who now has two baby girls of her own. "Are you OK? Dad told us what's happening tomorrow. This is good, right? Maybe they can figure out what the hell is wrong with him! How long has it been, like two months, that he hasn't been able to breathe properly? He's in the right place now. They'll know what to do, right?"

I honestly have no idea, but try to sound confident, knowing full well that Sheldon would minimize the severity of the situation so the girls wouldn't be frightened. "Yea, this is the best place for lung issues, so I'm sure it will be OK!" I offer comfort but not without wondering if my words sound as hollow to her as they do to me.

"Dad's asleep, Mom. Let's go down to the cafeteria. Did you eat today?" Mica takes my arm and leads me towards the door.

She drove with me last night as we followed the ambulance that transferred Sheldon from Norwalk Hospital. The ambulance, for some reason, kept the inside lights on. It was disturbing that I could see him in that sad state, and I insisted that it must be uncomfortable for him with the blaring brightness. Mica, ever the voice of reason, calmly responds, "It's OK, Mom, I'm sure he's sleeping, and it's bothering you more than it is him."

"Cas, let's go downstairs to get some coffee." Cassie moves towards us, with her notebook, asking for details of our conversation with Dr. Takyar, and I am comforted, beyond words, to have my girls here with me. The snack bar is open all night, and I notice that, in addition to sandwiches and muffins, they offer sushi, which seems so random. I have no appetite, but the girls encourage me to eat part of a corn muffin and a cup of tea.

The conversation doesn't stray far from Dad's situation and that the kids are asking where Poppy has been. Not to mention, Lila, our Shih Tzu, who is moping around, sensing that there is something wrong.

"I don't get it, Mom!" Cassie has been diligently searching the internet. "His doctor couldn't tell that he was breathing less and less?"

Hearing this, I immediately blame myself. "I know! I should have insisted on taking him to a pulmonologist." I take responsibility, although I can't help but blame Dr. Renser for not recommending it.

When the girls leave, I take the elevator to the 9th floor, still uncomfortable because I am at the Smilow Cancer Hospital Medical Intensive Care Unit. I remind myself that there is NO CANCER, and I find some comfort in those words, thinking of my father, who died of lung cancer at 66, the same age Sheldon is now.

I walk in softly, thinking he is asleep, but he says, "Hey!" I sit next to the bed in the dim light and take his hand.

"How are you feeling?" I whisper, knowing full well what the answer will be.

"Like shit!" he says, and we both chuckle.

As we hold hands, I can't help but wonder if I am overreacting as I choke back tears. "I'm scared, Shel!"

It takes some effort to speak, but he pats the bed and attempts to give me some space. I lie down next to him as best I can, without interfering with the tubes and wires. He reaches for my hand, and we lie still, but I sense that he is dozing before long.

I listen to the forced breathing behind his mask, and each choked breath is a stab to my heart.

When he moves, I realize that I dozed off too, and as I acclimate myself to the surroundings, I respond to my husband as he squeezes my hand. I focus on the fact that, in a few hours, they will perform some surgery and they will fix him. *They WILL fix him. Right?*

The speed with which he has deteriorated in the past few days concerns me greatly. Although I take comfort in the fact that we are in this hospital, I can only imagine his discomfort and fear. The description of the VATS thoracic surgery scheduled for the morning is frightening, but since he has not breathed normally in weeks, our options are few, and we must rely on these professionals.

When he squeezes my hand, I see his face behind the oxygen mask and, through my own tears, I look at his brimming eyes. Assuming that he is afraid of the procedure, I try to reassure him. But, he shakes his head as he struggles to speak. I lean in towards his raspy effort.

"I love you," he says so quietly that I can barely hear him.

I choke up, "I know...I love you, too..."

He is very still as he gathers his thoughts and whispers between tears.

"Joanie".

I wait and he sobs as he struggles to breathe. After a short exhale, he squeezes my hand and continues,

"We have had more love in one day than many people have in a whole lifetime."

I crumble and I break after my fortitude of the weeks preceding this moment. We cry uncontrollably, that massive cry when you feel deep in your core that the entire world is about to implode.

# VANNA (Joan) - Chianchetelle, Italy - 1954

I open my eyes and my first thought is, *today is my birthday*! I am seven years old! But my excitement soon turns to sadness. This will be my last birthday in this bed, in this house, in this town..... I will celebrate my 8th birthday in America. It's difficult for me to picture living in a different place. A place where my grandparents, aunts, uncles and cousins won't be.

I get up trying to be quiet so that I don't wake my sister or the baby. I tap my brother's shoulder as I pass by. Michelino wakes up right away and even though he acts annoyed, he doesn't linger in bed because he knows it's a school day. We both tip toe across the floor, but the baby still starts to cry. My mother comes in the room to pick up Gianfranco, while Maida, continuing to softly snore, doesn't even stir.

There, in the kitchen, laid across two chairs, are our school clothes. But the typical rush to get dressed and eat our breakfast *zuppetta* is interrupted.

"Buon Compleanno, Vanna," my mother says, holding

Gianfranco in her arms. She hugs me with her free arm and points in the direction of a small package. On top of the box is a letter addressed to me and I immediately recognize my father's beautiful large script.

I open the gift first. I think I know what it is and I am not disappointed. I take out a small blackboard and a piece of chalk and I write "Vanna DiGiovanni" across the board that perfectly fits my lap. I smile at my mother. "Grazie." She smiles back distractedly, while nursing the baby.

I become aware that the time is late so I help Michelino tear up the bread and pour on the milk. I put sugar in our separate bowls and we both use more than we should. As I eat, I open the letter from Babbuccio and it makes me feel as though he is sitting right here talking to me in his soft, gentle way. I miss him so much. The only good part about going to America is that we will be together again.

We finish our breakfast and gather our books. My mother kisses us briskly, returning her attention to the baby. Before I leave, I kiss the baby good-bye. I love how he smells and I look forward to holding him when I get home from school.

The school room is arranged in four rows with desks lined up side-by-side. Michelino sits near the back with two other boys. I am one of the youngest in the class and I sit near the front, next to a boy about my age. We always sit together because we need to share our books. But we all have the same teacher - Signora Brigida. I love school, which is why I wanted the blackboard and chalk. I can hardly wait to play with my sister because she is brilliant for her age and I just know she will love school too.

15

After school, we walk to my grandparents' house where the kitchen is always warm and something is always cooking. This is where the family gathers and where Mammina and the baby are already sitting in front of the fireplace. My aunts are busy moving around the kitchen. And my grandmother? I don't think she ever sits still.

Everyone takes care of each other. Zia Vittoria takes Gianfranco from my mother's lap and coos and kisses him. Zia Giovannella is trying to feed my cousin Enrico with a spoon. He is two years younger than me. He can't speak or walk and is strapped into a unique chair. I don't know what is wrong with him, but I know he is different. He can't play with us, so the rest of us kids don't bother with him too much.

I turn my attention to the immense cauldron hanging over the fire. "Nonna, sono pronte le mele?" *Are the apples ready?* They smell so good.

She gives me a little shoo with her dishtowel. "Esci, vai a giocare!" *Go out, go play!*

Banned from the kitchen, I run out the door towards the voices of my cousins and brother and sister. They are following my grandfather around the garden as he picks up branches and clears the garden for spring planting.

Papanonno directs us towards a spot where there are lots of dead branches and leaves. "Dovete pulire questo!" *Clean this up!* He opens his arms wide to show the area and then points to a small pile where we are to put everything. Some branches are large so we need to help each other and keep focused on the job. But when Nonno walks past me towards the field, I notice a little smile on his face. *Is he just getting rid of us with busy work?*

16

Before long, we clear the area and Michelino announces, "Oh fame," which reminds me that I am hungry too! We run, all together, into the house - towards the delicious smell of cooked apples. Zia Anna tells us to stop running and to quiet down!

Mammina has moved from the fireplace to the table. My mother is so beautiful. Her stylish hair is always in order, her nails are polished and she wears red lipstick. My aunts don't paint their nails or wear red lipstick. Neither does Giuseppina, the woman who cleans our house and does our laundry and ironing. More than once, I have heard my aunts refer to my mother as *La Greca*. I guess that's because she comes from Greece, but somehow it sounds like a bad thing.

"Mammanonna, le possiamo mangiare?" we plead. *Can we eat them now?*

She turns to us and offers an exaggerated scold, "Andate, andate!"

We all giggle but refuse to leave. As Zia Anna brings plates to the fireplace, my grandmother scoops out the best apples, and generously sprinkles them with cinnamon and sugar. We each take our dish to the long table where we eat greedily, and in no time, have a second helping.

"Andate! Uscite, uscite!" my aunt says while gathering the empty dishes. With full tummies and happy hearts, we run out the door to play until dinner is ready.

Raffaele sees my grandfather in the field and hoping for another job, we all run towards him. By the time we get there, Nonno is climbing a tall ladder that leans against the barn. He is halfway up when my cousin steps on the first rung. Nonno completely ignores us, so we are encouraged and begin to giggle as we climb the ladder behind Raffaele. I can't believe that my grandfather is not telling us to get down! We are lined up, one behind the other, with Pino, the youngest, at the bottom.

We laugh and make lots of noise, but our laughter is not loud enough to silence the roar of flatulence generated from my grandfather's behind - a stream of it, and directly in Raffaele's face. As part of his calculated plan, Nonno continues to act as if we are not there. Raffaele screams for us to get off the ladder as he frantically moves his face from side to side. Meanwhile, Pino finds that his three-year old legs are having difficulty making contact with the ground, so the process takes far too long. By now, we are all gagging, and poor Raffaele looks as if he will throw up. My grandfather's control is most impressive. He continues to fart and pretend that he doesn't know we're there.

When we finally escape the putrid smell, we run to the house and sit on the steps, laughing uncontrollably. Michelino is the first to try to fart like Nonno, followed by the other boys, including Pino. Nobody can come close!

When Papanonno comes inside for *il pranzo*, he washes up and sits at the head of the table. He never once mentions the ladder episode, or even that he saw us outside. But I notice a little smile on his face as he reaches for a handful of *cicole*. Mammanonna continues to fry more in boiling oil, drains them, and puts them on a large plate in the middle of the table where they disappear as quickly as they appear. They may only be little pieces of pig skin, but I think they are the most delicious thing I have ever tasted. But I think that for the rest of my life, I will connect them with farts.

Eventually, everyone sits down for *maccheroni, braciole and insalata*. Our meals are always noisy. We listen to what everyone has to say, even the youngest of us, although my uncles do most of the talking. Today, the talk is mostly about Pino, who is sitting on Nonno's lap.

Yesterday, Don Antonio, our priest, reprimanded Pino because he always needs reprimanding. Pino looked him right in his face and said, "vaffanculo." *Fuck you.* TO THE PRIEST! When we heard him, we ran away because we thought we would all be in big trouble. We weren't, but I think that Pino must be in trouble now! It made me happy to hear my uncles start to laugh. Zio Alberto, Pino's father, pretends to be angry, but he is laughing too! Sometimes, it's hard to tell what adults are thinking.

When we finish our meal, my mother puts the baby in the carriage, and Michelino holds one side while I hold the other. Maida hangs on to the back of my shirt like she always does when we walk together. As soon as we turn the bend, I can see that someone is standing in front of our house. Even from a distance I know who it is. He is tall and well dressed and he is our family doctor and my father's friend.

When we reach our house, he greets us with a big smile and ruffles the top of my brother's head, asking how we enjoyed our meal. My mother smiles her sweetest red-lipsticked smile. After a quick "hello," we proceed to run around looking for the lizard that Michelino said just ran past Maida's foot.

Before long, the sun begins to set and my mother tells us that we must go inside, and without argument, we obey. When we enter the chilly house, Mammina checks the brazier and sees that it needs more coal. It's Michelino's job to fill the brazier with coal from the metal box in the corner of the room, but today, Dr. Pallezzi helps with the chore. When the coals are lit, Mammina tells us to wash up for bed and to read a book. The baby starts fussing, so she changes his diaper and swaddles him with an extra blanket. With her back to the wall, she begins to nurse him. I notice Dr. Pallezzi looking in her direction. At first it seems strange, but then I remember that he is a doctor, and the one who delivered my baby brother.

Dressed in our pajamas, we brush our teeth and sprawl on the sofa. I read a story to Maida, and I don't stumble at all because I'm a good reader. My sister leans against me and looks at the pretty pictures in the oversized book. Michelino is only half listening as he plays with a piece of wood that he picked up when we were outside. I think he's making a cross to put on the grave of the next lizard we catch. We have a rule that if we kill a lizard, we have to be respectful so we bury it properly and say an entire prayer.

When I notice Maida's eyes begin to close, I realize that I am also tired of reading, so I close the book and say, "Andiamo a letto," *Let's go to bed.* Michelino takes his time and Maida, suddenly awake, takes the book to look at more pictures. My mother has since taken the baby to her bedroom and I go to her to tell her we are ready for bed. I find her sitting on the edge of the bed with Dr. Pallezzi, both of them smiling down at Gianfranco, who is resting in my mother's arms. My brother and sister show up at that moment, and my mother calmly walks us to our beds.

As I begin to doze, I remember the night Gianfranco was born on December 15ᵗʰ, just a few months ago. Babbuccio woke us in the middle of the night to tell us we must go to Zia Vittoria's house because, "Il bambino arriva!" *The baby is coming!*

Going to my aunt's house is not unusual, except this night, it was. Instead of going through the front door, my father pushed aside a large dresser, exposing a door that connected our house to Zia's! I never knew that door was there! He herded us through the small doorway and my aunt guided us all to her big bed. Before long, Raffaele and Pino woke up from all the commotion and they joined us. Soon, we were all wide awake and predictably playing and jumping on the bed. Curiously, neither my aunt nor my uncle came in to yell at us.

We were enjoying our fun until suddenly my mother's scream pierced through the walls and we all cowered under the blankets. It stopped as abruptly as it started, but it was not long before another one followed full force and even louder. And so it went for a long time until, eventually, everything was calm and still. Maida and Pino had fallen sound asleep, but Michelino, Raffaele and I were still awake. Zio told us to go sleep, and since all was quiet, I closed my eyes and dozed off.

We awoke to Babbuccio's voice, softly telling us that we had a new baby brother and that it was time to come home. Excited, I ran ahead, back through the connecting door, and straight to my parents' bedroom. There was Mammina sitting up in bed, holding the new baby in her arms and there, perched on the edge of the bed was Dr. Pallezzi. They were both looking down and smiling. It felt as though I had interrupted a private moment. But before I had time to react, Michelino came running in.

"Venite!" said my mother, looking up. She was happy to see us and she patted the space next to her on the bed. We climbed up next to her and I got my first look at the baby. He was the most beautiful creature I had ever seen. I touched his tiny fingers, and Mammina made a game of counting his toes. He had the face of an angel, and I was instantly in love.

After Christmas, my father goes to America to prepare for our family to join him. He told us he will find a house for us and he will be working for his brother, my Uncle Harry. I don't know much about America or New Jersey, where we will be living. Babbuccio told us it is big, like Benevento, where there are buildings, cars, and lots of people. When I asked my parents why we have to leave our home, my father said, "We will live where I can work, and my children can have a better future." I guess this all makes sense to them, but it is hard and sad for me to imagine not living here in Chianchetelle, near my cousins and grandparents.

Enrico and Domenico are my father's brothers, and they live in New Jersey. Zio Enrico and Zia Maddalena, his wife, came to visit us a few times. One time, he brought his car on the ship, and he drove it to Chianchetelle from Naples. Michelino said it was a Buick from 1949, but I don't know anything about cars except that it was very big and black and shiny. All the kids sat on the hood, hanging on to the sides. My uncle drove it up the hill to my grandparents' house! I was worried that someone might fall off and get hurt, but he moved very slowly, and nobody fell, and we had so much fun! I guess we will also have a car like that when we live in New Jersey, America!

My uncles each own an embroidery factory in a town called West New York. I practice pronouncing the words so I can be ready for America. I even write it on my blackboard and make my brother and sister practice it with me. My father works for Zio Enrico in his factory, which is called "REX Embroidery."

My mother explains, "Fanno belli ricami!" *Embroidery.* She says that it is sold to clothing manufacturers in New York and is used on blouses and dresses. "During the war," she explains," the machines made patches for American soldiers' uniforms because it was the law that they had to make them in the United States."

Although I write them on my blackboard, sometimes it is hard for me to understand many things. My father is a watchman, so he operates large machines. He also puts the patterns into them. "The patterns are big rolls of paper with the design punched into them with tin holes." My mother is very good at describing things with her words, but sometimes I still have a hard time hard visualizing, just like I can't imagine living anywhere else in the world other than my house here.

"What day is Babbuccio coming home?" I ask. We are all lying on my mother's bed while she nurses the baby.

"Vanna, I told you yesterday, he is coming home next week, on Tuesday."

I already have this written on my blackboard. "But what is the date?" I ask her.

"Go look on the calendar," she says as she adjusts the baby.

I know she is just sending me away because I talk a lot, and she probably wants to relax while she is nursing the baby. Zio Alberto calls me *mosca cavallina*, horse fly, because I am always asking questions and circling the adults. My other uncles laugh when he says this, so I guess nobody minds and, besides, I can't help myself.

I wait for Maida, and she jumps off the bed. In the kitchen, I take the calendar from the nail and flip pages until I get to June.

Maida points to Tuesday and says," It will be June 8th when Babbuccio gets home!" I turn the calendar so we can look at the front page, and I remember the first time I saw it when Uncle Harry sent it to us. We could not stop gawking, just as we are doing now. The picture on the front, smiling back at us, is the face of a man who is eating a huge piece of watermelon! We have never before seen a person whose face is black and shiny. My mother says that there are many different people in the world, and some have skin color which sometimes is not the same as ours. I understand because there are some other skin colors among the people who live in our village, but we don't know anyone with skin this color. We especially love his big white teeth and agree that we can't wait to see more faces like this in New Jersey, America.

Today, my aunt and uncle stopped at our house on their way to Santa Margherita church for a wedding. I beg them to please, please, please let me go with them, and my uncle calls me "mosca cavallina," laughing at his old joke. My aunt tells me she will take me if I put on a beautiful dress and promise to stay quiet in church. I promise!

The wedding mass is very long, and my mind wanders, but I try to focus and listen to Don Antonio. Suddenly I have a disturbing thought! *How can two people promise to spend the rest of their lives together?* I start to worry about it, so I tap my aunt's arm, and she leans down to let me whisper in her ear. I notice she rolls her eyes, maybe because I promised that I would not speak in church. But this is important! "Zia, what happens if the bride says no?"

Without missing a beat, she responds, "If she says no, she has to take off her dress and run out of the church in her slip!"

Oh my! I hope she knows that! I wait until I hear the groom say "yes" and then hold my breath until the bride responds "yes!" and I exhale, very much relieved.

Maida and I take out the calendar every day the week before Babbuccio comes home and we mark every day with drawings of pretty flowers. The square that shows June 8th is filled with stars and hearts and it is very colorful. We wait all day, but there are delays and we fall asleep before he arrives. This morning I woke up to a kiss on my forehead and I opened my eyes to the smiling face of my father. I did not realize, until I started crying, just how much I missed him.

We are leaving Chianche on November 1ˢᵗ. I look at our watermelon calendar and see that it will be Monday. Mammina said I don't have to go to school this whole week to prepare for our journey. I help pack the trunks with our clothing and some things from the kitchen, mostly the aluminum pots.

I also ask if we can bring our six beautiful storybooks, and, although they are large, Babbuccio says, "Prenderli!" *Take them!* I sit on my bed and, looking down, ask about taking that, but he shakes his head no.

"Everything is ready in America, and your new bed is waiting for you to sleep in it!"

I have slept only in this bed as far back as I can remember, so I feel a little sad. My brother and sister don't look unhappy to me, but maybe they don't realize they won't take their beds either.

During the last few weeks, we have spent a lot of time with our grandparents, and they hug us and play with us even more than usual. I guess that is because they are used to having us around, and they will miss us until we see them again.

Today is Monday, and I am wide awake while it is still dark. Babbuccio said we all had to wake up early this morning because Naples is far away, and we have to get on the ship that will take us to America. Soon everyone is up and moving around fast.

Mammina nurses the baby and Babbuccio makes *zuppetta* for us and *un caffe* for my mother and himself. It is barely light, but my grandparents, aunts, uncles, and cousins are all outside our door offering hugs, kisses, and tearful good-byes as we pile into two cars to go to the port.

Maida and Michelino bicker and make a lot of noise, my mother fusses with the baby, and I watch my father quietly wipe his eyes. I take his hand, and he holds it tight. Everything is confusing even though I try to understand it all. One thing I know for sure is that I don't want to go to New Jersey!

Zio Attilio asks Michelino to come to talk to him before we get on the big ship. I suppose Zio wants to say a special good-bye to Michelino, and everyone knows he is his favorite.

When we finally board the ship, we have to stand in line to show our passports. My father has his own, and my mother's passport has a picture of her and the four children. It is sunny and hot, and the line moves very slowly, so we all take off our jackets, except for Michelino. He is standing next to my father with a solemn look on his face and his eyes stare straight ahead. He never even unbuttons his long gray wool coat, and I can't believe he is not feeling the heat like the rest of us.

I have never been on a ship before, and everything looks tremendous and very fancy. But, the cabin is small, and we all have to sleep in it. Babbuccio says, "We will be just fine! We are only sleeping here for seven nights, and there are a lot of spaces on the ship that we can explore when we are not sleeping!"

As he speaks, he carefully helps remove Michelino's coat, and they both check the inside pocket. I move closer as they examine the dry branch of a grapevine plant to ensure there is no damage. My father places it on a shelf at the top of the small closet. I don't understand why he is so secretive, but he turns to us and, placing a finger to his lips, says." Shhhhh!" Now I know why my brother was so careful to keep his coat buttoned. That was so brave, and I won't tell!

Dinner is in the beautiful dining room, where there are white tablecloths and fancy plates. Waiters serve us our food and pour water in our elegant glasses. Everything tastes good, and we get pastries for dessert. After dinner, we walk around the deck, and the kids walk ahead. Gianfranco saunters holding my mother's hand, but mostly my father carries him. It is fun because my parents don't stop us from running. My father tells us there are three swimming pools on the ship, similar to the one we see here. We have never before seen a swimming pool, and it is beautiful, but it is too cold to go in it. Someone said that the first-class pool has heated water! I have never heard of such a thing, and I can't even imagine it! Also, I don't know what first class means.

Today, we met a boy named Michael. He is a little older than me, and he lives in America. To my amazement, he can speak both Italian and English correctly. Michelino says that the boy taught him how to say *legno*, "wood" in American, by tapping on the railing. So Michelino already knows a word in English, and now he knows that when we get to America, his name will be Michael. I wonder if I will have an American name too.

By the third day of the voyage, we are no longer in the Mediterranean. The Atlantic Ocean is exceptionally rough, and the ship rocks seemingly out of control on the waves. My mother has taken to the cabin because she is seasick most of the time. We go to meals without her, and we are very quiet when we come back to the room to sleep. My father brings her food, but she barely eats anything. Yesterday, they put a rope down the indoor deck's length, so we can hold on to it to keep our balance, and they also tied down the lounge chairs. The waves are so rough and the boat rocks so much that sometimes we sit for hours because it is impossible to walk around. Babbuccio says this is an adventure, but much of it is not fun.

This afternoon, the ropes holding the chair where I was sitting came undone and it slid across the deck! As it slid across the floor, the hand rope made contact with my face directly under my nose. The chair stopped when it hit the other side, but I have a big welt between my nose and upper lip. I cried like a baby, and Babbuccio was there immediately to hold me and bring me back to his chair's safety, which was still securely tied.

The days start to drag, although, thankfully, the sea has calmed. Finally, today, Tuesday, November 9th, 1954, we reach Manhattan Island in New York. I ask Babbuccio, "Che ore sono?"

He checks the watch on his wrist and responds, "Le otto e mezzo."

I will always need to remember the date and time because this is the most significant change I have ever made. I realize that we will live here forever, and we will never go back home because I can't imagine repeating this voyage and because I can hear my parents' conversations. The realization hurts my heart, and I quickly wipe away the tears in my eyes.

Michelino carefully replaces the grapevine in his coat pocket and buttons up. "Vieni!" he says. We find my mother standing at the railing with Maida next to her and Gianfranco in her arms. She looks sad as we approach the port.

"Eccola, La Statua Della Liberta!" my father says as he points to a beautiful, colossal green statue of a lady in robes holding a stone flame. None of us can speak! It is just as magnificent as he said it would be! I can almost hear her softly saying, "Welcome to America!" I have never seen anything like it, and it takes my breath away.

The port of New York is much larger than Naples' port, and I feel overwhelmed by the size of the buildings ahead. I take Mammina's hand as she smiles her beautiful smile. She looks much better today, but she still looks tired and sad. "Siamo arrivati…." she says softly.

Zio Enrico and Zia Maddalena pick us up with their two cars. I was surprised when my father told me that they have two cars and that my aunt drives one. The adults greet each other with hugs and kisses as we children wait for our instructions. Zio tells my father, "You and I will take the luggage, and Lula and the children will ride with Maddalena." Zia Maddalena is nice, but she is very bossy, but maybe that is just how American ladies are. Zio is older than Babbuccio, but they look very much alike. He smiles a lot and does whatever Zia tells him to do.

"Let's get something for the children to eat!" Zia says. I'm not at all hungry, but I don't say anything. Zio smiles as he instructs us to follow her, like little ducks, behind the mama duck. She leads us to a pushcart, where a man is wearing a hat and a big white apron. He stands on a little wooden box, and there is a long handle on each side of him, which must be what he holds to move the cart. There are two large wheels and one small one in front. There are bottles of a very dark liquid on a shelf, and I try to read the words written in a big red circle, "Drink Coca-Cola in Bottles."

The words coca-cola are easy for me to pronounce, so I whisper them, out loud. Right above that sign are words written in capital letters, "HOT FRANKFURTER AND ROLL 15 cents." I can't pronounce any of that! On a metal pole, and shading the entire cart, is a blue and red umbrella with writing on both sides that clearly says, "FRANKFURTERS AND COLD DRINKS." I understand now that drinks must mean *bevante*, but I have no idea what the rest of the words mean!

Zia talks to the man for a long time, and they both count heads as she points. I squeeze my way to the front to see what the man is doing, and I see a basket with many plastic bags filled with tiny soft loaves of bread. The man takes one piece of bread and holds it in his left hand. He slides a metal cover back with his right hand and, with metal tongs, reaches into a pot of steamy, dirty-looking water and takes out a skinny sausage. He puts it into the

Joan Isaacson

bread, which is cut in half the long way. My aunt points to some other containers and asks, "Do you want sauerkraut, onions, or mustard?" I have no idea what she is saying. It all sounds so strange, and the jars hold things I have never seen, so I shake my head *NO!* The man hands me the "Hot Frankfurter and Roll 15 cents," and I look at it suspiciously.

I wait until my brother and sister each have theirs, and I say to Michelino, "You taste it!" He responds by taking a bite of the bread and frankfurter. Maida and I wait for his reaction. He makes a nasty face, locates a pail, and spits everything from his mouth into the garbage.

We are about to throw ours out too, but Michelino says, "*Aspetta!* The sausage is not bad, but the bread tastes like *merde.*"

One by one, my brother, sister, and I stand over the garbage, throw out the bread, and eat the plain "sausage." It's not horrible, but it does not taste like anything I have ever eaten before. Zia gets us each a bottle of the black liquid, and I take a big swallow, assuming it will taste like licorice. I choke at the disgusting taste of the "Drink Coca-Cola in Bottles." I notice, however, that both my brother and sister are savoring the new American drink.

The ride to Palisades Park, New Jersey, where our new home will be, is not long. The baby is asleep on my lap as I look out the car window. I am amazed by the tall buildings and wide roads and many cars and traffic lights. When we get to Palisades Park, Zia tells us that this is the town where we will be living, and I am surprised at how pretty it is. There are lots of trees, beautiful houses, and a large building that she tells us will be our school.

When we get to our new home, Maida and I inspect all the rooms. I hold Gianfranco, so he doesn't get in the way as Michelino helps remove things from the cars. Soon everything is in the house and, within an hour, we watch my uncle and aunt drive away in their two American cars.

From the front window, I can see that as my mother is walking towards the door, my father takes her hand and turns her, so she faces him. Surprisingly, they stand there talking for a long time. He runs his fingers through his hair, and she puts down the small suitcase she is holding and begins to cry. He pulls her into a hug and looks like he is consoling her. Eventually, they come into the house, trying to look happy, even though I know something is wrong.

When my brother and sister fall asleep, I come out and sit next to Babbuccio on the couch. My parents stop whispering when they hear me come in, and he puts his arm around me and kisses the top of my head. I don't have to ask what's wrong because he knows why I'm here. "Non ti preoccupare, Vannuccella," he says.

"Cos'e?" I ask, afraid that he is sick.

He hugs me and tells me, "Zio told me, on our way here, that he doesn't have work for me anymore." When he sees my worried face, he hugs me closer. I am so confused because the only reason we came to America is so Babbuccio can work! "I will find a job somewhere else, don't worry," he says softly. His voice is shaky, and he blows his nose, and my mother quietly leaves the room without saying a word.

# JOAN - New York, New York - 1968

This morning, it takes extra time to dress in preparation for my lunch "date." The black and white houndstooth dress with the bright yellow Eisenhower jacket is my pick. For the tenth time this week, I wish that I would gain some weight! At almost 5'6" and 106 lbs., my daily effort is to go up a dress size. When I am fully dressed, I examine myself in the mirror and tell myself that I look OK, so I take my purse and walk down the stairs and out the door.

I walk to the corner of Highpoint and Palisade Avenues to meet the bus from Weehawken to New York City. My neighbor is already waiting, and we greet each other as we do every morning. He is unusually chatty today, and I am only half-listening because I am thinking about my lunch with Sheldon. We get on the bus, and my neighbor sits next to me as he tells me about a disagreement he had with his landlord. I acknowledge his verbal diarrhea with an occasional uninterested "hmmm" or "really?" He continues to ramble as the bus makes its way down the hill that approaches the Lincoln Tunnel. The coffee on his

34

breath is bothering me so I lean my head back and close my eyes, hoping to end his chatter. Thankfully, he stops talking and I can gather my thoughts to recall the letter I received from Sheldon a few weeks earlier, when he asked to make the plan for today.

I am very much looking forward to seeing him. The war in Vietnam has shifted our peaceful little world. Many of the boys we know have either been drafted into the army or have joined other service branches. Sheldon has been in the Navy since 1965 and just returned from his second tour in Vietnam on the USS Enterprise. I think about him often, hoping he stays safe. I love his letters and that he calls me whenever he is off the ship. The last time he was home, he got tickets through the USO, and we went to see a Broadway show with Sammy Davis, Jr. called "Golden Boy." After the play, Sammy Davis sat on the edge of the stage and talked to the audience. It was beautiful and different! I don't know how he does it, but a night out with Sheldon always turns out special.

Last year he sent me a statue of the Madonna, carved in wood, from the Philippines. It is beautiful! The fact that it caused a predictable argument with Freddy, who happened to be there when I opened the package, did not detract from Sheldon's thoughtfulness.

"Why is he sending you this?" And so it begins!

"I guess he thought I would like it."

He can't stop. "The same guy you write all those letters to?"

"Yea, Fred. He's a nice guy who is lonely being so far

35

from home and he's my friend. What's the big deal?" I'm not surprised by the pissy attitude, which turns into an argument and a dramatic storming out and he undoubtedly stops at the closest bar, which is one of our problems.

My eyes open just in time to see the dividing line halfway into the tunnel where it says New Jersey on one side and New York on the other. The Lincoln Tunnel is dingy and dirty from all the exhaust fumes of the thousands of cars and buses that go through it every day. I remember my grandfather telling us that in the late 1930's he came to America a few times and he worked on building this tunnel. I once read an old quote by newspaper reporter L.H. Robbins regarding the "cast of characters" who tunneled beneath the Hudson River to build the first tube. He wrote, "Big Irishmen, Italians, Negroes, Poles and Swedes, ox-strong, rough-clad, and splattered with mud, plaster and red lead. A heroic race they are, they and the stouthearted Sandhogs, gamely and proudly doing Titans' work down under the tide, under the town, making the world more convenient for the rest of us." It's hard to think of my grandfather fitting the description of these men, but he was one of them. I can only visualize the gentle man with his grandchildren running around him or holding his hand, not the Titan digging under the tide. But, I suppose it was something he had to do for his family and, as always, I feel a tender love for him.

The bus makes its way into the Port Authority building and pulls into the assigned spot to offload its 49 passengers. One morning, when I had to sit in the very back row, I counted, out of boredom. My neighbor gestures for me to go ahead.

"Thanks! Have a nice day!" I smile at him as I step down.

I follow the crowd to the bowels of the building as I aim for the IRT Line platform. There are particular feels and smells to the subway station. It is a combination of the creosote, which the railroad ties are soaked in to preserve them, and dust from the steel brakes. I join the crowd of people that are already waiting for the 2-3 train. Every time a train enters the station, it brings a blast of air from the tunnel, which only adds to the smell. My train comes in less than five minutes, and I step aside to let out a swarm of people before I board with a quick visual search for a seat. As happens more often than not, there is no seat, so I stand, gripping the overhead strap.

I spend the ten minute ride examining the walls of the train car. On the wall facing me is the city's big subway map with all its different lines and stops, all color-coded. At first glance, it is overwhelming, but it is incredibly straightforward and useful once you establish your location. On the other wall, there are dull advertisements. There is an ad for Manhattan College complete with their "Signum Fidei" logo and another for Kramer, Lowenstein, Nessen & Kamin law firm.

Since I have no interest in either, I don't read the content, but instead I am reminded of the "Miss Rheingold" contest a few years ago. These same walls had photographs of beautiful girls for whom you could vote on little paper ballots. I can't help but sing the jingle in my head, "My beer is Rheingold the dry beer, think of Rheingold whenever you buy beer...la, la, la, la, la, la, la, la, la ...won't you try extra dry Rheingold Beer???" I can't remember the in-between part. I wonder why they stopped having that contest and if they still make that beer.

The familiar garbled voice from the speaker announces that the next stop will be Park Place. When we arrive, we stand five-deep facing the door, which will allow us access to the platform. After a momentary delay, it opens and stays that way for 21 seconds. We quickly step out so that new passengers can step in. I am immersed in both the echoed sound and reverberation of the station as I drift along with that unique New York energy which feels like a well-performed ballet.

I take the steep escalator up to the street and move quickly, keeping pace with everyone else, although I would love to stroll the five-minute walk to the office. I'll wait until lunchtime to enjoy some fresh air, and I'll suggest to Sheldon that we get sandwiches and eat our lunch in City Hall Park. The only thing spoiling my morning is the nagging thought that I have to have "the talk" with Freddy. Why am I still seeing him? The most straightforward conversations become a disagreement or an argument, and he pisses me off more than he makes me happy. What is wrong with me? But I won't think about this today!

"Good morning." I greet the guard sitting at the big reception desk. He flashes a bright smile as I move towards the elevator banks. After almost two years of working in this skyscraper building, I am still blown away by this lobby's magnificence. It fascinated me when I first saw it, and I was happy to find a lot of information in my encyclopedia.

It was built in 1913 by F.W. Woolworth for $13.5

million. It was described as one of the most beautiful buildings in the world because of its Italian, French, and Renaissance architecture with a Gothic steeple. There are 57 stories with fireproof and smoke-proof stairs, and 29 elevators. They built it with the same framework materials used in bridges so that it can withstand high winds. From the marquee in the lobby, I know that the F. W. Woolworth Company has its offices on the 24th floor. The Fidelity Bank has its office at the top of the beautiful staircase in front as I look past the desk. The vaulted ceilings in this lobby are genuinely breathtaking, and it has been called "The Cathedral of Commerce." One fascinating thing I found is that the building was fitted for gas lighting when built in 1913 since they weren't sure if electricity was just a fad. I found the salamander in the designs throughout the building. They used to ward off fires at the turn of the 20th century.

I take the elevator to the 11th floor and enter the doors that say Titanium Metals Corporation. It is not yet nine a.m., but many executive secretaries are already there to get their boss's messages and make their coffee before they arrive. I greet a half dozen co-workers on my way to the space I share with Norman Hauser and Frank Walsh, who is our boss in the Accounting/Tax department. I'm the first one here, so I turn on the lights and glance at my brand new Burroughs adding machine, which I am trying to master. There are two pink "while you were out" slips on my desk. One call is from Angelo Russo's wife and one from Freddy, which has a checkmark next to "urgent." I highly doubt it is urgent, but there is no place to check "pissed off" on this slip, so I guess it had to do. Angelo works in one of our warehouses. His wife calls for an explanation of either the hourly calculations or the tax deductions after each paycheck. Because she is a nice lady, I patiently go over the numbers with her every time.

I suspect that Freddy is calling to continue the fight from last night. I'm not in the mood to talk to him because I don't need him to spoil my day. I call Mrs. Russo so I can take that off my plate. Freddy can wait, especially since I'm going to end it for good the next time I see him. The argument last night was pretty typical of what we do.

"What are you so mad about?" He asks.

"I don't know, Fred, maybe the fact that we were supposed to go out Saturday and you didn't show up until 10:30, and you were drunk? Why would I be upset?"

He is incredulous! "What's the big deal? I met my friends and lost track of time. It's not like I didn't get here!"

And so it goes with this relationship. He drinks, and I hate it. He breaks promises and then sweet talks to be forgiven. I smell the alcohol on his breath as he tries to kiss me, and when I duck and push him away, he is furious." You are such a bitch!"

No more tears for me. I knew for sure it was over as I watched Dodie feed a pretend bottle to a pretend baby on "My Three Sons" while I sat in a dark house all alone, dressed for a date that never really happened. I was doubly pissed because Sheldon had asked me to go out that night, but I said no.

Frank Walsh walks in with that big smile and happy guy way of his. He has a positive attitude and a pleasant manner. He never complains about his commute from Yonkers, Westchester County, to downtown New York as others do. We talk for a few minutes about his three adorable kids and his sweet wife, Midge. I know his family is very religious, so I can appreciate the little stories he tells. Instead of playing "house," his kids play "church" and take turns being the priest.

We are still laughing when we hear Norm say, "Good morning." I can't help but think, every day, when he walks in, "*Damn, he is GOOD LOOKING !*" He is in his late 40's, tall and with just the right amount of grey at the temples. I used to be a little flirty with him, but I stopped when I realized that his friend Todd, who meets him after work, is his life partner. He is also handsome, and they look right together.

Ed comes in carrying the morning mail addressed to the Tax Department, and he places it on my desk. "Thanks, Ed!" I say, and I begin to sort it but notice that he is lingering. Ed is our mail-boy. He is in his forties with some mental issues, so he is a little slow, but he is a lovely man. His job is not very demanding, because the mail gets pre-sorted and he only pushes the cart into the offices and distributes it. When we are swamped with work and Ed offers to get lunch or coffee, we are grateful to let him do it.

I smile back and say, "How are you, Ed?"

"I'm great!" he says. "I am taking Sarah on a date this weekend!"

He sounds elated, and I would like to be happy for him.

The girls who are his friends have recently told me that they thought this girl was using him to take her places and not treat him well otherwise.

Curious about her, I ask him, "What is she like, Ed?" At this point, both Frank and Norm are in the conversation and we are anticipating the answer, which takes a few moments for him to assimilate.

He is earnest and responds thoughtfully," She reminds me a lot of you!"

Frank and Norman smile at me, and I think, "'Oh, *how sweet!*' but notice that he has more to say.

In that calculated slow way of his, he finishes his well-thought-out response. "She's just a plain Jane, the run-of-the-mill kinda girl."

We nod and smile, but when he is out of earshot, we three explode in a fit of uncontrolled laughter, and I say, "Noone has ever called me that out loud before !!" Sweet Ed!

My morning work keeps me extremely busy. I am deep in the throes of calculating a tax return whose numbers refuse to cooperate when my phone rings. Distracted, I pick up the phone. "Tax Department!"

"Joan, hi, it's Sheldon." When I check my watch, I see it's 11:35, which means that he will not be here for lunch if he is calling from New Jersey. "I'm so sorry. I slept late."

The first word in my head is *lame* as I scribble "asshole" on my yellow legal pad.

"There is no way I can make it in for lunch!" He continues with a sleepy voice.

I write the word over and over, about twenty times in

different directions and sizes. "Hey! No problem..." I say, letting him off the hook.

But he interrupts me, "Can I meet you for dinner?"

I hesitate, just long enough to rip the page off my pad, crumple it up and toss it in the garbage. That's more like it! He's a sweet guy! "Sure!" I say, "Sounds good."

Although swamped with work, I find myself checking my watch all afternoon, and I am looking forward to dinner with Sheldon. I haven't seen him for almost a year, although there were a few phone calls and lots of letters. Because I still live with my parents and younger siblings and I work in an accounting department, I sometimes wonder if my letters to him are annoying. Sheldon's are always full of great descriptions of exotic places like China, Japan, and the Philippines. I love his letters and often read them twice because he sounds lonely. Or maybe it is I who misses him.

At exactly 5:02 p.m., I am on Broadway, hailing a cab to take me uptown. I am more excited than I should be as I approach the Winter Garden Theatre on Broadway. The Hawaii Kai is like nothing I have ever seen before. The pretty hostess leads me to a table under a thatched roof where Sheldon is already seated.

When he sees me approach, he stands and hugs me. "Hey, it's terrific to see you!" I see my joy reflected in his handsome face.

"I'm so happy to see you."

I try to figure out what seems different, besides his new glasses. He is also looking at me as if trying to figure out how I might have changed.

"You look beautiful," he says in a low voice in my ear. And as he pushes in the chair, I feel myself blush violently.

I have a perfect view of the very cool bar for which this place is known. Sheldon points out the diorama of Diamond Head at Waikiki that shifts from daytime to nighttime. He also tells me the bar is called "The Okole Maluna Bar," which means The Bottoms Up Bar. "And back here," he says, "is The Lounge of the Seven Pleasures." I blush again. "They have entertainment every night that plays until 3:00 in the morning!" He tells me that this whole place was designed by a guy who creates sets for Broadway plays. As he offers information, I think that one of my favorite things about being with him is that he loves to talk. The other thing is that I love to watch his lips moving.

"My brother tells me that this restaurant is a hot spot." He laughs, "I wasn't sure I should trust him!"

I feel good being here, and I love listening to him. "Tell Bruce he suggested the perfect place. I love it!"

I tell him that I have never tasted Polynesian food, so he orders a tableful of unfamiliar dishes. I try every plate, delighted that everything is so tasty. "Did you like the far east countries you visited?"

He smiles, "There were lots of great things to see, but I spent a good portion of my time on the 'Big E' with about 4,500 other guys!"

We laugh as my emotions soar! I know I'm about to screw this up by allowing feelings that I shouldn't have.

This silly drink with the tiny umbrella is so sweet that I can't finish it, but I had enough to make me less anxious. Sheldon finishes a beer, and I notice he doesn't order a second. He focuses on every word I say, and I savor the attention. I suddenly know what is different about him! He's not holding a cigarette. "Hey, did you quit smoking?"

"I did!" he says proudly." One morning, I woke up feeling like a baby elephant was sitting on my chest, and I knew what I had to do. So I quit cold turkey!"

As the daughter of a smoker, I know this is not easy to do. "Good for you!" I say, appreciating his self-control.

The evening flies by, and we marathon talk, trying to fit in all our questions before we have to say good-night.

"Tell me about everybody...I know Mike and Linda and Madeline and Pete got married.

I tell him they are all doing well." Mike and Linda have a baby boy, and Madeline is pregnant." He is momentarily thoughtful. "I'm sure I told you in my letters," I say, confused at his sudden introspect.

He smiles, "Yea, you did! I'm just thinking about how happy they must be!"

He smiles his adorable smile, and I melt a little knowing he has such a kind heart. *Stop!* I reprimand myself for having these feelings.

"So, John and Maria, how old are they now?"

I have to re-focus for a second, "John is 15 and Maria is 9."

I am not surprised when he says, "I'm looking forward to seeing everyone!"

I sincerely responded, "Me too!!"

"How are your parents.....more specifically, your Mom?" He seems genuinely interested.

"My Dad is great and my Mom... well, she is still Lula, if you know what I mean."

He laughs. "How is everyone in your family?" I ask.

He sits back in his chair, looking as if he has just made a significant decision. I imagine that if he had a beard, he'd be stroking it. "My parents are moving to Florida," he says.

"Oh, how wonderful!"

He continues, "I'm getting out of the Navy in the spring, but I have no intention of moving south."

I get it! Who would want to leave the New York area? I am ridiculously happy to hear that he will not be going.

"You and I should think about getting married!"

I laugh at what is quite obviously a joke. But, his earnest demeanor tells me otherwise.

"I don't expect you to decide now, but I need you to think about it! I had lots of time to think when I was away."

I am completely mesmerized by his moving lips and by the words pouring out.

"Every time I stood in some exotic place, I asked myself, 'Who would I want to share this with me?' And the answer was always Joan!"

I find myself stupidly happy at the moment. "Although this rarely happens," I say, "I have no words."

He leans across the table, takes my hand, and looks directly into my eyes. "I will wait as long as I need to! Don't feel that I am pressuring you. I want you to know that I promise to devote my life to make you happy if you let me." In this crazy, whirlwind moment, I have never believed anything more!

# JOAN - New Haven, Connecticut - 2011

I walk alongside the gurney, holding his hand, trying to keep my tears in check. Last night was so emotionally draining that I know I can't go there again without completely losing my shit. So, I hold his hand and whisper encouraging words. The orderly pushes him down the elevator to the assigned operating room. We are resolved and hopeful that they will find the reason for the extreme deterioration of his lungs. He continues to struggle and breathes only with the aid of a ventilator.

We reach the assigned OR, and a nurse meets us at the entrance. The orderly stops me from entering, saying, "Sorry, you can't go any further than this point." Although I fully understand that I need to leave him at the double doors, I have this awful feeling that I shouldn't let him out of my sight, so I keep moving forward. A nurse gently touches my arm and speaks softly through her mask.

"Sorry, you can only go this far."

I kiss his hand, and he caresses my face, and neither of us speaks. I stand frozen as they take him through and as the doors slowly close and he is out of my sight, I whisper, "I love you!'

I make my way slowly back to the elevator, feeling as though I am out of my body and walking through jello. I know that this procedure has been done here hundreds of times, so why do I feel as frightened and anxious as I do? I can't shake this feeling because it is way deep down in my heart, and it is physically sucking the air out my lungs. I lean against the wall to catch my breath, grateful that the hall is empty. I close my eyes and wait until I can breathe normally again. When my lungs have air, I compose myself enough to move slowly down the long corridor to the elevator, which will take me to the intensive care unit.

Through the ninth floor's bustle, I witness a woman in her early twenties pacing the hallway. I feel completely drawn to her, so instead of sitting in the green chair, I walk past Sheldon's room and in her direction. She appears agitated as she stands in the doorway of a patient's room. When I peek into the room, I see that the bed is empty. "Are you OK?" I touch her back very gently.

She turns to me with extreme sadness on her face, and tears brimming in her eyes. "They took my mom!" she cries.

"I'm sorry," I tell her as I guide her to the waiting room. I offer the seat next to me, hold her hand, and allow her to cry. I feel her pain deep in my heart.

"She couldn't breathe, and they rushed her out!" she exclaims. "I keep asking how she is, but they say they don't know!" She is inconsolable!

"Is there anyone here with you?" I ask, afraid that she has to bear this burden alone. She tells me that they called her aunt and that she is on her way. She holds my hand tightly, and I don't remove it because I know that she needs human contact, even from a stranger.

"I'll wait with you until she gets here," I promise, and the poor girl looks relieved.

For more than an hour, we sit quietly next to each other, lost in our individual and shared misery. Eventually, I see a woman speaking with the nurse just outside the door, and the nurse points in our direction, so I assume this must be the aunt. Since the emotionally drained girl has fallen asleep, I gently tap her shoulder. She opens her eyes, knows precisely where she is, and runs into her aunt's arms.

"Thank you so much." the woman whispers, reaching as if to touch me as I pass her.

"We need each other," I tell her, and I continue down the hall.

I have not yet reached room 220 when I hear the wailful cry of the girl who just learned that her mother is gone forever. I feel disquieted, sad, and deeply exhausted as I walk into this already familiar room.

I close the door, turn off the lights, and sit in the big green chair. I pray and cry for the sad girl, the stranger to whom I feel so intimately connected, and I remind myself just how fragile life is and how quickly we can lose someone. Thoroughly drained, I turn on the T.V. and scroll through the channels. I check FOX News and see only worldwide turmoil. "Egyptian protesters demand change and accountability...At least twenty demonstrators killed in Syria..." I change the channel and start surfing. I see coming attractions for the next episode of "Homeland" and a ridiculous commercial for the best hemorrhoid cream on the market.

Eventually, I stop on The Disney Channel because it is precisely what I would be watching if I were in my regular life at home with my grandkids. I doze off, and I have a vivid dream in which I am Dora The Explorer, and I am telling the chocolate tree that I am lost, and I want to go home.

# ARGHIRULA -
## Athens, Greece - 1939

It is Sunday afternoon, and there is nothing to do on Makriyianni Street. I go to Effie's house as often as I can because there are always happy people there - and music! There is also a beautiful radio record player, which sits on its unique table in the living room. The table has a shelf that holds dozens of records, neatly protected in their jackets. "Let's listen to Vamvakaris on the record player!" I plead.

"Arghirula, NO! My parents might come home, and my father would kill me if he hears Rembetika! He hides that album in the back. I think it is illegal even to have it! You know," she lowers her voice, "it's about hashish!" We pretend we are shocked, and we laugh.

It is surprising that he has this record! Mr. Georgakas is a banker and a very serious businessman. He is a nice man, and he talks to us about politics and music and patiently answers our often silly questions. But he is still a father, so there are rules, even though we are grown women of 16. But, compared to me, Effie is as free as a bird!

She is holding out her magazine for me to see. "Look at him! He is so handsome, isn't he?" I look at the picture of Cary Grant. He certainly is handsome, but he's an actor, so I don't care.

"Let's do something! Let's go to the park!" I plead. "I'm bored!"

"We can go for a walk, but we have to be back for dinner because Giannis is coming!"

When I put on my coat, there is a pack of cigarettes that I forgot was in my pocket. Effie hid them there a few days ago when we went to Giannis' kiosk. He gave us the magazines and a box of Karelia cigarettes because he wanted us to go home and off the streets.

We walk about a half mile to the small neighborhood park in the opposite direction of both the house and Gianni's kiosk. We locate a bench under a tree, which faces The Acropolis high up on the hill but, in truth, you can see The Acropolis from practically everywhere in Athens. We sit next to each other, and each of us lights a cigarette. She is far more experienced, and I admire her as I cough and wipe my watery eyes. I am determined to be a modern woman and master this part of it.

"Does your mom know you are staying for dinner?" Effie looks so sophisticated with her legs crossed and the cigarette between her fingers.

"It's OK," I tell her, although I have no idea if it is. Nothing is OK at my house, so I would rather be in trouble later than miss a fun evening. I asked Tolis and am relying on him to tell my father. I take shorter drags on my cigarette and puff out most of the smoke. I feel elegant, like a movie star!

Effie asks, "Where are your parents today?" She likes my mother and is intimidated by my father, as are most people.

"Maria and Damaskinos Diocles Raftopoulos." I enunciate slowly, exhaling my last puff of smoke. We both giggle. "My mother is at the Jewish section again. I guess she is delivering another baby."

She nods, "I wish my Mom did something like that. It seems so magical, bringing a life into the world." Then she says dreamily," Imagine being married and having a baby?"

I reply honestly, "That does not sound good to me at all!" And it doesn't! I have no desire to care for a baby!

Two young boys run past us, loudly bouncing a ball between them. An old couple walks on the path very slowly, with their hands locked, and their steps matched. There is something about them that warms me. I can't imagine my mother and father holding hands while walking, and I realize that I have never seen them hold hands at all. In total contrast to my tender image of the sweet couple, in the distance, I see a priest who looks like my father, and the moment is gone. When a young woman walks past us wheeling a baby carriage, Effie asks to look at the baby as the new mother beams with pride. Eventually bored, I pull at Effie's arm, "Let's go! I'm sure your mom will want help with dinner."

We don't rush walking back to Effie's house. The day is beautiful, and I walk with a little extra swing to my hips. Papa would kill me if he saw me shamelessly and openly flirting with the soldiers who follow us, but that doesn't stop me from doing it. The streets are crowded with couples and families strolling and holding hands in the crisp fall air. The square is full of men sitting at tables sipping coffee and ouzo. Although there is talk of bad times for Greeks in other parts of the world, the feeling here is peaceful and serene. I thread my arm through Effie's and feel happy to be young and free, even if for just an afternoon, and before returning to my own house.

When we get to Effie's, we follow the delicious aroma to the kitchen where there is *fasolada* on the stove and moussaka in the oven. The side table in the dining room is full of olives, dolmades, and salads. The dining table needs a tablecloth and plates, and I offer to help prepare it, after a peck on Mrs. Georgakas' cheek. Effie asks, "What time is Giannis arriving? And Papa, is he home yet?"

She places a kiss on her daughter's forehead and replies, "Yes, your father is home, and your brother should be here shortly." She continues to fuss, as she always does when her son visits.

Effie puts a record on the player, and the music permeates this already cheerful home. I hear the bouzouki and find myself dancing around the table as I place down the forks. Effie takes my hand, picks up a napkin, and waves it, imitating the motions we have seen her father make. We sing the words, move to the music's rhythm, and lose ourselves in laughter. When we stop, the room is spinning, and as it slows down, I see Giannis leaning against the doorway with his arms crossed and a crooked smile on his face. We lock eyes, and I feel my face get hot. I'm not sure if I am embarrassed that he caught us being silly, or I am happy to see him.

"Eleftheria!" When Effie runs to him, he gives her a warm hug and she kisses his cheek. He picks up his mom and spins her around to the music's beat, and she cannot hide her pride in her only son. I feel the warmth of this beautiful scene of family joy.

"Arghirula!" As he turns from his mom, he places a kiss on my cheek, which I am sure is just an extension of the family greeting. He steps away quickly, but he is close long enough for me to know he smells good, like expensive soap.

"Hello, Giannis, how are you?" I barely whisper.

Mr. Georgakas hears the commotion and steps into the room. "How are you, Son?" he hugs Giannis. "Sit, sit! Retsina?"

"Yes, thanks, Papa".

Dinner is, as always, delicious, and conversation is light. "Arghirula, is Tolis still planning on opening a kiosk?" I'm surprised that Giannis knows about my brother's plans. Although they know each other, they are not close friends.

"He is!" I reply, "Maybe for no other reason than to put me to work." Giannis smiles, but I see that Mr. Georgakas is a bit more serious.

"Where did you girls go today?"

Effie offers as little information as possible. "We went for a walk!"

Her dad smiles knowingly. "I am aware." he says. "Perhaps, it would be best if you stay closer to home in the future. The streets are not safe!"

His son expands, "I hear it is a bad situation for Greeks in Russia right now, and things in our own country are changing."

They discuss some current politics until Mrs. Georgakas changes the subject, "Giannis, how is it going at the kiosk?"

Giannis responds," You know the life of a *peripteras!* It would be an insufferable job, if not for the game!

"The game?" I am so curious.

"Yes," he continues. "The game! I know what a customer is going to buy before he reaches the kiosk. You can tell from a distance which guy will buy which newspaper, along with what cigarettes. The game of telling them we are out of matches to sell them a lighter, or telling them we are out of bus tickets unless they are buying something else." His remarks entertain me, but at the same time, I realize it makes good business sense. I can see that Giannis is an excellent businessman and will remember his advice when I become a *peripteras* myself.

The conversation shifts to numerous topics and eventually back to one familiar one. "Giannis, the offer for you to join the bank is still open, and I know you understand that it is a great opportunity. I hope you think about it!"

Slightly annoyed, Giannis responds, "Papa, I know that you are happy there, but it is not for me."

Mr. Georgakas pats his son on the back, "I know!" he chuckles. "You have bigger plans!"

Talk never ends, and topics segue smoothly, as do plates. At the end of the meal, the men excuse themselves and move to the living room. Mr. Georgakas takes the record off the record player and turns on the radio. Effie and I clear the table and prepare dessert plates. Mrs. Georgakas measures out coffee and puts it in the copper briki, pours in water, adds a lot of sugar, places it on the stove, and turns on low heat. She pours the aromatic coffee into each cup and spoons the kaimaki foam on top. I bring the coffee to the men, along with a plate of diamond-shaped pieces of baklava.

Effie and I have our coffee at the table with Mrs. Georgakas, and Effie brings the magazines. She goes back to reading the article she had started. As I leaf through mine, I can hear the BBC report coming from the radio speakers. "The Moscow trials continue. Joseph Stalin calls for trials against Trotskyist and members of The Right Opposition of Communist Party of the Soviet Union."

Mr. Georgakas shakes his head. "Stalin is a madman and a megalomaniac. A few years ago, he tried to get Ukrainian farmers to collectivize and give up their land to work on government-controlled farms. Thousands of Ukrainians died when they resisted! And now many of our Greek brothers are detained and dying in The Soviet Union. There is no boundary to his lust for power!"

Giannis sips his coffee and nods in agreement. Static blocks some words, but the report goes on. "Hundreds of people shot by Soviet secret police....." There is now so much static that no words are audible. Giannis turns off the radio.

"It is a terrible time of unrest." he grumbles.

Within seconds, Effie puts a record on the player, and the room's mood is suddenly lighter. Back in the kitchen, Effie puts away the dishes as I dry them.

I hug Mrs. Georgakas. "Dinner was delicious. Thank you so much."

She kisses my cheek and suggests that I prepare to go.

"Giannis will walk you home, Arghirula. It is getting late, and you should not be alone on the street."

Effie is about to remind me to take my magazine, and we both giggle, knowing that my father would never allow it in my house. Mrs. Georgakas wraps a large piece of baklava in a white cotton napkin and says, "Bring this home for Maria." Mr. Georgakas and his son say good-bye, and Giannis appears at my side, holding open my coat. I slip my arms into the sleeves and feel very special.

"Thank you," I murmur.

He smiles as he puts on his black wool jacket. "Bundle up; it's cold!" He digs his hands deep into his coat pockets, and we walk briskly, without speaking. I'm unhappy that we do not have a conversation, but he acts very much like a big brother. When we reach my house, I am not ready to say good-bye. He says, "Kalinychta, Arghirula." He waits for me to go in and close the door, and I am very disappointed.

For a few seconds, I stand at the entrance and hear only silence and then the familiar swish of water and the clinking of brushes in a bowl. I don't even need to see the back corner of the room. There is a small window there and a curtain that separates the space where my father has his "studio." Without seeing him, I know he is dressed in black pants and a white shirt covered with paint blotches. The smell of linseed oil and turpentine tickles my nose, and it is the smell of our house for as long as I can remember. My father is an iconographer. He studies the saints and paints icons on walls in churches, and sometimes on wood. I have lived in Athens most of my life, but Mamma told me that, before I can remember, we followed his work and sometimes moved near the churches if his commission was long. My family lived in Lamia in 1922 when I was born.

"Papa, I'm home," I call out as I place the wrapped dessert on the table and slowly make my way towards my sleeping space. I listen for his response as I mouth it along with him.

"Kalinychta!" *Good Night!* I hesitate because I know there is more. "Prosefches." *Prayers!* Also predictable.

Hopefully, my mother will be home soon. She will ask about my day, and she will tell us about hers. At the stove, I boil water that I will add to my bath. I can hear my sisters in quiet conversation behind the old screen that gives privacy to the three mattresses on the floor. They greet me without looking up from their stitching. "Hi", they say, in unison.

I remove my shoes and socks, sit down, and purposely, without greeting them back, say, "Giannis walked me home," knowing this will shock them! They look up, and Elena says,

"Did Papa see him?"

They are always amazed that Papa's rules don't scare me the way they should. "Mrs. Georgakas made him walk me!" I giggle. "It's not the way you think." They exchange a look and a smile and go back to their work.

I love my sisters and brothers, but I also feel sad for us all. In this house, we don't listen to music or drink ouzo or sing or play games. We never hug! There is nothing but gloom, restrictions, and dark moods.

Eventually, I fill the old tub, add the boiling water, and bathe in the tiny back room next to the water closet. I go back to my mattress and put on my sleeping gown.

# JOAN - New Haven, Connecticut - 2011

I feel my cell phone vibrate a split second before it rings and, shaking off the remnants of sleep, I answer, assuming that it will be Dr. Kim. However, it is Rachel checking in. I tell her I am expecting a call from the doctor, so we speak briefly, and she makes me promise to call her immediately after I talk to the doctor. Her voice is soothing, and in the few minutes that we are connected, she puts me in a little better place.

I'm glad that I will be fully awake for the doctor's call, although it doesn't come for another hour, and by now, I am truly anxious.

"Good morning, Mrs. Isaacson. Dr. Kim here."

"Yes, Doctor?" I realize I am holding my breath, and I force myself to exhale.

"As you know, we took tissue samples of your husband's lungs this morning. We will be sending them to three labs and should have results within a few days."

Surprised, I ask, "A few days? That sounds so long!"

"I must make you aware that the reason he couldn't

breathe is that there is no air getting into his lungs. Lungs are supposed to be spongy due to the millions of alveoli inside them. These are tiny air sacs that have pores to allow for the diffusion of oxygen."

I am trying to keep up with his explanation.

"Your husband's lungs, however, are solidified. They are like rocks! There is no air getting through at all."

My head is spinning, and I wish the girls were here!

"We will have to leave him intubated and ventilated because he cannot breathe on his own."

*What is all this? Didn't they fix him?*

"We will also need to keep him in an induced coma."

I try as best I can to understand everything he is saying, but I'm stuck on "his lungs are like rocks." The doctor hesitates, waiting for some acknowledgment, but all I offer is "OK." I can't think of anything else to say.

"Any questions?"

*Only a million!!!* My brain is screaming, but I respond, "No. Thank you."

"Please take my number," he says. "If you have any questions, please call me."

I scramble for a pen and a piece of paper and jot down Dr. Kim's office number. "Thank you," I repeat."

I call Rachel's number to unburden the weight of the doctor's report, and she tells me that she is in the car with Cassie and Mica and just minutes away from the hospital. Just as I end the call, I hear the gurney approach, and I stand up to face the door.

An orderly and two nurses wheel Sheldon into the

room, shift him onto the bed, and hook him to an assortment of tubes. When I see Dr. Takyar at the nurses' station, I leave the room to speak briefly about Dr. Kim's report. When I return, I am relieved to see that Sheldon looks like he is just napping... except for the oxygen mask covering half his face, the tubes in both his arms and the urinary catheter, complete with bag, hanging on the side of the bed. I should be upset, but I feel better now that I can see him, so I smile at the nurses as they fuss to get him settled and under the blankets.

"Are you OK?" this one is Jennifer. I know because I heard the orderly use her name when they walked in.

"I'm fine, thanks." I respond, not sure why she is asking. When they leave, I pull the straight chair close to the bed, and when I take my husband's hand, I am surprised that it is toasty warm.

Mica and Rachel are here, and they check their father for their assessment. "He looks better than he did when we brought him here!" Mica says to Rachel, who is already sobbing.

"Where's Cassie?" I ask.

"She stopped to talk with the doctor." she points out to the hallway."

"Which one?" I wonder if it might be Dr. Kim.

"Don't know his name...the tall one whose face is all doom and gloom."

"Dr. Takyar." I know just who she means. I am so relieved to have them here.

"Mom, what do they say is wrong with him?"

I try to remember all the things Dr. Kim said, but

there was only one thing I remember clearly. "His lungs are solidified, like two rocks. There is no air getting in without the ventilator".

Mica examines the ventilator monitor screen and the two long hoses connected to the mask on her dad's face. On the opposite side is a bedside monitor, which looks like a small TV and displays the heart rate, blood pressure, and other vitals. Beside the monitor is the intravenous pump delivering medication into his vein and, hanging on the same stand, is the feeding tube that will provide his "meals" as long as he is asleep.

We turn to Cassie, anxious to hear the doctor's report.
"Diffuse Alveolar Damage, or Hamman-Rich Syndrome and the start of Pulmonary Hypertension." She tells us, reading from her notes. "He said it's a rare lung disease that affects otherwise healthy individuals who do not have a history of smoking. Like Dad's, the symptoms are pneumonia-like and sudden, and the result is a hardening of the lungs." She hesitates. "There is no known treatment!" This last part sparks a lot of questions and considerable agitation. "So, basically, we need to just wait...they will keep him in an induced coma until he starts breathing on his own."

So we wait, my beautiful girls and I. I feel more helpless than I have ever felt in my life, and they are my emotional strength, although I keep reminding myself that they too are suffering. I ask them to tell me about the children and the little stories that they readily provide lift my spirits.

"Mom, we'll take you home tonight, and one of us will bring you back here in the morning." I don't immediately approve, but the three voices of reason insist.

"Mom, he's asleep! ...back in the morning,... you have to!"

I know they're right. Kiddingly, I raise a hand to quiet them. "Yes, OK! Have I told you guys how much I love you? And, look, it's the five of us! Just the way we like it best, the Original Five." We laugh at our old family joke, and we pass around the tissues.

It feels crazy good to be home! The shower soothes the aches in my body from the uncomfortable sleep of the last few nights and the emotional distress of the past month. I keep the TV volume low, but I can still hear the audience laughing as Jimmy Fallon finishes his monologue. The laughter feels all wrong, so I turn it off. In my search of the bookshelf for something to get me sleepy, I find the old red velvet diary, which belonged to my grandmother. As I have done since I was four years old, I carefully leaf through the brittle yellow pages, a few of which have fallen out. The ink color varies slightly, some deep blue and some pale lavender, faded from the passing of more than a hundred years. There are many delicate pencil drawings of flowers and grapevines and, because they look similar in style, I wonder if one person may have created them. The first page is dated 1902, and the last entry is barely legible, but I think it is 1906. I carefully look at every page, searching for something of my grandmother's world as a young woman but, aside from dates and her name, I can't understand a single word since it is all written in Ancient Greek.

# MIRIAM (Maria) - Smyrna, Turkey - 1901

"**M**iriam, please stop crying! What you are asking for is impossible!" my mother tries to calm me, but I am far too upset to listen. Even as I know deep down that it is wrong for me to ask, it is hard to believe they will not let me have what I want. "Mama, why? Please, it can be my birthday gift?"

My mother dramatically holds her head and shakes it vigorously. "Your Baba would never say yes to this! Please try to understand, yavrum, my baby!"

But I don't want to understand! My parents are generous with gifts, and most often, there is no need for a special occasion. I can't stop crying, and I can see that Mama is frustrated as she paces the room.

"We will talk to Baba tonight..." she trails off as she leaves the room.

Baba rarely says no to me! I stop wailing and try my best to control the hiccups. I don't know why I am so desperate to have this necklace, but I know that I want it more than anything. I curl up on the large floor pillow and reach for my math notebook. I will finish all my schoolwork before dinner and not make Mama call me three times before coming to the table.

Baba is a Rabbi, a religious leader and a teacher. He does not have a synagogue, but he teaches in a specific room in our home. I'm not permitted to enter that room if there are students, but I can go in when there is no one there. When I was small, I used to sit on his lap while he read to me. I don't sit on his lap anymore because I am eleven years old, but he still likes to read to me, although he knows very well that I can read for myself.

Although Baba was my first teacher, I now attend the Omereion School For Girls and I have lots of friends of different religions. Some are Jewish, some are Muslim, but most are Greek Orthodox. All of our classes are in Greek, but each of us goes for separate instruction in our churches. My Greek friends are the ones who wear the pretty necklace that I want so much.

I hear Baba's footsteps as he approaches, and I jump up to sit on the chair closest to the divan to prepare for interrogation because I have made Mama unhappy. My eyes are still wet, so I wipe the sleeve of my blouse across my face and put my hands on my lap, just as he walks into the room.

"Melegim" he calls me, *Angel*, so maybe he is not as upset as Mama would have me think.

"Hello, Baba."

He comes to me and places a kiss on the top of my head. When he bends down, I notice that there is a lot of gray in his black beard. As always, he wears a black fez hat, which is starting to look worn. I have seen Baba without the hat, but aside from Mama, I don't think anyone else ever has. He wears black pants, a white shirt and a black jacket. Most often, he wears a black tie, but today he has already taken it off.

"Why have you upset Mama?" The question makes me cry. Baba sits quietly on the divan, and I know all too well that he will wait for my answer, no matter how long it takes.

Eventually, I choke out the words, "I want a necklace..."

Baba already knows, because he calmly responds, "You can have a necklace, Miriam, but not the one you ask for." He stands and leaves the room, even though I am still crying.

The house fills with delicious smells of dinner, and I know that Mama is busy in the kitchen with Refika, who has been helping in our home for as long as I can remember. I wash my face, but I plan on not speaking to them because I am angry with my parents. My father scowls at me because I am the last to sit, and he begins the before-meal prayer "Barukh atah Adonai, Eloheinu......" When he finishes, he asks, "Miriam, what did you learn in school today?" Without responding, I pout and look down at my plate. The soup smells delicious, and I am hungry, but if I eat, it will seem that I'm not angry.

A few seconds pass, and Mama says, "Miriam, answer your Baba!"

I feel the tears in my throat. "Baba, please ....." I am about to cry again when I see my parents exchange a look that makes me hopeful, so I say, "Today we learned about the Antikythera mechanism to study astronomy."

Baba smiles and says, "That is very interesting!" and turns his attention back to the newspaper article he has been reading. He reads it aloud to Mama as I only half listen because it is familiar and it is all that adults talk about whenever they get together. "Turkish nationalists... exiles...replacement of the Ottoman Empire...constitutional government...trouble...revolt...turmoil!" They discuss the many changes in our world as I slowly spoon soup into my mouth. I hope the conversation will come back to my necklace, but I won't bring it up again.

My father's low voice and boring subject make me sleepy, but I am suddenly alert when my mother says, "Miriam, Baba and I are going to discuss the necklace." I can't believe my ears! "But, sweetheart, you must understand that we are Jewish! We do not display crosses in our home, nor do we wear them!" I feel stinging tears return to my eyes. She takes my face in her hands and says, "You are a perfect girl, and we love you... so, we will talk it over and make a decision."

I am hopeful and overjoyed! "Thank you, Mama, Baba! WHEN can I get it?"

We all laugh, but Baba says, "Miriam, we have not said yes, only that we will discuss it."

I go to bed willingly, knowing that my parents will decide to give me the necklace.

Two days pass and they have not mentioned anything at all! I am miserable, and with every minute that passes, it becomes more difficult for me to wait. I won't ask about it because they are still discussing, but a beautiful necklace vision is always in my mind.

When the school week ends, I help Mama prepare the evening meal to begin Shabbat. I put two loaves of challah on the table for my father's blessing. We sit, waiting for Baba to begin the kiddush. Before he does, he gives me a small box, saying, "Miriam, my dear, we decided to let you have the necklace. But, please understand we are not in favor........." If he is still talking, I don't hear another word!

I barely slept last night because I am so excited for school this morning. The little cross sits perfectly around my neck, just above the opening of my blouse collar. My hands shake with excitement when I put it on, and I am incredibly eager to show my friends! I greet a few Muslim girls, and I admire the pretty shawls over their shoulders as I walk towards the small group in the back of the classroom. Lea and Abria are both Jewish, and I see them every afternoon at religion class. I also see them with their families at temple services once a week. The girls huddle with our Greek friends, and when I arrive, we hug and giggle and all talk at once. Joyously, I show Anik and Gisa that I now have a cross just like theirs, and we all remove our necklaces to compare them.

I am utterly surprised and heartbroken that their crosses are shiny and mine is not! They are not the kind of brilliant that comes from gold metal, but incredibly bright as though sunshine reflects from the inside. I don't understand! I look from Anik's cross to Gisa's cross, and they are both equally bright, although I seem to be the only one to notice how dull mine is. They don't see what I see, and I cannot explain it to them because I am sad and disappointed.

When I get home from school, Baba sits in his big chair reading, and Mama is seated on the divan embroidering. They both look up when I enter the room. "Miriam dear, did you have a nice day?" My mother smiles sweetly.

I don't respond because there is a knot in my throat, and I don't want to cry. I go to the big chair and hold out my closed fist to Baba. He puts out his hand, and I drop the necklace into it.

He looks at it, confused, and asks, "What's wrong, my sweet? Do you not like it?" I choke back tears and can't explain the misery deep in my heart. "It doesn't shine like the other girls', Baba. It doesn't shine at all!"

### ...One year later

The festival of lights is my favorite holiday. Tonight is the first night, and Mama has placed the menorah by the window. She puts the first candle to the right and the shamash in the center. As he does every year, Baba explains, "The eight candles that will be lit this week symbolize the miracle that occurred when the Maccabees reclaimed the Temple. The fighters found only enough oil to light a lantern, by which to read the Torah for one day. But, the lantern blazed for eight full days." It is always a good story, but tonight it makes me cry.

*Will I have to light candles by myself next year, without Mama and Baba?* I can't imagine how I will live without them, even for a short time. I don't want to leave. However, Baba said I must because there is too much danger here. If I were able to choose, I would stay with Baba, Mama and the threat. But, there will be no changing Baba's mind. He said I will be going to Athens, Greece, to a school named after

Saint Euphrosynos. Baba knows someone who is helping with getting into the school, and he said that I must be grateful that I have this opportunity.

"Our separation will be brief, and we will also come to Greece when our papers are in order," he tells me for the tenth time today.

The candles are lit and visible from outside through our front window, as is tradition. There are extra potato pancakes and jelly donuts on the table, and I eat more than I should, but neither of my parents stops me from doing so. Although it is much the same, everything seems different than in past holidays. We are alone and not with the usual houseful of friends. Mama and Baba both look tired and sad, so I will not complain about this necessary arrangement. Besides, I have another week before I board the ship that will take me to Greece. Baba has promised that he and Mama will join me within the year.

"Tomorrow, we will pack, Miriam. Baba got a steamer trunk, and it has lots of room so you can take everything you want." Her eyes are full of tears, and no matter how strong I promised myself that I would be, my emotions are in turmoil. Mama is holding me tight, and, through my tears, I see that Baba leaves the room with his head bowed low. Mama and I sit for a very long time and discuss what we will do when we are together again. Mama says, "When we arrive in Athens, you can show us all the beautiful places." We cry, and we talk, and we cry more. I have never felt so unhappy in my life.

My mother takes up her embroidery, but her stitches are unhurried and measured. Placed on the footstool next to Mama's chair, is the small wooden box where she keeps her needles and threads. She has been working on this long magnificent scarf for as long as I can remember. The color is the palest pink, and the fabric is beautiful flowing silk.

I hear my voice even before the thought is complete. "Mama, can I take your shawl with me?"

Mama does not hesitate, "Yes, my love! Someday, we will finish it together."

I can barely get the words out, "I'll work on it every day, Mama, I promise."

When Baba returns, he finds us clinging to each other in sad despair. He takes us in his arms, so we are all wrapped together as one. I have never seen my father cry, so hearing him now tears at my heart. When the emotional torrent subsides, my mother, still weeping, organizes the threads in the box. She lines up the needles by size, larger to smaller, pushing them through the white fabric. I watch her with total concentration, as if in a master teacher's presence and learning a critical lesson.

When Baba asks me to join him, I sit next to him and put my head on his shoulder. He gives me a box with a beautiful ribbon. "Charoume no Chanouka," he says in Greek, *Happy Hanukkah*. I open the box and find, carefully wrapped in a piece of blue fabric, a beautiful red velvet diary. In my father's hand, on the inside cover, is written: "You soften my heart."

# ARGHIRULA - Athens, Greece - 1939

I am out of the bath, about to start prayers, which consist mainly of being away from my father, when I hear the door open and the voices of my parents as they greet each other. If there is a touch between them, I don't see it. I can count on one hand the number of times I have seen my father kiss my mother. He treats her respectfully enough, and I believe that he loves her, but he rarely shows affection.

I scramble into my nightgown, move aside the curtain, and greet Mamma. "Are you tired?" She offers a weak smile but is visibly excited about her day.

"We helped two babies come into the world!"

She is beautiful, with her bright blue eyes and porcelain skin. Her hair is long and streaked with gray, and she wears it pulled back and rolled at the nape of her neck.

"Have you eaten, Maria?" my father asks, sitting at the table with an almost empty plate before him. I hate him and feel he is not genuine when he speaks nicely to my mother. Mamma rises early, and no matter how busy her day, there is always a meal on our stove.

"Yes, Diocles, I shared the family meal of smoked fish. There was much celebration today!" she says, "You know their last baby was stillborn…" she trails off, clearly thinking about her multiple stillbirths.

"Mamma," I offer. "Shall I make you tea? Mrs. Georgakas sent you baklava."

She smiles at me and says of her friend. "She is a skilled baker! Thank you, Arghiro', tea sounds lovely." The stove is hot, so I fill the briki with water and place a few tea leaves and stems in the bottom. As I wait for the tea to steep, I formulate the discussion I must have with my mother to let her know I will be leaving.

"Did you paint at Kapnikarea today?" she asks Papa.

"Yes," he says, "I should be finished in a few weeks." She nods her approval.

"I received a commission at The Church of the Holy Apostles in Thissio, and I will start in two months." I smile at the news that Papa will be away because our atmosphere changes when he is gone. Perhaps I don't feel the same urgency about leaving quite yet.

Papa was born in Elevsis, near the Albanian border. I know his mother's name was Eleni and his father's name was Basilis because this is where my brother and sister got their names. Papa speaks differently from Mamma, and she says he has an Albanian accent.

My mother was born in Turkey. She has not seen her parents since she was a young girl and never speaks about them. Papa and Mamma were married in 1906, one year before my father ordained as a priest. Mamma is a midwife, and she assists in the birth and early care of babies, most often in the city's Jewish section. We live a modest life and occasionally move to follow my father's work. His icons are on the churches' walls in many towns, including Lamia, Trikala, and Nomoy. I have heard stories of him painting in churches in Russia when he and Mamma were first married, although it is difficult to imagine my father as a young man or my parents being young and in Russia. But the thing that is hardest to believe is that they fell in love.

"The baklava is delicious!" Mamma says as she licks the honey from her fingers." She has cut the dessert into three pieces and generously shares, but Papa declines as he prepares for his evening prayers. He is the only one of us who prays more than once a day. Mamma does not pray with him, although I'm sure she speaks to God before she goes to sleep. I am sure that her thoughts are for my brothers because they no longer live in our house, and sometimes she does not hear from them for weeks. I know she will be adding me to her prayers soon when I will be gone.

"Arghiro', tomorrow you will go with me to visit Chana and her new babies. She needs rest, and we can help her get things in order."

Surprised to be invited and happy to be away from the house to speak with her about my plans, I respond, "Nai Γysika!" *Yes, of course!*

My mother is beginning to look older, and her hair has more gray. She never wears lipstick or makeup, and she dresses almost exclusively in black. Papa is sixteen years older than Mamma, but he doesn't look old, although this year, he will be 65. He is tall and thin, and his hair is almost all black. He is not a big eater, and he frequently fasts. They are so different that I often wonder about their union. When I get married, my husband will be young and fun-loving! I can't help but think of Giannis as I clear the dishes and retire to the bedroom, and Mamma and I say good night almost in unison, "Kalinikta."

I awaken to a tap on my shoulder, and I groan as I see that it is still dark outside. Mamma is dressed and ready to go. "Kalimera, Arghirula!" she chirps.

"Mamma..." I complain, "it's so early!"

She turns away. "Let's tell that to the babies!"

I put my feet on the cold floor and reach for my thick wool socks. I use the bathroom and get dressed as quickly as possible, and I hear Mamma in the kitchen. She makes coffee for us and places bread and cheese on a plate and the remaining piece of baklava. I eat a little of everything and greedily drink the coffee.

As we bundle in preparation for the morning chill, I notice that Mamma takes her newly washed shawl and puts it in her bag. The streets are empty, except for a few men going to their very early morning jobs and one slumped in a doorway. "How is everyone at the Georgakas house?" Mamma asks. I'm sure she is only making conversation to keep me from complaining again about the early hour.

"Mr. and Mrs. Georgakas are wonderful," I say."

"They are good people!" Mamma says.

"Giannis joined us at dinner," I tell her.

"It's very nice when a boy visits his mother," she responds, sounding slightly angry. Then adds, "I wish your brothers would visit more often. What are they doing that they don't have the time?" I know that she is not asking a question, which is her way of dealing with their absence.

"Mamma, you know Tolis is going to open a kiosk soon, and I suppose he has a lot to do to get that ready...." I trail off when I hear her grunt. We maintain a quick pace and only slow down when we arrive at a cobblestone street that leads to a small alley. When we come out to a more significant road, I see that this part of the city has been left unattended, with older buildings and broken streets. We pass several stores that have either just opened or are about to. Some shop owners are greeting Mamma by name, but, oddly, they call her "Miriam." She responds to that name as she smiles and greets everyone without breaking her stride.

"Miriam, stop on your way home, I have something for you." She thanks the baker with a wave and a smile, and keeps moving. Other shopkeepers say similar things to her, and I begin to understand that these are regular interactions.

I look at Mamma with new eyes. She has always been just our mother, taking care of everything in our house with her quiet, organized sweetness. I had no idea that what she does extends beyond the walls of our home. Yet, here we are, in this place that feels so foreign to me, but where she is so obviously at home.

We walk five more minutes, and I follow Mamma as she turns into an alley where the houses are so close that the clotheslines go from one building to the one across. In front of us, there are two sets of steps. On the right, the steps are very far apart, and it looks almost like a hill of stones. On the left, the broad steps get smaller as you go higher, and they lead to several doors. I notice that there is a small decorative case at each entrance, always on the right side of the door. I ask Mamma what they are, and she explains that Hebrew bible verses are written, rolled up, and placed in each *mezuzah*.

Mamma gently touches the mezuzah as she knocks on Chana's door. I am about to ask her why she did that when the door opens, and an older woman greets us with a big smile.

"Miriam, I'm so happy to see you! Is this your daughter?" she asks as she opens the door wider to let us enter.

"Yes! Arghiro' this is Kyria Levi, Mrs. Levi." Mamma takes my arm and leads me inside.

"Come in, come in!" The sound of a screaming baby fills the room.

Mamma puts down her bag, takes out the shawl, and drapes it over her shoulders. There is a young woman, about my age, lying in bed, and she looks thoroughly exhausted! She has light hair, and her eyes are greenish-blue, very much like her mother's and, actually, very much like my own mother's. I have always thought that Mamma looks very different from Papa. Her skin is light, and her eyes are blue, unlike Papa's olive skin and dark eyes. When I was small, I often pictured my mother as an angel and my father as the devil.

Mamma beckons me to join her as she walks to the kitchen sink and proceeds to scrub her hands as she nods for me to do the same. As I dry my hands on a clean hand towel, she calmly picks up the crying baby, wraps her shawl around him and coos until he is calmer. She asks me to pick up his twin sister, who is also starting to stir and complain.

At first, I am clumsy compared to Mamma, but as I adjust her in my arms, I find it very natural to hold her. I can't help but think that these poor little things have to adjust to the world, and it is only their second day here.

"Did they suckle?" Mamma asks the women.

"No, not really! Both babies seem to be having trouble holding on, which makes me think that Chana might be the problem." Mrs. Levi whispers.

Mamma nods in agreement as she walks to the bed. "Chana, let's feed your babies!" The poor girl looks so exhausted that it's hard for me to believe that she has the strength to do it. But, she seems determined as she lifts herself on her elbows. Mrs. Levi arranges the pillows behind her and puts one under Chana's right arm to lean on to feed on that side. The baby boy struggles several times, hungrily trying to latch on without success, and I see a tear of sad frustration roll down Chana's cheek. Mamma calmly places her index finger in the baby's mouth, and the baby greedily attaches. Ever so gently, Mamma places her finger next to Chana's breast, and the baby grabs the nipple, just as Mamma slips her finger out of his mouth. He continues to suck, and the feeding has successfully begun. Chana's first reaction is a brief shock of pain, but it only lasts a few seconds, and then both mother and baby look peaceful and happy, and the tears on Chana's face are now joyous.

I continue to hold the baby girl as she waits her turn, thinking how beautiful and small she is. I enjoy this new sensation, and I can't wait to tell Effie. I hear Mamma speaking softly with Mrs. Levi.

"Chana's breasts should be engorged by now since the babies are not eating. I am concerned that her milk supply is low. The more they eat, the more her supply will build up." Mamma reaches into her bag and takes out a fabric pouch. "Give this to her every eight hours, until we see that it helps. I will bring more in a few days.

"Thank you!" Mrs. Levi is so grateful. "What is in the tea?" she asks.

Mamma itemizes the herbs in quick succession as if she has provided this list many times before, and I understand now that she probably has! "Red raspberry leaf, nettle leaf, fenugreek, fennel, alfalfa, chamomile, and dandelion. Put it in your briki and boil it for five minutes. You can add honey to sweeten it."

Mrs. Levi takes my mother's hand, and gratefully says, "Thank you, Miriam!"

Mamma returns to Chana's bedside and points out that the baby is calmly sleeping, and his mother has renewed color in her cheeks.

"Chana, I will take him, but I think your little girl is hungry too. Are you ready for her?"

The girl smiles and says, "Neh!" *Yes!* as I bring the now wailing baby girl to her mother. Mamma uses the same method to latch this baby onto the other breast, and everything is calm and peaceful in this room full of love.

We leave with a promise to return in a few days and that they should send for my mother if there is a need before that. We walk the same route back, but much more slowly as Mamma stops and visits almost every shop and kiosk owner. She has been carrying the black cloth bag all day. Besides the shawl, the bag also contains the "Miriam tea," wrapped in individual cloth pouches, which I have seen her sew, but never thought to ask about their purpose.

She truly is an angel as she glides through this place that is unfamiliar to me and calmly greets these people who look so much like her. New mothers and grandmothers welcome her healing pouches, and she fills her bag with cheese, jams, bread, fruit, and other treasures in return. Our last stop is to see Sage, the herbalist. Here, Mamma reaches into her treasure bag and retrieves a piece of cheese and a jar of honey and gives them to Sage in return for the valuable herbs that make up her special tea.

Walking home, I can't stop asking questions. Mamma laughs. I see her in a very different light than ever before. She is a healer! People respect her, hang on to her words, and heed her advice. I have never loved her more.

# JOAN - New Haven, Connecticut - 2011

The alarm startles me at 7:00 a.m. I try to clear the head fog, and it takes a minute before all the events of the last week hit me with full force. I had a dreamless sleep last night, with ten milligrams of zolpidem and the monumental cry that left me completely depleted.

This morning, melancholy, I shower and dress for another long day ahead. The heavy feeling lingered from last night but is somewhat lifted by the beautiful sunlight pouring into my room. Our room! Within seconds, a flood of tears weighs upon my heart once again.

When I peek next door, I'm happy to see that my grandchildren have not yet left for school. As he has done since he was a baby, Adam kisses me twice, and Gia gives me one of her 20-second hugs, which soothes me immensely.

"Nana, when is Pop coming home?"

I choke back tears and tell them, "Soon!" And, since this answer is enough if you are ten and eight, they proceed to gather their signed papers and lunches. She shoves everything into her backpack, and he meticulously places every item in proper order, one by one.

My son-in-law greets me with his big sweet smile and gives me a much needed hug, "You OK, Mom?"

"Yea, I'm good, Mike."

He starts the coffee, I kiss the tops of the kids' heads, and they all walk out to the school bus at the driveway's end. When Mike returns, he asks, "Do you want me to drive you to the hospital today?"

"Thanks, honey, I'll drive myself."

"Are you sure, Mom? I don't mind!"

I often forget that I didn't raise him myself. He has an uncanny memory, and I often tell him that he is an old soul. "I want the freedom of having a car so that I can come and go."

He nods, "I get it! Let me know if you change your mind." He pours us each a cup of coffee, I give him a peck on the cheek, and I go back to my house as he goes into his home office

I meticulously pack two pairs of stretch pants, underwear, socks, and four tops that take me fifteen minutes to choose. I fix the bed with all eleven pillows, every one unnecessary except for the one on which I sleep. I take a long time examining the room, making sure that it is perfectly tidy. I check the bathroom, put away everything on the counter, and spend ten minutes spraying Windex and wiping until everything sparkles. Downstairs, I check the shelf for a book that I have not read, and not seeing any, I pack the Kindle. I put my bag and purse by the front door, go back to the kitchen, place the two dishes and one coffee cup from the sink into the dishwasher and proceed to scrub the counters, sweep the floor, and end with a quick mopping. Looking around, I'm satisfied that the house is "company ready." I laugh out loud at my cruel joke, and I don't need anyone to tell me that I am on the verge of a mental breakdown.

I see that the traffic is light going northbound as I cross the overpass bridge on Newtown Turnpike. I barely merge onto the Merritt Parkway when the tears begin. I talk to myself out loud and blast the radio. After five minutes, I turn the radio off and talk to myself again. "He will be fine, just as soon as they figure out what to do for him!" I blast the radio, but the louder the radio, the more loudly I cry!

With a pounding headache, I finally reach the hospital parking deck and claim a spot. Before leaving the car, I pull down the visor to check the inevitable damage, and I'm shocked to see the tired old lady looking back. I pinch my cheeks, put on lipstick, and compose myself as best I can. The walking bridge puts me in the lobby, but I turn left out the front door and down the street instead of going to the check-in desk. Just as I hoped, the smell of coffee in the tiny Dunkin' Donuts takes away the edge. I automatically order a medium coffee, extra light, with cream, no sugar while searching for the perfect doughnut.

Back in the hospital, I take the elevator to the 9th floor and ICU Room 220, and as I walk down the hall towards the door, I have a vision of Sheldon sitting up in bed, saying, "Let's get the fuck outta here!" Although it is no real surprise that nothing has changed, I am nonetheless a little disappointed that he is motionless with his eyes closed. He is clean-shaven, and the bedding is white and crisp.

The monitors are still in place, and the tubes and bags are connected just as they were yesterday.

I put my overnight bag behind the big green chair and sit in the straight one next to the bed. I take his hand and kiss his cheek as I whisper, "I'm here, Shel." Still hopeful, I look for a response from his face and the monitor screen, but of course, there is none.

Because Yale-New Haven is a teaching hospital, there is a constant stream of doctors coming in and out of the room. Generally, they greet me, look at the records, glance at the monitors, and leave. I couldn't tell you most of their names; however, the nurses have become our friends. Jen is a family favorite, and she's the one who shaves his face.

She told us, "I noticed he packed his toiletry bag, so I figured he would be happy with the grooming!" It is so touching!

The day nurse comes in now, checks his vitals, smiles at me, and proceeds to tilt him slightly to his other side, as they do every few hours. She is still fussing when the girls walk in. Cassie greets her, "Hi Carrie!"

Carrie responds, "Hi" as she leaves the room without another word, which seems slightly out of character.

I turn my attention to my daughters, "Hey! I'm surprised to see you all here! Where are the kids?"

Mica explains, "Holly and Matt both came to watch them" and adds, with a little smile, "all together!" All I can do is imagine the crazy noise of my six grandchildren in one place, but remind myself that Uncle Matt and Aunty Holly are incredible.

Cassie tells me, "Dr. Takyar called and said he wants

to talk to us. I thought you knew, Mom." If someone told me, I don't remember.

"Maybe they are going to take him out of the coma!" Rachel says, hopefully, as she holds his hand. "Hey, Daddy," the all-too-familiar tears are in her eyes.

"We have over an hour before the meeting, so let's walk to the food trucks and get something to eat," Cassie suggests.

"You guys go ahead, I'm not hungry." I am a little thrown off from my usual schedule. Typically, this is my time to wait for doctors to walk through, for visitors to appear, for my husband's eyes to open magically.

"Mom! You're coming too." Rachel takes my hand to have me stand.

"OK," I concede, "but let's be sure to get back in time for the meeting..." I barely start the sentence when I see all six eyes roll!

We walk out of the main door and across to Cedar Street. I am blown away by the number of food trucks lined up on both sides, maybe 40. If you can dream up food, they have it here; arepas, falafel, Ethiopian, Indian, Japanese, Italian, and burgers and hot dogs. It is a buzz of activity and crowds of people, including doctors and nurses, line up at every truck.

The atmosphere is festive, the sun is shining, and the air is crisp. I have a peaceful feeling that I have not felt in weeks, which makes me believe that good news is coming. As difficult as it is to decide, I choose the Moroccan truck because I have never tried it before. I wait behind three tech-looking guys who seem to know what they are ordering.

"What's good?" I ask the young man in front of me when he offers me a smile. He seems happy to share his knowledge.

"The lamb and couscous are excellent, and the chickpea tagine is great too."

I smile my thanks and wait for my turn. When he steps away, I move up and order the tagine. The Moroccan man in the truck pours a scoop of the aromatic chickpea soup into a cardboard container, and I can smell the cinnamon, cumin, and cilantro. "Thank you."

The benches are all taken, so we decide to go back inside the hospital, pleasing me. We show our ID tags at the main desk, where we often see the same receptionists. The one whose name tag says Grace, repeats her daily comment to Cassie, "I just love your sequin bags! I see you have the silver one today!"

Cassie's sequin bags are a constant source of entertainment for everyone who knows her. She received a gold one as a gift and purchased a second one from Coach directly. But she loves them so much that she got a few knockoffs that look surprisingly similar, at a much gentler price.

"I want you to have this one!" Cassie says. She reaches into the shopping bag she has been carrying and takes out the blue sequin bag. "It's not Coach, but it's fun!" Grace is beyond excited and inspects the purse with "oohs and aahs."

We ride the elevator to the ninth floor and go to the ICU family waiting room. It is unusually empty today, with just a few people sitting in chairs and one couple sitting on one of the couches. We spread our lunch treasures on the table, sit in the four available chairs, check our phones, and proceed to eat what turns out to be the tastiest food I've had in weeks. We speculate on the different things the meeting might be about and discuss possible scenarios, including lung transplants, which Cassie has been researching.

We are cheerful, fed, and watered when we go to Sheldon's room and put away our jackets and belongings. We give him our kisses, and Cassie retrieves her notebook to prepare for the notes she will inevitably need to take. At the nurses' station, Mica says, "We have a meeting scheduled with Dr. Takyar. Can you tell us where?"

The nurse looks at her notes and sweetly responds, "Down the hall, last room on the left" as she points over her left shoulder.

We locate the room and find it empty, with the lights on. The space is incredibly small. There are four chairs against one wall, facing another four on the opposite wall. We choose the four chairs on the right and sit, feeling optimistic and excitedly ready for some good news.

Dr. Takyar walks in and occupies one of the center chairs. Because he is always so severe, the girls refer to him as Dr. Doom and Gloom. He doesn't disappoint today as he introduces us to the other three lung specialists he has brought with him. The names are on their white coats right above the left pocket, which holds pens, and they each wear a lanyard with a tag on it. We are so ridiculously close that if we stretched out our legs, our feet would touch. Of course, everyone is sitting perfectly straight, and Cassie has her notebook on her lap, prepared to document.

Without hesitation, Dr. Takyar begins, "As you know, Sheldon's condition is unusual. He has Acute Interstitial Pneumonitis and Diffuse Alveolar Damage" There are so many words, "acute respiratory distress.... prognosis..." But I can't help my focus on the small woman to Dr. Takyar's right. I know I should be listening to the doctor, but I am completely mesmerized by this young woman's body language and her angelic aura. I glance at the name stitched on her coat, Rebecca Bird. How very fitting. I try to force myself to the present, but I am in a trance as my eyes fix on that one small tear falling down Dr. Bird's face. Just as the lone tear reaches the corner of her mouth, Dr. Takyar's words explode in my brain.

"Arrange for those close to him to come to say their last good-byes. He will not be waking up."

# JOAN - Weehawken, New Jersey - 1968

"Yea, Mom, it smells great!" I agree with my mother. She stirs another handful of rice into the boiling milk as she tilts her head in the direction of my 15-year-old brother's bedroom to indicate what smells so good. My mom is an incredibly good cook, but not much of a baker, so rice pudding is her version of a *dolce*. However, the aroma to which she is referring is the sweet smell of incense.

She often lights the little incense pyramids in front of her saints' statues on her dresser. John likes to burn it in his room too because he loves the smell too. He even takes the little plastic Jesus from church for my First Communion and puts it on his dresser. So happy that it's for Jesus, my mom once gave him a box of the little pyramids. He was beyond pleased because the pungent odor of the incense camouflages the smell of pot.

When Marilena walks into the kitchen, she is immediately put to work, stirring the rice. Mom prepares the cinnamon sticks, cuts the peel from a large lemon and puts it all into the milk, along with a large handful of sugar.

She lowers the flame and gives the mixture one more stir before covering the pot.

My mother is an excellent cook, and my parents' social life revolves around dinners in our home or at homes of their friends, often including the entire family. Our family doctor, Dr. Sanmole, has a standing invitation and has dinner with us almost every Wednesday evening. He sits at the head of the table, one of my parents on each side, and they chat and laugh and share a glass of wine and generally end with espresso coffee. He even shares some of his mother's Sicilian recipes with my mother. She fusses over these meals and somehow manages also to look beautiful while serving them. Over the years, he has remained in our lives both as our doctor and their friend. His wife and children do not socialize with us, although I was invited to their summer home in Ortley Beach for a week to babysit for them a few summers ago. Madeline did the same the following summer.

Since today is Sunday, everyone will be here. I set the table with ten dishes and ten napkins as Marilena follows with forks and knives. "Vanna, You have one plate too many!" my mother says, looking towards the table and knowing full well that I do not.

"Mom, I told you yesterday that I invited Sheldon for dinner." She grumbles something as she returns to stirring her rice pudding. I hear the rustle of paper bags as my father comes home with his Sunday morning treasures. Food shopping for my dad is more like a religious experience than providing nourishment, so he takes it very seriously.

It is doubtful that bread from the pastry bakery could be as good as from the bread bakery, so he makes the rounds. Peeking out from one of the bags is his Sunday paper "Il Progresso Italo-Americano." Marilena runs to him, kisses him, and takes a sack.

"What did you get me?"

He smiles that unique smile that he reserves for her, "Aspetta!" he says, laughing and knowing full well that she will not wait. She giggles and starts to rummage through the bags, finds her treat right under the newspaper, and pulls out a bag filled with penny candy and bubble gum. I notice she puts the Swedish Fish back at the bottom of the bag, without telling him that she doesn't like them. She is not about to break the magic of this ritual between her and her Babbuccio. My mother, still grumbling about something that I can't make out, goes back to the stove, stirs the sauce, and places the fried meatballs into the already meat-laden pot.

I take a piece of the fresh bread and hold it out to her. She spoons some sauce on it and shoos me away. I step away gladly, although I hear her as I walk away, "Non ti capisco!" *I don't understand you*

"Mom, you have known him for years and have always liked him, so why are you doing this now?" This conversation is not new.

"Because he's Jewish! He can be your friend, but nothing more!"

I leave the kitchen and sit in my room to avoid a fight before my brother and sister get here, or Sheldon for that matter. She exhausts me! I turn a few pages in my grandmother's journal, and I wish to read the ancient script, but I can't. So I can only guess what my grandmother said in 1944, when her daughter, my mother, married the enemy, the Italian sailor occupying their country. Maybe she didn't say anything nasty because she was a kind and loving mother.

I hear Pete's voice first when he teases my mother, and she giggles like a schoolgirl. Madeline looks at the table and asks, "Are Mike and Linda coming?"

I hear my mother, "Yes, they are... and so is the Ammazzacristo!"

Everyone responds in unison! Pete rolls his eyes, and Madeline quietly says, "Mom, I can't believe you can even let that pass your lips!" My father just shakes his head, Marilena starts to cry, and Johnny takes this opportunity to scoop a meatball out of the sauce because he's so hungry. I pretend I didn't hear her, although I passionately hate her right now. I know she will become June Cleaver, the perfect mother, when we are all together. I refuse to let her spoil my happiness today! Soon Mike and Linda arrive, bringing hugs, smiles, and baby Michael, the sweetest little boy.

When the doorbell rings, I press the buzzer to unlock the front door downstairs, and I wait at the top of the steps, watching Sheldon climb them two at a time. "Hey," He holds my gaze for a minute, and I feel the still-new sensation that warms me from head to toe. As we share a tender kiss, I know that my mother does not have the power to take this away, no matter what she says or does.

We join the others in the dining room, and as he greets everyone, he gives my mother the lovely bouquet he has been holding. She thanks him offhandedly and, with barely a glance, passes them to Marilena, who goes to the cabinet to find a vase. I measure up my mother to guess how this will go with her, but she is entirely composed and almost radiant. Of course, she is, and why not? Her world is perfect, right here, as all five of her children are together in her home. I sometimes wonder if she might be a little insane.

My dad loves to be in the kitchen. When I ask if I can help, he points to the antipasto platter that he just finished preparing with Marilena's help. I carefully take it and put it on the dining table, treating it as a work of art. The thin salami is perfectly rolled, as is the prosciutto. Slices of mortadella and soppressata fill the left side in between sections of provolone cheese. The olives are a perfect blend of colors, and the roasted peppers have extra garlic that Dad has meticulously minced. It is a masterpiece! He joins us in the dining room and pours glasses of wine for himself, the men, and Madeline. John declines, along with Linda and me. My mother extends her glass and says, "un dito," *one finger*. He pours a little into her glass, gives the same to Marilena, and places the oversized Fortissimo bottle on the floor next to his chair. As we all take our seats around the table, Sheldon stands back to see where I am and takes the chair next to mine.

In typical Italian fashion, everyone leans over to serve themselves from the platter. Linda is about to reach for the bread, but notices there is no butter on the table. "Mom, do you have butter? I'll get it!" We all teasingly reprimand my mother for forgetting Linda's favorite "food."

As Sheldon sits back patiently waiting for everyone else to fill their plates, I whisper, "I'm so happy you're here." He reaches under the tablecloth and rubs my leg, sending an electric shock through my body. I take a quick look around the table, making sure that everyone is busy with their appetizer frenzy, and I lean towards him and kiss him on the lips. He is surprised but kisses back passionately before I pull away. Mom looks up a split second too late, and she can't be sure she saw what she saw. Linda walks out of the kitchen with the butter pretending she did not notice. However, Marilena knows what she saw and gives me her adorable "I know" smile, and I think to myself, not for the first time, that I like having her in my corner.

The noisy chatter makes it seem like everyone is talking at once, but we are also listening, which is the magic of the Italian family. There is no shortage of stories and jokes and never a lull throughout the antipasto and first glass of wine. The girls and I clear the table, prepare the macaroni bowls, and serve the boys and Mom, who has declared herself done for the day. Dad is in the kitchen, directing and checking on the remainder of the meal.

I sit down, just as Sheldon says, "I heard it was pretty bad in Newark last summer with those riots...were you guys involved?" Pete defers to Mike, and we are rapt as Mike tells his story:

"It was the middle of last July and Linda was three months pregnant. We decided to go away for a few days, so we booked a Wildwood hotel on Friday, July 14th. Just before we got down the shore, Linda turned up the radio and said, 'Did you hear that, Mike?'

Hear what?

She pointed to the radio, but whatever report there was had ended. I turned the knob, trying to get more news, but there was only music. Having been in the car for three hours, we were anxious to go for a walk, so we checked in, dropped our bags in the room, and walked towards the ocean. We were on the boardwalk just a few minutes when we heard an announcement from overhead speakers that we didn't even know existed.

'All National Guard is activated and required to report to the Newark Stadium immediately!'

They announced it over and over. We couldn't believe it! We knew there were problems in Newark the past few days, but assumed it was a police situation. The whole thing started two days before when two policemen beat up a black cab driver. There were rumors that they had killed him since witnesses saw them dragging his bloody body. They hadn't killed him, but they beat him and brought him into custody. Around midnight, two Molotov cocktails hit the 4th Precinct and right after that, the first group started looting the stores on 17th Avenue, and it just blew up from there!

Linda and I had to check out of the hotel. When we explained why we had to leave, the manager told us he would refund our money. We drove three hours back home and, after dropping Linda off, I reported to the stadium. By Friday afternoon, there were thousands of national guardsmen and state troopers in Newark, and the rioting lasted four days. Twenty-six people died, and I don't know how many hundreds were injured. I think there were close to 1000 arrests."

We are all absorbed and saddened by this familiar story. Sheldon said, "When I first heard about it, it was referred to as the 'worst civil disorder' in the history of New Jersey!"

Pete chimes in, "Yea, it was, and there were millions of dollars in property damage in the city."

We all respond at once, "Wow!" "Holy shit!"

"It was horrible!" Mike goes on:

"I'll never forget how we each had to grab a gun! By the time I got there, they were out of rifles, so I was handed a .45 ACP, and I was directed to a bucket of bullets and instructed to fill my pockets! We couldn't believe it! As we walked out, almost as an afterthought, they told us that there were snipers on the roofs and in apartment windows. They told us that the streets would be dark since the guardsmen, who were first to go out in the streets last night, shot out every streetlight. It was a long five days!"

We switch to much more pleasant subjects and enjoy the delicious food on the table. We remove the macaroni plates, and Dad brings out the pork roast on a big platter surrounded by roasted potatoes. They taste slightly of lemon, thanks to my mom's Greek recipe. There is also a large bowl of meatballs and all the meats that were in the sauce. The salad, seasoned by my dad, or Marilena, I'm never sure which, is a little heavy on the oil. Sheldon can't believe there is more food! I noticed he was lingering over the macaroni. "I thought that was the entire meal," he whispered.

"Save room for dessert!" I tease.

Dinner is delicious, and the atmosphere is pleasant if you don't count the daggers that I sometimes catch from Lula, my sweet mother. *Can she give it up?* Sheldon laughs when the espresso comes with the oversized plate of pastries from Rispoli's Bakery. It is hard to choose between the cannoli, Napoleons, sfogliatelle, pignoli cookies, and babas. I am browsing the choices, when he reaches over and takes a miniature cannoli for himself and places a pignoli cookie on my plate, with a look that says, "This is what you like, right?" This guy blows my mind! That would have been my exact choice.

# JOAN - Weehawken, New Jersey - Summer, 1968

"**M**y parents are coming to New Jersey next week." I'm sitting at the kitchen table with the cord of the phone stretched as far as possible. My parents and sister are in the living room, watching Bonanza.

"Oh, that's great!" I say.

"My father wants to take everyone out for dinner." I come from a family that never goes to restaurants. Going out for us would be to go to someone else's house for dinner. "Can you come?" he asks, sounding hopeful.

"Sure!" I say, and I am already thinking about what to wear to a "family dinner." "Will you wear your uniform?" We both laugh before I even finish the question.

"I want to tell my family about us!" he says.

I am only half joking when I say, "What do you want to tell them, exactly?"

He chuckles. "I want to tell them that I asked you to marry me, and I'm waiting for your answer."

*Why is he so sure of himself, and exactly why am I waiting?*

"You can let me know when you decide." He hesitates,

"About the dinner, I mean!" he says, and I laugh. "And, hopefully, you can stay at Bruce and Joyce's for the weekend!" Oh sure! That should go over well with my mother!

When he was home on leave a few months ago, Sheldon bought a 1959 Chevy Biscayne, red and white, which he leaves at Bruce's house in Old Bridge. Everything seems effortless, and he is consistently dependable. Because it is a whole new experience for me, I often expect something to go wrong, or that he will let me down, but he never does. I am sitting on the bed, talking to Marilena, when we hear the doorbell. She jumps up, and I tell her Sheldon is not coming up. "I'm meeting him downstairs." She rolls her eyes towards the kitchen, where my mother is making more noise than necessary. I use the bathroom, check my face in the mirror, and take my overnight bag.

I poke my head in the kitchen, and say "I'm leaving!" but she just grumbles something in Greek that I can't understand, and I leave without asking her to translate. She has barely spoken to me since I told her about my plans. Marilena has gone ahead, and I see she is already sitting on the step with Sheldon as they chat away, and it warms my heart that they like each other.

I hear him say, "Did you find a telescope?" They seem to be picking up on an already-existing conversation where she dreams of being an astronomer. Funny, I never knew this before!

"No, I didn't, I don't even know where to look!" she giggles. When I tell her we have to go, she hugs me and runs back up the five outside steps and through the first door. I notice she has put a wedge in the inside door so she doesn't have to buzz to get back in. Clever girl!

We share a kiss and walk a block and a half to where Betsy is parked. One of the drawbacks of living in this area is that it's always hard to find a parking space, so we often have to circle a few times. "How are things?" he asks, tilting his head slightly towards my house.

I know what he is asking and respond, "Well, the aspirin I just took should help." He laughs. "Seriously, she is either spewing her bullshit in three different languages or giving me the cold shoulder. I'm never sure which is worse!"

As is his way, he doesn't get upset at the things that I tell him. "She'll get used to the idea, just give her some time." But, I am truly angry with my mother, and I was not kidding about the headache she gave me this morning as she ranted her cruel remarks, before she froze me out.

"The car looks so clean!" I admire the shiny chrome.

"Joyce cleaned it inside and out!" He unlocks the passenger door and holds it open for me. I climb in and put my bag on the back seat. As I turn around, I notice that the driver's door is still locked, so I lean over and unlock it. He gets in, starts the car, puts his arm around me, and pulls me in close for a proper kiss. "I missed you," he whispers. I feel all my tension release as I kiss him back, and I wish that we could just stay right here forever.

The ride to Bruce's house seems short because there is no lack of conversation. Mostly, Sheldon is talking about the guys who are with him at Oceana Naval Air Base. He is caught up in stories about his Navy buddies in Virginia Beach and being on The Enterprise or in the Philippines and Hong Kong. Now and then, he glances over or reaches out and touches my hand.

Judy greets us at the door. She is beautiful, with her

reddish-brown curls, blue eyes, and a big smile with perfect teeth. After a happy-to-see-you hug, she leads me to the living room where everyone has formed a circle around two-year old Dawn. She is entertaining them with her goldfish stories as Joyce adjusts herself on the couch to better accommodate her eight-months pregnant body.

Sheldon's mom, Nettie, is petite and put together. She is less than 5 feet tall, and fashionably dressed with perfect hair, which she has styled every week. His dad, Hyman, is a little overweight and a little sloppy. I have met them both before, so their dynamics as a couple are not a total surprise. They don't seem to communicate much unless it is under their breath or with a sharp look.

I enjoy catching up with Judy while Sheldon talks mostly to Bruce. Every time I look his way, he is often looking at me and either winks or smiles. As I melt, I know that my feelings are already beyond my control. It's a pleasant change to be here in Bruce's big house, where we are free to either hang with everyone or go outside or to another room where we can talk and kiss all we want.

When the babysitter arrives at 6:30, we leave in two cars, and we get to The Robert E. Lee 10 minutes early for our seven o'clock reservation. I am learning that the Isaacsons don't like to be late. The restaurant is large, and the menu is enormous and lists everything from burgers to lobster dinners. Bruce immediately begins to order, and, in no time, the table fills with mussels, clams, and Italian appetizers. "Mom, they have the fried shrimp you like," Judy says, and turning to me, "...and the scallops are excellent here!" Judy and I order the scallops, Nettie gets the shrimp, and everyone else gets lobster. Sheldon, his father, and brother are experts at cracking the lobsters, and the crustaceans are picked nearly clean. Sheldon's father pays the check, which must be substantial, and I am surprised that no one even attempts to contribute towards the bill.

Joyce suggests that we stop for a drink before going home, and I am amazed at her stamina. The music is loud, but there is a curved bar with enough stools to seat everyone, so it's a winner! Sheldon pulls his stool very close to mine and, when the bartender asks, he orders a beer. He looks at me questioningly, and I tell him I'll have the same. The 5th Dimension's "Stoned Soul Picnic" is blasting... "sassafras and moonshine"... and conversation is practically impossible, so we enjoy the music and kiss and touch hands. As I finish the beer, he orders two more, and when I finish my second one, he leans towards my ear and asks, "How's the headache?" Due to the combination of beer, loud music, and the thought of my mother's pissy attitude, there is dull pain. When I gesture that it is slightly there, he calmly reaches into his pocket and brings out a tiny piece of tissue paper, in which he has very carefully wrapped two aspirins. He hands them to me, and says," I brought these for you, just in case."

I suddenly have this incredible moment of clarity where I can see his heart. It is almost physical, and I see his goodness as an aura around him. The loud music is gone, as are the voices, and the harsh lights are softer. Very clearly, I see us together as a snapshot from an old camera, and I know my future is full of love.

When I return to the present, I say, "YES!" He can't hear over the noise, and he asks me to repeat. "YES!"

He squints his eyes in question, "Yes, what?"

Magically, the music pauses between songs just long enough to say, "Yes, to the question you asked me." He kisses me. I'm sure he heard me the first time and already knew what the answer would be.

He very seriously says, "Tell me again tomorrow when you're not half drunk!" I'm sure he just wants to hear me say "yes" a fourth time. God, I love this guy!!!!

# MARIA - Athens, Greece - 1903

"Girls, please take your seats!" Sister Eleni is very young, and the girls don't fear her very much. Although they go to their seats, they don't end their chatter and only stop talking when she taps the desk, three times, with her ruler. When the room is quiet, she smiles sweetly, puts her arm around my shoulder, and introduces me to the class. "This is Maria! Everyone, please make her feel welcome."

Many of the girls smile and greet me out loud, "Hello, Maria!" Welcome, Maria!"

"There's a seat here, Maria!" Like echoes, I hear them as I try to come to terms with the fact that I am no longer Miriam and that I am no longer Jewish. I tell myself that it is temporary, and I know that when Mama and Baba get here, we will once again celebrate the Jewish holidays.

"Soon" Mama had responded when I asked the question for the tenth time.

"When will you join me?"

I look around the room and see a dozen girls of different ages, all with dark hair and eyes. Most schools are for boys, but this school is only for girls, and I know that my father's friends arranged for me to be here.

"Yassas," *hello*, I say in perfect Greek, and they greet me as if I am Greek and I am greatly relieved that I have no explaining to do. Sister Eleni gives me a gentle push towards the available seat, and I obediently take it. Although the girls are smiling and friendly, I don't feel like I belong, so I find comfort in losing myself in the workbook when the first lesson starts.

Both Ancient Greek and Demotic Greek are easy classes since I have already studied them with Baba, and as long as I work a little extra every day, I can also get through the arithmetic. The religion classes, however, are more complicated, and I find that I have much catching up to do since my classmates have already learned about the New Testament. Baba taught from the Talmud, and I was his perfect student, but it is of no use to me here. I am becoming an expert at pretending to mouth the words to Greek Orthodox prayers and only partially answer questions. The girls and their chatter often rescue me as they inadvertently answer for me.

I have two new friends who have been friends with each other since they were five years old. Agni is beautiful, with big brown eyes and very long lashes. She wears her hair in a thick braid, and she is sweet, shy, and most often reticent. Olga has dark curly hair, which she leaves loose and makes no effort to contain. She is very talkative and generally doesn't care if anyone is listening. I like her very much, so I hear most of the time.

Our school day starts at eight o'clock right after breakfast and ends at one o'clock in the afternoon. The classrooms have gas lamps that we light when we use the room. I found that if I get to class early, Sister asks me to "light the gas." I love the popping sound it makes when the flame catches. We eat the principal meal at two o'clock in the dining hall, whose large windows make the room bright even on a cloudy day. Our afternoons are filled with a rotation of chores and mandatory study before we gather for evening prayers. After a light meal, we retire for the night.

We have to use candles to walk around when it gets dark, and the candles are in a box with matches on the end tables next to our beds. To avoid dripping wax on the floor and furniture, we cannot light them often, only if it's very dark or an emergency. It's easy to get used to the dark, especially since some light comes in from the gas lamps on the street outside our windows. At night we are required to use the chamber pot in our room to relieve ourselves instead of using the lavatory down the hall, but most of us break that rule.

When the moon is full, light shines like a magic ray through the only window in my room. Like every other night, I put a straight chair in front of the window, not far from the brazier full of burning coals, and I take out the silk fabric that Mama gave me. I carefully unfold only the section on which I am working, and I leave the rest neatly folded in the small wooden box at my feet. Because the moon is unusually bright, I know that it will be a long night. There are times when the light is so dim that I work slowly, almost by memory. But on a night like tonight I work for many, many hours. I want Mama to be proud of me.

As I sew, my thoughts wander to a time not too long ago when I sat in front of the fire with Mama and Baba in Smyrna's house. When the fuzzy memory becomes a clear image, I find that it is hard for me to breathe as the air leaves my lungs and makes my chest feel as if it will explode! The torrent of tears is so great that I can't see the stitches, so I carefully remove the silk from my lap and entirely give in to my misery.

I received one letter from Baba two years ago when I first arrived in Athens. Mother Thekla handed me the envelope with the single folded sheet, and I will forever recall the sad look on her face. I have read and reread it a thousand times, and I see the tear stains of a little girl on it. "It will not be long before we are together again. Be good and know that Mama and I love you more than anything in the world." I rarely look at it now, and I no longer cry if I read it. I sometimes close my eyes to remember them, but more and more often, their faces are difficult to envision, and their features are blurred. I wrote a letter to them this morning before class. I gave the letter to Sister Eleni so she can arrange to send it to them, although I have some doubts that it will reach them. She took it with a smile and slipped it into one of the magical pockets buried deep in her habit.

Today is my 14th birthday. Agni and Olga are up before me, and I hear them tiptoeing around the room. Since I assume they're trying to surprise me, I lie still with my eyes closed and pretend to be sleeping. The sun pours onto my bed when the girls open the shutters. I roll over as if just waking up, and they giggle and give me kisses. "Xronia Polla, Maria!" *Happy Birthday!* they exclaim in unison. They make me happy, and they are the best friends I have ever had. I jump out of bed, wrap myself in the blanket, and sincerely return their warm hugs.

"We have a gift for you!" Agni says. Olga gives me a tiny package wrapped in brown paper and tied with Agni's hair ribbon. They are giddy with excitement as I untie the ribbon, open the wrap, and carefully unfold a sky blue fabric. Tucked in the folds is a beautiful gold cross! It is similar to the ones they wear every day, and it is slightly larger than the one Mama and Baba had given me so long ago. It is amazingly shiny, even more so than the ones my classmates wore in Smyrna! It is magically bright, and my friends' love fills me with joy, although my heart aches. Agni and Olga are confused when tears roll down my face as I place the thin gold chain around my neck.

"I have something to tell you," I say. I know we will get a demerit for being late for breakfast, but I need to share my truth. We sit on my bed, and as I open my heart, they cry along with me.

When I finish my story, I know deep down and without a shadow of a doubt that I will never again see my mother and father.

# ARGHIRULA - Athens, Greece - 1940

**M**y plan of leaving my father's house did not go well and, when I felt his anger would turn towards my mother, I decided to stay. He mostly ignores me, but he has become fanatic about my absences. Even though we share minimal conversation, he is acutely aware of my comings and goings.

It is a beautiful October day. The summer was hot, mainly because I had to stand outside the kiosk almost every day when Tolis needed me to cover him. Today, I'm bored, and I read the magazines until someone stops to purchase cigarettes or a newspaper or candy. Our kiosk is smaller than Giannis', who is on the other side of the city center. Giannis has plans to expand his booth, and he will add a shop when the opportunity arises. I leaf through the latest fashion magazine, and I imagine myself in the coat with the oversized fur collar that the model wears. The picture looks like it is in Russia on a snowy mountaintop.

I am intrigued and lost in thought when I hear Effie shout "Arghirula!"

We embrace and as always, I think how good it is to see her. "Come for dinner tonight!!" She jumps right to the point. "Can you?"

I am distracted by Tolis as he approaches with his arms full of merchandise. "I want to!" I say as an idea is forming.

My brother is not a tall man, but he is healthy, and there is something about him that makes you feel that he is in charge. Tolis greets Effie as he gets busy, stocking and rearranging items all around the kiosk. He stands on the wooden box and hangs things on the highest shelves. "How was the day?" he asks.

"Practically nothing!" I respond as I pull the cash box from under the low ledge. He laughs as he always does when he sees me do this and says,

"What are you worried about?"

I place the box on the counter, where I know it will stay until he closes for the day. "Effie invited me for dinner!" I have my reasons for telling him. He takes his time and continues to organize.

"Does Papa know you will not be home?" he asks.

"I was hoping you would tell him! I want to go, please, Tolis."

My father has so many archaic beliefs, and the smallest infringement on his rules makes him upset. I know that Tolis is playing with me and making me beg for something that he will do anyway, but I need to hear him say that he will. He continues to busy himself with the stock. Effie and I wait anxiously for his response, and I know we are annoying him by standing so close to where he is trying to move around. Finally, he says, "Malista, malista, I will tell him! Help me here!" We are so happy that we do everything he asks, and I wonder how I would ever survive my life without my brother.

Effie is talking without taking a breath. "Alessandro this, Alessandro that, Alessandro, Alessandro...." she can't say his name enough because she is so crazy about him, and I have never seen her happier. We walk quickly, as she is anxious to get home to change and fix her hair before he arrives. For me, knowing that Giannis will be there is reason enough to hurry.

Mr. and Mrs. Georgiakis are, as always, cheerful and hospitable. The table is ready, and all the beautiful smells imply that dinner is too. Effie practically pulls me to her room and starts to take her favorite dresses out of her closet. She holds them up so I can help her choose. She settles on the blue one and quickly hands me the red one. "You wear this!" I start to protest, but she insists, "This is a special night! You know that Alessandro asked Papa for my hand today, so tonight is a celebration!'"

"Do you think your Papa said yes?" I tease.

She reaches in a drawer and pulls out the box of powder and lipsticks. She finds a little tiny brush and a small piece of charcoal, wrapped in brown paper. The inside of the wrapping is all smudged black. She tells me to sit, and she starts to work on my eyebrows. She touches the brush to the charcoal and, ever so lightly, brushes each brow. I tell her to go natural because I don't want to look overdone, and my eyebrows are dark already. Done with the brush, she puts it to the side and reaches for the lipsticks. We open a few of them and decide on a beautiful red shade. She puts some on her finger and dabs it on my cheeks, rubbing lightly in circular strokes. She is so expert at doing this, and I am happy to be included in her excitement. She stands back to check her work the way I have seen my father stand back to review a painting in progress. "Your hair!" She brushes it and twists it and pulls it up, then behind my ears. She finally lets it fall and fluffs the curls with her hands. "Not much to be done with this." We both laugh, but she seems satisfied "Put on the dress and shoes before you look in the mirror."

She reaches to the floor of the closet and pulls out two pairs of black shoes. "Choose! Put on the stockings first!" I do as I am told and finally slide on the dress, turning around.

"Are the seams straight?"

While she checks my seams, I choose the suede shoes that wrap around the ankle. I loosen the strap to allow for the half size difference, although they still feel snug.

"You look beautiful!" She points to the mirror, "You can look now." She steps back and waits for my reaction. I stand in front of the full-length mirror and barely recognize the woman looking back at me.

"Oh, Effie! I look so pretty!!" The dress hugs my hips and bosom so perfectly as if it were made just for me. I turn to the side to check the perfect seam going up my stockings.

Effie gives me a quick hug, "Eisai ekthamvotiki!" *You are stunning!* she says emphatically. In the short time that I admire the new me, Effie Is already dressed and putting her silky hair up in a perfect knot. She is so elegantly beautiful, and she is the most selfless person I know. I feel closer to her than to my sisters.

When we are entirely dressed, Effie produces three different red lipsticks which, I know from the fashion magazines are all the rage! I hold them up, one at a time, next to the dress, and find the perfect match. We lean towards the mirror at the same time, and as I color my lips, I yearn for my friend's brother's attention.

Everyone, including Alesandro's parents, is sitting around the radio when we walk into the living room. Mr. Georgeakis has his ear close to the speaker. The others also lean in to hear the report crackling through the imaginary tunnel. "At 3:00 a.m. this morning, twenty-eight of October 1940, Emanuele Grazzi, the Italian ambassador to Greece, delivered an ultimatum from Benito Mussolini, demanding that the Axis Powers be allowed to enter Greece to take up strategic positions. Prime Minister Ioannis Metaxas has a simple response, 'Oxi!' *No!*"

The room is electric, with a joyous celebration. Alessandro jumps up and picks Effie off her feet and swings her around, kissing her passionately. Giannis laughs but holds my gaze a little longer than usual. Taking my hands, he steps back for a better look. "What happened to Arghiro'?" he says playfully.

I feel beautiful and empowered in my red lipstick and seamed stockings. "She grew up," I whisper.

Dinner is delicious, and most conversations are about how courageous the Greeks are and the fact that Metaxas stood up to Mussolini. "Did he answer with only the word Oxi?" I ask. It is a proud moment for our country. We return to the living room for coffee.

Mr. Georgiakis tries to tune in the radio for a long time and the static finally clears enough to hear, "Today,

Mussolini's army invades Greece..." before it comes back full force. We are cut off from further news, but since it is a celebratory evening, Giannis turns off the radio without additional effort to get a clear reception. And, pointedly, there is no discussion about what we heard before all the static.

Mr. Georgeakis pours champagne for each of us and toasts the happy couple. "In this time of turmoil, we must let love be our guiding light. Xronia Polla! A toast to your happiness, Eleftheria. Alessandro, welcome to the family. We wish you a lifetime of joy!" We all cheer and sip our drinks and bask in the joy of the moment. This occasion is just as unique as this family.

We try to push the horrific news to the back of our minds, but as the evening moves forward, the cruel blanket of reality wraps around us as friends and neighbors confirm that Italy has invaded Greece! *Are we prepared to hold off the Italian army?* The conversation is animated, but the topic is one, and the happy mood is indeed spoiled. Giannis says, "Arghirula, I will walk you home." I hesitate, wondering if I should change back into my clothes, but Effie catches my eye and nods towards the door.

I thank Mr, and Mrs. Georgiakis for their warm hospitality, give Effie a heartfelt hug, and tell her, "Nothing can make me happier than your joy!"

"I love him so much!" she replies earnestly and hugs me tight. "Thank you for being here tonight."

Giannis stops at the door to call out more good-byes as he takes my elbow and leads me outside. He takes my arm and slips it through his as we stroll towards my house.

"You look beautiful tonight, Arghiro'! You should always wear red." I put my head down because I'm sure that my face is red at this moment. It is out of character for him to speak so personally or be so close. We walk in slightly uncomfortable silence, but he keeps my arm snugly in place. The house seems very dark, which pleases me, so I will not have to hide the dress, shoes, and makeup.

When I find my key, Giannis takes it, and I step aside for him to unlock the door, but in doing so, we find ourselves face to face and, instinctively, we lean towards each other. I kiss him first. I know this because it is my very first kiss, and I have often wondered how it would feel, and I want to remember every detail. He kisses me back like Cinderella's kiss from Prince Charming. It's a gentle kiss, but I think it surprised us both, so maybe we weren't ready. Giannis seems about to go back to opening the door, but I take his face in both hands and give him a much better sample of what I think it should be. He responds instinctively and puts both his arms around my back, bringing my body close to his. Now, this is worth remembering! There are a few more kisses before he pushes me back at arm's length and holds my gaze for a very long time as if he is making a critical decision. "Tomorrow, I will speak to your Papa!" he says, and my heart soars!

We share a feeling of urgency because everyone knows that war is imminent, and things are about to change quickly. And, for me, the thought of being away from my father's rule is already liberating.

Papa is pleased that Giannis Georgiakis wants to marry his youngest daughter since he comes from a respected family and has aspirations for his future. He will take care of me, and he is a decent man, so it is easy to get Papa's blessing. Giannis wants to get married right away, so we plan a church wedding before Christmas.

"Do you love him?" asks Mamma.

I don't understand why she asks this! "Of course, Mamma! Don't you think he's perfect?"

"Yes, he is perfect in many ways." She seems lost in thought. "Arghirula, your heart is the only true guide, so you must always trust and follow it!" I have no idea what she is saying!

"Yes, Mamma, I will!" My mother is a wise woman, so I try to hear my heart in following her advice. It clearly says, "I can't wait to be married!"

# JOAN - New Haven, Connecticut - 2011

Room 102 on the fourth floor of Smilow Cancer Hospital at Yale New Haven is the "Reflection Room," and there is no lock on the door. I know because I have come here at all different times of day and night when I need to be alone, and I have always felt welcome. There is an ultimate peace within these four walls, an order that is missing from my soul. The room is unremarkable, with just straight chairs and paneled walls. There are no candles or incense or anything out of the ordinary, but there is something about sitting here that calms me. Is it because I know he is still here, in this building? I can walk to his room, hold his unresponsive hand, and pretend that he will be waking up at any minute and we will go home.

I lose track of time here, but time for me now has a whole new meaning. When I leave this place, when my life's love is gone, I will have nothing but empty time. I can't cry now! Not only because I might have shed every last tear, but because if I let even one drop fall, it will open the dam, and I am afraid it may never stop.

I am facing the door, so I see Rachel as she quietly enters the room. "Hey, Mom." She sits next to me and takes my hand, but we can't look at each other for fear of breaking down. "There are a lot of people in the waiting room...you won't believe how many ma...." she can't finish the sentence. She is crumbling, and I find myself consoling her, and before long, we are holding each other up and, at the same time, falling apart.

We are in this room for what seems like so much longer than the fifteen minutes that passed. We are spent but momentarily composed, so I say, "I think we should go up now." We walk down the hall on the fourth floor, holding onto each until we reach the elevator to take us to the ninth floor.

When we get off the elevator, I automatically walk towards Sheldon's room. Rachel touches my arm to turn me in the direction of the waiting room. "Go ahead, Rach," I tell her, "I'll be right there."

I walk down the hall towards room 220 and see my brother John leaning against the wall just outside the door. "Is Mike in there?" I ask.

I assume our brother is giving Sheldon a pep talk, to get better and get home. He has repeatedly told me, during this horrific time, that "He is not going to die!", although the doctors tell us otherwise.

We all have to get through this in our way, and he has chosen his. John, on the other hand, is inconsolable! "I can't do it! I can't go in there to say good-bye!" His grown-man tears are like daggers because I know they come from his heart.

"You don't have to go in, Johnny. Or, I can go in with you if that would help." Mike steps out of the room, and his eyes are still wet with tears.

He coughs to clear his throat and tells John, "Just go in and talk to him. I think he can hear us." John takes a step into the room and closes the door behind him as I give Mike a thank you hug.

This morning Madeline and Pete called together to check how I am holding up. The sound of their voices was soothing, but it didn't take long for the three of us to lose our emotional control and have to cut the call short. Pete is preparing for his second kidney transplant, so he can't come to the hospital. The pain of not being able to say his last good-bye to his "brother" is painful for us all.

The waiting room seats are full, and people are standing all around this sorrowful room that is calm yet so emotionally charged. I find my mother-in-law Nettie sitting with Sheldon's sisters, Judy and Lori. I ask her, "How are you, Mom?" How painful it must be for her to lose her son. It is unnatural, I think as she embraces me, crying. I am not sure that they told her the cold truth, but it seems like she might know. "Do you want to go see him?" She puts her tiny, arthritic hand in mine so I can help her up from the chair. I move the walker, so it lines up, and she grips the bars, standing but still significantly bent over.

Mica sees us walking out and comes to us. "Do you want me to take Gigi, Mom?" "I can do it."

Looking at her, I respond, "Come with us."

The walk down the hall is painfully slow because my 94-year old mother-in-law keeps stopping to ask questions related and unrelated to our current situation. Mica takes on the job of responding, which removes some weight from my shoulders. I need to be strong for others, and when you look at my composure, you can't tell that I am crying, kicking, screaming, and falling apart from indescribable anguish.

# JOAN - Weehawken, New Jersey - 1968

"What's the occasion for the party?" He's so damn cute. I could just visualize his face, and it makes me smile.

"No occasion. Just some friends and a few work people coming over. The house is hardly ever empty, but it will be this weekend. Can you come?"

He doesn't hesitate, "I'll make it work!"

By this, I know he means he has to get a ride from Virginia Beach to Old Bridge, which will take six to seven hours, stay overnight at his brother's house, drive an hour to Weehawken, and then reverse the whole thing on Sunday. He amazes me because everything is possible, and he never disappoints me. "I'm glad that you'll be here..." I trail off. I sit at the kitchen table, my feet up on the chair, leaning against the wall and playing with the long curly cord as I realize how happy I feel.

"Joan, I would walk all the way, if I had to."

"Funny," I laugh, but can't help but feel flattered." "Will you wear your uniform?"

He doesn't hesitate, "No way in hell!" I have only seen him in his uniform once when he first joined. I laugh too, knowing that his answer would be negative. "Listen, I have to go... I'm running out of change!" I can hear the clicking sound just before the operator will ask for more money.

I quickly say, "Good Night," just as he says,

"I'll call you tomorrow...same time?"

"Yes, bye"

"Bye. I love you." Click. I wish I had time to respond.

"The Beverly Hillbillies" has just ended, and Marilena is already in her pajamas. She takes my hand as she walks past me to bed, so I walk her to the bedroom we share, and I sit while she gets comfortable. "Was that Sheldon on the phone?" she asks. "Yes, it was," I respond.

"Are you in love?" she giggles.

"Go to sleep!" I tickle her, and she laughs. I leave the hall light on because it lets just enough light under the door into the bedroom. Good question, baby sister!

My family rents the top floor of a two-family house on a pretty street. There are houses all along our side of Highpoint Avenue in Weehawken, and the United Water Company Hackensack Reservoir No. 2 is along the opposite side. The reservoir goes up to Palisade Avenue, where it creates the border to Union City. The Del Vescovos own the house, and they live on the first floor.

The house, built in 1900, is haunted by a friendly old couple. I have never seen them, but others have, and their description is always the same. She has gray hair pulled back in a low bun with many wrinkles, and she wears a black shawl. The old man wears a dark brown wool coat, and his white hair peeks out from an Irish cap. I have never seen them, but this is the typical description.

In my commute to New York every day, I have become "bus friendly" with a girl about my age, and our chats are very general and not too personal. One day, she asked me where I live and when I told her I was at 208 Highpoint, she seemed to hesitate briefly with a little chuckle before she asked, "Have you seen the old lady?"

Not surprised, I tell her, "My brother's friend bolted out of the house when he saw an old lady standing by our front door, just inside the apartment. How do you know?" I asked.

"We lived there many years ago. One day my brother was washing his hands and, when he looked into the mirror, an old lady was watching him. When he spins around, she is gone! But, he knows he saw her!"

We are sort of nervously laughing when I tell her, "My mom felt one of them tickle her feet one night, and my dad once got punched in the side. They seem more playful than mean." She agrees.

I have a lot to do to get ready for my "mod party" Saturday, but most important is my outfit. To be "mod," you have to wear bold colors or short skirts...really short! Twiggy is the most popular model right now and, although I could never wear it, I love her eye makeup with the bottom lashes drawn on her face! I am having an outfit made by Rosie. She makes her patterns based on whatever you can dream up. Today, I am picking up the outfit I dreamed up.

"Hey, Rosie! How are you doing?"

She opens the door wide, "Come in, come in!" She's kind of quiet, so I know the baby is sleeping. She goes softly into her sewing room and, within two minutes, comes out, proudly holding up my outfit.

I try to keep my voice down, but I'm squealing with excitement. "Rosie, it's perfect! Just the way I pictured it!"

Rosie is so proud of her work, as she should be. If her circumstances were different, she could be a fashion designer and high-level seamstress. However, in this life, she was born in a small Italian village and married her husband, Joe, who works as a stonemason and they moved to America for a better experience. Luckily for those of us who know her, Rosie uses her talent in her little sewing room in the back of their rented apartment in Union City, New Jersey.

It is rare for our house to be empty, and I enjoy the half hour alone, dressed in my "very mod" outfit and ready for my guests. Before long, the house fills with music, noise, some of my favorite people, and some people I hardly know. Sheldon walks in with a few people who were ringing the doorbell when he arrived. I greet my work friends, and Sheldon hangs back until I'm free, takes my hand, and gives me a quick kiss. "Look at you! You look beautiful! The outfit is very cool!" I feel warm all over when he looks at me.

I also feel a tap on my shoulder, "Joan, where can I find soda?"

I give Sheldon a pleading look and point to the living room, asking him to mingle. He knows several people from high school, so he starts making his way through the growing crowd.

When I return to the room, I notice he has found a spot on the couch and has put on his sunglasses. I wouldn't be surprised if he is exhausted and just wants to nap. But, he sees me and waves. "So, this is 'mod'? I had no idea," he chuckles. He stands, removes his sunglasses, and takes a quick survey of the room. I follow his gaze and I take in the oversize daisy patterns and psychedelic colors. The girls are in either mini skirts or bell bottom pants, and a lot of the guys are in turtle neck shirts. I turn to comment, but he is no longer looking towards the room, but slowly, slowly, looking me up and down. "You look great!"

I feel his hand touch mine and that now familiar electric charge shoots through my body. I think I love this guy! Do I even know what the hell I'm doing feeling like this? I can't help but see my mother's face before me, with her judgemental look. Someone has turned up the music, and the entire room seems to sway to the Moody Blues' "Nights in White Satin." Sheldon is, holding my gaze and singing the words, "Cause I love you, yes I love you, Oh how I love you....." I play along and sway to the sexy feel of the music. As I am about to lean in for a kiss, someone touches my arm to greet me.

I'm happy the girls from the office made it since I know it was far for a few of them who live in Long Island. I turn to introduce them to Sheldon, but he is with a group of guys from high school, and they sound as if they're catching up with old stories. There are many people to greet, and I enjoy the small talk with some people I have not seen in a while. I'm in a casual conversation when someone tugs at my arm and guides me to the opposite side of the room "Here's a leg!"

The outfit that Rosie made for me is lame silver metallic with one long bell bottom leg and one "hot pants" leg. The top has one long sleeve, and the other side is sleeveless. Someone leads me to the dining room's far wall, where the artist has set up his station. I kick off my sandals and stand on the chair just vacated by my friend Nancy, who is now sporting a colorful flower on her shoulder. The art is quite good! "Hey, Joan... up here, up here! You have the perfect canvas!" Laughing, I give myself over to the creativity of Joe Strenk from advertising who is diligent and detailed in his art.

I refuse a "doobie," and a glass of wine quickly replaces it. "Thanks!" I take a sip and hand the glass back, laughing, happy in the knowledge that I am having fun at my party! This masterpiece takes some time, so I occupy myself by looking around the room from my unique perch. I see people I have known for years and people I have never seen before all mingling and enjoying.

In the corner, on the floor leaning against the wall, I see my little brother John and his friend Lenny passing a joint. I am surprised that he's home! When we make eye contact, he quickly looks away. Damn! I will talk to him as soon as I get off this chair. I knew my sister went with my parents, and I just assumed my brother was going too.

Joe Strenk from Advertising is diligently working on my leg and flirting with the girls who are waiting for their turn. I turn towards the voices of a big group, and when I look in the boys' direction, I find that bodies block my view. I try to get on my tippy toes, but Joe reprimands. "Hey, Joan! Stay still!" So, I do as told, but I am no longer enjoying myself.

I half expect Sheldon to come to check out my leg, but he doesn't, and I can't see him in the crowd. After what seems like an eternity, Joe tells me that I can look at his work, and I am delighted to see the intricate flowers painted from ankle to thigh and under the hem of my hot pants. There is much detail in the flowers, buds, and leaves. "This is beautiful, Joe!"

He smiles proudly. "Yea, it's groovy!" he says as he turns to the waiting line of leggy ladies in mini skirts.

I glance towards the wall where my brother had been as I walk to the couch where I left Sheldon. He is sitting on the arm, talking to a girl that I don't know, and I can't help but feel a little jealous. When he sees me, he stands, takes a step towards me, puts his arm around me, and squeezes me. "Where were you?" I show him my leg, and he admiringly says, "Wow! It's beautiful! But it was already impressive before. How does he do this? I feel bathed in sunshine.

"Can I talk to you?" he says as he turns me away from the people around us.

"Is everything OK?" I ask, a little apprehensive. He nods that all is OK.

"I hope you don't mind, but I walked your brother to Lenny's house, and he will stay there tonight." I am so surprised that all this happened while I was stuck on my easel-chair. "There's a lot of stuff going on here, and the boys were getting into it. I think they were either drinking or smoking pot when I told them we had to leave."

Surprised, I ask, "And they agreed to go?"

He laughs. "Not really! But, I asked them what time did they think Chief Barakat was coming!" George Barakat, the police chief, is our next door neighbor and not on the "guest list."

"No, you didn't?! You are funny! And they bought it?"

We are both laughing, "Honestly, they were pretty stoned and believed everything I was saying. They couldn't get out of here fast enough!"

Tears fill my eyes, partly from relief and partly for this guy being who he is! "Do you think they'll stay at Lenny's?"

He winks, "Oh yea, Mrs. Balacco was there and was already making them popcorn and dishing out ice cream before I left. They won't be awake long, I guarantee it. And you can relax because I searched the entire house, and there are no remaining siblings."

As I thank him, the radio finally stops tuning and lands on Herb Alpert and The Tijuana Brass. Sheldon puts his arm around my waist, pulls me very close and sings along, "You see this guy, this guy's in love with you... yes, I'm in love... Who looks at you the way I do when you smile? I can tell we know each other very well..." He kisses my neck and then my ear and slowly pulls me closer. My knees buckle, and I honestly wish everybody would go home. When we kiss, everything stands still, and all sound disappears. I see a million colors and know that I am where I belong, and as I come slowly back to the present, I know that I am totally and completely in love with this guy!

# MARIA - Athens, Greece - 1905

The new girls stand perfectly straight at the front of the room as Sister Eleni introduces them. They are cousins about the same age I was when I came here. Olga and I welcome them, but Agni is quiet and distracted as she has been for the last few weeks. I privately asked her if she is well, but she doesn't share her feelings, unlike Olga, who always talks openly. Olga's heart is on her sleeve, so her thoughts and opinions are never a mystery. "Do you know what is bothering Agni?" Olga says. "I think she is upset because she has to get married, and she does not want to."

Surprised to hear this, I ask, "Who is she going to marry? I didn't know she was in love."

Olga lowers her voice, "Her father made an arrangement when she was very young, and he will have to honor it when she becomes 16."

I visualize beautiful Agni in a white wedding dress, holding the arm of a handsome young man. "Has she always known that she would have to marry her father's choice?" I ask, fearful that my father might have made a similar arrangement.

"She has known for a long time, but she has yet to meet her future husband."

For some reason, I feel sad for her. "I hope she's happy" I say, from the bottom of my heart. "Olga, has your father also chosen your husband?"

"No, our family doesn't do that," she says and I am relieved!

When we gather for dinner, I offer Agni a hug with no request for conversation. She smiles her beautiful smile, and I pray that she will be happy. After all, what will happen when we are no longer living here? Having a husband and a home doesn't sound bad. It's better than being a nun!

I don't have many classes to attend this year because I have been chosen to accompany the sisters who visit the sick. I am happiest during this part of the day when we see babies and children and sometimes visit older people who live alone and need medicine, food, or a bath.

"Maria, are you ready?" Sister Dimitria peeks her head into my room, without breaking her stride as she walks down the hall. She has substituted her traditional daily habit for a simple black dress, sizable white apron, and black scarf to cover her hair. On a long chain around her neck is a large crucifix and there are rosary beads attached to her belt. The symbols of the Greek Orthodox Church have become a part of my daily life, but I often miss my mother's menorah and her beautiful table on high holiday and, mostly, I miss her smile.

"I'm ready!" I respond, reaching for my sweater. I walk

at a quick pace to keep up with her long stride and, when we arrive at the street, I ask, "Who are we visiting today?"

She explains, "We are assisting in childbirth this morning! The mother has been in labor for hours, and the midwife is there."

I am both excited and nervous because I have never seen a child being born. "Oh my!" I pull the sweater closer and instinctively quicken my step.

Sister Dimitria laughs as she catches up. She tells me, "We will be there on time!" But, I am both worried and nervous.

When we arrive, Sister taps on the door but she opens it and walks in with me trailing behind her. The house is small, and the bed in a direct line to the door. "Oh, good, you're here!" the midwife calls out. We scrub our hands in the kitchen sink and we stand behind the woman in labor and Sister gently begins to massage the woman's lower back.

The midwife gives instructions to the mother-to-be on using her breath to make the pain more tolerable and then comes to the foot of the bed and places a pillow under her feet as she gives me instructions on what I am to do. "Give her second and third toe a gentle but firm squeeze and then release... like this.

"Entaxei." I respond ready to take on this simple task."

"Do this on both feet, and I will let you know when to stop." She explains, "This will warm her and it may speed up her slow labor."

Once we are in our positions, the midwife takes her time examining the mother, who is biting down her teeth to cover a scream as she tries to breathe through another stabbing pain. The midwife seems satisfied that all is in good order and tells us that this baby is not in any hurry to arrive. The woman looks extremely tired. The rest that she gets in between the labor pains is energizing, but it is not long before another pain wracks her body, and it all starts again.

I concentrate on massaging her toes and try to avoid looking at this poor girl's tortured face. I place my thumbs on her arches, and the midwife acknowledges this with a look of surprise as she nods. "That's perfect!" she says. "When she is having a contraction, hold your thumb at the center of the arch, apply firm pressure, and move your thumbs in a circle." As this seems very natural, I understand what I need to do.

When she is between contractions, I rub her legs and watch her face relax, almost as if nothing is happening.

We work efficiently and quietly for about an hour when the midwife exclaims, "You are crowning!...push! push!" I find myself holding my breath. "Now, stop pushing, breath, breathe. That's good. Perfect!" I exhale! I can see that another pain is coming and hear the midwife, "OK, push again... a huge push! Perfect! More! Keep pushing! Don't stop!"

I can't breathe! I might faint, but I continue to rub the mother's left leg, ever so gently, although I realize that this leg might be holding me up. "Maria, look!" the midwife tells me to come around and watch. The baby is coming! The midwife places both her hands firmly on both sides of the baby's head and turns it gently, so the face is up. A few more pushes and the baby's shoulders and body slide out along with the cord, which is still attached to the mother.

The midwife gently guides the newborn and tells me to take the scissors and to cut the cord. "Right here, she whispers." I am nervous but overjoyed as I cut.

Sister ties the umbilical cord and takes the baby to the table to clean it. The midwife cares for the mother and, within minutes, she is holding her perfect baby girl. I crumble to the floor, exactly where I was standing, and I feel tears fill my eyes, head, and heart. I just witnessed a perfect miracle, but I miss my mother and I find that I can't untangle those two thoughts.

# MARIA - Athens, Greece - 1906

Agni has been married since Christmas, and she lives with her husband Constantine, in a large house in a nice neighborhood on the other side of the city. Olga and I visit whenever we can get a carriage ride by Stavros, the delivery man who brings the nuns' supplies. We might see her more often, but we do not feel very welcome by Agni's husband.

Constantine is not friendly and not especially attractive. He is not much taller than Agni with dark brown hair and a thin mustache, and he usually looks as if he just ate a lemon. We visited last month and, although she was happy to see us, she seemed nervous and anxious.

Today we will stay for two hours because Stavros has deliveries to make. We tell Agni many stories about school, and Olga asks, "How is it to be married?" Olga is ever so interested. Although Agni seems uncomfortable with the personal questions and often looks towards the door, Olga presses on. "How was it the first time? You know….!." I am embarrassed by the question but not surprised when, in a barely audible whisper, Agni responds,

"Scary! Not just the first time, every time!"

Agni shows us her beautiful house with pretty carpets and sturdy furniture. Everything is correctly placed and reflective of excellent taste. I'm not sure precisely what Constantine's work is, but I know he was on the Finance Committee of the Olympics in Athens in the spring.

The Olympics' opening ceremonies were like nothing I have ever seen before, and it was a day I will never forget! That April morning, the city was electric with anticipation, and wagons made their way through the streets leading to the stadium. We saw cabmen brush up their carriages, preparing for the remaining eight days of the games. Olga and I, along with two of the younger girls in our charge, walked towards the stadium, and, although we were not allowed to get very close, we could see the "evzone," the King's guards who were lined up, shoulder to shoulder. There were thousands of them, from the stadium entrance and all along the top. They were there to prevent people from stepping over the wall. They were a fantastic sight to see, with their white skirts and tights, fancy black and gold vests, red caps, black scarves, and shoe pom-poms, complete with rifles leaning on their left shoulders.

His Majesty King George, accompanied by his sister Alexandra and all the rest of England and Wales' royalty, was there. The soldiers saluted, and the royals bowed their heads in recognition of the cheers. Flags waved frantically as the crowd's voices exploded! They grew louder and louder, and it sounded like all of Athens was cheering. The audience was from many different countries, and masses of people passed in front of the royals.

However, we couldn't see them or any of the games. We had heard there would be running, long jump, shot put, javelin, boxing, and equestrian events and that a high number of countries were present. With Germany, England, America, Australia, Belgium, France, Hungary, Italy, and more, there were easily 100,000 people inside and outside the stadium.

The day was like no other that I have ever experienced, and the spectacle was spectacular! At two o'clock, we met with Agni and Constantine, who had been there all day. She was wearing a beautiful shawl around her shoulders and head. It had lovely gold threads running through the soft silk fabric and trimmed with a delicate black and gold fringe. It was the suitable shawl of a lady of great stature, and I admired her elegance.

Agni was gracefully quiet as she stood next to Constantine without touching him. She fussed greatly to keep her shawl from sliding off her beautiful hair. However, while everyone was preoccupied with the spectacle before us, the silk shawl slid down, and in the few seconds, before she quickly set it right, I saw the purple and green bruises on the side of her face close to her right ear. She was aware that I noticed and gave me a pleading look, as if to say, "Please keep my secret."

Today, weeks after the games, Agni is happy to see us and leads us to a divan and two chairs near the window. "Agathe, please bring the coffee!" she calls out as we walk through the corridor. Before long, we are served by her ancient domestic, who barely acknowledges us. The table is lovely with plates of perfect koulourakia with sesame seeds.

There are also diples and halva, galaktoboureko, and a bowl of yogurt and honey, topped with toasted almonds. Agathe, without a smile, carries in the copper briki and pours us each a cup of dark aromatic coffee.

During the visit, I can't help but remember the bruises on Agni's face when we last saw her. I worry about her domestic situation. "Is it hard," I ask, "to be the lady of the house?"

Agni smiles her mysterious smile and answers an emphatic "Neh!" *Yes!*, with no further explanation.

We have been here for almost two hours, and Stavros will pick us up soon to return to school. "Agni, what do you do all day?" Olga is honestly curious.

Agni reflects as though she has not thought about her daily routine and answers as if she is seeing it for the first time. "I sleep late and dress for the day. My husband comes home for the mid-day meal, so I help Agathe prepare. After he leaves, I embroider and read. If the weather is mild, I walk with Agathe, but she usually can't walk too far. Soon the day is over, and Constantine is back for our evening meal."

Olga is fascinated by this schedule and says, "It sounds wonderful and very romantic."

Agnis' quick response does not surprise me. "It is not! It is quite stressful." I haven't mentioned Agni's bruises to Olga, and I probably never will, but the pain in Agni's eyes is real, and I am helpless to give her any comfort.

Olga repeatedly looks at the clock, and I am surprised that she is anxious to get back to school and even more surprised when she comes out of the bathroom with her cheeks rosy and her lips pink. Did she pinch her cheeks? "Stavros should be arriving at any minute, Maria. We should be ready!" She tries to look past the drapes and out the front window. As I finish the coffee, Agni fusses with the plates of pastries. She calls Agathe to wrap a package for us to take.

"Thank you for your visit," she says, and I can see that she means it. The sweet calm that was once in her eyes seems to have disappeared, and my heart hurts for my friend.

Stavros is already waiting outside, and he waves when he sees us. Olga practically runs down the steps and climbs quickly into the carriage. He extends his hand to help her as he moves over so she can sit next to him. "Thank you," she softly whispers, never taking her gaze off his handsome face. It is a sweet moment, and I now understand why Stavros is always around and offering his help. Why did it take me this long?

I sit on the bench in the back next to the supplies. "Good afternoon, Maria!" he greets me with a big toothy smile. He is good looking in his crisp white shirt and the kapaki covering most of his reddish curly hair. He is talkative and funny, and today he tells us a story about a customer. As always, he is thoroughly entertaining and it is good to be in the sun and away from the gloom around Agni and her home.

The streets are filled with people strolling or in other carriages, enjoying the afternoon sun or delivering their goods. Stavros keeps the horse in check, so the ride home takes longer than it should. If I tilt my head slightly to the right, I see that their legs are touching, as are their hands. When we get to the school, Stavros offers me a hand, and I step down. Olga lingers with an offer to help him unload the carriage, and she dismisses me with a look.

When I enter the front door, I see Sister Ariadne move towards the door to assist in emptying the cart as she usually does. I stop her, "Olga is helping with the supplies. I don't think further assistance is required!" Sister does not hesitate and gladly returns to her embroidery. I glance back as I close the door, and without a doubt, see Stavros pull Olga very close and give her several tender kisses before he starts his work.

# ARGHIRULA -
# Athens, Greece - 1942

My sister Eleni is snapping the ends off string beans and placing them in a pot. "Be prepared for a painful first-time experience," she says, out of the clouds.

"What are you talking about?" I know what she means, but it upsets me much to hear her discuss it, especially since she has no first-hand knowledge.

"What do you think is going to happen, Arghiro'? Do you understand your duty as a wife?"

When I ask my mother, she says, "Do not discuss this with your sisters!" She explains things in medical terms. "Arghiro', we have talked about this before, do you not remember?" I do remember, and also remember that I was only half-listening, but she never mentioned pain!

"Mamma, you told me about female and male anatomy!"

She smiles, "Exactly, child...so you understand! A good man will be gentle and patient, so you do not need to worry."

I can't help but think of my mother and father and

their first time as husband and wife. Was she afraid? Was he gentle? I have to think about something else because this is very disturbing. I know that many girls are already married by age 19, and I know that my father and brothers have sheltered me. The only person I wish to discuss this with is Effie!

Our wedding preparations are quick and modest, as expected during these turbulent times. When you are the daughter of a painter with many children, there are limited funds, even though both Giannis and Mr. Georgakas have offered help.

Effie is always cheerful, but especially so now. "Today, you will truly become my sister, and nothing can make me happier!"

I hug her warmly as I agree, "I feel blessed too, and I will be a good wife to Giannis, I promise!" We talk about many things, but when I ask her about pain, she looks as confused as I feel. I don't think Eleni knows what she is saying!

The wedding is small, with just our immediate families in attendance. We have a traditional ceremony at our church, and our mothers share in the preparation of the wedding meal. We celebrate with retsina and champagne that Mr. Georgakas had for a special occasion, and, although my father does not drink it, he seems to be enjoying the day. I notice that the music in the background is very classical and almost religious. I realize how much consideration there was by Giannis' family not to offend my father with music that he does not allow in our own home.

Giannis is attractive, intelligent, hard-working, and a good provider. However, though he is sometimes sexual, he is never sensual. I think of Effie and Alessandro and how they can barely keep their hands off each other, reaching out for a kiss or a touch. I expected us to be like this, but, sadly, we're not.

Giannis spends most of his time reading or working out numbers in a binder. I don't ask what he is calculating any longer, since the first and only time I asked, he dismissed me with "nothing for you to be concerned about...it is for our future."

Since Effie has moved to America, I have no one to discuss my feelings of joy and disappointment. I often write to her, and I miss her with all my heart, but I don't mention private thoughts about my husband because, after all, once you write something down, it is like shouting it to the world. I don't know how many letters reach her, and I only receive occasional notes from her.

In her last letter, she said, "San Francisco is a beautiful city, and I hope that someday when this world goes back to normal, you and Giannis will visit us. Right now, we are feeling the pain of war with both our current situation of the United States and Japan and the disturbing news that comes to us about the hardships in our beloved Athens. Although the Japanese attack on December 7ᵗʰ was on Pearl Harbor, our city fears attacks on our coastline. There are guards at the Golden Gate Bridge, and we are subject to blackouts in the city. There is much yelling on the streets to shut off lights, as some people do not comply. I pray a lot, and I am very homesick."

Although I feel her loneliness, I know that she does not truly understand how dire the situation is in Greece. She says she gets most of her information from propaganda movies, and I am confident that her parents try to spare her from the truth of what it is like since the Axis occupation in June of last year. It is difficult to discuss the famine and the executions and the fear in our everyday lives.

I have not discussed my cold marriage with my mother or my sisters. Even in these dreadful times, I expected more from my marriage. I wonder now, more than ever, what my parents were like when they first married.

We live in a two-room flat not far from his kiosk, and Giannis works long hours. I go to bed alone and fall asleep long before he comes in. He stays up into the morning hours to do his numbers or read his books. He says, "Someday, I'll open a big store, and we will move to a proper house." I believed in his dream when we were first married, but Greece's situation has changed so drastically since last year. It is almost impossible to visualize the future in any way other than what it is now.

A few months ago, the announcement I heard on Athens Radio as we gathered around Gianni's father's radio, still rings in my head: **"You are listening to the voice of Greece. Greeks stand firm, proud, and dignified. You must prove yourselves worthy of your history. The valor and victory of our army has already been recognized. The righteousness of our cause will also be recognized. We did our duty honestly. Friends! Have Greece in your hearts, live inspired by the fire of her latest triumph** and our army's glory. Greece will live again and be great because she fought honestly for a just cause and freedom. Brothers! Have courage and patience. Be stout hearted. We will overcome these hardships. Greeks! With Greece in your minds, you must be proud and dignified. We have been an honest nation and brave soldiers."

A day after this announcement, on April 27th, the German tanks drove straight to the Acropolis in our beautiful city and raised the Nazi flag. The soldier on guard duty was ordered to remove the Greek flag. He obeyed the order and took it down but refused to hand it to the invading Germans. Instead, he wrapped himself in the flag and jumped off the Acropolis, where he died. We didn't know this soldier, and I wonder if it is just a tale. A few days later, as the German flag waved on the Acropolis' uppermost spot, two Athenian youngsters climbed up at night and tore it down.

The city is in a state of extreme poverty since the Axis forces have taken everything! We are hungry, food comes in meager rations, and it is not uncommon to see people collapsing on the street from sheer hunger.

I work at Tolis' kiosk every day since Tolis is elsewhere with meetings and things that he does not discuss with me. I see him every two or three days when he comes to collect the few drachmas from infrequent sales and restock the limited inventory.

Tolis and Basilis are part of the Resistance, the same group responsible for removing the German flag from atop the Acropolis. I'm uncertain what this group does or my brothers' roles, but I know that the life we knew before is forever gone. I trust that they will learn how to stay safe because my mother worries about them and they are responsible for keeping us from starving. The Germans came and took practically everything for the Reich but, because my brothers are no strangers to the black market, we survive.

Today, I arrange and rearrange cigarettes and gum packs to face the street better. Most of the customers are Italian or German soldiers, and there is a distinct difference in attitude. The Italians are friendly and flirty, always smiling and trying to speak Greek. Most often, the Germans are stiff and straight and speak only German, expecting everyone to understand them.

We Athenians can hear the soldiers march way before we see them. There is a disparity in sound between the Italian army and the German army when they approach. If it is the German soldiers' distinct goose-step with their marschstiefel, marching boots with hobnails under their shoes, we run into our homes and lock the doors. If it is the softer march of the Italians, we Greeks stand outside and wave, sometimes holding children up on our shoulders to do the same.

"Omofri kopela!" *pretty lady!* I hear a friendly greeting with an Italian accent. "Good morning, Francesco!" He stops by most mornings and buys cigarettes, but today he hands me a paper sack with four apples. I am thrilled and thank him profusely. He is in the Italian Navy and is always in uniform, although I wonder how he ever passes inspection with his scuffed boots and his hat askew on his head. But he is cute and always so happy. He repeats the same thing he says every day, "Please tell me you left your husband!" We laugh at the joke as he takes his cigarettes and tells me to keep the change. He is always the best part of my day!

A few days have passed since I have seen Francesco, but just as I am thinking about him, I hear his cheery voice greeting me as usual, "Omorfi kopela!" *Beautiful girl.*

Happy that he is here, I look up from my magazine and see that he is not alone today. He turns to his friend and says, "I told you that I would introduce you to Athens' most beautiful smile!"

His friend is very handsome and neat, especially standing next to Francesco. He wears a perfectly ironed uniform, and his hat is precisely in place. I notice that he has a few extra stripes on his sleeve, so assume his rank is higher than Francesco's. Ridiculously, my heart skips a beat, and I feel tongue-tied as I greet him with a handshake. "Piacere!" he says with a little smile. "Sono Clorindo!"

I feel a charge when he touches me to shake hands, but I calmly respond, "Charika gia tin gnorimia." *Nice to meet you.*

What in the hell is wrong with me? He is Italian, the enemy, and I should hardly be socializing with either of these men. But, instead, I feel like kissing him! For a few minutes, he practices his Greek and helps me with some Italian words. All too soon, another sailor comes towards us in quick strides and says something to the men. They quickly offer their good-byes with a promise to return as they follow instructions and walk towards what must be an emergency.

I am crestfallen! I watch them leave with my eyes fixed on Clorindo until he is totally out of my sight. I feel feverish, and I must talk myself out of my stupid instant attraction to a man that I know is the enemy and will probably never see again. Not to mention the fact that I am a married woman!

# ARGHIRULA -
# Athens, Greece - 1942

My mother continues to deliver babies in the Jewish section, which has suffered significant losses. She tells stories of German soldiers that are everywhere, and how the Jewish people are interrogated randomly. She says that what remains of the population lives in extreme fear and the community is suffering very much. Every day they are removed in vast numbers, their properties confiscated, and all must wear armbands showing the yellow Star of David to mark them as Jewish. My mother does not get paid, since no one has anything to barter. But babies keep coming, and new mothers need help, so my saintly mother continues to do her work, but the pain and sadness of the people is taking its toll.

Even in our changing world, I appreciate the sky and the sun's warmth in my precious Athens. I pretend that tomorrow Effie and I will be at the beach as I try to clear my mind of the horror that has become our day-to-day life. I also pretend that my marriage is good. Giannis does not want children, so he takes precautions on the rare times

149

that we are intimate. I no longer seek intimacy and feel dispassionate when we come together, but I assume this is how all marriages are behind closed doors.

"I don't like that you walk alone to the kiosk!" Giannis says as he prepares to leave for work. I scoff, with more bravado than I feel, "I am at the kiosk alone the whole day!!"

"It's not the same as walking the streets filled with soldiers. Arghirula, you know the difference!"

There is something about his concern that irritates me! I tell him that Tolis is walking with me, and this seems to satisfy him. He has done his job as a dutiful husband, and he is off to work with no more than a chaste kiss on my cheek.

I clean the kitchen, make the bed, and prepare myself for the few hours that I will be a "periptero" keeper. Although it is a mild day, I take a sweater and scarf when the sun hides behind the clouds. Tolis arrives promptly at 9:30, and I ask if he wants a coffee.

"Sigouros!" *Sure!* he says as he steps in.

My brothers bring food to my parents and coffee for us, and no one questions where or how they get it, including my father. The black market is undoubtedly part of their world and they keep our family alive when many around us are starving. There have been countless deaths in the city, including people that we knew, due to the famine.

We walk in total silence as my heart aches at the sight of empty retail shops. They were cleared out and "purchased" at no value by the Germans. The troops took everything from women's stockings to electrical equipment, and the goods were shipped home to the Reich. Shops, small factories, hospitals, and drugstore supplies were taken, according to my brothers. I see abandoned buses and trucks everywhere! The Nazis even took bicycles from the people. Thousands of them! Our beautiful Athens has been disabled and destroyed, and there are times that I am surprised that the sun still shines.

We walk past the body of a child in a doorway. She looks like she is sleeping curled up in a tattered coat. I feel death all around us, so I pray and try to hold back my tears. Tolis takes my elbow to cross the street, but as I look back, I see the emaciated body of a young man stripped of his shirt, revealing a skeletal torso. Stupidly, what mostly strikes me is that his pants pockets are inside out. Evidently, someone thought not to waste a ration ticket that will never be used by him.

My crushed heart and broken spirit make me weak, and I lean against Tolis as he puts his arm around me. "Hang on, Arghiro'!'" his voice cracks, and I know he is overwhelmed with our current lives' grief. Unable to discuss the horror of what we see every day, we are emotionally raw, and the insufferable pain around us is palpable. When Tolis serves a customer, an Italian soldier who is making a fair attempt at speaking Greek, I don't look up from my magazine because I don't want to see the enemy's face, after what I saw this morning.

Soon my brother begins to fidget as he moves things around on the racks. "Go wherever you need to go!" I tell him. "I'll be OK. But, please come back to walk me home." He hesitates only slightly before he leaves. I watch him move away and think, not for the first time, that he has a good heart.

When Tolis comes to walk me home, three hours later, I tell him, "I have not seen Mamma all week, and I'm sure she wouldn't mind seeing you too." He doesn't argue as I turn in the direction of my parent's home.

"I have something for her, anyway."

We walk hastily and in silence and with our heads down, fully aware that you never know how you might anger a Nazi. When we pass the graveyard, it repulses me to see the bodies dumped there. I turn to Tolis, eyes wide, and ask, "Why?"

He takes my elbow to quicken our pace as he explains, "It is better than leaving them in the streets."

I choke up and cover my face with my scarf, trying to avoid standing out as I keep my posture straight. "There have been hundreds of deaths every day in Athens since December, and the future looks bleak."

"I worry about Mamma and Papa." I say, "Do they have enough to eat?"

He shakes his head, "Barely. Basilis and I can give Mamma just enough food to keep her and Papa alive, but it is difficult."

I feel ill as our lives' truth becomes more real, and I feel melancholy deep in my soul. My heart hurts for Athens, the Jews, the Greeks, the bodies on these streets, and my loveless marriage.

We open the door to our parents' tiny house, and I smell the turpentine, which tells me that my father is painting. In the kitchen, the sloshing water's sound stops immediately as my mother realizes that Tolis is here. Her face cannot hide the joy of seeing her son. When I wrap my arms around her, I feel how thin she has gotten, which only adds to my misery. "Did you eat today, Mamma?" She nods yes and points towards the table where I see only a pathetic loaf of bread, made mostly from corn flour, which has a small piece missing. Also missing is half of the boiled onion that is on the metal dish.

She looks warmly at Tolis and says, "Basilis was here yesterday and brought a few things, thank God. We are so grateful."

My mother asks about Giannis, and, with all that I want to tell her, I only say, "He is well." Our visit is short, as we need to get home before curfew.

"You can stay at my house any time you want, Arghiro'. I think you know that."

Happy that my brother is perceptive, I respond, "It might be easier sometimes." And that is the start. Instead of going home, I stay at Tolis' a few nights a week. At first, Giannis accepts its convenience since the apartment is right near Toli's kiosk. But it does not take long for him to be annoyed that I am not coming home, although I know he loves his solitude.

Tolis, my brother, friend, and confidant asks me, "What's wrong, Arghirula?"

"Instead of feeling light and happy, I feel heavy and burdened," I respond.

Do you think it's just this crazy time of war?" he asks. "Most of us are not happy now, for many obvious reasons. But, only you can know what is in your heart".

With his support, I feel emotionally liberated and free to analyze my feelings. For the first time in a long time, I believe that I can indeed follow my heart and I know that I must talk to Mamma.

My mother and I sit at her table and drink tea she made from the mint leaves she dried last summer. It warms me, and the words flow smoothly. "I know he is a good man, Mamma, but I am often happier away from him than when I am with him." Mamma nods her head as if this is not a surprise to her. I don't know why, but she is always so wise.

"You must follow your heart, Arghiro'. Your head may tell you something different, but it is still the heart that should lead the way." I cry. She continues, "Giannis is a good man, but perhaps, he is not the man that is good for you."

I have to ask her, "Mamma, why have you been married to Papa for so long? You are so different, one from the other."

She answers the question I have asked myself since I was a little girl, "Arghiro', your Papa and I love each other very much, and I can not imagine my life without him. Can you imagine your life without Giannis?" she asks.

I close my eyes to reflect as I honestly ask myself. The answer is to Mamma as much as it is to myself, "Yes, Mamma...I can imagine that, and I welcome the thought."

Getting a divorce is not difficult in Greece in 1942, provided we both confess repentance and state that we are sexually incompatible. Giannis takes care of the paper process, and I only have to sign to be free. Yesterday, I moved my things to Tolis' house and already feel settled and more at peace than I have been in a long time.

# ARGHIRULA - Athens, Greece - 1942

Sunday afternoon, sitting at the table with hot black tea, which he brought home yesterday, Tolis tells me that he will close the kiosk. "It is almost impossible to stock it, and there is no profit." I'm not surprised and often wondered how we have kept it open so long.

"I understand," I tell him with concern.

As if reading my thoughts, he says, "I have a friend who can use help with typing for a publication."

I clearly understand that he is talking about an underground paper. "Yes!" I am thrilled at the prospect!

He is quick to admonish, "Arghiro', this is not something to just occupy your time! It's essential and secret, and you must be prepared to follow strict instructions. It is not like working a kiosk!"

"I am fully aware of the situation here, Tolis," I tell him solemnly. "I will do whatever is needed!"

He seems appeased and holds up two fingers. "Two weeks !" The knot in my chest loosens a bit, knowing I will soon be off the street, where it feels more unsafe every day.

I equate the pain and death all around us to my failed marriage and wonder if things might have been different for us in another time or place.

My walk is considerably shorter from Tolis' house than Gianni's but, since Tolis is not at home, I walk alone to the kiosk. The blue sky is a canopy over the city, and sunbeams reach down like loving arms. If I could keep my head lifted, it would be the perfect day but with my head down it is gray and distressing, and I pass three destroyed buildings.

In the rubble of what used to be a jewelry shop is a man who looks very old. I cannot avoid walking past him, and as I get closer, I see that he is much younger than I first thought, but he is dying of hunger. He looks directly at me with empty eyes and collapses before me. I am again reminded of the horrors of this war. I am 20 years old but feel far older under the weight of this life.

Only one Greek soldier stopped by to get cigarettes about an hour ago, so time is moving slowly. I have read all the magazines twice, and I have written a letter to Effie. So, although I just cleaned them the other day, I think I should wash the windows. This chore helps take my mind off the things that weigh heavily on my spirit. I find old newspapers and the bottle of vinegar stored under the board on the back wall. I soak the newspapers with vinegar, step on the wooden box and stand on my toes to reach the high square. It's no surprise that much dirt has accumulated in just a few short days. It sickens me to think that this same air we breathe is from destruction, fires, and dead bodies.

I feel a large hand under the skirt of my dress! When the hand cups my bottom, I momentarily freeze as it squeezes me most disgustingly, and remains invasively touching me before being retracted. In anger and without clear thought, I spin around and, in what feels like slow motion, slap my aggressor!

I see the grey-green color of the uniform, the dark green collar, the braid across one pocket, and the SS insignia. His blonde hair shakes from my strike's impact, and his steely blue eyes show the unexpected shock. He grabs my arm in one swift movement and pulls me down so that my feet hit the ground. Out of nowhere, another soldier appears and holds my wrists together behind my back. He keeps me so tight that the pain that starts at my hands creeps up my arms, shoulders, and head.

Frozen with fear, I keep my eyes lowered and focused on the tall black boots in which the soldier pants are tucked. Ridiculously, I am mesmerized by their perfect shine!

I catch a glimpse of my attacker's hat, just as he snatches it off the ground. The black visor, double cord, and red piping all scream "German officer!" and fear clutches at my heart as I think of a dozen recent stories of Greeks suffering at Nazi soldiers' hands, for far lesser crimes.

A strong arm pushes me down to the wooden box. I sit stone still and focus on the men's boots. "Was ist passiert?" the soldier asks the officer.

My attacker says, "Sie schlud mich ohne Grund."

I know that the liar is blaming this incident on me, and I can barely breathe. As he pulls me up to my feet, I keep my head down, and I see a figure leaning against the building across the street, lighting a cigarette. I recognize Tolis, who is looking directly at me with his finger against his lips, miming "Shhhh." Thank you, God! My pounding heart beats just a little slower, although fear still cripples me.

They parade me through the streets. I feel detached from my body as I do what they tell me, and I know there is a shorter way to get to German headquarters, but realize that I am an example for others. I keep their pace and stay in step, although I am increasingly angry at the situation's injustice. I want to lash out and kick this soldier who is just following orders, but I heed my brother's warning and do not speak as I keep my eyes down.

No one dares to interfere, and many people step aside. A bicycle passes us very close to the curb as a military truck rumbles past him going too fast. The truck tires screech and the man is thrown off his bike about 100 feet in front of us. He seems stunned but sees us approaching and quickly stands up and runs in the other direction, leaving his mangled bike where it fell. I imagine that my captors and I are a scary sight.

Looking down, I cannot help but see bloodstains on the ground in more than one place, and I know that I am passing the square and I know thousands of Jewish men dressed in their Shabbat best were rounded up and taken here just a few months ago. They were tortured in broad daylight in the blazing sun because the Nazis said they needed to see which men were fit for manual labor. Some were put to work paving roads, but many disappeared or were shot as they tried to escape.

Sadness for the Jewish community fills my heart. I also grieve for Greece, but, at this moment, I feel frightened and sad only for myself. I won't fall apart and know that Tolis will help me. Please, dear God! I think of my father and hope he will pray for me, and I think of my mother, and I choke back tears and concentrate on ignoring the pain in my wrists.

I am embarrassed about being held as I walk down Ermou Street like a criminal. I know I can't do anything but keep my eyes down and obey. When my captors speak to each-other, the soldier asks questions. The officer angrily snaps his brief answers until the soldier stays quiet. I have enough presence of mind to understand that things can, and probably will go wrong. There is just one thing that keeps me still breathing, and that is the sensation that someone is following not far behind and, although I can't look, I know Tolis is there.

The building, which is our destination, used to house a bank and a shipping company, but the German army now uses it as a headquarters. As we approach the ornate front doors, I see the Acropolis in the sky on top of the rocky hill. It never loses its magic, and I appreciate the name that means "top of the city," maybe for the first time. *God, please don't let this be the last thing I ever see again!*

When we enter the building, the officer walks ahead, and he turns down a hallway to my right. The soldier pulls me roughly through the doors, down a corridor, and into a small room. He pushes me towards a chair and says, "Sitzen!!" I am alone with the soldier in this tiny room that smells like stale smoke. He is young and nervous, and he avoids looking at me and does not speak to me. I sit straight up and watch him like a puppy waiting for a command. He settles into a scuffed old desk where he shuffles through an endless stack of papers. He lights his first cigarette, and when it is consumed to where he can barely hold it without burning his fingers, he begins his ritual of lighting another. He lights every new cigarette with the one he has just smoked and continues to do this for an interminable amount of time as my throat gets constricted and my eyes burn.

Since there is no clock, I have no idea how long I am sitting here. I cover my nose with the back of my hand, and, when he senses movement, he turns in his chair to face me. Our eyes lock, and for a brief moment, I see what might be sympathy but, after a squint from the smoke, I see the steely look return to the gray eyes, and I once again cast mine down.

Voices crash through my fog and, since there are no windows, I have no idea how long I've been here. The fact that I must adjust my back tells me it has been a while since I have moved, so I sit up straight without looking at anyone. There are three people in the room. My instinct is to cry, but something tells me I should not show weakness. I control the tears by talking to myself and physically biting my tongue. I recognize the officer's voice and know the soldier is still at his desk.

The new voice is that of a woman and, from my vantage point, I see she is wearing a uniform with a skirt, short boots, and wool socks. She stands in front of me, "Komm mit mir!" and then in very distorted Greek, "Ela mazi mou!" *Come with me!* I find some relief in her effort and hope that she will help me! I don't speak but respond to her tug on my arm by standing up. We walk down the very long corridor to a door that opens to a dark staircase leading to a basement. Although I felt slightly comforted that I am with a woman, I realize now that I am terrified.

"Chreiazomai to banio" *I need the bathroom.* I look at her as I make my request, but she barely glances at me. She leads me down a gray and dingy hallway to a door covered with streaked blue paint, opens it and points. As I enter, she positions herself in the hall just outside the door.

The room is tiny, with peeling walls and a putrid smell. As I look around for a toilet, I see graffiti everywhere. "Long Live Greece" is written in charcoal and large print on the wall facing me. Way up high, in a smaller script and possibly written with lipstick, it says, "piss on Axis." There is smudged writing on every wall, but I search for a commode feeling the urgency of my situation. I find only a hole in the floor, and I am disgusted at what I have to do in this filthy place. I maneuver the skirt of my dress while I bend my knees and squat knowing that I have no choice. I manage and wonder what could be worse as tears sting my eyes. Looking around for something to complete this process, I find only an old newspaper within my reach. I tear off a piece and finish my business as I hold back sobs.

As incredible as it seems, I hesitate to leave this disgusting room to delay what can only be a worse situation. I eventually gather myself, step out and exhale since, along with everything else, I have been holding my breath.

The dingy hallway is so narrow that we can't stand side by side. My keeper guides me by holding my arm so close that I smell the combined odors of her bad breath, cheap soap, sweat, and fear. It doesn't take long for me to realize that the smell of fear does not come from her. It comes from me!

At the end of the longest hallway I have ever seen, we approach our destination. The original door to the room has been replaced by metal bars, crudely hung and possibly homemade. But, regardless of their odd shape and the way they are attached to the wall, they look strong. "Geh weg von der Tur!" The guard tells the three curious women to move away from the entry as she uses a key to open the large lock. She gives me a little push and slams the gate behind me with a loud bang.

This room smells only slightly less putrid than the bathroom. I expect the space to extend to my left, but I see that it is minimal. I turn to the guard for instructions, but see only her back and the low boots with wool socks, as she is already halfway down the corridor that suddenly seems incredibly short.

I count seven women of different ages and sizes, who all look as if they are starving or freezing and possibly both. A few are wrapped in filthy blankets and are either sleeping or feigning sleep. Most of them look emaciated, and no one seems to notice that I'm here. I see the back corner where there is a hole in the floor, similar to the one I just used down the hall. To my right, and very close to the entrance, is a rolled-up army blanket and a dirty pillow. I sit on the floor and lean my back against the wall, trying my best to avoid the disgusting pillow. I curl myself up, facing the wall, but soon feel cold to the bone and have no other choice but to reach for the foul-smelling blanket.

I lie still for a very long time and pray that I will fall asleep and, by some miracle, survive the time until they take me out of here. *Please, God, don't forget me.* This looks like a place where others are lost. I implore Mary, the mother of God, to watch over me and bring me back to my own mother.

My father's prayers suddenly make sense here, and I pray with abandon and all my heart. Eventually, the gate clanks and two guards walk in. They move past me as I peek out from under the smelly blanket without moving my body. One of the guards is carrying a large jug. The other takes a pot of horribly smelling soup and a basket of thick pieces of black bread. My stomach growls as I realize I have had nothing but coffee all day.

I watch, lying very still, from my corner as the women hold out tin cups for soup and aggressively grab the stale bread. They slurp the broth, some more noisily than others, but all hungrily. The guards do not engage in conversation with the women. One of them hands me a cup and points to the food, offering it. I take the cup but shake my head "Oxi," and they move on.

The women greedily eat and drink their meager offering, and I think that it may be their only meal of the day. When they empty their cups of soup, they pour from the jug where I see a yellow tint to the water. Although I'm starving, I'm afraid to get up and find myself pushing further into the wall with no attempt to partake in either food or conversation. I know I will need to drink water before long because I need to stay awake. I close my eyes, still pretending to sleep, and try to escape the reality of where I am as the possibilities of what will happen next spin through my head.

The night is long, and I fall asleep but startle myself awake every time I doze off. My exhaustion is real, both physical and emotional, but I know that I need to stay strong in this hell. I feel the tears on my face, and it is an effort to hold back the scream in my throat. I continue to pray for Mother Mary to watch over me, although it is easy to believe that She has forgotten me altogether.

Naturally sleep overpowers me, and eventually, I am startled awake by loud stomping footsteps in the hall, accompanied by voices. I stay motionless, not knowing what to expect, but they open the gate and walk past me with purpose. They stand over one of the women's prone bodies and call her by her name, but she does not respond. One of them takes her arm and roughly pulls her up to her feet. She is entirely emaciated and cannot stand on her own, so they each grasp an arm and half drag her out, shutting the gate behind them. Both relieved and disappointed that I was left behind, I don't want to think of the poor woman who has probably seen her last day on earth.

# MARIA - Athens, Greece - 1906

Although I know that if Sister catches us we will both be in trouble, I often cover for Olga when she sneaks out to meet Stavros. It's hard to say no when I see how blissful she is because of him. His visits to the school are the best part of the day for both the girls and the nuns. Stavros' sweet, friendly manner and kindness for every person he engages make everyone feel special. He remembers everyone's name and often brings little gifts that he knows someone might like, like a flower or a particular stone. No matter what he brings, it always seems perfect. It pleases me that Olga has found such a wonderful person to love and who loves her equally.

She usually goes out right after Vespers and before night prayers. We are encouraged to attend all the prayer hours, but the sisters are more lenient if we miss the night prayers instead of morning prayers, assuming that we are studying or reading in the evening. Although there is always a Mass at Matins, there is only a Mass at Vespers if a priest shows up. So, often we just sing and return to our rooms. Since Olga has offered to help Stavros unload his carriage of supplies he has brought for the kitchen, I go to the prayer hour alone.

I see that there will be a service tonight, since as I walk to the seat I usually occupy, I pass several priests lining up on the altar. Father Theodore regularly performs the Mass and, on occasion, students assist, but tonight there is one priest who does not look like a student. I can feel his gaze on me even after I have passed. I turn as I take my seat and he is still watching me. I cast my eyes down and straight ahead to the altar, feeling myself blush uncontrollably.

When the mass ends, I practically run out of the chapel, speak to no one, and go to my room. Sister sees me and stands in my doorway, asking, "Maria, are you feeling ill?"

I respond, "I think it is approaching my time of the month." She nods her understanding and leaves me to my confusion.

Olga comes in right as Sister leaves. "I can't believe no one has caught you yet!" I tease.

"I know!" she responds. "I guess I am an expert at helping unload carriages!" We laugh. "The sisters come looking for me to send me out to meet Stavros! It is the best of all worlds!" She is radiant, and I am very happy for her.

"When will you tell your parents?" I ask.

She has her answer ready, "I have to tell them soon because I am afraid that I might get pregnant." I am shocked!

"What are you saying? Are you sleeping together?"

She says, "Well, we never have enough time to sleep." She has always been a rebel.

"Olga, please be careful!"

"Don't worry, we love each other, and he is going to

speak to my father as soon as he can show him that we have a decent place to live and that he will be able to provide for me."

She asks, "Is everything OK with you?"

Surprised that she is always so perceptive, I ask, "Why?"

"I don't know... something is a little different."

I begin to recount the strange incident in the chapel. Since she is a hopeless romantic, her only question is, "Is he handsome?" I feel myself blush, and that is all the response she needs.

Mother Thekla the Abbess is the first person I met when I arrived here, and I have been under her care since. I know I am a favorite, but I suppose that is because most of the other girls have families, and I do not. This morning I am summoned to see her after morning prayers. I can only think that she wants to speak to me about Olga! So I mentally prepare excuses to justify her absences. "Good morning, Mother "I stand right at the entrance, waiting for instruction.

"Come in, come in, Maria!" she says, and I am glad to see she is not scowling! She has a wrinkled face because she is very old, but her eyes are bright, and she has a beautiful smile. She points to the chair that faces her desk, and I sit with my back straight. After small talk about my classes and overall health, she asks, "How old are you now?"

Although I know that she already has that information, I answer "Sixteen."

She smiles, nodding her head. "There is someone whose eye you have caught and who would like to speak with you, with your permission and blessing."

I know immediately of whom she is speaking, and I try to visualize his face. I sit stone still because I don't know what my proper reaction should be.

She watches me closely, trying to read my response. "Because your father is not here to speak for you, I hope you do not mind that this falls on me." I suppose that "this" means choosing a husband for me. I look down and nod my head.

She continues, "When we took you in, it was with the understanding that, at the proper time, I would arrange a match for you. I know this young man personally, and I can vouch for his sincerity and good intentions." I listen very carefully. "He is an artist. His education is in iconography, and he is a very pious man." I cannot think of anything to say, so I wait silently. "Do you hear me, Maria?" I nod, and she says, "I understand this is sudden, but you should make a decision soon, and please feel comfortable discussing it with me. Do you know of whom I am speaking?"

I carefully respond, "I do."

Mother is relieved that she does not have to worry about this part of the process. "He is ready to be ordained, but chooses to marry first, so please try to make a decision promptly." I surprise myself that, although they discussed so much without my input or consent, I am not opposed to meeting the handsome stranger.

Should I be uncooperative or rebellious? If I am honest, I am not disturbed by the attention but rather pleased by it. I think of Olga and Stavros and how happy they make each other, but when I think of Agni and Constantine, it frightens me that this could be my future. Mother has to repeat herself. "How do you feel about a formal introduction?"

In all honesty, she smiles, and I answer, "I have no objection to an introduction. Does he know about my origin?"

She smiles and says, "That is your story to tell if you choose to."

She has told me this more than once. I don't ever speak of my origin, although, in my heart, I will always be Turkish and the daughter of a Rabbi.

It has been four years since I have seen my parents. The news of pogroms during this time leaves no doubt that they were killed, among other Jews. My memories of my parents are losing their intensity, and it has been some time since I have cried myself to sleep. I have only told Olga and Agni that I am Jewish. Because we shared everything, this secret would have been too big to keep! Everyone else thinks I am a Greek orphan born in Turkey. I recite the Greek Orthodox prayers required here at school and even in my most private moments, these are the prayers that I say.

Tonight I ask God to make Diocles Raftopolous a good man, like my father. I already know that he is handsome and tall. I suppose I am lucky that an educated man has chosen me. "Please, God, let him be kind!" I whisper to myself.

"Which one is he?" Olga is bubbling with excitement.

"Let's see," I tease. "He is the one wearing a black tunic and a black kamilavka on his head!" Because, of course, they all wear the same thing, we giggle.

She can't help but create the fairy tale. "A prince will come, love you, passionately, and be gentle and kind."

I know that she is talking about Stavros, but I say, "I hope so, Olga." I can't help but think of Agni and her unkind husband.

It is comforting to know that I am allowed to choose or, minimally, agree. Unusual as it is, Reverend Mother was quite clear that I can wait if I do not feel a connection. She indicated that Diocles may not have been the only man inquiring about me, but that he is her choice. These thoughts are disturbing and too close to Agni's situation for my comfort, but I think my future path is limited, and I am grateful that I am under Mother Thekla's wing.

I put on my black skirt but, instead of the dark blouse that I would typically wear to service, Olga convinces me to wear my pretty white shirt with ruffles at the neck. I have never worn this blouse, as it never seemed the right occasion, but I suppose tonight can be considered unique. "Olga, I need help plaiting my hair."

She instantly jumps into action. "Why must you wear a braid?" she wants to know.

"Because I am going to church, and I am about to be introduced to a priest!" I laugh nervously, and she says,

"You have the most beautiful hair!"

"Even if that were true," I say, "I must wear a shawl, anyway."

She agrees to do a simple braid, although it does not look the same as when I do it myself. She takes my hand and turns me slowly, pleased with the results.

"Thank you, Olga." I mean that from my heart. "I am a little afraid," I confide in my friend.

"Of course you are! But, no one is forcing you to be interested. Follow what your heart tells you. I promise you will know." I realize she is referring to herself as much as me. "Which veil will you wear? You must wear one of these tonight!"

Olga unwraps the two lace shawls that I brought with me from Turkey. I did not understand, at age 12, why my mother insisted that I take her veils. It is clear now that she knew far more than what we discussed, and she knew the years would pass, and I would become a woman.

"I am more comfortable wearing the same veil as the other girls."

Even as I say this, I touch the shawls and feel warm with my mother's memory. I don't want to be sad now, so I quickly choose the white one. Olga places it carefully on my head, and I wait for her approval.

"Perfect." She says as she holds up the looking glass for me.

Since it is too early for service, I reach for my mother's embroidery and unfold the portion which I am currently stitching. I will busy myself until it is time to go to chapel and Olga, always alert, sketches pretty flowers on the pages of my diary and waits quietly with me. The rhythm of the needle and thoughts of the strange man I am about to meet blends with the vision of my mother's angelic face. Absorbed in the joy of feeling her presence, I miss a stitch, and the needle pricks my finger. I react, but not in time to prevent a tiny spot of blood from staining the shawl.

It is faint and blends in with a dark pink flower and so inconspicuous that no one will ever notice. But, I will always know exactly where it is and when it happened.

"Maria, the bell!" Olga jumps up and checks me from head to toe. She pinches my cheeks and dabs my lips with raspberry that Stavros brought her, and I allow it. We join the others in the hall. As I look at the younger girls walking to Mass, I realize how changed we are from when I first met Olga and Agni, and I miss our youthful, carefree days.

As we pass the tall windows in the main hall, I find myself in awe of the spectacular sunset. I gaze to the heavens and pray that my parents are looking at the same sky. Although there is no conversation, Olga stops with me, and I know she knows my thoughts, and I am ever grateful to have her as my friend.

The chapel is in the center of the abbey, and its beauty amazes me. As I walk into the narthex, a novice gives me a candle which I light in front of the "Mother of God with Child" and I say a prayer. "I put myself in your hands, Holy Virgin, and promise that I will be open to and true to myself."

The beauty of the icon moves me, not only for its content but also for its talent. I admire the other images covering the walls. Although I see them every day, I am drawn to their messages and linger to savor the quiet of the moment The sound of giggling girls coming towards the chapel pierce through my meditation, and I also move along.

I am decidedly nervous, but I walk to the nave and find my position in the spot that Olga has saved for me. The candlelight is dim and soothing as we face the intricately carved wooden pulpit. Five nuns are standing in a circle around the podium, and they begin by reciting liturgy before breaking into song.

Although the music is beautiful and the words familiar, I struggle to follow the hymns because I am distracted by only one thing. I bow my head as I shift my gaze in the direction of the deacons standing directly in front of the four seminarians. At first glance, they all look alike in their black robes and kamilavkas, black hats. I look from one face to the other, in search of him. All eyes are cast down or closed, except for those of Diocles Raftopoulos. He is already watching me, and although his lips don't smile, his eyes do.

Since we sing Saturday Vespers, the entire service lasts less than an hour. But for me, that hour moves incredibly slowly. When the service is over, Mother Thekla summons me across the room, acknowledging me with a nod. As I approach, she smiles sweetly, and I am so grateful for her emotional investment in me, and I promise myself that I will show her my gratitude someday. "Maria, you are a vision of youth and innocence, and I am proud of you!" I blush but take her extended hand, and she leads me towards the enormous doors that open onto the patio garden.

The nuns are strolling on the various paths, with hands tucked in their robes' deep pockets or holding prayer rope rosaries. Diocles is standing next to a cement bench under a flowering pear tree. I expect Mother Thekla to stay with us, but she walks back the way we came after she makes a quick introduction. I realize that we will be watched only through a window directly above us. The position is so perfect that I am confident we are not the first couple to meet here.

When I stand before him, he is quite tall, and I have to lift my chin to look at his face. It is a strong, handsome face with deep-set eyes, dark brows, straight nose, and a trimmed beard. Since he has removed his kalimavkion, I see that his black hair is curly and long enough to be pulled back and tied low at the nape of his neck. He looks younger than I expected. "Yassou, Maria," he says with a slight smile.

"Yassou, Diocles," I respond, feeling tongue-tied.

He steps aside with a small bow, and I sit on the bench. He sits next to me, leans down, elbows on his knees, and folds his hands together. He holds the plain cross hanging from his neck and looks straight ahead without speaking. I sit quietly with my hands on my lap and wait for a sign from him. After a lengthy silence, he says, "Thank you." It is a whisper. I lean forward to look at him, and he turns his face towards me. "Thank you for not ignoring my feelings." I feel suddenly shy, but much less nervous.

"Maybe I'm only curious." I tease, and he smiles.

"Shall I tell you about myself?" His earnest demeanor is soothing, and I feel warm and safe as if I have always known him. But, I am afraid that everything will change when he knows my history.

I shake my head slightly and respond, "Let me tell you my story first, Diocles. After you know mine, you can share yours, if you still wish to."

As I begin to tell, my gaze follows a pear blossom that has landed on his shoulder. "I am Turkish and the daughter of a Rabii." I see the surprise in his eyes. We are silent as he absorbs my words, and I wait for a sign from him.

He reaches out slowly, takes my shawl, carefully removes it from my head and across my shoulder. He folds it neatly and places it on the space between us on the bench. "You are beautiful," he says. He clears his throat and says, "Please tell me your story."

I look into the distance as I recall my childhood as clearly as I can. Speaking of my parents is like a gentle balm, and having someone with whom to share my secret is more soothing than I ever imagined. He only interrupts if something is unclear, but I lose myself in the joy of bringing together my two worlds. When I finish, I turn to him and attest to the feeling that he has been watching me. In response to my story, he quietly reaches for my hand and nestles it carefully in his.

# ARGHIRULA - Athens, Greece - 1942

The loud clanking of the gate startles me out of my cold and uncomfortable sleep. I have to move my legs in two different directions to stimulate the blood flow. Although I slept, I feel exhausted and am grateful for the dirty water offered by a female guard. She is not the same as last night, and she looks sad as she looks around the room. Another guard is standing just outside the bars, and I see him impatiently make a gesture to speed it up. The female guard extends her hand to help me get up, and I gladly take it.

The gate is opened, just enough for us to get through and is then immediately shut and locked behind us. She turns to me and asks," Do you need the bathroom?" I'm surprised at both the offer and her perfect Greek.

"Where are you taking me?" She does not answer but stops at the same room I had used yesterday to relieve myself. For obvious reasons, I hesitate to go in but, since I have no idea where I am going or for how long, I'm grateful for the opportunity. The room is no less disgusting, but without the surprise factor, it is slightly more tolerable.

She waits with the male guard right outside the door, and I can't help but compare the shine on his boots to those of my attacker. I don't need to do a close inspection to know that they do not come close! As I climb the dark stairs that took me down here yesterday, I hope for freedom but fear a terrible fate waiting for me. Since I have no choice in the matter and the guards set the pace, him in front, and she behind, I keep my head down and do what they tell me.

When we eventually reach the top of the long staircase and the guard opens the door, I am shocked at the bright sunlight streaming in from the high windows in the front of the building. I take a deep breath to remove the stench from down below, but cigarette smoke permeates the air, so it is hardly cleansing.

There are occasional loud voices, but conversations are muted and confined to small groups for the most part. No one is curious, and barely anyone looks in our direction. They take me to a hallway with a row of chairs against one wall. Men sit in some, but most are empty. I sit at the end, as instructed, and the female guard positions herself next to me. I don't know what happened to the male guard, but he is no longer with us.

I watch as people enter and exit the door that faces me across the hall. Some men are in suits, and some look like poor locals, but German guards escort most. I have seen the same man going brusquely in and out more than a few times. I only saw one woman brought in, but it has been a long time, and I have yet to see her come out.

Since no one speaks to me, I can only assume that there

is some sort of military tribunal inside that room, and they are bringing me here for judgment and punishment for my crime against the German pig. I'm angry, frightened, and helpless as my fate is at these cruel people's hands and based on the untrue story twisted to make my attacker the victim. I have no chance in hell for this to end well, and I am having difficulty breathing and feel faint.

The guard takes my arm, "It is time, come!" she says, in perfect Greek as she guides me into a large, noisy room. This room looks like it might have been a vault when the building was a bank, but now there are rows of benches facing the room's front. There is a high platform with a large desk where a judge sits between two flags; the black, red, and yellow striped German flag and the red and white Nazi flag with the swastika in the circle.

All my senses tell me that I am right to be afraid, but I can't help that I also feel angry. The guard directs me towards a bench, and I wait, with eyes cast down and hands folded on my lap as she stands at the back of the room with other guards. There is a camaraderie between them, which feels misplaced in this environment of fear and intimidation.

I sense someone slide into the bench next to me. Prepared to move away, I hear the low familiar voice, "Arghiro'!" and I stay in my place. I look into the precious faces of my brothers Tolis and Basilis, and they each take a seat, flanking me. The bottled up tears come all at once with the release of my fears.

Tolis puts his arm around me, "You have to compose yourself." he whispers.

"I know!" I respond as I bury my face in my hands and bend over with the sensation that I might genuinely faint as a result of being relieved, afraid, and hungry.

"Arghiro', you will be called before the Judge shortly." Sobered, I listen carefully to his instructions. "When you get there, all you have to do is keep quiet." *I can do that!* He continues, "You have to pretend that you don't understand a word of German! Can you do that?" I nod yes, still choking back tears. "Arghiro', it took a lot for us to get this done." He nods towards Basilis. "So, you must understand that it is important for you to pretend that you are dumb! When he asks you a question, respond briefly and without expanding. Yes and no are perfect responses."

Of course, as much as all this goes against my grain, I understand that I could have been shot right on the spot, so I enthusiastically agree and say, "I understand, Tolis!"

He gives me his handkerchief and points to my face, so I wipe my tears, blow my nose, put the square in my pocket, and sit quietly, waiting for the bench's instructions. Eventually, I reach for my brothers' hands, and we sit like this as their love energizes me and, although still afraid, I feel very much protected.

When the deputy calls, "Arghirula Raftopoulos!" My brothers nudge me to go towards the judge, with some encouraging words, but mostly words of caution. I walk past dozens of people who are waiting, and I stand before the judge. A soldier, who must be the interpreter, is to his left, and I am next to the officer who attacked me. Instead of looking at the smug expression on his stupid face, I concentrate on his boots, which are still disturbingly shiny.

"What happened yesterday?" The judge looks directly at me as he asks the question. *Was it only yesterday?* Although surprised to be addressed first, I am ready.

"I was standing on a box, wiping the kiosk's windows, and a man attacked me." The judge does not react, either because he already knows the real story or doesn't care. "Is the person that you are accusing in this room?" It is repeated in Greek, although I understand the judge perfectly well.

I want to say many things, but I respond, "Yes," as instructed by my brother.

"Can you point to him?"

At the risk of making eye contact, I turn my head towards the officer and point, looking right into his eyes.

There is a smirk on his face, and I have to look away to keep my promise to my brothers and play "dumb" rather than spit at him. The judge addresses the officer. "What happened?" There is no longer a translator, but I can understand.

"I was walking past this woman's kiosk, and she attacked me for no reason!"

I can not believe my ears! The room spins out of control, and I hear someone yell, "HE IS A LIAR !" Of course I know that I am the one who said it as I see the shock on the judge's face. Although prepared to let me walk away as my brothers arranged it, I understand that the judge has to change direction.

"I see you understand German, Miss Raftopoulos," he says calmly, looking directly at my face.

The room is hushed since my outburst. Everyone watches the judge, including me. *Oh, God, what have I done?*

After an eternity, the judge leans towards me, and his eyes say, "why could you not keep your mouth shut?"

"Your punishment, Miss Raftopoulos, is that Kapitan Lutz will slap you as you slapped him!" The judge barely finishes his sentence when I feel Lutz's backhanded slap across my face. It is a full and painful man's blow.

My head snaps back and forward again from the impact, and I know that if he could, he would have used a closed fist. I am stunned and dizzy and outraged. When I turn to strike back at the disgusting Nazi, I feel four strong arms lift me off the floor and take me away kicking.

I stopped breathing in my rage, and I don't exhale until I am out of the building and on the street. Although I don't know how I got here, I sit on the steps, with an exhausted brother on each side. They both laugh nervously, "As pame spiti!" *Let's go home!* they say simultaneously.

# MARIA - Athens Greece - 1906

Diocles has a quiet, smooth, and level voice, which reminds me of my father's. He leans over, elbows on knees as he occasionally holds his cross, and then releases it. He looks straight ahead as he recounts his personal story. "I am the 12th of 20 children, and I was born in 1870 in Elefsina, on the Albanian border, about 18 kilometers from here. My family is Arvanite, and our origin is Greek-Albanian. In my house, we spoke both Greek and Arvanitika. I studied for the priesthood near my town, as did my brother, who is an ordained priest. I came to Athens to study art, which disappointed my parents," he chuckles. "I have a brother who is a magician, and I believe he too has disappointed my parents. My passion and training are in Iconography."

He glances at me to see if I understand what an iconographer does. I nod and say, "Earlier today I admired the beautiful 'Mother of God with Child.'" He smiles, looking very pleased, and a little surprised.

"That is a beautiful work! I painted, on that same wall, some of the minor icons."

I smile and say, "You are very talented."

He looks at me, without speaking for a few moments and feeling his gaze's warmth, I am delighted. When he breaks the spell, he looks straight ahead once again and clears his throat. "I often travel, because my work demands it. If there is an opportunity, I work for months." I know he has purposely stopped speaking so that I might absorb this.

I ask the first question that enters my mind, "Do iconologists take their wives with them?" I feel my face grow red at my presumption, but I can see the smile even before he turns to face me.

"Yes, Maria, they often bring their wives and children as well." He teases as he looks directly into my eyes.

I feel the heat rise to the roots of my hair, and I drop my gaze. We sit quietly for some time, and I realize that I have been touching the cross that hangs on the thin chain around my neck.

"Maria! Diocles!" I am startled by Mother Thekla's soft voice as she approaches. I pull up my shawl while he sits straight and stands in one smooth motion, just as she reaches us. He takes my hand as an indication that I too should rise, and, when I do, he promptly releases it. "I hope you had a nice visit," she says.

Diocles bows his head, "It was lovely. May I visit again?" I am thrilled that he has asked to see me another time and equally delighted at Reverend Mother's response.

"Saturday would be a perfect day for a walk of the grounds." And then, almost as an afterthought, she adds, "If you are free, Diocles."

He responds, "It will be my honor!"

My head is buzzing, and I barely hear them making

meeting arrangements. He offers a small bow and walks towards the abbey, in long strides, as he replaces the kamilavka on his head. Mother Thekla tells me that she will meet me after breakfast Saturday morning and asks earnestly, "Do you feel he is a good man, Maria?"

Afraid to break the spell, I simply respond, "Neh" *Yes, Mother.*"

I light the candles in my room, knowing I will not embroider tonight because there is no light through the window and because I want to relive the evening in my mind before Olga gets here with her inevitable barrage of questions. My thoughts are of Diocles Raftopoulos and his kind demeanor, and the fact that he has chosen me. I give in to sleep as I envision his handsome face and artist's hands, and I dream of visiting exotic places with my husband.

Olga's questions start immediately when my eyes open, "Do you like him?" I sit up with my back against the headboard, pull my knees to my chest, and hug them. She is sitting at the foot of the bed, waiting.

"I do like him... very much," I reply dreamily.

"Will you marry him?"

"I expect that I will if he wants me."

She doesn't stop asking questions and demands detailed responses until breakfast is over, and class begins. She is my sweetest friend, and I love her.

"Agni is expecting a baby!" Olga is out of breath as she catches up to me on the way to evening Vespers. She has seen Stavros today, and he carried the news. I can't help but visualize the hopeless sadness that is always in Agni's eyes, but there is nothing more special than a baby.

"How wonderful!" I say, but Olga shakes her head.

"She is heartbroken about it!"

Today is Friday, and it has been, without a doubt, a very long day. Although I go through the motions of routine things, my thoughts are elsewhere. Classes are just a blur, and I have to be called twice, in two subjects, to answer a question that I had not heard. I don't taste any of my meals, and I can't concentrate on the service tonight.

I look forward to sleeping so that tomorrow morning can arrive.

"Please let me help you with your hair after you wash it!"

I laugh at Olga's excitement. "I will only be sleeping on it, so why bother?"

She shakes her head and asks, "Do you know how beautiful you are?"

In response, I say, "I never thought about it!"

She goes on, "Look around at the other girls, including me. We all look similar, with our dark hair and dark eyes. Your hair is like gold, and your ivory skin practically glows." I do not want to think about my looks so much and would like for her to stop.

"Olga, I will let you help me with my hair!"

When I wash my hair, Olga is ready with cut strips of fabric that look like a pile of rags. I roll my eyes, but do not argue with her because she is determined. Directing me to the chair where there is the most light, Olga begins the tedious process of separating my long hair into thin sections. She wraps and twists each section with the cloth strips. I am so amazed at her tenacity that I relax and let her work, although it takes a long time. When she finishes with every section, she places a cotton towel around my head, encasing it. "I will finish it tomorrow before breakfast. You should get to sleep so that your eyes will look rested!"

To my surprise, I am not uncomfortable placing my toweled head on the pillow. I lie still, but I am too anxious to fall asleep. I get up and bring the chair closer to the light coming into the window, reach for my embroidery, and begin my private prayer to Mama and Baba.

# ARGHIRULA - Athens, Greece - 1942

"Arghiro', we have to tell them!" Tolis and I have been arguing over this for over an hour.

"I wish you would just go talk to them alone!"

He shakes his head as he walks to the stove to make coffee. He looks over his shoulder to be sure I'm listening. Of course, I understand. The thought of being out on the street terrifies me, but not as much as telling my father what happened yesterday. He will blame it on my red nail polish! "We must tell them together, so Mamma sees that you are well."

Walking briskly, I wrap my sweater against the chill. Usually, it is a struggle to keep up with Tolis' long stride, but he slows down today. I feared that I would feel exposed and afraid on the street since it seems that there are more soldiers in German uniforms than usual. But instead of feeling nervous, I feel angry as if every one of them has done something wrong. Gratefully, most don't even look in my direction.

The door to my parents' house, which is usually open, is locked today. "Poios einai ekei?" *who's there?*

"Arghirula."

We hear her unbolting the door, and I wonder if that secure lock was always there, or if my father recently added it. Her embrace brings me solace, and I try to hold on a little longer, but she guides me towards the table and sits facing me as if she knows she is about to hear something unpleasant. Tolis follows and my father comes from behind his screen, although I do not receive an embrace from him. Tolis accepts a black-market coffee and begins by saying, "There was a little incident, but you can see we are both fine....." He proceeds to tell them, from the start, with some help from me, and ends by saying that they escorted me out of the courtroom. There was no mention of where I slept the night before, and my parents do not ask.

My father looks older today, a little drawn. His hair and beard are still black with a few grey streaks, although his body looks healthy. His eyes look sad and worried, and I can barely remember ever seeing them that way. My mother has many questions about what happened, but mostly about how I felt during that time. "Were you afraid, Arghiro'?" "Were you hurt?" Have you been taking care of yourself?" My father only sits and listens without comment. I can't help but wonder if he blames me somewhat for what happened.

Happy that I visited with my mother, some of the tightness in my chest is relieved. "We will stop at the cafe for ouzo," Tolis announces, and, although I would prefer to go home, I appreciate his support, so I agree to it.

There are not many places left in the city that have not been destroyed structurally or by lack of funds, products, or patronage. Tolis enters the taverna to shouts of recognition and welcome, and I like being in his company and meeting his friends. "Mateo, this is my sister Arghirula." I smile and take the offered hand of the owner. He is also the bartender, and I'm sure he is also the cook and floor-scrubber.

"Welcome!" he says with a big smile and prepares ouzo for Tolis. He lifts an empty glass towards me, "You too?"

I nod, "Efcharisto!"

We take the table next to the window, and Tolis points to the chair that faces into the room as he sits opposite me, so he has a view of the street. Tolis clinks my glass and says, "Yamas!" *to our health!*

I repeat "Yamas" and sip the liquid that looks like a cloud, and I am grateful to my brother for making things better. "Papa seems softer, don't you think?" I ask, curious to see if my brother noticed it too.

"The war has changed us all, Arghiro'?" Pointedly, he waits for my response, and I am aware of how much I have changed in the past two years.

Half to myself, I respond, "Toso alithes!, *so true!*"

Although Tolis is usually anxious to run off somewhere, he is exceptionally relaxed today as if he has nowhere to go. I soon realize that the business he has planned is coming to this taverna. His name is Lucas Barbas, referred to as LB. He is tall for a Greek, with fair skin and coppery color hair. Tolis orders another ouzo as he makes the introduction. "This is my sister Arghirula...that I told you about." I extend my hand, and LB gives me a firm handshake, which leaves no question that he is a man in charge. The conversation, inevitably, is about the conditions of our city and our people and our suffering. I am somewhat contributing, but when the discussion becomes about people I am not familiar with, I become lost in thoughts of my recent events.

"Are you a good typist?" LB addresses me and, because I have not had time to think, I respond honestly.

"I'm not fast, but I'm accurate."

He smiles at my honesty and asks, "Do you know who we are?"

Once again, I respond truthfully, "Oxi, *no.*"

Now, he laughs and turns to Tolis. "I see that you are an expert at keeping secrets, my friend!"

At my questioning look, LB explains, "We have an underground publication called 'Rizospastis,' *The Radical.* The newspaper originated before the war, but it is now a Greek resistance paper of the Greek People's Liberation Army." I nod and listen, trying not to seem too excited, but I am thrilled at the prospect! "We always need help." LB offers a smile.

Tolis asks. "Where would she need to go?"

"We have a space in the basement of 33 Adrianou Street." Tolis nods as he knows the building. "Three or four girls type there every day, and the organizing and layout are also in this location. We have the newspaper finished by a printer, who remains anonymous, but is a friend of the Liberation Army."

Tolis approves of the location since it is only a few blocks from our house, and he says that I can walk it alone if there are times he can't be there. When he sees my frightened face, he gives me a look to say, "You will be OK!"

LB continues, "We have limited funds, so the pay will not be much. We all work primarily voluntarily for the cause." The thought of actually getting paid anything at all makes this that much sweeter.

"When can I start?" Tolis and LB laugh, and I take a sip of my drink, slowly savoring the taste of anise, to hide my embarrassment at being so excited. LB seems happy with my enthusiasm,

"Why don't you come tomorrow morning and see what you think?" He takes a piece of paper out of his pocket and hands it to me. At a glance, I see the address of the building and the person I must see. Once again, as I sip my drink, I can't help but be grateful for my brother.

The noise level increases and eventually explodes as the music begins, just as I start to relax from the drink. I see that all the tables are full, and many people are also standing, and I hear the distinct sound of the Rembetika music from the far corner. There are different instruments, including a bouzouki and a guitar, but mostly, I lose myself in the grave, raspy voice of the singer as I hear the theme of the song. Every word is not intelligible, but it is about our troubled times, as he describes hunger, poverty, and our people's pain.

The doors are tightly closed and monitored, and we are confined indoors. I remember when we would sit at the outdoor tables with people pouring out of the cafe onto the sidewalk. Painfully, I remember that these are different times, and the music makes me miss Effie and mourn my failed marriage.

"Another?" LB shouts, offering another drink.

"Neh, efcharisto *Yes, thank you*," I respond at the top of my voice.

LB and Tolis are in deep conversation, but I barely hear them. I observe the crowd and see that Italian soldiers and sailors outnumber the locals. Although we see them on the streets, it feels different from being in the same space and jovial together as the ouzo and retsina are flowing.

There is a lightness that, although a fantasy contained within these walls, gives me a needed reprieve from my tormented thoughts. I let the ouzo warm me and feel my head get fuzzy. Enjoying the moment, I smile back at an Italian sailor vying for my attention. Tolis, seeing all, grabs the leg of my chair and with one quick pull, turns me away from the room. Thrown off-balance, I am now facing the window and the street just as he intended. Although disappointed in my changed view, I sit back, sip my drink, and lose myself in the beautiful, forbidden music.

# JOAN - New York, New York/ Weehawken, New Jersey - 1968

I think I am in love! However, my mother finds every opportunity to remind me that I would be making a terrible mistake to make this relationship permanent. The one consolation is that she didn't think Mike should marry Linda either. The thing that my mother loves most is her children. However, her nature is selfish, and when the time comes that these children share affection with an outsider, Mom has a hard time coping. Pete is the exception because he pays an incredible amount of attention to her, and she probably likes the fact that he is Italian. My father loves everyone, but unfortunately, my mother can bring him over to her side if she puts in the effort.

My mother works at Vincent's Jewelers on Bergenline Avenue in West New York. My father will drive her, and one of us will pick her up at 6:00 p.m. I don't have my own, but my father's car is always available, although there is hardly anywhere I can't get to by walking or taking a bus. My mother also uses the bus during the week.

We are all in the kitchen, which is a little crowded. My

father is making toast from Italian bread. He piles it up on a plate, and Marilena spreads butter on it, but it is usually too cold for the butter to melt. Since everyone is on the run, nobody cares, and I add grape jelly to mine before eating two pieces.

Today I have a 12:30 appointment at Vidal Sassoon in New York City for a haircut. I am splurging and spending much more than I ever have on a cut, but, determined to grow my hair longer, I will spend the $30 to have it appropriately shaped. The salon is very upscale, and I feel a little out of place, but the staff is friendly enough, and I don't have to wait long to get shampooed. The hairdresser's name is Sandy. "You have to grow it a little longer to get it cut into a bob!"

Fully aware that it is still on the short side, I ask, "Can you shape it while it is in the process of growing?"

She looks hesitant, but says, "Let's do a perm!"

Surprised, I ask. "Did you notice that I have curly hair?"

She is so sure of herself, "I understand, but we can control the curl with a perm."

I hear someone in the hall, "Vidal, can you come to check this?" and Vidal Sassoon's response,

"Be right there!"

Completely smitten that he is here and so close, I tell Sandy to go ahead and perm, even though I know that my cost for today has just doubled

I am relieved when we are finally ready to comb out, and I am truly horrified at the result of this too long process.

My head looks just like a black poodle, and I hate it beyond words! "Are you kidding?" I cannot control myself.

"You don't like it?" Sandy keeps touching the curls gently with both her hands. "It came out perfectly, and just the way I pictured it!"

I am in tears, "You have to get rid of it!" I plead.

She seems stricken because she is so proud of her work. Meanwhile, I don't want to step out into the street. She becomes agitated, and I am not helping the situation. We are both teary and, in my typical fashion, I am feeling sorry for her. "Listen, Sandy, I'm sure you did a great job, but this is not what I came here for, so please tell me what we will do!"

She concedes, after conferring with her boss. "You will have to come back next week because I will burn your hair if I put any other chemical on it today. We need to use a relaxer." *Next week??!!*

"I will come back next week, but as early as possible." Fortunately, they can give me an appointment for Wednesday at 4:30 pm. I am sure that Frank will be OK with me leaving work early to get the train uptown to get here in time. They do not charge me for the perm, nor will they expect me to pay to remove it.

Sheldon laughs when I tell him how my day was, although I fail to see its humor. "You look beautiful, no matter what!" Where's my mother when he says things like this?

"I don't like the way I look at all right now!" Then softer, "When do you get to come home?"

"No leave for a while," he explains, "but I have a

three-day pass coming up in a few weeks. I hope you'll be at home." His voice is music to my ears.

"I will most certainly be here," I promise.

It is closer to three weeks before he gets home, which is OK because my hair is heading back to normal.

"Good morning." He sounds sleepy.

"Hey, you're up early!" I tease. I look at my watch and see that it is 9:10.

"I know, but I got here really late last night... this morning. We had to wait for two guys to get off work before we could head out." He continues, "But, I just need to shower and drive up anytime you say." I love him!

"Listen..." I say," Bob is home this weekend too, and Laura asked if we want to go out with them later." Laura and I have been friends since high school. We tried our first cigarette together in the balcony of The Mayfair Theatre. She enjoyed it, and I choked and hated the taste.

Sheldon doesn't have to think long. "Sure, sounds good!" He likes Laura a lot and, even though Bob, who is a Marine, is a bit of a jerk, he likes him well enough, and they are always fun, and I feel the same way. "We thought we could go to Tedesco's for pizza and mussels and then to The Shadows to have a drink." He seems distracted,

"Yea, it all sounds great! Any plans you make are good for me. I'll see you in a few hours, depending on the traffic." Then, "I love you."

I don't hesitate, "I love you too!" Oh, that feels so good, because I do!

# MARIA - Athens, Greece - 1906

My sleep last night was brief and disrupted by many dreams. I awaken at the crack of dawn, hours before breakfast, and open my red velvet diary. I leaf through the pages of greetings and poems written by my friends for the last four years. I read through the rhymes and notes and admire the delicate flowers. Olga has meticulously drawn on many of the pages. The realization that I will soon leave this life behind me feels both bitter and sweet.

Olga eventually rises and goes behind the curtain to the chamber pot with her eyes still partially closed. She is surprised to see that I am already awake. "Did you sleep well, Maria?" When I shrug, she examines my face. "Come sit!" she says, pointing to the chair. "We will finish your hair!" She shows me the first strand removed from its casing, and it is surprisingly pretty. She is swift in her labor, and, before long, I can feel the soft curls frame my face. "Get dressed before I finish, and then you can look." I put on my walking dress, which is dark green and understated, except for the lace inserted at the high-collared bodice that comes in at my center. Olga surprises me with a black velvet ribbon to tie at the waist. I put on my stockings and low-heeled walking shoes and look to Olga to finish my hair before we go to breakfast.

She quickly gets dressed and is excited in her own right, since her parents are coming to visit and, most importantly, they will meet Stavros. Olga runs her fingers through my long hair, gathering it loosely at the nape of my neck. She produces another ribbon, very similar to the one around my waist but much more narrow, and places it across the top of my head tying it in the back. She carefully uses a comb to pull some waves of curls in the front and pins a small branch of blossoms on the band and over my right ear. I can see that Stavros has helped her find these treasures, and I appreciate her vision and love.

When she holds up the looking glass, I am overjoyed, and Olga is very proud, "You look like a princess!" We laugh at the comparison, but I genuinely feel royal as I glide to breakfast.

I eat a bowl of yogurt with almonds and a koulourakia. I sip coffee and a glass of water and then wait impatiently for Mother Thekla. She finally arrives, and as we make eye contact, she smiles as I approach her. She takes my hand and turns me one full circle. "You look lovely, Maria. Can I assume Olga had something to do with this?" It is more a statement than a question.

Diocles stands when he sees us, although we are far from the bench under the pear tree. As we approach, he says "Kalimera, Igoumeni," *Mother Superior* to Reverend Mother, and does not look at me as they exchange pleasantries. I feel mildly disappointed and hope that he has not cooled towards me in the two days since we first met.

Mother Thekla points to the walking path, and Diocles steps forward with his hands clasped behind his back and waits for me to stand next to him. The Reverend Mother remains until we have walked about 20 meters before she begins to follow, and I am grateful that she is giving us so much privacy.

"You are the vision of an angel," he says. I look at him, but he is looking straight ahead, and since I am indeed blushing, I am glad of that.

"Olga insisted." And as an afterthought, "and I did not stop her!" We both laugh, and I exhale, extremely conscious of his physical presence beside me. He adjusts his stride to match mine as we synchronize our steps. The sun is shining, and the spring flower colors are more vivid than I ever remember them before.

"Did you sleep well?" I am surprised at this rather personal question, but respond honestly,

"No, I did not! I had a sleepless night." He chuckles, "As did I!"

We walk further as this seemingly unimportant, but very important, exchange hangs between us. I fully understand the seriousness of his intention.

"Why have you not yet taken your vows?" I would like to get my questions out of the way.

"I have always known that I would marry someday, but have never before found myself drawn to a woman enough to take her as my wife. If I take vows before I marry, I would have to vow celibacy."

I change the subject because I am not prepared to discuss

the topic of his celibacy. "Do you plan on preaching?" He glances at me,

"I will not preach. I am an iconologist, so I will continue to paint." We are quiet for some time, and I happily find that the silence between us is comfortable, and the energy in the space between us is palpable.

"Would you like to sit?" he asks. I look back towards Mother Thekla and notice that she has also stopped and is sitting on a small bench way behind us. I follow his gaze to the large rocks and follow him. He finds a flat rock that looks as if others have used it for this very purpose for centuries, and he positions himself so that he is facing me, with our knees almost touching. I feel lightheaded and savor the look of him, as I somehow know that I can see past the man's stern exterior. "Have you thought about me?" His question surprises me, but I feel I should be sincere.

"I have." I respond and then, boldly, ask, "And you? Did you think about me?"

His eyes soften as he says, "I have thought of nothing else, Maria."

We don't run out of topics, although many moments are silent and reflective. When I look back at our chaperone, I see the white veil of a novice. Sister Anna has taken Mother Thekla's place, and from the relaxed way in which she is looking at her book, I see that we will not need to rush today. She glances up, barely lifts her hand in a wave, and goes back to reading. As I turn to Diocles, I notice a bird perched way up high on a tree and hear the high ascending call and then the "chac-chac-chac" chatter.

I point out the pretty little bird with black and white

markings, the long black tail, and the big voice. "It's a Magpie," I tell him. "I love listening to them."

He smiles, "I have never seen one! Or perhaps I just never noticed, but I will now."

I feel happy to share my knowledge. "It is a brilliant bird," I take a deep breath and say, "And they mate for life!" As we hold each other's gaze, we know that we have just made our commitment.

Diocles meets me every evening after Vespers, and we walk, if the weather is compliant, or remain in the chapel, always under the watchful eye of one of the sisters. Soon after our greeting tonight, as we sit in the back pew he tells me, "Maria, I have received a commission to paint in a church in Russia." These are not words I wish to hear, and I immediately feel the tears spring to my eyes. He sees my reaction and hands me the letter. "I received it just today." Although my vision blurs, I see that it is from The Transfiguration Cathedral in Odessa, signed with an illegible signature, and authorized by Tsar Nicholas II, for the Pre-Conciliar Commission of Odessa. I scan past all the unnecessary words and instructions to see the date that this will occur. I turn to face him with tears I cannot hide, after seeing that he is to report 15 July 1906.

"How long will you be gone?" I am devastated that we will be separated so soon.

"It is an important job, and I would be working, with a team, on the iconostasis, the icon screen. I am certain that it will take many months to complete."

He takes the letter back and puts it in his pocket. He tenderly takes both my hands into his own beautiful artist's fingers and says softly, "I love you, Maria." He reaches up and gently wipes a tear from my face. "I want to be with you for the rest of my life if you will have me." I feel breathless and try to rein in my many emotions. I was afraid that he would leave me and, in honesty, that further stirs my love for him. I miss my parents and wish they were here to confirm my belief that he is a good man and give us their blessings.

I am unhappy to be the reason that he will not take this excellent opportunity to go to Russia to fulfill a dream. But, I sit quietly with my hands in his and thank God that he has sent him to me.

When we hear the bell calling for the girls to retire to their dormitories, we rise and walk, without speaking, towards the main doors, where I will leave him. I face him and look up into his eyes. "I will have you, Diocles."

His face lights up with joy and a look that asks, "Are you sure?"

I smile and say, "Yes!"

He takes both my hands, raises them to his lips, and gently kisses each one separately. "I promise to make you happy each day of my life, as you have made me happy this moment."

I am on a cloud and cannot concentrate in anticipation of seeing Diocles at Mass tonight. He is there when I arrive, and we watch each other throughout the incredibly long Mass. When the service is over, and we greet each other, it is with a very different feeling. "Good evening, my future husband." I smile up at him. It is hugely disappointing when he does not immediately respond with words of love.

It is evident that something weighs on his mind, and I hope and pray that he has not changed his heart.

"Maria, I would like to discuss something that has been on my mind all night, enough that I could not sleep." He takes my hand and guides me to a bench away from other ears. I cannot speak because I fear that last night's magic spell might have disappeared and that he is going to Russia and will find someone else to love. In his mellow, soft voice, he says, "There is no reason that we cannot marry immediately! In that way, I can take the commission, and I will take my wife with me." We both laugh nervously, remembering our conversation.

I ask, "Really? When?" *Did that sound forward?*

He is pleased. "I will speak to Reverend Mother tomorrow. Neither of us has a family to attend, and everyone we care about is here so we can merely apply for a city license."

I feel giddy! "Nai Fysika!" *Yes, of course!* I am thrilled and incredibly happy.

He suddenly looks somber. "Come with me!" he says as he takes my hand and leads me to the garden's doors. He does not let it go until we reach the pear tree. I sit where he directs me, and I watch him as he fumbles in his pocket. He produces a small box and gets down on one knee. "Will you honor me by being my wife?" My emotions are visible as tears fill my eyes.

"Yes, Diocles, Yes!" He opens the box, reaches for my left hand, and places a plain gold band on the fourth finger. It is the most beautiful, most shiny piece of jewelry I have ever seen. "I vow to wear this for the rest of my life, Diocles, and I vow to love you just as long."

He smiles, "Maria, I pray that this is what you want. Will you be happy to commit your life to me and make a home for us and bear my children?"

I suppose I have not thought very seriously about the dedication and devotion that marriage requires, but I don't feel afraid. When I look into my imagined future, I see him, big and passionate, and full of love for me. And Baba is standing behind him with a hand on his shoulder.

# ARGHIRULA -
# Athens, Greece - 1942

3 3 Adrianou Street is only a short street away, but Tolis insists that he accompany me today. He plans to walk me into the building, although I have argued that he treats me like a schoolgirl! He does not concede to not going with me, but gives in to the time we leave the house, so I am a half hour early to the appointment. He grumbles just enough for me to complain, "You invited yourself, after all!"

I am grateful that the walk is so short. Destruction is practically everywhere, and I feel cold in my heart at the very personal realization that there is nothing but pain, poverty, and death all around me. The fact that Tolis can stay cheerful and often bring me out of my sadness is proven today as he arranges for me to embark on something new.

At 8:55 a.m., we enter the beautiful neoclassical building and locate the staircase. The lobby is spectacular, and, most probably, the only reason the Germans have not taken this building is that it is small compared to others in the area. I walk next to Tolis, who seems to know where he is going, and I am surprised when we walk down two levels.

We reach a door that is not marked, and Tolis knocks four quick taps. "A man's voice asks, "Poios einai ekei?" to which Tolis responds,

"Raftopulous!"

The door opens immediately, and a man greets us wearing black suspenders and shirt sleeves rolled up to his elbows. He seems to be in his 50's and has a mass of gray hair. "Ela, Ela!" he instructs us as he steps aside and quickly closes the door behind us. We are standing in an empty room with walls full of bookcases, which, except for a few old and torn ones, are void of books. They are filled, instead, with pieces of broken wood and destroyed construction materials. I am confused as I look at the paper in my hand.

"I was looking for Xaver," I say, sounding skeptical, as I once again look around the room.

With a little smile on his face, Tolis introduces us. "Xaver, this is my sister Arghirula."

Xaver takes my extended hand and, without hesitation, walks me to the bookcase straight ahead. "Pleasure," he says. He reaches his arm behind some rubble, and the cabinet to the right opens slightly into the room. Tolis enters first, and Xaver nudges me through and follows close behind.

We enter a much larger room filled with tables of all sizes, which, although at first seem to be randomly scattered, are very clearly marked with letters and numbers, which mean nothing to me. There are a half dozen men with similar rolled-up sleeves as Xaver, some with suspenders and some with garter bands on their upper arms, but all in white shirts. In one corner of the room are many small boxes closed at the top, and there is a large wire basket on wheels, brought in through a doorway leading into yet another room. I note that the bucket is full of typed pages.

Xaver seems much more relaxed on this side of the bookshelves, and I am beginning to understand this organization's seriousness. "LB likes your brothers very much." I realize that they are all part of the resistance.

I am a quick study, and typing comes easily to me as do proofreading and editing the grammar. The content of the publication is stories written by various reporters who support the clandestine media. All press systems, Greece included, have been put under the control of German Minister of Propaganda Joseph Goebbels, therefore all the allowed news is censored. More than once, I hear that we play a crucial role in informing and motivating resistance, and we are creating an "intellectual battlefield." Our goal is to share information to help build solidarity and strengthen morale even if, at times, we are creating a platform to stage uprisings.

Within this group, the camaraderie is like nothing I have ever experienced before, and I am happy to be part of it. "Good morning, Arghirula!" Xaver greets me. The drill is the same every morning. I knock four times, and he lets me in, and no matter what time I arrive, he is already here. He is the keeper of the key, and, for understandable security reasons, none of the staff has one. I pass through the secret bookcase, past the collating room, and to my desk.

"Kalimera," I smile at Thea, and she smiles back, shyly, "Kalimera, Arghirula."

There is already a handwritten article on the table next to my typewriter, which means that a reporter dropped it off during the night in the alley's assigned metal milk box. I remove my coat, hang it on one of the large hooks on the far wall, drape my sweater over the back of my chair, and immediately begin working. Within a half hour, the room is filled with voices and chairs scraping the floor as other girls take their places before their typewriters.

There is much conversation about the topics of the articles, comparing the seriousness of some as opposed to the satire of others. Our job is to type and pass on to LB, the editor, to review and make changes before they come back to us for the final typed draft. I have never met the people who do the printing and assume that they are purposely anonymous.

We are encouraged to walk around every few hours and drink from the ample supply of water on the table in the corner. There is no lack of chatter among the girls. Some know each other, but most, like me, have been brought in by an organization member. Thea and Sofia are sisters, close in age, and a year or two older than me. Alexandra is older and worked for a lawyer before the war. The lawyer has left Greece with his family, and she is not sure where he has gone, but because he was Jewish, it is difficult to know if he is gone or in hiding.

We eat our meager mid-day meal together, and if it is not too cold, we step out into the alley for fresh air before we return to our seats. Since there is a constant paper exchange flow as articles rotate, I don't usually see the same story that I originally typed, and this suits me since it allows me to read almost everything submitted. It is a smooth and well-organized operation, and I marvel the first time I see the finished product. It is a fantastic accomplishment for such a small group.

There are two movie theatres in Athens, and they are open sporadically and at irregular hours, due to the fear of bomb alerts. One has been relinquished and used for the entertainment of the German soldiers. The other cinema shows movies from different countries but the titles are in German, Italian and Greek. The films are mostly German propaganda newsreels showing that life in Greece is peaceful under their protection. Movies are banned if they are from a country that is hostile to the Axis forces.

"My uncle is getting us tickets for the cinema, Arghirula. Sofia and I are going, and we are inviting some others." Thea looks around the room to see who is there. I hesitate because the tickets typically cost 4,000 drachmas.

As if she read my mind, she says, "The tickets cost 500 drachmas!

"The Voice of The Heart" is playing at The Esporos. I am very excited because I would love to go to a movie and also because the girls include me. The theatre is open tonight!

"Thank you, I would love it!" I say as I open my purse to produce the 500 drachmas required for the ticket.

It is such a busy day that it seems that no time has passed, and the workday is over. The girls are all tidying their spaces and gathering purses and jackets and meeting in the first room. "Xaver, can you please tell Tolis that I went to the cinema with the other girls?" My brother and I have an unspoken agreement, where he happens to be walking past my building every evening when I leave, and I always act surprised that he is there, and we walk home together.

"Of course!" Xaver says, "stay safe!"

It is unusually cold tonight, so we are bundled in our coats and scarves as we walk against the wind. Although it is two weeks before Christmas, the city is drab and dark and not festive, which should make us sad. But, the girls walk fast and arm-in-arm against the chill, and we are jovial at the thought of losing ourselves in a fantasy that will block out our day to day misery such as the article I typed today about the destruction and demolition of several cemeteries in Athens. The German forces took the ancient tombstones as building materials for sidewalks and walls.

"Hurry!" says a distant voice. We quicken our pace and meet at the entrance of the theatre, welcoming the relative warmth in the lobby. There is a small group of young men waiting for us. Sofia makes quick introductions, and we all smile politely, but we are anxious to find our seats. It is surprisingly crowded, so we separate into small groups. I sit with Alexandra and two young men whose names I do not remember.

"Do you know them?" I ask Alexandra, nodding my head toward them.

"No, I just met them tonight too, but I think the taller one is Niko."

The first thing we see on the screen is a clip from an upcoming movie. It looks like a romance film, and I can't help but think of Effie and the movie magazines we read. I miss her with all my heart, and I miss my youth, although I am not yet 21.

They announce that the film will be showing in this theatre in January 1943. Hopefully, Sofia's uncle will get us tickets. Before the feature movie starts, we are subjected to a very long propaganda movie about how well the Greek people are doing during this war. There are scenes of children laughing and dressed impeccably, going to school. There are scenes of farmers working their land. There are scenes of the hustle and bustle of city life in Athens. Can this be what the world is seeing? These blatant lies? I am not sure whether to laugh or scream! I look at Alexandra and see a tear falling down her cheek, and I reach over to take her hand, consoling her as I console myself. I wonder, sadly, what our future can hold. I must write a letter to Effie! Whether or not it ever gets to her, I must write it.

Since most of us live within the same area, we agree to a quick coffee at the closest taverna before the dreaded 10 o'clock curfew. "Arghirula, do you know Niko?" Alexandra asks since we are seated next to each other.

I shake his hand, "Charika gia ti gnorimia," I say. *Nice to meet you.* There are lots of names called out as we all try to meet while ordering coffee and ouzo. The owner seems happy to have this small crowd, since the taverna is otherwise empty. Niko is cute, and he tells me that he paints for fun and, although a very different type of art, I tell him about my father.

"Is he also a historian?"

"I suppose he is in a way...he is an avid reader," I respond. I have barely finished the sentence when I see my brothers enter and walk directly towards us. There are lots of familiar greetings, and everyone shuffles chairs to accommodate them. I am happy to see them here and especially glad that Basilis has placed his chair between Niko and me, so I don't have to discuss my father anymore.

# ARGHIRULA - Athens, Greece - Christmas 1942

The negative energy of our city is unavoidable. Cold weather adds to the gloom of the sad people walking to church today. Coats hang from their shoulders because even our healthiest is too thin, starved, and hungry. We spend the better part of Christmas day in our very crowded church, and my father is happy to have us all together. My sisters, Elena and Aphrodite look pious in their black veils, and I fidget only slightly less than Tolis. Looking at Basilis and Christos together, I try to see a resemblance between them and my father. I don't see any, except for the large ears that I have also inherited from him. My sisters are both lucky to have Mamma's delicate ears.

My mother's 46 years show in her silver streaked hair and thickened waistline, but her tranquility remains her strength. My father looks younger than his 62 years. He stands very straight, and his hair is still black, although it is beginning to recede in the front. He keeps his beard and mustache trimmed, and his look, as always, is rigid and stern. Today he is dressed like my brothers in a suit with a white shirt and dark tie. Mamma is covered entirely in black, and her skirt and blouse have no distinctive touches to make them look any less drab, and I cannot help but think that she dresses like a widow. Her face is that of an angel, and her eyes have a twinkle that has always been there.

We look like the perfect Greek family. I try to put aside the reality of our beautiful Athens' ravaged streets while we are in this holy place. After service, we walk to my parents' small house and feast on the "bounty" that my brothers have provided from who-knows-where. "We tried to get a leg of lamb, but couldn't." Basilis sounds apologetic as he portions out the delicious smelling, lean chicken. The chicken is not enough to satisfy this crowd, yet it must be shared. I see my father discreetly pass on his portion, and I know that Mamma will boil the bones into a broth for tomorrow's meal. Mamma has also made fasolada from the dry beans that Tolis brought her, but I can't help but notice that there are barely any vegetables in the soup. On the table is a large baked onion and two small loaves of bread that look pale and not well risen.

"This is a true feast!" Elena says to my brothers, "Thank you. And thank you, Mamma, for being a good cook."

My mother shrugs, "These days we fast during the day, and we starve at night... and we are luckier than most, thanks to your brothers."

As I take in my family, I feel the full weight of what this war has done to us. Can it be that my parents have aged so much in such a short time and that in that same short time, I have been married and divorced? Will our lives ever be simple again?

"Are you still typing?" Mamma knows nothing about where I work or what I do, other than type." She doesn't ask questions of her grown children because she doesn't want to know. On the other hand, I think my father knows far more, but there is no open discussion, as is his way.

"Mamma, Tolis said that you went to the Jewish section a few weeks ago. Was it terrible?"

Her beautiful eyes fill with tears, and she barely whispers, "It was."

My mother recently visited the section of Athens, where she has brought many children into the world. My father strongly objected, but she insisted that she had obligations because it was Chanukah's feast. To my surprise, instead of forbidding her to go, he accompanied her, and she was able to see a few of her old friends. But, they were devastated at the decay of the community since the occupation. She has not returned, but she prays for these people of whom she is so fond.

Neighbors, friends, and Giannis stop by to pay their respects. He looks like he has aged in the past year but has a look of maturity and self-confidence. "My parents send their love," he says to my mother. My brothers pat him on the back and shake his hand, wishing him a good holiday. "Kala Christougenna," *Merry Christmas*, he says as he gives me a chaste kiss on the cheek. It feels no different than a kiss from my brothers. I'm sure he felt the same, very much as it did in our brief marriage.

# MARIA - Athens, Greece - 1906

Reverend Mother wrote a letter stating that I am a ward of the church to acquire a marriage license since I have no birth certificate. I never before thought that no papers or records of any kind accompanied me when I was brought to the school five years ago. The only things that I have are the things I carried - my mother's embroidery, and the velvet diary. My entire past is stored only in my memories, and I never before needed validation.

Mother Thekla, taking on the role of my family, arranges for the chapel's wedding ceremony. She provides a beautifully simple white dress, which was donated by a generous parishioner. "My mother offered to get you a veil!" Olga says," If you would like." I know she is emotional about the sudden planning of my wedding and the fact that I will be leaving and will be away for her marriage to Stavros.

"Your mother is sweet," I say. "But I am hoping to wear my mother's silk shawl."

She is thrilled! "Did you finish the embroidery ?" I am proud that I finished it and happy that the timing has worked so well.

"I just finished it a few days ago, when we had all that sun coming through the window. I worked all day because the light was so good, and as I was folding it to put away, I could feel my Mama near me!"

Olga says, "It makes me cry thinking about your mother. I know you miss her terribly."

I hug her and say, "Olga, thank you for being my sister." We compose ourselves, and Olga is once again excitedly planning,

"Stavros will get us flowers! I will ask him today since there is not much time." I am so happy to have Olga at my side.

"Thank you, Olga. What would I do without you?." It does not take long for the tears to well up again. Although I will only be in Odessa temporarily, I will no longer live here, nor will Olga.

I remember my first day very clearly and, since this has been home to me, with each passing day, my early childhood becomes more and more blurred in my memory.

We are wiping tears when Sister peeks in the door. "Maria, Reverend Mother needs to see you!" I don't hesitate, and I stand up, blow my nose, glance at Olga as if to say, "I have no idea!" and walk quickly to Mother Thekla's office. She is expecting me and smiles as I enter.

"How are you, Maria?"

respond, "I am very well, Mother. Thank you."

"Is Olga helping you get ready for your ceremony?"

I smile, "She is very accommodating and makes me joyous to be preparing."

"Diocles is a good man, and I think you are wise to be

217

giving him your hand. Of course, the sisters will miss your help in assisting with the babies." I had thought about this part, and it saddened me.

"Oh, Mother, I will miss that so much!"

I can't help but think of the precious babies brought into this world and the young mothers who suffer through excruciating childbirth but come away with the most beautiful reward. "Perhaps, when you settle back in Athens, you can help them again, whenever time allows." She smiles sweetly.

"There is nothing I would want more, Mother, thank you!"

"I will pray for your happiness and feel blessed to have known your goodness and your grace. Your mother and father would be extremely proud of you and will watch over your marriage and your future children." Here she hesitates and sweetly asks, "Is there anything that you would like to discuss? Do you have any questions?"

I immediately respond, "No, thank you, Mother."

I barely make it through the brief exchange of good-byes before taking my leave. I almost laugh aloud as I think of how shocked Reverend Mother would be to know how much I know. After all, Olga has supplied mountains of information regarding this very subject, whether I wanted to listen or not.

I will not see Diocles until Sunday, the day of our wedding. Although it is January, the weather is perfect, and every day leading to Sunday makes me feel warm and hopeful. Diocles has arranged for a sea passage to Odessa, and we leave on Monday, the day after our ceremony, as husband and wife. He has reserved a room in Piraeus for us to stay our wedding night to be ready for sailing at early dawn, and I will admit that I am nervous, but not afraid to start my new life with this man.

Surprisingly, Olga is up before me on Sunday, and when I open my eyes, I am amazed that I slept so well last night. I roll over and take a few minutes to gaze at the simple white dress with the newly ironed shawl, which will be my veil. It is such a pale pink that it almost matches the dress. The slightly darker pink embroidery of flowers cascades down the length, and I can see the needle in my mother's hand as she creates their beauty. I can also easily spot the more flawed work that I did as a young girl before I too found the mindless flow that completed it beautifully.

"I'm glad you had a good sleep!" Olga is busy with the headband as she weaves fresh white and pink flowers together. She finishes with a scattering of baby's breath as she tells me they are the symbol of purity of emotion and long-lasting love.

"I dreamed of my father, Olga." I did not even realize this until I started speaking, but slowly, the whole dream becomes vivid in my mind. Olga, my beautiful friend, moves her chair closer, ready to listen as she continues her delicate work.

"I was walking with my father in the garden. This garden here, not in Turkey, and I am fully grown, not a little girl." I feel warm at the memory of the dream. "Because it is a lovely sunny day, we walk for hours, very close, our shoulders almost touching, and eventually, the sun begins to set, but we are still walking and talking. I don't know what we talk about, but I know my heart feels very light, and I do not feel the heaviness that I usually feel when I think about my parents. There are beautiful flowers all around us, brighter and more colorful than anything I have ever seen before. It feels like we will walk forever, but just as the sun takes its final bow, Baba takes my hand and walks me to the pear tree. Diocles is standing there, tall and smiling as we approach. He puts out both his hands, and I take one, and my father takes the other. I smile up at him for a brief moment as a petal from the pear blossoms lands on his shoulder. I turn to smile at Baba, but he is gone. The strange thing is that I still felt happy!" I look at Olga, as she has stopped her work and is crying quietly, and as I reach for her hand, I feel the tears on my face, but I know they are tears of joy.

# ARGHIRULA -
# Athens, Greece - 1943

A lexandra is a few years older and much more sophisticated than the rest of us, so she is my inspiration. Today, she brings a bottle of red nail polish, the same as the color on her nails, and asks if anyone wants to try it. Surprisingly, I am the only one interested. We take our meal break, and she and I rush to a secluded corner where we will not be disturbed so that the nail painting can occur.

"Alexandra, my hands look so beautiful...you are an artist! Thank you!"

She laughs, "Maybe it is a form of art! Just look at how lovely they are!"

I need to let the polish dry, so I take a walk through the rooms, waving my hands the whole time. Xaver shakes his head and says,

"There are just too many women in this place!"

I enjoy typing the rest of the afternoon because I love watching my fingers move on the typewriter keys.

"Papa will not be happy with you!" Tolis says as his first reaction to my beautiful nails.

"I don't care what Papa thinks!"

He shakes his head, and he looks a little angry. "Arghiro', you are a grown woman, so you can do what you want, but Papa will not like it!"

"I know," I respond, trying to appease him, "I will make sure he knows you had nothing to do with it!" He gives me a stern look, and we both laugh at the ridiculousness of this unimportant thing while we are in the middle of grief and pain and death every minute of every day.

When we get home, and before he leaves, I ask him sweetly, "Tolis, do you think you can get me a bottle of polish? And please make sure it is red!" His amused look is all the response I need!

Tolis is gone more often these days, and he still does not discuss what occupies so much of his time, but it becomes apparent to me that he has power in the underground. If he did not know the right people, I indeed would not have gotten off so quickly before a German Judge. It is still difficult to walk past a German officer in uniform without distrust and fear, and my initial reaction is to check the shine of his boots.

Occupying soldiers infest the city, both German and Italian. My mother is uncomfortable on the street, so she spends her days in the house with my sisters.

"Mamma, let's at least sit outside the door. It is a beautiful day!"

She agrees, and we step out as she wraps herself in

her old shawl. "Pame!" *Let's go!* She sounds almost angry. The sun is shining, and Mamma lifts her face slightly in response to its warmth.

She sits in the straight-backed chair, and I take a chair from the table and place it next to hers. "Mamma, what's wrong?" I ask when I notice that her head is down.

"Arghiro'." When she looks at me, I see that she has been crying. "Arghiro'," she repeats, "Half the people in the Jewish section are gone, and I hear they were sent away in groups. Some have run into the mountains, and others hide in Greek homes, which is so frightening. Everyone will suffer if the Germans find them!" She bows her head and almost whispers, "There are camps...." she trails off.

I wait for her to go on, but she is quiet for a long time. "What kind of camps?" I can barely hear her between her whispers and tears.

"The Germans call them concentration camps, and they take Jews by trainloads to these places." She is having a hard time breathing.

"I know, Mamma. They take them to resettlement camps, and I know it will not end well for many of them. We have seen it first hand on our very streets."

She is slightly shaking her head, "It is not the same... the camps are killing camps!"

I feel her agony. "Yes, Mamma, I know so many Jewish people are dying in these camps."

Her voice gains a little strength, "Oxi, Arghiro'...these are extermination camps! They put people into chambers and kill them with piped-in poison gas!" I listen in horror! *Can this be true?* "Sometimes," she continues, "they are taken off the trains and told that they are at a temporary

223

transit stop and would soon continue, but these are also death camps, and people are killed within hours…hundreds of them, thousands. We hear that some of the stronger men are kept alive to work for the Germans to help with the extermination process and remove the corpses." I am horrified!

"Mamma, how do you know of this?" I have never seen my mother so agitated.

"The priests…" she says. "The priests see and hear much more than us, and your father said they were discussing it yesterday." She cries into her shawl, and as much as I try to console her, I feel the full impact of her pain. I can't help but see the babies' faces that she helped bring into the world, their young mothers, and the people who loved my mother so much.

I can hear them calling out to her, "Maria, I have something for you!" as she walked with her precious herbs. I have no words to take away her pain, so I sit still and hold her hand.

I smell the paint when my father opens the door and stands directly behind our chairs. He quietly puts his arm around my mother and, at the same time, bends down and places a kiss on top of my head. This occurrence is so rare that it only saddens me more, and I can no longer hold back tears. I squeeze my mother's hand, as I feel her lean into my father's embrace. I have never before seen my mother so broken.

# MARIA - Athens, Greece - 1906

Reverend Mother takes the place of my father in accompanying me to the door of the chapel. Diocles is standing at the entrance facing me, dressed in his cassock and holding a single white rose. His intent gaze is on me as I approach. I take note that he has cut his hair and trimmed his beard very close to his face. We stop when we reach him, and I look into his eyes as Mother Thekla puts our hands together. Reverend Mother taps his arm to remind him to give me the flower as she steps away. As he hands me the rose, he leans down and whispers, "You look like an Angel."

Olga is our koumpara, and I see her waiting next to Christos, a fellow seminarian of Diocles, who is the koumbaro. Although this is the same room I come to every morning and every evening, today, the chapel looks extraordinary and beautiful. Although there are friends and acquaintances, I can't help but be sad that neither of us has a family to share this day.

When we approach the altar, we stand straight before the priest, and I feel both nervous and happy. The priest, Father Pappas, acknowledges us with a small bow of his head. He puts out his hands with his palms up, looks down, and begins, "Blessed before you, God, both now and ever and into the ages of ages, let us pray that you bless Damaskinos and Maria." I feel giddy that Father Pappas uses the wrong name for Diocles, and I glance at him, but he is standing perfectly straight and looking directly at the priest, so I do the same. "They stand before you, God, with their friends as witnesses as they pledge to enter into an indissoluble bond of love." He looks up, reaches his hands towards us and continues, "It is the love of God that has brought you together to be married and bear children. He will watch over you throughout your marriage and into oneness in mind."

He takes the ring off my right hand, asks God's blessings upon it, and blesses us by touching our foreheads. He makes the sign of the cross above our heads. He says, "The servant of God, Damaskinos Diocles Raftopoulos is betrothed to the servant of God, Maria Papanicolaou in the name of the Father, Son and of the Holy Spirit." I realize that Diocles and I know very little about each other.

Christos, our koumbaro, takes the ring and places it on my right hand's fourth finger. I am slightly overwhelmed by the full meaning of this commitment and feel blessed that I feel happy. I cannot help but think of how joyous Olga will be when she commits her life to Stavros and, at the same time, how sad Agni is in her loveless marriage.

When the prayers end, the priest takes our hands and joins them together. I am comforted by Diocles's touch and as I turn to look at him, I see that he is already looking down at me. We both smile with shared joy.

The priest recites a reading from St. Paul, "Live in

love as Christ loved us and handed himself over for us. Be subordinate to one another out of reverence for Christ. Wives should be subordinate to their husbands as to the Lord. For the husband is head of his wife just as Christ is the head of the Church, he himself the savior of the body. As the Church is subordinate to Christ, so wives should be subordinate to their husbands in everything. Husbands, love your wives, even as Christ loves the Church and handed himself over for the sanctity of her, cleansing her by the bathwater with the word, that he might present himself to the church in splendor, without spot or wrinkle or any such thing, that she might be holy and without blemish. So also you, Damaskinos, should love your wife Maria as your own body. He who loves his wife loves himself."

Before the next reading, Olga hands us each a lit candle, taking the rose that I am holding. Christos walks behind us and places on our heads two thin crowns, which are connected with a white ribbon and have been blessed by the priest. These crowns symbolize the glory and honor bestowed upon us by God, and the ribbon symbolizes our unity. The stefanas are then exchanged three times from my head to his. The crowns remain on our heads during the reading of the Gospel, which tells of the marriage in Cana at Galilee, where Jesus turned water into wine. We each get a cup of wine, and we sip three times, as is traditional.

Still wearing our stefana, Diocles takes my hand and we walk around the altar three times to symbolize our first steps as a married couple. Olga and Christos walk close behind us, holding the stefana in place. Father Pappas blesses us, and, when the ceremonial walk ends, and the crowns are removed, he separates our joined hands by using the bible to remind us that only God can break this union into which we have entered. He says, "What God has joined together, let no man separate."

Diocles takes my hand, and with joy we move to the table to sign the act of marriage. We are congratulated, hugged, and kissed by dozens of our friends and fellow students, and I feel a bit overwhelmed. Diocles and Reverend Mother have arranged for anapsyktikà, *refreshments*, in the dining room, and the guests slowly leave the chapel and walk in that direction.

Diocles takes my hand, guiding me in the opposite direction and out the doors that lead to the garden. "Where are we going?" I ask as I try to keep pace with his long stride.

"We will celebrate with everyone in just a few minutes." He takes me to the pear tree, and I know this is where he will seal his promise. "I would like to kiss my bride," he says as he bends to kiss my lips with a passion that I would not have predicted, and I kiss him back with a hunger I did not know I possessed. "I want you to know that you will always be at my side and that I will love you and protect you until the end of my days. I can promise this because each time I look at you my heart softens." I love him; there is no doubt for me.

"Who is Damaskinos?" For a second, he seems surprised at the question but realizes that I don't know.

"A few years ago, I was baptized on the eastern bank of the Jordan River in Israel. It was in the same spot where John the Baptist baptized Jesus." I am fascinated by this man.

"Describe it please, since I can only imagine how wonderful that was."

He continues, "It was one of the most spiritual things in my life, and I feel blessed to have been there. But, it is a story for another time!" He takes my hand to join our guests, and I know that I will always, obediently and lovingly follow my husband Diocles Damaskinos, no matter where he leads me.

# JOAN - Westport, Connecticut - 2011

The most comforting thing to our family is family, and our togetherness is usually associated with food. There is no exception in these dismal days of hospital room waiting, and my brother Mike shows up with an excessive amount of the best sub sandwiches from Tommy's Taste of Italy in Woodland Park. You would think that my appetite would be gone, faced with my reality, but somehow biting into this sandwich gives me great comfort. Having family around me softens the edges of my extreme grief, and there are moments that I act as I usually function and momentarily forget that I will soon be a widow.

Cassie's ability to research has always been a strong point, but never used more effectively than during this challenge. She stands in rounds outside her father's room, and I am amazed that the doctors treat her like one of the students. Dr. Takyar listens intently to any new information she brings and when she asks questions, she receives answers from him regarding the course of action. I understand that her way of coping is to be proactive, and I am grateful to this great hospital and staff for allowing her to be so.

I hear them talking, but barely engage because my mind is numb. Why am I not screaming or sobbing or praying? I am here and not here, no past or future. I am in a place that is new to me. But, I give in to it feeling that my girls will carry me emotionally. Their voices are like a faraway echo, but I see them just a few feet away. I am included in their conversation but have nothing to contribute. "We can't just sit back and just accept it!" Rachel is adamant.

"Of course not!" Cassie says. "But we have to figure it out ourselves. They will only follow procedures, and we need them to step out of the box. Jen told me that we could recommend whatever we want, and they will follow up and mark it 'per family's request.'"

Mica chimes in, "It's probably an insurance thing." They all agree. "Cassie, you diagnosed this thing even before the doctors gave it a name!" Mica reminds us.

"That's why we have to keep doing the research...what if there is something we are missing? Our window is so small! He's asleep, but he is alive right now. Maybe they can do something for him while he's in the coma." Cassie is googling on her iPad as she speaks at high speed. Rachel is sobbing, and I am in a fog. "We have to wait until they clear the infection that he got when they did the thoracic surgery. They failed to give him something that was supposed to prevent infection." Cassie says.

Mica is annoyed, "Really, what the fuck?"

Cassie is still searching, "It's just a minor thing in the big picture," she says. Everyone is temporarily quiet and sitting around the bed where their Dad is lying and dying, and all hooked up to medications that I can't even pronounce. I am back in my big green chair, taking in the scene and wondering where these girls get their strength.

"Mom!" I must have dozed off in the comfort of having the girls here and the fact that they have taken the reins, and I am allowing them to do so. "You have to come home tonight. You can't possibly be getting any decent sleep in that chair!"

"I can't leave him...you know that!"

Rachel holds my hand and cries openly. "Just come home tonight. Sleep at my house if you don't want to go home. I will drive you back first thing tomorrow. Anibal will be home with the girls."

I eventually realize that I am better off letting the girls make the decisions, and where I sleep should not be another worry added to their already full plate. After just a few more proddings, I agree to go home tonight, so I gather my things, unplug my phone charger, put everything into my bag and take my jacket out of the tiny closet. I put everything on the green chair and walk to the bed, past the monitors and tubes, absentmindedly reading the labels on the drip pouches. One that catches my eye is "Propofol." Why does that sound so familiar?

The girls have said good-bye for tonight and are outside the room speaking with the nurses at the station. It is very dim in this room, with most of the light coming in from the hallway. I sit in the chair next to the bed and carefully take Sheldon's hand without lifting it so as not to disturb the tubes in his arm. I bend over and kiss his face, where I can, around the intubation contraption. He feels warm as usual, and his face has a slight stubble. I bend down and put my head on his motionless hand. "I have to go home to sleep, Honey, but I will be back early tomorrow." I feel empty and hollow. "They are telling me that you are not going to wake up from this, but the girls are not going to accept that without a fight. We have raised some pretty amazing women. I will take a little bit of the credit, but you are the best father, and they learned so much from you." I was hoping to avoid tears, but here they are." They have your grit and tenacity, and they will not sit by meekly." I weep as I struggle to breathe. "I cannot live without you, I know you know that, and I can't think beyond this moment. I love you so much." I know he can hear me. I just know it!

I stand up and turn on the iPod that is sitting propped up not far from his right ear. My brother John suggested playing his favorite doo-wops so, if he can hear, he can enjoy what he would listen to at home. The nurses know, and they make sure it stays in place and on. I gather my things as The Duprees sing "You Belong to Me." I leave him with a kiss and whisper through tears, "I'll see you in the morning. I love you" I stand up, wipe my face and blow my nose just as it hits me where I have heard of Propofol .... it's the drug that killed Michael Jackson!

I am drained, tired, and quiet on the drive home. The girls talk nonstop about their schedules and the kids, but mostly about what to do about their father. Cassie says, "If all else fails, we have to see if he is a candidate for a lung transplant." This is not a new conversation.

Rachel asks, "What about the steroids that you mentioned yesterday?"

Mica agrees, "That should be what we push for right now!"

"Yes," Cassie agrees." Definitely!"

"Mom, are you sure you don't want to come home with me?" Rachel says as she steps out of Mica's car and heads towards hers.

"No, Honey... I'm fine (internal laugh)." We all hug and Cassie and I walk to the house.

"Mom, get some sleep. Everything will be OK."

Nothing will ever be OK again, I think, but I say, "I know, Honey. Thank you for everything you're doing." We know we can't make eye contact, but I kiss her and walk in the front door as she walks the 50 feet to her front door.

The first thing I do when I come into the house is open the door that connects the two places. I want to be home, but not alone, and I hope the kids are loud when they get up in the morning. I walk around in circles in my spotless kitchen and absentmindedly leaf though my mail, without really seeing anything. Lila walks in to say "hi," and I bend down to pick her up, walk to the couch and sit with her on my lap. I don't know how she knows, but she is pathetically sad, looking at me as if asking me when he is coming home. I know dogs don't cry like humans, but the sadness in her face tears down my barrier, and I lose it, bending down into her soft furry head. She doesn't move away and lets me cry for an hour until I release her. She stays on my lap until I gently put her back on the floor so she knows she can go back to sleep in Cassie's bed, her nightly ritual.

I have to get upstairs, but the staircase looks insurmountable! I stand frozen at the bottom for a long time. I finally force myself to walk up the first five steps, but when I reach the turn, I look up at the remaining seven steps and feel faint. I have to sit to catch my breath and cry and pray that my nightmare is just a bad dream. When I think I can breathe again, I climb the rest of the way to the top of the stairs and head down the hall to the bedroom. I feel as though I am moving through a thick cloud and in slow motion, but I am here, and I cannot entirely fall apart, not yet, while he is still breathing, even if only artificially and through a machine.

The shower is soothing, removing a little of my stress, so I feel somewhat calmer getting into our meticulously chosen, beautiful king-size bed. It has always been a joke for us since we spoon when we sleep and combined, we use the equivalent space of a twin bed. It does not take long for extreme sadness to engulf me, and I cry myself to sleep. I dream of us when we were young and newly in love.

# ARGHIRULA - Athens, Greece - 1943

The bitter winter has given way to a very mild spring and although life is still dismal, at least the temperatures are pleasant. It does not help that I spend my days at work reading and typing things that are depressing and angry. It seems as though we have been stripped of so much, that the smallest of good deeds make for a joyous occasion. Today, Tolis brought home a bottle of red nail polish! "If it were a diamond, it could not please me more!" I hug him. "I feel liberated from the generosity of my friends, and I will have beautiful nails for the rest of my life!"

Tolis laughs and says, "Let's hope your life is longer than that bottle of polish!" We laugh halfheartedly. "That was not an easy thing to get, so use it sparingly!"

I will be 21 years old in a few weeks. Age these days seems to be just a number, and birthdays are celebrated by exchanging small portions of food in place of gifts. One of my greatest pleasures is the cinema and due to a stranger's generosity I can enjoy this rare treat when there is a new movie. "I hear that they will be opening the outdoor cinema early this year because of the mild weather," Sophia reports.

"Oh, that is wonderful!"

I remember the evenings when Effie and I enjoyed the outdoor movies, and it makes me miss her so much. I can't allow myself to feel sad because my heart will break for so many people who have lost loved ones to this pathetic war or who have someone fighting in it. I am grateful that my family is still intact and grateful that Effie is safe in the United States, but I fear every day for my brothers, although I fully understand that they must do what they do.

"Arghiro', we are planning to go to Therinos on Saturday. Do you want to join us?" Sophia is excited to be making plans.

"Nothing would please me more!" I tell her honestly. "Do you know what film is at the cinema?" Not that it matters.

"The Voice of the Heart," she says. "It is brand new."

"What is it about?" I am only curious. It would not matter at all what they show. But, she is happy to tell me because someone she knows has seen it and told her. I do not interrupt her, although it is too much detail, and possibly the ending will be spoiled.

"A man is released from prison after having served a lot of time for the murder of his wife's lover. He meets a young couple who wants to get married, but the mother of the girl is against the marriage. When the man realizes that the girl is his daughter and her mother is his wife, he makes an important decision." I pretend to hold my breath in anticipation. Sophia laughs and continues, "He agrees with his wife that he will disappear from her life as long as she allows the couple to marry."

It sounds just frivolous enough to be entertaining, and I am happy to have the opportunity to go. Living in an occupied city, where our destinies are in the hands of evil has changed each one of us. The enemy imposes rules, but the traditional rules of our families and friends are non-existent, and there is an unspoken feeling that getting old, like our parents, is unlikely for many of us. People our age, like my brothers, survive our misery by being members of organized youth groups. In February, we went as a large group to a house in the Ampelokipi district for a meeting of EPON (United Panhellenic Organization of Youth), and delegates from ten different youth groups were in attendance. There were rooms filled with young people, many too young, and it made me sad to see them having to live their childhood this way.

The main agenda was to recruit members to fight against the occupying forces whenever and wherever needed. Ten youth organizations were listed on the flyers:

1) The Federation of the Communist Youth of Greece (OKNE);
2) The Socialist Youth (SEPE);
3) The Friendly Society of Youth (FEM);
4) The Free Girls (LN);
5) The Nationalist Youth Union (LEN);
6) The United Youth Workers and Employees (EEN);
7) The United School Youth (EMN);
8) The Union of New Fighters of Rumelia (ENAR);
9) The Sacred Battalion of Thessaly (TIL); and
10) The Peasant Youth (AN)

"We will fight for the freedom and independence of our country and the solution to problems facing our youth. We will fight towards national liberation, education, joy, and culture. You are all welcome and encouraged to fight in our ranks!"

In a fleeting memory, I could see black, gleaming German officer boots, smell the disgusting toilet, and feel the sting of the slap across my face. The speaker was so animated and because I didn't want to miss a word, I brought myself back to the room and put that horrific memory back in the deepest recesses of my mind, where it had been lying.

Many joined on the spot, including brave young women. Christos noticed my extreme interest in the speakers and my response to the energy they create among the attendees. "Arghiro', you are already part of this with your work, so you have been contributing for months!"

Tolis picked up on the conversation, "Don't even think about it! You are fine with what you're doing. Lots of others would want to do what you do!" So without allowing one word of protest from me, the decision was made that I would not get swept up in the electric enthusiasm in the room. "Besides," Tolis teased, "You might chip your nail polish!" We all laughed, but I also wanted to cry.

A few weeks have passed since the youth meeting, and we have heard that there was a call for all youth to support EAM and EPON in a demonstration in the streets today. We step out mid-day and can see that demonstrators are filling the streets. "They are demanding the rescinding of the proposed 'mobilization' of the Greek people to supply

Hitler's factories with a Greek workforce." LB tells us there are people packed in the streets as far as we can see.

Banners and black flags wave everywhere. We return to work, and the street noise is muffled only by the many walls in our building, but the energy of the people stays with us all afternoon. LB returns just as we are ready to lock up, and he is very excited. "We were successful in occupying the ministry of labor!" There's a loud whoop from our group! He continues, "We set the mobilization lists on fire in the streets!" We all let out a loud yell, with everyone embracing, shaking hands, or slapping backs. "Hitler and his apprentices were forced to withdraw the law concerning civilian mobilization!"

It is the best news we have had in a long time, and all our hopes are attached to these groups, who seem fearless, and we are certainly encouraged by today's outcome.

Twenty days have passed since the successful demonstration, and Tolis is up early and already quickly drinking a coffee when I wake up. "You can go back to bed," he says. Then, as an afterthought, "And stay home! Do you hear me? Arghiro', stay home!" I am still fuzzy from sleep, and he is talking so fast. "Do you hear me?" he repeats.

"Calm down and tell me what is happening, please! I hear you, and I will stay home."

Tolis calls back as he steps towards the door. "There is a demonstration today against the order to mobilize our people into supplying Hitler's factories with Greek manpower."

"I know of the order, but did not realize there is going to be a demonstration today," I tell him.

He turns to face me, "I did not want you to know, and I do not want you to go!"

I begin to protest, "Why?" but he cuts me short.

"Arghiro', there will be thousands of demonstrators there today, so you know there is bound to be trouble. Just stay in the house and read a book or paint your nails. I will tell you all about it when I get home later." He hesitates, "and tomorrow, you will type of it!"

I am miserable that I have to stay home, as this is usually a feast day for the Greeks. March 25th is the celebration of the War of Independence against the Ottoman Empire in 1821. Also, the church celebrates The Annunciation, when the Archangel Gabriel visited The Virgin Mary to tell her that she would become the mother of Jesus Christ. March 25th is precisely nine months before Christmas. My family has always gone to church on this holiday of course, and it has always been a day of the gathering of friends and family. But it will be a much different day today, even if I weren't a prisoner in my house.

Tempted to disobey, the urgency of my brother's orders and the pallor of his face keep me locked in for the remainder of the day. The day is long and frustrating because there is no way for me to know what is going on or if my brothers are safe. I can't see anything outside the window, but at one point in the day I hear a barrage of gunshots, and I am terrified, but I have no other choice than to wait for my brother to come home to know what is going on. "Dear God, please keep my brothers safe," I say out loud.

241

I cannot sleep and although it is very late when Tolis comes home, I am wide awake and full of questions. "Is Basilis OK?" He assures me that he is safe and back home.

"Can you make me a coffee?" he crashes down on the sofa.

"Tell me!" I press as I reach for the briki and our small supply of coffee.

"I will tell you all, but first, thank you for listening to me and not leaving the house. It was a terrible day!" He starts his story. "Last night, the EPON members wrote all different slogans on the walls calling for the Greek people to intensify their resistance against the forces of the occupation. Thousands of them put wreaths on the graves of our national heroes, but the Greek police attacked them. Today, there were hundreds of thousands of people in the city with shouts 'to live in freedom!' Patriots showered Greek flags down from balconies, thousands of them!"

"I wish I could have seen that!" I think to myself, but don't say a word.

He continues, "The appointed place for the demonstration was at Syntagma Square, and by eleven o'clock, the square was packed with demonstrators holding a huge banner with just three words - FREEDOM OR DEATH! There was a man with a megaphone constantly announcing slogans like 'Death to the fascist invaders!' and 'Down with the traitorous government!' and 'Long live March 25th!'"

I say, "It sounds exciting !"

He shakes his head, "Oxi!" *No!* He continues, "At this point, occupiers and Greek collaborators try to disperse the crowd with firemen's hoses filled with water and ink and by attacking the crowd with rubber truncheons. We were firm and united and opposed them for a long time." I know there's more, so I wait for him to take a breath. "Suddenly, the base murderers open fire with rifles and tommy guns, and many people are hit, including a man ten feet away from me!" He chokes back tears and clears his throat, "The blood of many Greek patriots once again stains the streets of our city, mostly young EPON members." I can feel the tears sting my eyes. He doesn't take a breath, "There were hundreds of people arrested, and rumor has it that they will go to concentration camps." He looks drained, and my blood runs cold from his recount and at the thought of the camps, based on the stories my father recently told.

Tolis stands, "Thank you for the coffee. I have to get some sleep. I will be leaving early tomorrow, so please be careful about going to work. I will meet you after." I can't believe he will be able to sleep at all and, although I am so tired, I wonder if I will be able to sleep myself.

The mood at the office today is sad and quiet, and, of course, we found many articles about the events of the last two days in the box in the alley. Everyone is more busy than usual, and even our breaks are quiet and reflective. The brightest part of the very long day is saying good night and confirming that we are going to meet for the movie tomorrow. Tolis is already waiting for me, leaning against the building smoking a cigarette. "Can I have one?" I ask him. He reaches into his pocket, without hesitation, and shakes out a cigarette, puts the pack back, and hands me his lit cigarette so I can light mine. We stand leaning on the building, and I use the excuse that the smoke is getting in my eyes to cry at the joy of seeing him unharmed and the culmination of the last few days.

"Do you want to stop for a coffee?" he asks. I am meeting some people at the taverna and Basilis will be there too.

"Yes, please. It is amazing how life just goes on, isn't it?" He nods his head in response, and there are no further words needed.

We enter the taverna, and the music and voices are equally loud. It takes only a moment for Tolis to find the others, and I spot Basilis with a pretty girl sitting very close to him. I hardly ever see my brothers with ladies and never thought much about it, but this girl is nuzzling his neck, and he is all smiles and very responsive. When he sees us, he raises his glass to welcome us. As we approach, he stands up and offers me his chair, which I take since there are no others. He introduces me to Olga, but he has to repeat my name twice because the noise in the room is so loud. She smiles sweetly and asks if I want a drink, and I readily accept it. Basilis looks so happy, and I am glad that there is still love in this mess of a world.

I relax and feel the tension leave my body as I look around. There are nearly as many civilian women as there are men, which is a sign of the times. But, it always surprises me how many Italian soldiers are in the mix with Greek soldiers. They seem comfortable with the language and the people, and it looks as though they are always telling a story or laughing at someone else's story.

"What are you thinking about, pretty lady?" I turn to see Niko, and he is all smiles and looking handsome, but by now, I am on my second drink, since they seem to turn up in front of me.

"Hey, Niko, how are you?" I haven't seen him since the last time we all went to a cinema. I don't have anything else to say, so I ask, "Are you going to the movie tomorrow?"

He smiles his great big smile and says, "Yes, not much else to do."

Before long, Basilis and Olga say good-night and leave holding hands.

I look around for Tolis, but he is with a group of other men in a very animated conversation. I feel exhausted from my sleepless night, long workday, and too much ouzo, so I am ready to leave, well before curfew. Niko seems to read my mind and follows my gaze to my brother. He offers, "I can walk you home since I'm leaving anyway." I am grateful and stand up and walk to Tolis.

"I am going to go home, Tolis." I tilt my head towards Niko. "He said he would walk me home." Approving of my companion, he allows it.

"Be careful and lock up behind you!"

We walk the few blocks, and all the while the conversation is flowing. Niko is a nice person, and it is nice to chat. He asks about my family, "I know your brothers, but are there more of you?"

"Yes," I tell him. "There are six of us, three girls and three boys. And you?"

"I am an only child." he chuckles, "I always wanted brothers and sisters, but it was not my choice to make." We laugh.

"What do you do?" I ask.

"When the war started, I was getting my law degree,

245

but, sadly, I had to stop because my family could not afford the tuition any longer. They owned an appliance store, but the Axis forces took everything, and they had to close, and my father has been in a deep depression since. I teach Ancient Greek at the lykeio, *the secondary school.*" I am impressed with this man, who seems so humble.

"Did you tell me you are a painter?" He seems pleased that I remember.

"Yes, I do paint."

He does not ask me if I have a job, and I don't mention it, and I am glad that I do not have to explain. When we get to my house, I ask him if he would like to come in for a coffee, and he kindly declines, probably more for fear of my brothers than anything else. "I'll see you tomorrow!" he says as I turn the key in the lock. I wave back, close the door, and lock it securely. Tomorrow, I will have breakfast with my mother. I have not seen her in over a week and, although she knows I'm safe, probably needs to see me.

It is a beautiful Saturday, and the sun is warm through my window. Tolis is already awake and reading the newspaper when I come out of my room. "Kalimera..." he mumbles, distractedly. It amazes me how little he sleeps!

"I am going to see Mamma this morning," I inform him, hoping he will join me.

"Poly kala." *Very well.* He continues to read casually as I put on the water to boil for coffee. "What are you doing the rest of the day?" he asks, still leafing through the paper.

"I am meeting the crowd at the cinema after I leave Mamma. But don't worry, I will be back home before curfew!" He stops reading the paper, folds it, and puts it on the table. "Would you like some coffee?" Suddenly, he seems anxious to get ready to go.

"Oxi, efcharisto", *no, thank you.* I see him in the half-open door to his bedroom as he fixes the bed linens and tidies up the room. I smile to myself as I realize that he is getting ready for company, and I know full well how he has had to adjust his life to allow me to live here.

"You know, I am thinking of staying at Mamma's tonight! It would make her happy."

He says," Einai entaxei," *that's fine,* without much emotion, but I think I saw him do a little dance step of joy!

I pack a bag with my toothbrush, clean underwear, and a blouse that I can wear to church tomorrow, as I am sure my father will expect me to join them. I suppose he assumes that if I am not with them on Sunday morning, I am going to a church closer to my house. Which, of course, I do not do! The walk to their home is quite long, but the day is sunny and just the perfect temperature and, since I am in no real hurry, I pretend life is ordinary and begin to lose myself in thought. But, of course, I need to be sharp and watchful, and I need to be sure I don't do anything that might anger an idiot German soldier with a gun. I am surprised that my brother is letting me walk about alone, but I know his mind is elsewhere today. Because of the beautiful weather, there are lots of people on the street and children playing close to their front doors. It is hard to believe there was so much turmoil in the city just a few days ago, but this has become our new daily life.

There are more foreign soldiers than there are Greeks on the streets. Most of them are German, and many are Italian, with their very different postures and attitudes.

My walk is uneventful, and I arrive at my parents' house undisturbed. I hear the scraping of chairs when I knock on their door and my father's voice, "Poios einai ekei?" *who's there?*

"Arghirula," I respond loud enough so he can hear me.

The door opens immediately and although his lips are as stern as ever, his eyes are smiling, and he steps aside to let me in. As he closes the door with his right hand, he places his left hand on my back, and I feel touched by this small show of affection. Mamma is already in front of me when I step in, and she openly embraces me, obviously happy to see me. "I worry about you," she says softly.

"I know, Mamma because I worry about you too."

We enjoy the morning, and I convince them to take a walk to the park, surprised that they both agree. Many children are playing, but staying close to their parents. Couples or pairs walk the babies in carriages, and I don't see many women walking alone, just one or two, and they seem to have a specific destination. There is a group of young people gathering and greeting each other, possibly for a picnic. If you could take away the many soldiers stationed everywhere in the park, you might think this is a typical day in an ordinary city in regular times. But we all know it is not.

I arrive at the theatre long before the movie is due to start and am surprised to see Niko already there. He smiles his big handsome smile as I approach and says, "I was hoping you would be early."

I think I blush, and I greet him warmly and say, "Thanks for walking me home last night! I didn't even hear my brother come in. I assume it was pretty late, so you saved me!

"Thank you for allowing me to walk you home," he says graciously. He is just too good! "Would it be OK if I sit with you today?" I am looking forward to poking fun at the movie with my friends, but do not want to be rude to this nice man.

"Sure!". We make small talk until, eventually, the crowd gathers. The girls are all in a group, and I follow them to their seats, with Niko walking close behind. I let the girls go ahead, and I sit in the next to the last seat in the row. Niko is happy with this arrangement and sits in the aisle seat.

The movie is predictably funny, even in parts that are supposed to be serious. Sophia is next to me, and we chat and giggle a good portion of the time, but I try to include Niko whenever I can. Of course, we must sit through the longer-than-ever propaganda movie first, so we enjoy "The Voice of the Heart" that much more because it lightens the mood and our very souls. About halfway through the film, Niko reaches for my hand and, because I am not totally surprised or totally against it, I let him hold it for the remainder of the movie. It is a lovely feeling to be touched and, I assume, desired.

# MARIA - Athens, Greece - 1906

Our wedding festivities are simple but extremely joyful. Everyone here is someone who loves one of us, or possibly both of us, like Mother Superior. She is like a proud mother and expresses her joy often, to us and to anyone else who will listen. She stands next to me and whispers, "Can I see you alone, please?" I excuse myself from my new husband and the others and walk to Mother Thekla's office with her. "This will be brief," she promises, "No need to sit!" She reaches into her desk drawer and retrieves an envelope. She hands it to me and says, "I have been holding this for you since the day you came here. The person with whom your father arranged for your safety and care brought this for me to hold until you left us. You can consider it a dowry for your marriage, or keep it for yourself if you think you might someday need it. There were no instructions on how you should receive it, only when."

I have never handled money or even thought about it, so, without opening the envelope, I ask Mother Superior to hold on to it until I leave later today. After she slips the envelope into her pocket, I return to the party arm in arm with her.

I am so happy to start a new life with Diocles, but slightly anxious about spending our first night together as husband and wife. However, when Diocles comes near me, he touches my face, and when he places his hand on my back, I feel a spark, and again I feel anticipation and joy. We say good-bye to our guests, including Constantine and Agni, who is full with child, but no less sad than the last time I saw her. "I hope you have a baby girl and I hope she is as beautiful as you," I whisper to her.

Without a smile, she responds, "I pray that it is a boy." I fully understand and hug her tight.

"Thank you, Mother Superior, for all you have done to make this day so special and for the beautiful woman that you have given me. I promise to protect and love her for the rest of my life," says Diocles. He squeezes my hand, and I smile at him.

Mother hugs him, and when she hugs me, she says, "Remember, I have something that belongs to you." I had forgotten the envelope in Mother's pocket. I respond, without hesitation,

"Oh, yes! Please, give it to Diocles. He has pockets."

Olga waits at the door until we have spoken to everyone else and tells Diocles, "I will help Maria change. Stavros is outside in the carriage if you would like to join him." Diocles seems relieved that he can leave, and with a quick happy step, walks towards the front doors.

When we reach our room, Olga helps me to remove my veil and carefully folds it to replace it in the wooden box. She handles it gently and reverently, "I think this is the most beautiful shawl I have ever seen, and it looked perfect on you today." I have an idea,

"Olga, there is no need for me to take it to Russia! Please wear it for your wedding, this way it will be as though I am with you."

The tears that we promised we would not shed are here, and neither of us can control them. We cry as I remove my wedding dress and put on the walking dress that is hanging on the door. I take off my white shoes and stockings and replace them with black dress shoes and black hose, all the while sobbing. Olga is also changing into her casual clothes. "I know we will see each other before long, but it makes me so sad that you will not be here to be the koumbara for my wedding."

"I know," I respond. "But, knowing that you are marrying Stavros and that he loves you so much is enough for me. I promise you will feel my presence." I replace the dress on the hanger and hook it on the door to return to the generous woman who shared it, and Olga helps me pack the few remaining things in my carrying bag. We both realize that we will never be together again in this room, and when Olga leaves, there will be two new girls here who will share their deepest thoughts and laugh together and cry together as we are doing now. I know we have to go, but I hesitate and walk around the room, touching everything. I did not know how difficult it would be for me to leave this life behind. I will be back in Athens, but never again will I sleep in this room.

Diocles and Stavros are in an animated discussion when we reach them. They both turn and it is nothing short of beautiful to see their faces light up when they see us. The happier I am for Olga and me, the sadder I am for Agni. Diocles jumps off the carriage, helps me up into the back bench and turns to help Olga, but she has already climbed up and is sitting on the bench next to Stavros. Something looks different, and I notice the second horse and that there are thick blankets on the seats and that the carriage is overall clean and shiny. I realize that Stavros has done this for us as his gift. He is taking us to the port of Piraeus. The weather is perfect and just cool enough for the horses to be able to handle the trip.

I snuggle up to my new husband, feeling the comfort of his arms, and I feel both joy and sadness. He knows what I am thinking, "I know, Maria, I wish my parents could have been here too." I smile at his perceptiveness and reach up to kiss him. He returns my kiss passionately and then asks, "What is this envelope in my pocket?"

I had forgotten all about it and answered simply, "It is money. I suppose it is my dowry," I laugh.

"I did not expect you to come with a dowry! Why did you not open it?"

I shrug my shoulders, "Because I don't care about it, and you promised to take care of me. So it is ours, and you can open it if you want to." He doesn't speak for a long time and pulls me closer to him.

"I don't know what good thing I did in my life for God to believe I am worthy to have you," he says.

Spending time with Olga and Stavros is by far the most pleasant way to travel. The horses' clop-clop serves as background music to our never-ending conversations as subjects change, as the men are animated and the girls laugh at their seriousness about politics and the world. The two hours pass quickly, and we are now in search of the hotel in which Diocles' friend has reserved a room for us.

The Theoxenia Hotel is within minutes of the port where we will board the ship at 7:00 a.m. tomorrow. We arrive at the hotel just before dinnertime, and Diocles asks the receptionist, "Is there the possibility of dinner for the four?" as he points to the beautiful dining room that we can see from the lobby.

"Yes, absolutely" A table will be ready for you in a half hour. "Can someone take our trunks, and hold them for our departure tomorrow?"

"Yes, Sir!"

A valet appears from nowhere and goes out to the carriage with Diocles and Stavros. Within minutes, the trunks go into storage, and our bags are brought up to our room, while Olga and I sit in two beautiful chairs near a fireplace with a lovely, blazing fire. The men return looking refreshed and suggest we go up to do the same, so we head up to the room. "This place is beautiful!" Olga is so excited. "I wish we were staying too!"

We laugh, and I say, "Me too!" only half kidding.

"Diocles is a good man, Maria. All he wants to do is make you happy, and this is a perfect example!"

I speak from the heart, "He certainly does make me happy... just being with him makes me happy."

She smiles and says, "I understand."

Our dinner is dear, but it must end soon because Stavros and Olga must get back to Athens before it is too dark. "I will not cry!" Olga says as she hugs me. You will be back before long, and we will raise our babies together." The thought of this makes me happy, and I give her a tight hug.

"You are a sister to me, and I love you." We both cry.

The room we are to sleep in is beautiful, with a marital bed which reminds me of Mama and Baba's bed in Turkey. Diocles blocks me from entering and says, "I must carry you in!"

I stop walking and ask, "Why?"

He is so sure of himself, "Because it means I will protect you from the devil." We laugh, and I gladly let him pick me up. I do not tell him what I have also heard about this tradition and that some say it started when, in ancient times, young girls did not want to lose their virginity, and men carried them to hold on to them so they would not run away.

At the moment, I don't want to think about either. Although I am apprehensive, I appreciate the fact that I listened to Olga's secrets, and having delivered babies, I have an understanding of human anatomy. Also, I am so incredibly happy that I love this man and feel his love in return.

He puts me down over the threshold, closes the door, and locks it. He is so gentle and attentive that I lose myself in his kisses and embraces. As he kisses me, he slowly removes his clothing until he is only wearing his pants. He releases me and sits on the edge of the bed as he asks quietly, "Can I look at your body?" I am already opening my blouse as I say,

"Will you look with the eyes of an artist?"

"No," he responds, "Only the eyes of a husband in love."

# ARGHIRULA -
# Athens, Greece - 1943

Being at the outdoor cinema is by far the most fun that I have these days. I miss Effie and those wonderful carefree days, but since I know they will never return, I enjoy new friends and the attention of a few boys, even if most of them seem so young. Niko is the exception, and although I like him very much because we can discuss things that interest me, my feelings towards him are similar to what my feelings were for Giannis.

I was 13 years old when Cine Thission came to the city. It is in the Thission neighborhood, and the views of the Acropolis are spectacular from here. For some reason, the stars seem to shine brighter and are more abundant in this spot. Our group meets at the far back left because the best view is from here. There is a vast area where we have placed our blankets and, since we have to wait until dark, we are sitting on the ground talking and laughing and pretending as if there is no misery, pain, and hunger around us.

There are many blankets discreetly separated, but close enough, so the atmosphere is that of a massive picnic, and everyone is friendly and somewhat loud. I take a look around at my "neighbors" and see that there are many couples sitting alone and other blankets are overcrowded with friends, women, and men mixed, and there is a smattering of uniforms of all kinds. Still, the camaraderie is un-warlike, and it is just young people enjoying a beautiful evening. There are picnic baskets on some of the blankets, and I have a fleeting thought, "Where are these people getting food?" But, of course, I know there is a black market, and I have heard that the Italian soldiers are generous with supplies from their commissaries. I also notice the discreet passing of wine and ouzo bottles, including within our small group. Niko has been in an animated conversation with Alexandra, and they are sitting close behind me. "It is inevitable that there will be a civil war....." I hear Niko going on and on about the unrest, but I try to shut it out. Reading articles every day, I am happy to step away and not think about the war for tonight.

On the next blanket is a group of men and women about my age and two Italian sailors dressed in their white uniforms. They are all laughing because the sailors are telling them something that no one in the group can understand. They keep repeating the same thing over and over, and they attempt to find the right Greek word, but continue to fail, which sets off another round of laughter before they try again. I find myself smiling at the comical exchange. I pick up my ears to see if I can identify what they are trying to say. "Il mio villaggio ha molte pecore e capre!" The soldier has a pleasant laugh, an undeniable sense of humor, and the support of his friend. Their small audience is trying to repeat the words and doing a terrible job, while everyone laughs and passes around the wine bottle.

I am so thoroughly enjoying this exchange that I find myself laughing out loud. The soldier who is not doing the talking notices me and steps out of the group, taking the two necessary steps towards me. He has a big smile and a friendly demeanor. "Lo capisci?" *You understand?* he asks. Still laughing, I nod my head, yes. He leans down and grabs my hand, to make me stand up, and leads me to the group. The soldier who is telling the story has had his back to me, but now turns in response to his friend. "Clorindo, questa parla Italiano!" I begin to protest, but we suddenly recognize each other, and he seems so happy to see me!

I can't believe that, in this great big city, with all of its chaos, God has blessed me with seeing him again! My heart is beating at high speed and I am momentarily speechless. He takes my hand and kisses it, saying, "The most beautiful smile in all of Athens! I came back to your kiosk the day after we met, and the day after that. I realized after a half dozen attempts that it was closed permanently. I wanted to find you, but I didn't even know your name! "He looks directly into my eyes as if we are the only two people on the earth, and the feeling of an electric shock once again shoots through me from his touch.

The crowd is demanding a translation, so we need to turn our attention to them. To clear things up, I say, "No, no, I don't speak Italian, I just understand a little!" The small group is welcoming and all talking at once.

"Pecore... what is that?" The tall girl asks.

"Provato," *sheep.* I tell her. Another round of laughter follows.

"And, I think capre is gida, *goat*, but I'm not sure."

The curly-haired man says, "Of course, that would make sense! So, he says there are more sheep and goats than there are people where he comes from." Problem solved. Everyone is patting each other's back and nodding their understanding at this revelation. I laugh along with them, and I am a hero for solving the big mystery.

Clorindo pats his friend on the back and says, "Good job finding her!" There is more laughter as someone hands me a bottle of wine, which I decline. Clorindo points to a spot on the blanket, offering a seat next to him, but I suggest my blanket and say,

"I am with my friends."

He looks in their direction and smiles his understanding. My heart flutters when he smiles at me. His hair is dark and combed straight back, and his eyes are chocolate brown over a straight nose with just the right bump at the top. I also notice he has beautiful ears. I probably linger just a little too long, and he asks again, "Are you sure you can't sit for a bit?" His Greek is choppy and interspersed with Italian, but he emphasizes by adding hand gestures.

I look at the blanket with my friends and see that Niko and Alexandra are even more animated than before to solve Greece's problems. Clorindo follows my gaze and asks, "E il tuo fidanzato?" *Is he your boyfriend?* When he sees my confusion, he points to me then to Niko and then to his heart.

"Oxi," *No!* I respond almost too quickly. His smile is genuine, and he seems determined that I now sit with him. I take the spot he indicates, and we sit very close because space is limited. He is so near that I can smell his cologne, which is very pleasant. "So, goats and sheep?" I tease him.

He laughs. "Mikri poli," *small-town* he says with a look as if he misses it. "More goats and sheep than people!" I try to visualize such a small town, but it is hard to conceive. He points to himself and says, "Sono Clorindo DiGiovanni." Then looks to me and asks, "Tu come ti chiami?

I respond, "To onoma mou einai Arghirula Raftopolou."

He asks me to repeat it and tries his best to pronounce it. When I correct him, he tries a few times again and eventually gets it right, but I hear him mumbling it quietly to himself as if trying to memorize it, and the gesture touches me.

The film is about to start, and everyone gathers belongings and finds seats. I walk in my group's direction, but Clorindo takes my arm and asks, "Kathiste mazi mou?" *Sit with me?* Without hesitation, I raise my finger to say, "one minute" and walk to my blanket to gather my sweater and purse.

I tell those closest to me, "I will be sitting right over there." A few nods and Alexandra gives me an OK sign, telling me she has an eye on me. Clorindo takes my elbow, locates two seats, and guides me to them. There is no lack of self-assurance on his part, and I feel oddly happy. I will think about the fact that he is the occupying enemy later, and there is also the probable fact that I will not see him again after tonight. Right now, I am very receptive to his attention and plan to enjoy this evening, which has already gotten better than I expected.

The propaganda movie is ridiculously long and full of blatant lies, and the main feature is a German short film with Greek and Italian subtitles, but very little substance. I suffer through it without complaint because I enjoy being outside and with Clorindo and pretend that this is everyday life. He leans over during the film and asks, "Ti piace? *Do you like it?*

I respond, "Oxi!" *No!* and we both laugh, as I gladly inhale his scent.

When the film ends, there's an hour before curfew, so we do not rush to leave. I find my friends and keep them within my vision so as not to be walking home alone when it is time to go. Alexandra waves and I wave back.

Between his limited Greek and my much more limited Italian, we are enjoying our conversations. His Greek is far better than I thought, and I realize now that he was playing with the group earlier. "Do you mind if I smoke?" So sweet to ask.

"Not at all."

I expect him to pull out a pack of cigarettes, but, instead, he produces a pipe and a small pouch of tobacco. He packs the tobacco gently into the bowl, lights a match, slowly sucks on the end in his mouth as the match flickers and slowly, ever so slowly, ignites all the tobacco. I have never seen anyone smoke a pipe, so I am mesmerized by this small ritual. He is watching me from the corner of his eye and smiles at me after his first puff. I look in his eyes and feel a little tingle in my body. *What is wrong with me? This is the very last person that I should find attractive!*

Giacomo approaches us, pointing to his watch,

"Clorindo, dobbiamo andare!" *We have to go!* Clorindo glances at his watch.

"Tu vai," *go ahead*, he responds, looking over at the other two sailors waiting. Giacomo is surprised. "Sei sicuro?" *Are you sure?* he asks.

"Si, Si, andate!"

I have never met anyone who is so unhurried as he continues to puff on his pipe and make small talk, although, eventually, I tell him I have to leave to get home before curfew. "Posso accompagnarti?" *May I accompany you?*

Nai tha ithela afto." *I would love that!*

I see Niko and Alexandra standing on the fringe of the crowd, and I motion to them that I will walk home with my new friend. They nod in understanding and walk off together. Are they holding hands? Clorindo taps the tobacco out of his pipe onto the ground, stands, and reaches to help me up, and I put on my sweater. I no sooner get one sleeve on, and he is holding it up to slide my other arm. I will say that he is attentive!

The crowd at the movie is significant, and everyone leaves at once. I notice that I am not the only local girl walking with a sailor or soldier, and I take it as a sign of this insane time. It does not feel that there is a future for us, and the present is smothering with the horrific reality of death and famine. And so I justify my attraction to this man and try not to think beyond the moment.

"Are there really more sheep and goats than people in your town?" I am curious.

He laughs, "I would hardly call it a town, more of a village." He uses lots of hand gestures to explain, "No tall buildings, or cars or tavernas or big squares!" He is encompassing everything we walk past, trying to explain. I have a hard time visualizing this place.

"What is it called?"

He chuckles as he says, "Chianchetelle."

I ask him to repeat it, but no matter how many times he does, I can't come close to pronouncing it. I just picture it as a place of storybooks, where there is a princess and a prince and probably a villain too. "It is close to Naples, about an hour away." I remember Naples from my history books, but would not be able to locate it on an unmarked map.

We are so engrossed in talking about ourselves that we reach my house in no time, and we have to say good night so he can report to his barracks. We linger at my door, and he asks, "Ti bacio?" *May I kiss you?*

It is not my first kiss, nor will it be my last, so I whisper, "Si," and he laughs. He pulls me very close and holds me tight as he gently places his lips on mine and kisses me with more passion than I have ever felt before. I can smell his tobacco and his cologne, and I feel dizzy with pleasure.

"Posso vederti Lunedi?" *Can I see you Monday?*

I don't have to think, "Si, Si!" No translation is needed. He writes down my building's address, and we establish the time that I will be free from work.

Tolis is not home tonight and told me he would be leaving tomorrow and would be away for a few days, which is a good thing because I don't want to talk about my evening. The chances that Clorindo will show up Monday are pretty slim, and I'm sure that I am not the first local girl he has walked home and kissed. Although I am not naive about this crazy new world, I can't help but think about his handsome face and that incredible kiss. Even in my deepest recesses, I toss all night and know that this is not a relationship that I should hope for or pursue. I fall asleep smelling tobacco mingled with cologne, and I dream of a tiny village with lots of sheep and goats, with very few people, and me walking there with him.

Although I have lots to do, the workday moves slowly, and I feel a little disconnected and anxious. "Do you want to join us for a coffee?" Alexandra asks, pointing to the small group already leaving.

"Not tonight, thank you. I have to go home." I respond casually.

I use the bathroom, scrub my face, brush my teeth with my finger, make sure my specially chosen outfit is in order, comb my hair, and carefully apply my lipstick. I know my nails look perfect because I have been checking them all day. I like what I see in the mirror.

I am ready to step out, although I suddenly have doubts. Sadly, oh, so sadly, he is not standing there when I walk out. I look in every possible direction, and he is nowhere in sight. I recheck my watch, although I know the time and know I have allowed extra minutes. He is not showing up! *How could I be so stupid?* Like a schoolgirl, I trusted his fake sweet personality, and I let him kiss me on the street like a "porni!" I will be 21 years old in just a few weeks, a grown woman, but I reacted like a silly girl. Lesson learned. I wait only a few minutes and then start to walk in the direction of my home.

I can't help but feel extremely disappointed, and I

berate myself for falling for some stranger's charm and believing his sweet, stupid, chopped up words. I feel the tears sting my eyes and wipe them away as I walk a little faster because I don't like being on the street alone.

I hear voices way behind me and feel that there is some commotion, so I move more quickly because any activity on the street can result in someone being shot on the spot. My gut reaction is only fear, so I increase my pace and keep looking down, aiming to take myself away from any possible danger. I hear man-sized steps running in my direction, and I am indescribably stricken with fear as I visualize the shiny black boots. As the footsteps come closer, I know that this time, I must defend myself, and as I feel the rage rising, I spin around aggressively and defensively, with the manicure scissors from my pocket clutched tightly in my fist. I promised myself that no German will ever touch me again without a fight.

It takes a few seconds after I turn to see beyond my rage, and I find myself looking at the white uniform that has now come to a stop only a few feet from me. "Lypamai poly," *I am so sorry.* I am shaking with relief and ridiculously happy to see Clorindo's handsome face.

"Ola kala!" I say, almost crumbling, and I mean it from the bottom of my heart, which is still racing uncontrollably.

"I tried to leave on time, but I had to address things that kept coming up. I am sorry that I was not here when I said I would be." He is working so hard at explaining with his Greek and Italian all mixed in with hand motions. He makes a writing motion with his right hand, and I understand he must work in an office.

We walk very closely, and our hands are almost

touching. "What do you do?" I need to have some everyday conversation while waiting for my heart to go back to a regular beat.

"I am a procurement officer..." here he stumbles trying to explain, but he is so creative with hand motions that I understand.

"Ypefthynos promitheion ?" I ask.

"Yes, Yes, that's it!"

"So, you are in charge of getting food for your barracks?"

He gathers as many words as he can and responds, "Yes, my team gets food and supplies for the troops in the barracks when we are here and for the ship when we are at sea."

I am curious, "Where do you get food here? It feels as though there is none to be had."

He looks uncomfortable with the topic but says, quietly, "Arghirula, we are AXIS, and much is available to us." This obvious brutal truth and the agitation that I still feel bring angry tears to my eyes, and I remind myself that he is the enemy, and I should not be here with him. He notices that I am upset and takes my hand, "It has nothing to do with us!" he stresses.

There was never a time when I have felt happier, but I can't help feeling torn. He gently takes my arm, stops walking, and turns me to face him. "I am very sorry about your country and its people, do you understand me?" I nod in response. "This is my job, but not my choice or the wish of most of the men here!" I think of Giacomo and Francesco and some other men I met at the kiosk, and I know he is telling the truth.

"Can we walk in the park?" he asks, and I quickly agree.

I admit that I will go anywhere to be together, knowing how sad I felt when I thought he was not showing up. I say a little silent prayer that we do not run into my brothers.

As if he reads my mind, he says, "Do you have a large family?"

I think for a second and say, "Mother, father, two sisters and three brothers. There were others, but they died." I intentionally make no mention of my brothers' connection to the underground.

He seems amused, "I am from a family of six children, also!"

I don't know why, but I am surprised that he comes from a large family. "All from the village with more sheep than people?" We both needed to lighten the mood with laughter.

He spots a bench under a tree and away from the paths, pointing to it with a questioning look. It is perfect, and I pick up my pace, so we can occupy it and not lose it to some other couple who might be hiding from brothers. He releases my hand as we run to the bench, and I immediately miss his touch.

During our conversation, I have occasional reflective moments when I feel I can read his mind. We have created our language, and it feels as though we have known each other always, but it saddens me to know that this feeling will someday end, for many reasons. My family will never allow it and, eventually, he will need to return to his village with the sheep and goats and, possibly, the girl he left behind. What am I doing?

As the sun begins to set, it surprises me that we have been here for so long. "Hai fame?" *Are you hungry?* he asks.

I am surprised to realize that I have an appetite, and I am glad to prolong our day. "Si, ho fame," I laugh. "ma... non lavoro per te?" *No work for you?*

Understanding correctly, he responds, holding up two fingers, "Due giorni senza lavoro!" and I appreciate that he has two days' leave.

He knows his way around and has a specific destination in mind, so I follow his lead and, when he reaches for my hand, I am thrilled to give it. Near the Acropolis, I take in the glory of the Parthenon at the top of the hill. It is lovely tonight, and I feel like I am in a fairytale. He sees me look up and says, "Che bello, il Partenone dell' Acropoli!" I smile in agreement as he goes on, "Until yesterday, that was the most beautiful thing I had seen in Athens."

I turn to him with a sarcastic remark ready on my lips in response to his obvious line, but when I look at him, there is nothing but sincerity in his eyes. He pulls me a little closer and places a gentle kiss on my forehead, sending an electric charge down to my toes. I step back, but he holds my gaze, and I cannot avoid what is happening, so I drop my eyes and let him retake my hand. We turn down Athanasiou Diakou and halfway down the street we stop at the doorway of an old building. When we enter, I can hear music, loud voices, and more than one person calls out, "Clorindo!!" My first thought is that he always brings girls here, so I feel a little uncomfortable. With a firm grip on my hand, he leads me towards several tables, mostly occupied by Italian soldiers, many civilians, and, surprisingly, a few German soldiers.

He locates a table for two in a corner towards the back and points to tell the waiter that we would like to occupy it. Without breaking stride, we reach the table, and he pulls out one of the chairs. "Un bicchiere di vino?" he asks as the waiter approaches.

"Malista," I smile at him. I don't want wine, but I do want to be here sitting with him. The wine arrives almost immediately, accompanied by a plate of tiropites and dolmathakia. I smile at the waiter and ask, "Pou einai to banio?" He points to a nearby door, and I excuse myself from the table.

Alone in the bathroom, with the door securely locked, I look at myself in the mirror and say, "What are you doing?" and I can see, in my mind's eye, the faces of my father and three brothers, all scowling and angry. Of course, they would be furious to know that I am falling in love with the enemy, but they cannot understand, and somehow, I will keep this secret!

I use the toilet, wash my face, and re-apply lipstick before returning to the table. Clorindo stands up to pull out my chair and sits facing me. "Sei veramente bella, lo sai?" I understand what he says, but pretend not to and ask him to repeat it. He laughs and says, "I think you know what I said!"

Clorindo and his friends must often frequent this place because everyone seems to know each other, and the fact that it is off the beaten path makes it comfortable for these men who are so far from home and in a place where they don't want to be. The camaraderie in the room is contagious, and it is comfortably similar to being with Greeks, although it is difficult for me to remember a truly happy gathering of Greeks. My mind goes back to those early days at Effie's parents' home with music, excellent food, and laughter. I also cannot help but think of Giannis and how, once again, I would be disappointing him.

Clorindo sits back in his chair and lights his pipe, but never takes his eyes off me. I am more physically thrilled by this simple gesture than I was at any time in my marriage, and I wonder briefly, *Should I stop this from going any further?* But, before I can finish my thought, he leans towards me, takes my hand and kisses it, just like a scene from a film. Although the gesture is surely trite, I am thrilled to the point that I can feel my body temperature rise, and I know that I am blushing. Of course, he notices, smiles, and says,

"Sei dolce." *You're sweet.*

I can't help but think that he has used this line before, bringing my temperature down as I compose myself. He looks disappointed when I take my hand back, so we both pick up our forks and eat. I look up at him and ask, "Sas aresei to elliniko gafito?" *Do you like Greek food?*

He does not hesitate and responds, "I like everything Greek!" Which brings another flush to my face.

Sailors of all shapes and sizes stop to say hello with occasional pats to Clorindo's back, and others look at us from a distance and wave, and they seem cheerful and happy. I laugh and shrug my shoulders, referring to the blatant teasing, and he says. "Sono cretini!" *They are jerks!* But, he laughs too, and the mood is very light for the moment.

"I don't think we should be together." I mean this when I say it, and I am surprised that I say it out loud.

"Perche?" *Why?* he asks, although we both know the answer.

"Eiste o echthros!" I say simply. *You are the enemy.*

"Do I feel like your enemy?" he asks.

"Oxi," I reply. We stay quiet, and I look down at my lap, but I can feel his eyes on me. "No, you feel nothing like an enemy!" His smile is spontaneous and so beautiful. "How long will you be here?" I ask, bringing us back to reality.

"I don't know..." he answers honestly. "But, can we just like each other for now, while I am here?" The world is such a terrible mess, and the thought of not seeing this man, who makes me so happy, is much more depressing than anything my brothers can do to me. "I think we already do like each other." We are in full agreement!

We have about an hour before curfew, and we stroll in the quiet evening and return to the same park and bench we sat on earlier. Although the weather is balmy, the air smells of sulfur, blood, and flesh, which are a bitter reminder of our reality. I don't mention my olfactory acuity on the assumption that he sniffs the air just as I do, but my sisters have always told me I have an overly sensitive nose.

Although there are lots of armed soldiers in the park and on the street, the bench is free. I feel protected in the company of an Axis soldier, but fearful that I will encounter someone I know. We sit and whisper about mostly unimportant things. "How old are you?" he asks.

"I will be twenty-one in a few weeks. And you?"

"I am twenty-six," he replies, "but feel much older," he

laughs. I understand exactly. "When is your birthday?" he asks.

I try to respond in Italian, but mess it up a bit. "Il venti-cinche."

He corrects me, "Il venticinque? In due settimane?" *In two weeks?*

"Malista."

He asks about my parents, "I tuoi genitori, sono vivi?" *Are they alive?* I am not surprised by his question because I told him that I live with my brother.

"Si sono vivi!" I try to describe what they do. "My father is an iconologist, and my mother is a midwife." He seems impressed, which pleases me.

"Mio Papa e un contadino." *My father is a farmer.*

But then I wonder if he may think that my father is an oncologist. "Do you know what an iconologist does?"

Now he looks slightly confused "He is a doctor?" he asks.

"No," I laugh. "He is an artist and paints icons in churches."

"Ah, si, capisco!" He does not seem any less impressed, which makes me smile.

I say, "He is also a priest." Now he looks confused.

"But he is married with children, how can that be?"

"In my religion, priests can marry, but then can't rise beyond the priesthood's first level. He and my mother were married before he was ordained." It is new to him, but he understands.

"Your parents sound interesting," he says. "And your brothers, are they artists too?"

I pause, then respond, "They are very artistic, especially Basilis and Tolis."

"And are you an artist?" I laugh, "No, not at all... none of the girls in my family have any talent!"

He gives me an exaggerated lecherous look and says, "I bet that is not true!" And, again, my face turns red.

Because of curfew, I must get off the street, so we begin to walk towards my house. He takes my hand and holds it firmly as if I might run away. I mildly wonder if I should, for my salvation. But, just as that thought enters my mind, he stops me, turns me towards him, and very lightly kisses me. My knees feel weak, and I respond wholeheartedly. When we get to my house, he stops, wondering if I will invite him in. "I will make you a coffee if my brother is not at home." I tell him. He smiles like a little boy tempted with candy. I open the door slowly and check inside the door for Tolis' shoes and jacket, but see everything just as I left it. He told me he would be away for a few days, but I don't want to take the chance he came back early. I am not yet ready to deal with him and this situation.

Clorindo follows me into the house, removes his hat, puts it on the end table, and sits at the kitchen table, looking very much at home. I take out the briki to make coffee, and he watches closely every move I make. "In Italia, non si fa cosi' il caffe," he says. I cannot imagine coffee being made any other way than in a briki! He continues, "Usiamo la macchinetta Napoletana." He tries to describe a pot that holds water in the bottom and coffee at the top. He keeps making a boiling and flipping motion, which just confuses me. I remember the group trying to understand the sheep and goats as we laugh at my confusion. I wonder if he is

273

teasing me, but I don't care. I just love his laugh and his attention.

We sit at the table for hours, our discombobulated chatter never ending. The sound of his voice is like music. The conversation, of course, turns to current conditions in the war, and he says, "Things are changing quickly, and there is fear that Italians will not be safe here much longer." I am slightly annoyed at this statement.

"Of course, the Greeks have not been safe for years!" I snap. He is sympathetic, but he is only explaining the reality of something I have not had reason to concern myself. I tell him, "My brothers are both in the underground!" He looks surprised.

"Things will not be suitable for them, just as they will not be good for the Italian military." he says quietly.

I don't want to discuss this any longer because it will spoil the evening, so I change the subject. "Tell me about your family!" He is glad to change to a happier topic.

"My two older brothers, Enrico and Domenico live in America, in New Jersey." I think of Effie, and for a moment, I wish that we also lived in America. "My sisters, Vittoria and Giovanna, and my youngest brother, Attilio, all live in Chianchetelle, as do my Papa and Mamma." He goes on, "I was born with a twin sister, but she died at birth. Mia Mamma' e morta', *died*, when I was less than a year old." Everything sounds so sad to me, but he tells his story and does not seem unhappy. He seems very fond of everyone.

Suddenly, he looks at his watch and says, "E tardi!" He stands and takes my hand. He pulls me close and kisses me, much more passionately than he did on the street, and whispers, "Mi piaci davvero," I *like you!*

I want to keep him here forever, and I want to tell him that, but instead, I say, "I have been married and divorced."

He hesitates only a second and, looking directly into my eyes, asks, "Do you love him still?"

I answer, with no hesitation, "Absolutely not!" and, although I don't say it, my honest response would be, "I love YOU!"

"Domani?" he asks.

I hesitate because I am working tomorrow, but instead, I say, "A che ora?"

"I will get you at 8:00, and we can go to the beach." He kisses me again, this time lingering much longer, and I know that I will not be able to reverse these feelings that are so new and wonderfully frightening. I respond by kissing him back with all the passion that is in me. He allows the interaction for a few more minutes, but pulls away, and holding me gently in his arms, says, "Dobbiamo capire un sacco di cose!" *We have to figure out a lot of things!*

I get the gist of what he is saying, and I know he's right, but I realize that I will do whatever it takes never to let him go. I believe the universe has brought us together, and making my family accept him is just something that will have to happen. He kisses me a few more times, and I kiss him back fervently, wishing that he would not leave.

"Lock the door!" he says as he steps out. "Ci vediamo domani!"

# MARIA - Athens, Greece/ Odessa, Russia - 1906

I have packed everything securely in the same trunk that brought my things from Turkey to Athens, less than five years ago. So much life has happened in these years that it is difficult to remember that I was once a little girl. Although the faces of my Mamma and Baba are ever in my mind, they sometimes mingle as one. Besides getting dressed this morning, I don't have much to do, since Diocles has made all the arrangements and is managing the paperwork and the loading of our trunks on the ship.

The walk to the pier where we will board is not long, but maneuvering the trunks on the borrowed cart is a chore. The cart is too small, but we are grateful to use it since it was the only one available. When we reach the ship, two crew members take the trunks, and Diocles returns the cart. I am on the boat, sitting on a bench, hands folded on my lap with my back against a wooden wall, watching the crew's comings and goings, and feeling somewhat useless. Diocles spots me and walks in my direction. He is so tall and handsome, and my heart reacts as I watch him approach. Without control, I blush at thoughts of last night. Surprising myself, I look forward to being alone again tonight.

"Are you well?" he asks, touching my cheek.

"I am just a little warm!" I explain.

He accepts that with a smile and says, "I had the trunks brought to our cabin, so I can take you there if you like before we sail. But, we will want to be on the deck to see Athens as we depart. When we pull further away, you will see there are three natural harbors."

I look around and ask, "Are there no other passengers?"

Seeing only some sailors scrambling to prepare to leave, he says, "Actually, I met a couple going back home to Odessa after having lived in Athens for many years. And also a professor, traveling alone, who will be making his home there and working at the university." At my confused look, he explains," This boat is a cargo ship, and weeks ago it carried a load of grain from Odessa to Athens. Now, it goes back, much lighter, with books and educational materials. There are limited cabins, and some of these ships have none at all. We are lucky that the timing worked so well."

Many ships sail through the Saronic Gulf in the Mediterranean, and there is something reminiscent of the boat I sailed on from Turkey to Athens, although I know that I have blocked out parts of that voyage from my mind. I mostly remember a sad and lonely little girl, crying in absolute misery. In total contrast to that memory, nothing can make me sad today on this ship, which has the name Moskva. It is not storybook pretty in its appearance, and much of it looks rusted, but there is some evidence of what it once was that reflects in the wood, which remains highly polished and looks like it gets attention.

Regardless of the condition of the ship, today it brings me extreme joy mixed with apprehension. We are to remain in Russia as long as the work takes to complete, and since Diocles has not seen what it entails, we are open-ended in our plans to return to Athens.

"What is your prediction, or guess as to when we might return?"

He looks out at the skyline of Athens and says, "You have become my whole world, so time and place do not matter to me. I had no idea I could feel this way, and I welcome this feeling I have never known before." He puts his arm around my shoulders, and I move closer as we watch the city get smaller and further and further away. "Are you concerned about the amount of time we spend away from Athens?" He looks at me.

"I am not!" I respond, and quickly add," because I love you too!"

They reserve the entire bottom belly of the ship for cargo. We walk down just one level from the upper deck to a small corridor where there are doors on both sides, which must be staterooms. Our door is at the end and on the right, in the direction that Diocles is pointing. When we arrive, he uses a key to unlock it and steps aside to let me enter first. It is by far the smallest space I have ever seen, not much larger than a closet. The cot is attached to the wall, and it is smaller in size than my bed at school. They have elevated it so that our trunks fit under, and we can open them, as Diocles is demonstrating now. I notice that a good portion of his chest contains brushes and various rolled canvases. In the corner, there is a wood panel behind which there is a commode. There is also a small shelf on which rests a metal pitcher filled with fresh water. It does not take long to inspect the cabin, and he is watching me intently to see my reaction. I smile at him and say, "It's a good thing that we like each other!" to which he responds,

"I was concerned about you, but I can think of nothing better than to sleep so close, even if only for four nights." He takes my hand, and we quickly return to the top deck to join the others as the ship pulls out of Piraeus's port.

The sailing vessels and docked steamships become smaller and smaller as we pull away. The hill has many tiny rooftops, and there are many simple buildings and warehouses closer to the pier. Diocles has his arm firmly around my waist, and we stand quietly as the anchored ships shrink, and we move further from the port. Eventually, he whispers, "Our first adventure as husband and wife," to which I respond, almost inaudibly,

"Our second."

He kisses the top of my head and pulls me closer.

The cabin is exceptionally stuffy during the day, but it cools down in the evenings and into the morning, so sleep is comfortable enough. We leave as soon as we wake up to join the others for breakfast, but we find ourselves often drawn back, even if just for passionate kisses. It is challenging to have so much time on our hands and not feel the pull of the lovely privacy that the little cabin provides. Diocles retains the schedule of his daily prayers and has a strict routine. Although he asks me to join him, I believe that he likes his solitary sessions, so I only join him for evening prayers. But, if there are no prayers involved, I follow him quite willingly.

Although it is early July, the deck's air feels refreshingly cool, especially when we reach the Bosporus Strait and enter the Black Sea. The crisp sea air awakens my senses. I can't help but think that my transition from schoolgirl to wife and lover suits me quite well. I stretch my legs out and lean against the same spot where I sat when we boarded this ship, and I read my book of poems.

I am alone and don't expect to see another person unless I move around the ship. I do this every day when Diocles goes to the cabin to say his morning prayers. I close my eyes and think about my parents and can't help but wonder, once again, what happened to them. There is a small part of my heart that will forever be theirs, and I can't help but think that my easy acceptance of change may directly result from my childhood, especially the extreme event of my transition from Turkey to Greece. I remember only harmony and good feelings in our home and, fortunately, also in the care of the nuns and Mother Thekla. Sadly, Mother Thekla's wrinkled face is now more vivid in my mind than my own mother's beautiful smooth face. Because he often comes to me in dreams, my father's face is handsome and kind and more clear in my thoughts.

Our meals are not extravagant. Although our sailing companions maintain their privacy during the day and late evening, we eat and socialize as a group in a standard dining room. At these times, Diocles enjoys conversation with the professor, Nikolai. Since he is a man of science and Diocles is a man of God, they rarely agree, and the discussion usually becomes animated. On the other hand, I enjoy less complicated conversations with the older couple, Leonidas and Dorothea, who are married over 25 years. Naturally, one of my first questions is, "What is the secret to a good and long-lasting marriage such as yours?"

They smile fondly at each other and use the words that I would have expected, "Trust, loyalty, acceptance," and a few I had not thought of, "compromise, effort, and humor."

As Leonidas turns to join the conversation between the other two men, Dorothea leans closer to me and whispers, "....also, good sex is important!" I am surprised at her comment and feel my cheeks heat up. She goes on, "... and remember, he should love you more than you love him." Well, I certainly learned a lot today! I glance at Diocles, and he is already looking at me in that way that he does. I smile shyly, because of my current enlightenment as he tilts his head ever so slightly in the direction of our cabin.

I decline coffee when the steward offers, ask Diocles for the room key, and excuse myself for the evening. I briskly walk to the cabin, wrapping the sweater around me against a sudden gust of wind. I am barely undressed and in my sleeping gown when I hear the gentle tap at the door. I unlock it, and Diocles steps in and removes his clothes even before the door locks behind him. Does he love me more? I don't have time to think about who loves whom more right now, but there is love in this tiny room.

The Black Sea water is dark and not as pretty as the Mediterranean, but we are more than halfway through our journey, and Diocles seems anxious to arrive. He is due to report for work on July 15th, which will give us a few days to settle into the offered rooms. My father used to speak of Odessa and the difficulty of the Jews in the late 1800s. I have not been a Jew to anyone other than myself since I arrived in Greece, but I will always be Jewish in my heart. When I ask him, Diocles tells me that there is a substantial population of Jews in Odessa, and the first synagogue was built there nearly 100 years ago. There is also a university and an opera house, which have been there for almost as long. "I think you will love it!" he says as we look out into the expansive ocean. He continues, "It is a beautiful city, and the thought of coming here without you saddened me." I kiss him with pure love in my heart, thinking how grateful I am that God has chosen to bring us together and I know that I will follow him to the earth's ends.

I see from a distance, as we approach Odessa, that there are three ports, and the old lighthouse is the first structure to welcome us. Dorothea and Leonidis are excited to see their native home, and they hold hands as he wipes away her tears of joy. It takes so much longer than it would seem to pull into the port, and this extra half hour gives the professor an opportunity to tell us the story of the unrest in Odessa the year before.

"In April of last year, fear of a pogrom prompted the national committee of Jewish Self Defense to urge Jews to arm themselves to protect their property, and non-Jews were threatened with armed retaliation if such a pogrom occurred. Although it did not occur until October, fear of one emerged in June, and Cossacks shot several workers on strike. The next day, large groups of workers stopped working, and an unruly crowd attacked police with guns and rocks. The battleship Potemkin arrived in port with a mutinous crew that very evening and thousands of Odessans went to the port to show their support to the sailors. During the afternoon, a crowd started to set fire to wooden buildings and to raid warehouses. There was much chaos, and the military blocked off the harbor and fired into the crowd. Strikes, disorder, and the Potemkin's arrival caused the death of many people at this port." He points straight ahead towards our destination. "The incident, blamed on the Jews, was reason to disarm and search all Jewish apartments in the city. So, even though the pogrom did not happen in June as feared, the anti-semitic environment had been formed, and it was enough for the October Pogrom.

I am relieved that his description of this horrifically sad event is cut short by the mate's shouts, "Prepare your belongings. We will be entering port shortly!" But, the professor finishes his story because he has a captive audience in my husband.

"They are not sure how many Jews died in those three days, but possibly close to 1,000 and thousands were injured. There were millions of rubles in property damage, hundreds of ruined businesses, and thousands of families forced into poverty."

I need to step away, and I pretend to be checking that we have all our things to prepare to disembark. I am so saddened because I know that my parents probably suffered a similar fate. Diocles comes to me and takes me in his arms. "I'm sorry," he whispers. I hold him close and cry from extreme sadness, but I know the others only think I am crying tears of joy at our arrival, and they will never see the truth.

The rooms provided us are spartan but clean and more spacious than I expected, in an ancient building just a few streets from Cathedral Square, where Diocles will be working. We spend a few hours organizing ourselves, but soon take to the streets to explore our surroundings, and the first point of interest, naturally, is the church. Transfiguration Cathedral is more than one hundred years old and is just spectacular with a top cross bell tower. The white marble icon screen is in the side chapel, specifically where Diocles will be painting. We need to locate the curator to get access to the chapel, and we find him easily.

Ivan is extremely old and slumped over. He introduces himself and asks, "Can you state your business?"

Diocles shows his papers and says," I am an iconist here to work. I begin Monday, but I would like to see the chapel today, if possible." Ivan smiles graciously and is happy to oblige, but moves very slowly and deliberately. "He must be 90 years old," I think to myself and am reminded of Mother Thekla.

"I believe a young man is assigned to work with you," Ivan says in perfect Greek.

"Yes," Diocles responds, "I will have an apprentice, but have not met him yet." We walk, ever so slowly, to the chapel door, and Ivan unlocks it.

The glory of this room is enfolding and breathtaking. There is gold all around, and on the wall before me there is a design that looks like grapes. There are images of saints behind the vines that my mind cannot take in all at once. Mixed in the gold, I see silver and bronze, and there are six arches, each with a large icon of a saint. Above the white marble screen is a spectacular image, much larger than the others, of Jesus, Mary, and Joseph. The moldings all around the room are extensive, intricately carved, and trimmed with the same blue as the ceiling. The screen has many faded or missing icons, which need to be restored or replaced, but the frames are still there. Looking up is like a clear night sky filled with gold stars, and the chandeliers perfectly catch the light. The room's highlight is an icon of Jesus holding a bible, which covers the entire ceiling.

I am engulfed in this spectacular chapel's beauty when I feel Diocles take my arm. He has been measuring and inspecting the space where he will be working, and I notice that Ivan is gone. I come out of my reverie to see him smiling at me. "It is beautiful, is it not?"

I say, "It awakens all my senses."

He is pleased.

"Take your time here," he smiles." Then we will walk in the square."

The temperature outside is somewhat oppressive after the coolness of the chapel, but the square is lovely. There are benches along the paths that wind around an inner circle where there is a giant statue, although I cannot see from here who it represents. We take our time and walk about, enjoying the view of the beautiful cathedral square. The further we walk from the cathedral's columns, the better perspective we have of the multiple domes and steeples that top it. Many people stroll in pairs, and there is a small group of young women in straw hats, animated in their speech, who laugh frequently. For some reason, I believe they are sisters.

Eventually, Diocles finds a bench, and we sit, looking around at what will be our neighborhood. He leans forward, resting his elbows on his knees, and it reminds me of the first time we met and how far we have come is such a short time. "How long do you think we will be here?" I ask.

"Looking at my project, I would say possibly six months or so." He looks at me earnestly and asks, "Do you think you will be happy here?"

I don't have to think long to respond, "I will be happy wherever you are."

He seems preoccupied. "Maria, when we go back to Athens, I will be ordained."

I am not surprised, although, since the last few months have been so hectic, I had not thought much of it. "Of course!" I respond, "This has been your plan all along." He takes my hand. "Is there something I need to do?" I ask. I sincerely want to know if I am required to have an active role. His smile is beautiful, and he squeezes my hand.

"No, my dear. Just be at my side."

I feel tears in my eyes. "I will be there forever," I promise. He suddenly jumps up, still holding my hand.

"Let's go see the Boulevard Steps! They are a sight to see!" I have no idea where we are going, but he is familiar with the surroundings. On the route to the steps, we walk down a smaller street called Ulitsa Gospitalnaya, and just as it suggests, we pass a large hospital which occupies four city blocks.

I ask Diocles, "What is this building?"

He responds, "It is the Jewish Hospital, but it serves others as well."

I feel so drawn to it. "Do you think babies are born in this hospital?" I ask.

"Yes, of course, they are, probably every day." He looks at me knowingly and knows what is on my mind. He suggests, "Maybe you want to see if they take volunteers? You will have many empty hours in your days." He is so agreeable, and I am overjoyed that he does not minimize my work and passion.

"I will come back next week." I squeeze his hand as a thank you.


We eventually arrive at the steps, and from where we look down, I realize that I saw them from the ship when we arrived. Although I was curious about the massive staircase leading up when I spotted it, we got caught up preparing to disembark, so my focus shifted elsewhere. Now we stand looking down the stairs. "It looks so different from here!" I say.

He explains, "From this vantage point, we see only the landings and the steps are not visible to us, but when you are at the bottom looking up, you can only see the steps and the landings are invisible." I am amazed at the precise construction that would allow this.

"How many steps are there?"

He explains," There are 200 steps in total. The top-level, where we stand, is about 12 meters wide, and they get progressively more extensive, with the bottom step being over 21 meters wide."

We eventually turn back towards the square, and right near the top of the steps, there is a bronze statue that sits on a marble pedestal. It is impressively set against the crisp blue sky. I ask Diocles who he is, and he tells me that Duc de Richelieu was the governor of Odessa in the early 1800s. "We can come back one day and walk the steps down and back up if you like."

I look forward to exploring this beautiful city. "Let's go home," he says, taking my hand. I am only too glad since the early rising and long day has exhausted me. "Are you hungry?" he asks as we spot a cart straight ahead. We have not eaten since breakfast, so I readily agree that we should have something to eat. The cart sells *bichki* and *stavridas*, neither of which sounds familiar. On inspection, I see they are both small fried fish, and they smell incredibly delicious. I point to one, and the big woman with the scarf on her head tells me it is mackerel as she expertly turns an ordinary piece of cardboard into a cone and fills it with the aromatic fish. There is plenty to share, so Diocles pays her, and she wraps the fish in paper, and we take our aromatic treasure as we find our way back home.

As we near the bottom of the cone plate, I realize that I have eaten most of the fish. I look at Diocles, but he does not seem to have noticed and is calmly surveying our surroundings. "We have a full day tomorrow when we can explore the city together, and then I will begin my work."

I smile up at him and respond, "And I will start being a wife and prepare your meals." He only nods his head in agreement and seems quite preoccupied.

# JOAN - New York, New York/ Weehawken, New Jersey - 1968

I am alone in the office today. Norm is on vacation, and Frank is at an all-day meeting with the executive officers. Other than an occasional phone call, it's a quiet day, and they are minimal since the girls at the switchboard are mostly taking messages. I have gone to the switchboard room twice so far and looked at the pink slips for both of the men, to see if I can handle any issues. Much can be taken care of quickly, so I tear up the papers and throw them in the garbage.

I am eating an apple that has been on my desk since yesterday and looking forward to lunch. I rushed out of the house this morning without eating because I woke up late and didn't want to miss the bus. There are stacks of papers that need filing, and this is the perfect day to get caught up, so I bring my chair to the filing cabinet, drag over the first box and start, in alphabetical order.

Lost in thinking about nothing more than the ABC's, I barely hear the tap on the open door. I turn on the second knock after I have found the appropriate spot for the file.

I expect to see one of the secretaries here to get some paperwork or one of my friends to see what I am doing for lunch. Instead, I am looking into Sheldon's adorable smiling face! It feels like Christmas morning, and I cannot contain my joy! I jump up and hug and kiss him. "What are you doing here?" I still can't believe this guy!

He says, "I got out early and got to New Jersey late last night. It killed me not to call you, but I wanted to surprise you and take you to that lunch I owe you." Then, as an afterthought as he looks around, "Can you go?" Within less than a minute, I move things around the room, straighten my desk, unplug the calculator, and turn off the lights as my workday is over!

"I'm all yours!" I tell him as I grab my purse and jacket, and I mean it from the bottom of my heart.

We take the elevator down to the lobby, and he asks, "Where do you want to go for lunch?" I know exactly where I want to go!"

Let's get sandwiches and eat across the street in the park." He seems both surprised and pleased with this idea as we head to the deli down the street. He orders, "Corned beef and pastrami on rye with extra mustard." I asked him to go first because I am still thinking. And, finally, a decision,

"Roast beef on a hard roll with butter." I am not sure whose face registers more shock, Sheldon, or the deli guy making the sandwiches.

Sheldon says quietly, "Joan, this is a Jewish deli. They won't put butter and roast beef together."

I am slightly embarrassed, so I quickly change my order to "with mustard," since I'm not sure where mayo fits into this rule. Everyone seems to breathe a sigh of relief at my fix. I watch the deli man make the sandwiches and wrap them in waxed paper with expert precision.

We walk in perfect sunshine until we reach the park, but at a glance, we can see all the occupied benches, so we stroll, carrying our meal. I watch an old couple because there is something so sweet about them. I find myself basking in their good vibe as he takes her hand to help her up and keeps holding it as they stroll away. It is the picture of true love. As Sheldon claims the bench, I wonder if he saw what I saw or felt what I felt.

We unwrap our sandwiches, and the smell of mustard immediately overwhelms me. I start picking at my lunch, which being Italian, I hate to do. Sheldon meanwhile is savoring his sandwich and says, "The problem with being out of the New York area is that they just can't come close to making a sandwich like this! I missed it so much."

My sandwich is now totally apart to get rid of anything that was touched by the mustard. I end up with a half slice of bread folded with only pure roast beef. Delicious! I am so focused I don't see him watching me. I smile sheepishly as he laughs. "You are crazy!"

I laugh too and say, "I'll know better next time!" He leans in for a kiss, to which I respond to too quickly, so I get the dreaded mustard taste anyway.

"Do you have the whole weekend off?" I say, hopefully. I can't help but wonder if everyone that is in love feels the same way. Every word, every movement, every smile is perfect, and I feel like a different person when we are together.

"Yes! I hope you don't have any plans that you can't change." He winks.

"I do not!" is my quick response.

He seems thoughtful. "Besides, I think I need to talk to your father." *Am I ready for this?* "And your mother, too!" he continues." I am a little apprehensive. "We love each other, and we don't want to be apart, right? So, the sooner they get used to the idea, the better."

I nod, "You're right!"

He points to two pigeons bobbing their heads and walking on the path. "See, that's us! Watch! they move together and don't move away from each other." I look at the birds, and I see that he is right, they stay together and eat whatever bits of seeds or food they find on the ground. We watch them quietly for a long time and see that when one moves, the other moves too, almost blindly following each other. When the entertainment moves on, he asks, "How are things going with your Mom?"

Although I hate this topic, I appreciate that he is always himself with her, and of course, she has known him for years. She is the one who has turned against him, although he never changed his respectful way towards her. I have noticed that she has been better lately. We argued the other day, and the conversation was unimportant and stupid, and I can't even call to mind how it started, but I know she brought me to tears. I said, "I hope you understand that what you are doing pushes me towards him instead of away! Sometimes I don't know if I really care for him or just want him because you fight me. You are not letting me think straight!"

She relented, but couldn't let it go. "You will not fit into either world!" I let her have the last word because for the first time, I realized she might be talking about her own life and not mine.

The Frick Museum is on 70th Street and Fifth Avenue. I have never been here, and it is also Sheldon's first time. He recently read about it and thought it might be fun to see it before leaving to go home. It is super easy to navigate the city by subway, so we make our way here by early afternoon. I can tell immediately upon seeing the mansion that I will love it, and I am not disappointed as we enter. The antiques are breathtaking 18th century French, and the art pieces include works by Rembrandt and Renoir, some still hanging in the original spots. It's the former residence of Henry Clay Frick, a successful steel industrialist, built in 1913. The space on the second floor where he, his wife Adele, and their daughter Helen had their bedrooms are now galleries. The third floor housed their servants - all 27 of them! According to the information posted, Helen is still alive and still philanthropic. She is about 70, lives in Pittsburgh, and she never married. It is a vast mansion but worth the two hours that it takes us to see it all.

We have worked up an appetite by now, and I am surprised about the time, and I am starting to feel anxious about getting home. "Are you planning on talking to my parents tonight? Not rushing you!"

We both laugh, but he quickly gets serious. "I think we should get it over with." he says, in brutal honesty. "If they truly object, I guess you will have some thinking to do."

The reality of this is a little disturbing, but there is no doubt in my mind that I will follow my heart. At the same time, I know my parents and, although my mother can be overly opinionated, my father is the world's most gentle human being, so I am not truly worried. She will come around! Sheldon, the ultimate planner, has parked his car near my house, and we take the bus from Port Authority to Weehawken.

"Should we talk to them together?" I ask, willing to take his lead.

He thinks for a bit and says, "If they will both talk to me, I can do it alone." I feel relieved and squeeze his hand with appreciation.

When we get to my house, it is no surprise that my parents are both at home, as are Marilena and John. I admit to being a little nervous, but my father asks Sheldon if he wants a glass of wine, and he accepts. Does my father suspect? After all, he is a smart man. "Sheldon ti vuole parlare." I say to him, and he gives me a knowing look. I turn to my mother and say, "You too, Mo." She seems a little less receptive. "Marilena, do you want to go for a walk with me?" She jumps up with a happy "YES!" I ask, "John, do you want to come too?" letting him know he should leave.

He says, "No, I'm going to Lenny's."

My sister, my brother, and I come down the steps and out to the street where we all walk to Lenny's house, which undoubtedly annoys John, but since he doesn't talk to us, we're not sure. He doesn't break stride when we get to his destination, but just bounces up the steps and knocks on the door. "Bye, Johnny, have fun!" I call out, teasing him. He raises his hand with a quick wave or a universal hand gesture, not sure which.

"Is Sheldon asking Mom and Dad if he can marry you?" Marilena asks.

"How do you know this stuff, aren't you nine?"

She giggles, "Yes, but I'm not stupid! Why would he be talking to them by himself?"

I give her a little hug. "Yes, that is what he's doing."

She looks at me. "What if she says no to him?" She seems truly worried, and I realize how it appears to her.

"Honey, we are getting married no matter what Mom says. He is just nice to follow an old tradition, but we already know, between us, that we are going to spend our life together."

She is excited but skeptical. "Will you be Jewish too, when you get married? Mom won't like that part!" I laugh at her brutal honesty.

"Marilena, I already am Jewish ...and so are you, and so is she!" I can see it is time to explain a little family history to her. "Besides, you know none of this matters when two people love each other, right?" She nods her head yes, but I can see that this is one of those times that she's glad she is a kid instead of a grown-up, and I agree.

Marilena and I walk around for about an hour, and I figure that, however it went, it is over and done, so I take her hand and we go back home. The upstairs windows look as they did when we left, and it is ridiculously comforting as we climb the seven outside steps to the first door. My keys are already in my hand, and I unlock the first door, change keys, and unlock the inside door. Marilena stomps up the interior stairs to our apartment, I believe as a warning to those inside that we are home. I would laugh, but I must admit that I am a little nervous and hope that my mother was civil. I'm not worried about my father because he can't help but be kind, and he has never been my problem in this situation.

We walk into the apartment to voices, Sheldon talking, and my mother translating any parts that my Dad might not understand. My father's grasp of the English language is minimal, even though he has been in the U.S.A. for fifteen years. On the other hand, my mother is fluent in Italian and English, in addition to her first language, Greek. One of the first things she did when we moved here was to register for night school to learn the language. I realize, the older I get, what a bright woman she is.

"Cosa dice?" my Dad asks my Mom.

"Dice che sara' finito con la Marina a Marzo." *His Navy service will finish in March.* I think my father likes the fact that he is a fellow-sailor.

My mother asks, "Do you have a job when you are out of the Navy?"

Sheldon says, "I do not have one yet, but I will. Right now, the U.S. Navy is my job." Way to go, Shel!!!

Marilena runs in and sits next to my father, and I take a chair from the dining room and place it next to Sheldon. Finishing an earlier conversation, my mother says, "I am in the store tomorrow. Come before it gets busy." I look from one to the other to figure out if they are discussing what I think!!

He takes my hand and says to my parents, "Thank you, I promise to make her very happy."

My mother smiles and says, "I believe you."

*What the fuck, Mom? Were you testing me?*


"Just pick out the ring you like and forget about it!" I laugh, "Why don't you just surprise me?" He looks at me and knows I am kidding.

"I know better!" he says.

We spend an hour in Vincent's Jewelers, with my mom, trying different settings and looking at stones. The experience is quite surreal because my "crazy mother" has done a 360 about this whole thing and is all caught up in the perfect ring.

I know what I want! Doesn't every woman know from the age of 12? A solitaire diamond set in plain gold and the stone's size doesn't matter. She slips a few sizing rings on my hand and says I need a size 4-½, "I like the six prongs, instead of four, what do you think?"

"I think it's weird how much you have changed your tune," I say to myself. Why did she have to put me through that in the first place?

"What did you say to them?" I ask my future husband. He laughs, "Nothing they didn't already know! They love me!" We choose the ring, and my sailor boy makes arrangements to pay it off on a store account and will bring or mail money to my mom every month when he gets paid by Uncle Sam.

We go back to my house and are thrilled to realize that there won't be anyone around until after three when the kids get home from school. We rarely find ourselves alone anywhere, and we are already kissing as we walk in the door. The kissing and touching feel amazingly good, and it keeps going as we take off our jackets and move, still kissing, to my bed. He is so incredibly patient and respects my Catholic girl, daughter of Lula's refusal to have intercourse before marriage. However, the things he teaches me today are magic and tender and loving and oh so gratifying for us both.

# ARGHIRULA - Athens, Greece - 1943

I wake up very early and realize what mixed feelings I have about seeing Clorindo again today. I lie in bed, wide awake, and think about what I am doing. I could just not answer the door when he arrives, and he would just quietly go away, I suppose. He would be free to go home to his village full of family and goats, or possibly find another Greek girl to like, but this is the part that is so disturbing. I wish I could talk to my mother about this, but what could her advice possibly be other than "RUN!" I think of Olga and Stavros and their joy and Agni and her sadness. In a time that we have no idea what tomorrow will bring, or when we hear bombs in our city, and we cannot be out on the streets at night, what is the difference who I love? I don't have the energy or the will to fight my feelings.

I doze off, and I see his handsome face in a dream. He is standing there in his white uniform and extending his hand towards me. I wake up just as I reach him and realize I only have a half hour before he picks me up in real life.

"Where are they?" I ask myself as I rummage through

the limited clothes in my wardrobe. When Effie moved to America, she gave me some clothes she was unable to take. There are a pair of pants somewhere in here, and they will be perfect for today. It will be too cool to go swimming and, anyway, I don't swim. I locate the pants and, once again, admire Effie's taste. Pants are the newest thing, and, although you see women in them in the movies, none of the girls I know wear them. All except Effie, of course! She was always a trendsetter and so elegant. I put on the pants, and I love the look. They are loose at the top because of the style but fit perfectly around my waist. I wear my pale lavender short-sleeved sweater and, at the last minute, a string of costume jewelry pearls. This hair will be a problem today because curls and sea air do not agree, but since it is getting a little longer, I can style it somewhat, by running a comb through it.

He is precisely on time, and he takes my breath away with his beautiful smile. "Come in!" I open the door, and he maneuvers a picnic basket, so they can both fit in the doorway. I inhale his scent as he passes me. "What do you have?" I have an image of him walking the streets with the basket, and it is slightly comical."

Abbiamo il vino, pane, formaggio, e fragole!" He holds up the basket as I try to interpret the contents - wine, bread, cheese, and strawberries! A Feast! He is magical, and every doubt I had, just this morning, flies out the window.

Instead, I say, "Eisai agapi!" *You are a love.*

He laughs and responds, "Lo so. Te l'avevo detto!" *I know, I told you!*

I take a sweater, and he takes my arm. As we step out of the door, an old military truck pulls up, and I am only slightly surprised that he leads me to it and helps me climb into the back seat after he carefully places the basket on the front seat. He sits next to me and says, "Matteo, quest' e Arghirula." He points to the driver and says," Matteo."

I lean forward to shake his hand, but he is a bit rigid or shy, so I lean back and say, "Piacere." He nods his head and grumbles something I can't understand.

*What am I doing sitting here in this vehicle with this man?* I am grateful that we are not visible to the people on the street, and I will pretend that this is OK and that my brothers will not kill me when they find out. When he takes my hand, I know for sure that I will pretend just that for now!

There is no one on the beach for a few reasons. It is only the beginning of May, and the temperature, although pleasant, is not warm enough for swimming, and it is 9:00 a.m. He helps me with a hand on each side of my waist and puts my feet on the ground. He retrieves the basket, in addition to a large blanket and another pouch. Lastly, he removes a large jug. When done, Clorindo asks me to wait and walks to the driver's side, evidently to give Matteo instructions to pick us up later.

I help him carry his bounty, and he finds a spot on the beach near a cove and very much secluded, which makes me feel that he has done this before.

"E molto bello qui," I say in Italian, to which he responds,

"Sei molto bella tu!"

He takes the blanket, spreads it out on the sand, and places the basket and satchel on two corners. He points to the jug and says, "Acqua" and puts it near the rocks where it is coldest. It is still chilly enough where I need to keep on my sweater, and I am so glad that I have pants so I can sit comfortably on the blanket. "Vuoi fare una passeggiata?" he asks, moving his pointer and middle finger in a motion that looks like legs walking.

"Ne!" I say and think to myself, "I would walk to the ends of the earth with you" as we remove our shoes.

The Athens sun is bright, and the sand feels refreshing and soft in my toes. He takes my hand, and we stroll for a long time, and my thoughts are only of the joy I feel right now, today, at this moment. I turn to look at him, and he seems lost in his thoughts, and I admit that I love the look of him, his hair, his skin, and the beautiful bump on his nose. As we walk further, the ground gets a little rocky, and since we are barefoot, we turn and retrace our steps back to the blanket. When the sun starts to feel warmer, I remove my sweater, and I don't miss his glance at my breasts. He seems slightly embarrassed that he got caught, but does not turn away, and instead smiles with a little twinkle in his eye as he takes my hand back, and we continue to stroll.

Incredibly, we have walked quite far without running into another person. I have never been here, so I have no idea if this is how it is typically, but for me, it is the happiest I have felt in a very, very long time, and I savor the solitude. "We are the only ones here! Is this how it is usually?" I ask him.

He shrugs his shoulders and says, "I don't know. I have never been here before!" I know it's crazy, but it makes me so incredibly happy knowing that I am the only one he has brought here.

Since we have earned the rest, when we reach the

blanket, we come tumbling down on it. I immediately roll my pants to my knees because it is getting warmer still. Clorindo watches every move I make, and I know I am blushing, but I smile at him and ask, "What?"

He doesn't hesitate and says, "Hai delle belle gambe, anche se sono un po 'arcuate." I can immediately translate the part about "you have pretty legs," but I stumble on the last word. I squint my eyes and ask, "What does 'arcuate mean?" He laughs and, with hand motions, I understand that it means 'bowed." I make a pouty face, but he leans in and kisses me, and I don't hesitate to kiss him back. I didn't realize until this moment that I have been anxiously waiting for this, and my need is visceral. We kiss and touch, and he feels so familiar that it is hard to believe that I have only known him for such a short time. I feel like we have been together forever, and I respond to every kiss and every touch. He embraces me, and he holds me, and we snuggle and lie back and eventually fall asleep. When I wake up, I am wrapped securely in his arms, and I know that I need to be here forever, as long as forever might be for us.

The satchel holds a white tablecloth and thick drinking glasses that look more like jars. Clorindo spreads the tablecloth on top of the blanket and removes the bread from the basket but, having only a small cheese knife, he tears it with his hands. The cheese, wrapped in a white napkin, is cut into pieces, and he makes a little pile. The strawberries, carefully wrapped in butcher paper, are in a white towel. When he unwraps the last napkin, he reveals a cured meat that I have never seen before. He puts a small piece on a chunk of bread, adds the cheese, and places it in my mouth. My tastebuds awaken to the most delicious thing I have ever tasted! These are luxuries! And this man gets these treasures. I will remind myself later how terrible this situation is and how things are bound to go wrong. But, for the moment, with the ocean waves and the sunshine, as I reach for a strawberry and Clorindo hands me a jar of wine, the world stands still, and I believe this is some version of heaven.

"Il tuo nome." he says, "Your name is too hard to pronounce."

I laugh, "You are the first person ever to say this!" He seems surprised.

"Quando penso a te, ti chiamo Lula." *When I think of you, I call you Lula.* I translate to Greek and take his face in my hands.

"Mi pensi?" He kisses me but seems genuinely surprised that I ask him if he thinks of me.

"Ti penso ogni minuto!" *I think of you every minute.* He is using hand motions and kisses to emphasize.

"Chi e Lula?" *Who is Lula?* I tease.

"Lula e la mia futura moglie!" *She is my future wife!*

He smiles, but looks very serious. I have to translate the word moglie, so I ask him, and he thinks hard then says, "gynaika!" *wife!* I feel tears in my eyes as he holds me. What are the chances that we will ever be husband and wife? In this world, in this situation, in this war, how long will we be able to pretend that this is in any way normal or acceptable? But, for today, I will be Lula, Clorindo's future wife.

There is very little that we don't discuss sitting on the blanket or strolling the beach, but the truck shows up at

6:00 p.m., and the day will eventually come to a close. We bask in our love, and we feel the heat between us, even when we are not touching.

Everything is loaded back into the truck, and we ride quietly back towards my house, holding hands and nodding off from the rocking motion. When my eyes open, I orient myself and realize we are a few blocks from my house. I suddenly feel claustrophobic. "Can we get out here and walk, please?" I ask him. He immediately understands and calls the driver,

"Matteo, ci lasci qui, per piacere?"

The truck pulls to the curb, and Clorindo steps out, helping me down onto the sidewalk. I take a deep breath, and I taste the smoke and rubble in the back of my throat, which is probably magnified by the fact that the air at the beach was much cleaner. "Are you OK?" he asks as I try to catch my breath. I am not!

"You know my brothers will kill you when they find out about us."

His spontaneous laugh is like music. "Do you think I came all this way to be killed by your brothers? If so, then it will be my destiny!" He kisses my hand, holds it, and we walk in the direction of my house.

As we pass the Taverna, he says, "Vuoi un caffe'? Fear grips my heart as hunger twinges my stomach. We are too close to my house, and I am sure that one of my brothers, possibly both, are there right now. He tugs me along as if this is all normal, and we are two lovers free to love as we want. I pull his hand to stop him. "My brothers might be in there!" I say fearfully. He stops and faces me.

"Lula, we can't go back with our emotions, so we need

to move forward. If your brothers are here, we can tell them today." I let myself be led by him, realizing that he might be both crazy and right.

The taverna seems quite crowded and is extremely noisy. I do a quick visual scan, praying I do not see my brothers, and exhale when I am confident they are not here. Clorindo, meanwhile, is moving quickly, with me in tow, towards the end of a long table where there are two empty seats. He makes eye contact with the waiter, pointing to let him know that we will take them. "Ho fame!" he shouts, "Tu?"

I realize that I am hungry, but can't imagine what food is available here in this Greek Taverna. I already know that most coffee recently is ground roasted chickpeas, but it won't be long before there won't be any of those. To my surprise, they offer an egg lemon soup, which turns out to be delicious, although thin, with barely any rice. But there is plenty of lemon taste. I savor the familiar taste and watch Clorindo enjoy the soup as he practically inhales it.

I can't stop looking at him! He awakens all my senses, and he fills me, but I know, at the same time, that he will break my heart through no fault of his. My failed marriage did not break my heart because Giannis never filled it in the same total and complete way that it is now. I need to be prepared to lose him, and it makes me extremely sad. He watches me for a few minutes as if reading my every thought and says, "Cos'e? *What?* I snap myself back to the present and my surroundings, taking another quick look around the room and towards the door.

"Tipota! *Nothing!* I respond. I don't want to remind him again that we are doomed.

"Arghirula!" I hear voices calling my name, and I turn to see Niko, Alexandra, and a few others. We are noisy with our greetings and happy to run into each other.

"This is Clorindo," I introduce them all by name, and he is his charming, witty self. Niko and Alexandra indicate that they remember him from the outdoor cinema. A few Italian sailors who know Clorindo join us and the crowd, grown considerably, is upbeat and friendly.

The door frequently opens and closes as people enter and leave. The crowd is thicker than ever when I think I spot my brother coming in. Because he is short, he disappears in the multitude, so I lose sight of him. My panic is real because I am not emotionally prepared for this now, with all these people here.

Clorindo is talking with his friends, not more than 10 meters away, Alexandra is in the middle of a sentence, and Niko is standing between us. I turn my attention to her, just as Tolis approaches and taps my shoulder. I turn as if surprised that he is here. "You're home!" I say, and I hug him, genuinely happy that he is safe, although not thrilled that he is here.

"Malista, I have not even gone home yet!" he says. He looks from me to Niko as if he understands what I am doing here and I take Niko's arm and, bless him, he acts as if this is normal. I look at Alexandra, and she gives me a most understanding look.

"We were just about to leave!" I say with way too much enthusiasm. Clorindo is watching this interaction, and, although I know he understands what I am doing, he seems upset.

Tolis shakes Niko's hand, exchanges a few niceties,

and is distracted by someone who grabs him in a bear hug. Given the opportunity to exhale, I compose myself. I turn to Clorindo and mouth, "Synchorese me! *Forgive me!* He smiles, and I melt, knowing that I will have to face my family sooner than later, but not tonight.

To my utter amazement, as my brother moves through the crowd I hear him shout, "DiGiovanni! Is that you?"

And the surprising response from Clorindo, "Tolis?" They are so genuinely happy to see each other that it takes some time for my mind even to try to understand how this could be. Am I just imagining it? They chat and laugh in the broken Greek that Clorindo does so well and the hand motions they both do until Tolis takes Clorindo's arm and leads him to me. "Synantiste tin aderfi mou! *Meet my sister!*

Clorindo plays along and reaches out and shakes my hand, but wiggles his fingers in such a way that my whole body tingles. I don't think I can do this! But, it is already in the works, so I suppose this is how it will go. "Piacere." he says simply, without a hint of recognition.

"Clorindo was my favorite Italian sailor at the kiosk! I used to get him tobacco for his pipe." I blush at the thought of him lighting that pipe. Tolis turns to him and says, "But, it was a long time ago, where have you been?"

Clorindo explains that his hours changed about a year ago, and the hours of Tolis' kiosk didn't work out, so he gets his tobacco near the base. I take the opportunity to introduce Alexandra and Niko to Clorindo, and I can see that my brother is happy that Niko and I are seeing each other. Clorindo gets the sham, but still gives me a little crooked smile, as if this might help!

I asked Alexandra if she will be leaving soon since we

are not far from curfew and she picks up on my cue, saying, "I am ready to go now." Alexandra, Niko, and I say good night to everyone, and we leave together. We are no sooner out the door than Alexandra, and Niko burst out laughing. She says, "How long do you think you can pretend?"

I feel like crying, "Not much longer, for sure. But, if you just help me a little longer, I can find the right time."

They laugh, "Of course! We understand that your heart wants what it wants." My beautiful friend Alexandra looks lovingly at Niko, and I understand what they feel and am extremely happy for them.

They walk me home, and I collapse on the sofa with a million mixed emotions and total exhaustion from the highs and lows of this day. What do I do, and when do I do it? I am sound asleep when I hear the key unlock the front door and then close quietly. I don't want to speak to my brother, so I pretend I am sound asleep and do not call out. I hear his bedroom door close, and I relax, although I have a fitful sleep for the rest of the night.

I get ready for work, and I am having coffee when Tolis comes out and says, "Good morning!"

I respond, "Kalimera. How are you? It is good to have you safely home!" And I mean that. He asks, almost immediately,

"Are things serious with Niko?"

I respond, "He is a wonderful guy!" Seeming satisfied, he drops that subject. We have coffee together and make casual conversation about our parents and siblings. When I am ready to leave, he asks,

"Shall I meet you after work?"

I respond, "No need. I won't be alone!" He nods his head in understanding, and I flood with relief. "I have to be away for another day or two, so I am glad I don't have to worry about you." I know he is busy, but I feel that there might be a lady taking up a lot of his time. All good with me!

Clorindo is standing outside the door when I leave work, and he is like sunshine on this cloudy day. We share a quick kiss, which feels like a promise for more, and I am overjoyed. He holds a basket in his hand and pointing to it, tells me, "Poche cose. Forse per tua mamma!" He brought food for my mother! He is an angel; there is no doubt in my mind. But, will they think he is the devil? Either way, I know the time will come that I will find out.

Meanwhile, I will follow my heart and hide our love. "Dove vuoi andare?" *Where do you want to go?* he asks.

"Sto spiti mo!" *To my house!* I respond without hesitation. I desperately need to be alone with him.

We do not leave the house all evening, and the magic only ends when he has to check into his base for the night. When he is gone, I spend every waking moment reliving every kiss, every word, and every touch. I know I will never tire of him and, without a doubt, will never let him go of my own free will. Whatever God has planned for us, I hope that it is together. He is there every day and, if my brother is away, we spend whatever time we can together. If my brother is home, Clorindo and I occupy ourselves by walking and going to the park or the Parthenon. Tolis does not ask questions because he assumes that I am with Niko, and he is happy to pass the baton.

The summer is magical for me, but the country is suffering more than ever, and Athens is in shambles. Clorindo explains that things are going to change drastically, very shortly. "We must tell your family about us, Lula." I know this is true, and I plan to tell Tolis alone and, once he accepts the inevitable, he will help me with the rest of them.

In July, Benito Mussolini, the Italian Tyrant and partner of Adolf Hitler fell from power. His successor, Marshal Badoglio, surrendered Italy unconditionally to the Anglo American Allies. We know that significant changes are coming, and I feel the urgency of what I must do!

I tell Tolis that I need him to meet me after work at the Taverna because there is something essential that I must discuss with him. "Tell me now!" he says as I am about to leave for work.

"Tonight, Tolis!" I insist. "It is probably the most important and hardest thing I will ever have to talk to you about, so please, we have to do it this way."

He looks at me dubiously, "Are you pregnant?"

I open the door to leave and call back, "No, I am not!"

Clorindo and I arrive first and take seats at a quiet table in a corner. He holds my hand and says, "Your brother is a good man, and he will understand."

I'm not sure, but I smile at him and say, "I'm ready!"

Tolis walks in, and I wave to him. He reaches us with a big smile on his face as he sees Clorindo and automatically reaches out to shake his hand.

"Where's Niko?" he asks.

"This is your question?" I am dumbfounded! Nobody speaks for what seems like an hour, but it is just a few short minutes. I know he is processing this scene; after all, he is a smart and worldly man.

"Giati, Why?"

I laugh. "Do you think we can know why?"

He sits and places his head in his hands. "Did I do this?" He wants no part of it, of course! So, I release him of his potential guilt.

"Oxi, Tolis, we already knew each other when you introduced us. It was never Niko. It was always Clorindo!" I recount the story of our meetings and the natural progression of our relationship. We deal with the questions, the anger, the tears, and love within the first fifteen minutes. I feel cleansed, and Tolis is angry, but not unreasonably, much to my surprise.

"What do you two think you're doing, though? You know this can't end well!"

Clorindo responds, "Tolis, I don't have all the right words to tell you how much we love each other. Whatever we have to do to stay together, we will do it. Forse Dio ci aiutera." *Maybe God will help us.*

There is not much left to discuss, and we are all properly drained. Tolis has a revelation, "Is this where Mamma has been getting all the food?" This depressing reality brings us full force back to the uncertain present.

"Tolis, no matter what happens going forward, please give us your blessing." Clorindo and I sit very still, and I know I am holding my breath.

"You have my blessing," Tolis says as he abruptly stands and leaves without another word.

# MARIA - Odessa, Russia - 1906

I have inquired at the hospital several times, and after being sent from one person to another on multiple occasions, today I meet Ruth. I explain, "I hope to volunteer my services to help with either childbirth or new babies," I tell her, slightly frustrated by my impossible mission. Ruth is fluent in Greek, so it is easier for me to explain what I am offering, and she tells me that the three failed attempts were very much because of a language barrier.

"We so desperately need extra hands with deliveries, newborn babies, and new mothers!" I am overjoyed!

"I can come here during the day, when my husband is working, but would not be able to help at night. And, our stay here is temporary, as I explained earlier." She quite clearly understands and is very grateful for any help I can provide. "I will come back tomorrow morning, if you like," I tell her.

"Efcharisto!" *Thank you!* She seems genuinely pleased.

We have been here for less than a month, but time seems to be moving quickly. Diocles works long hours at the church and returns when the sunsets and the natural light is gone. Our routine has a smooth flow, and I work around his schedule to help at the hospital. "Are you happy with the progress of your work?" I ask him today as we sit facing each other in our kitchen. He spoons the beet and cabbage soup that I have learned to make from our landlady Natasha. It has become his favorite and, since I can make a large pot at a time, it is also my favorite for convenience, although I don't savor the taste as much as he does.

"As you can imagine, this work needs to be perfect, so it is prolonged." He puts another spoonful of soup in his mouth. "And you?" he asks. "Are you enjoying the hospital?"

I don't hesitate at all, "I love it! Being with the babies fills my heart. Sadly, there are so many that are extremely weak and malnourished, as are their mothers. There is nothing sadder than when one or the other does not survive. But, many of the women only need help to learn how to nurse their babies, and, when we are successful, it is most rewarding."

He smiles at me and takes my hand. "You are a true angel." I feel myself blush both at the compliment and his touch.

Natasha has invited us to join her and her husband, Sidor, for dinner after Mass on Sunday, and I am looking forward to my neighbors' company. We step out hours before the service is to begin and enjoy a stroll towards the magnificent church. The warm day is a welcome change from the days of gray skies and rain we have had the past few weeks.

"Let's walk the steps before Mass!" he sounds like a little boy.

"Really?" I ask. "It sounds exhausting!"

He laughs, "Who's the old person here, you or I?"

I take the challenge, and he takes my hand as we head to the Potemkin Stairs. When we reach the top of the steps, we look out at the harbor, and I remind myself that we are only visitors to this beautiful city and that our life together will soon begin back in Athens. Without warning, he walks briskly down the steps, and I quickly catch up. Before long, we are racing each other, and I more than keep up with his long stride and feel wonderfully invigorated by the exercise.

Hearing him laugh is like music, and my heart sings. In the past few weeks, he has been intense and sometimes quiet and withdrawn. I know that his work is difficult, so I try my best to leave him to his solace and prayers as much as I can. The stairs are magically void of people, so the world is ours for now. When we reach the bottom, we need to catch our breath, and we laugh like children. He takes my hand and turns me toward him, holding me close. I turn my face up, hoping for a kiss, and not only am I not disappointed, but he treats me to a number of them. Is it appropriate for the priest and the midwife to kiss in public?

He turns me to the stairs and points towards the top. I can see the beautiful statue of Duke de Richelieu. Diocles tells me that the figure has been there since it was unveiled in 1826 and is the first statue erected in the city and done by Russian sculptor Ivan Petrovich. The view looking up the stairs is spectacular, and I fully appreciate its beauty. I turn to Diocles and ask, only half jokingly,

"How do we get back up?"

The walk to the top is much longer, but we take it slowly, and we stop at some of the landings. When we reach the middle landing, we rest by sitting to the far right. From here, the view is perfect in both directions. When I look up, I see that the stairs narrow progressively, and all I can see are steps. But looking down, they widen to the bottom, and all I can see are landings. It is also just the perfect spot from which to enjoy watching other people. A middle-aged couple walks down cautiously, holding hands. A father carries a small child as a young family makes its way down, calling out to two children who run ahead. Three teenage boys hold a blue banner, one on each end and one in the middle. They have paced just right so that the banner billows as they catch the wind, looking like they are under a parachute. When we get to the top, we stroll towards the church, with plenty of time before the service.

"Would you like to see the chapel?" he asks.

"There is nothing I would love more!" I tell him.

The chapel is just as I remember it from the first day we were here, but the screen where they are working is protected and surrounded by very high scaffolding. It is open enough to see the work in progress, and Diocles proudly points to the work he is currently doing on the apostles. He points them out, one by one, and names them. "Peter, John, James, Andrew, Philip, Thomas, Bartholomew, Matthew, James son of Alphaeus, Simon the Zealot, and Jude (Thaddeus) brother of James."

I have been counting silently and ask, "Why are there only eleven?"

He looks at me like a proud father. "Excellent, Maria! The twelfth was Judas Iscariot, who was replaced, after Christs' resurrection, by Matthias. Neither is here."

I take time to look at each one and appreciate the talent and beauty. "Can you show me exactly where you are working? The exact place where you last touched with your brush?"

His laugh is genuine, and he puts his arm around me and whispers, "You are so special." He takes a very long-handled brush and reaches up high, pointing to John's blue robe, saying. "John happens to be my favorite, and, at the moment, I am working on his garments, right here!" He gently touches the spot where he has last painted, and it moves me for some reason. The delicacy of the chapel's restoration stirs me, as does the gentleness of the man who is my husband.

The service is long, and as always, I remain quiet and still, although I feel fidgety long before it is over. Diocles, on the other hand, savors every word and every movement. He is lost in his prayers, whether they are silent or spoken, very much as he is when he prays on his own at home. When the congregation leaves, we step back out into the sunshine and quickly return home to prepare for dinner.

I ask Diocles to taste one of the koulourakia cookies I made yesterday, and he says it is delicious. Since I do not consider myself a good baker, I am glad but also bear in mind that his approval might be encouraged so that I train myself to be a good wife in the bedroom and the kitchen.

We walk down the stairs and turn to the right into the short hallway that brings us to Natasha and Sidor's apartment. We are precisely on time, and they, immediately after Diocles knocks three times with his knuckles on the thick wooden door, open and stand together with matching, welcoming smiles. The door is opened wide, and as we enter, I hand Natasha the tin filled with my cookies. Natasha is about ten years older than I, and Sidor is ten years her senior. She is about my height with an ample bust and long, dark hair pulled back and rolled into a bun at her neck's nape. She wears a dark skirt and white blouse with an apron tied at her waist. Sidor is almost as tall as Diocles with a matching beard. However, Sidor's hair is very thin, unlike Diocles's full head, and he is twice the circumference. They shake hands vigorously, and Natasha and I embrace in greeting. We are escorted to their living room and assigned seats on the sofa.

"It smells delicious!" I say, pointing in the direction of the kitchen.

"Pelmeni," Natasha says as she assists Sidor to serve us drinks. "Vodka?" Diocles declines, and Sidor points to the beautiful decanter with brownish red liquid.

Diocles says, "Kvass, Thank you."

I have never seen this drink, and Natasha, seeing my confusion, explains. "We make the kvass ourselves and prefer it to vodka" I am interested, and she continues, "We make it with fermented black bread, ginger, lemon, raisins, sugar, beets, and berries."

Diocles extends his glass towards me, "It is quite tasty, you should try it, Maria."

It tastes like cider, but with a little punch to it, I suppose from the fermentation. It is quite delicious! "I would love a glass. Thank you."

Natasha and Sidor sit side by side, affectionately, as their hands occasionally touch. The conversations are diverse.

"How do you like Odessa, Maria?" Sidor asks.

"Everything is very different from Athens, so every day there is something new to see and appreciate," I respond honestly.

"Have you walked the steps?" Natasha asks.

Diocles and I quickly glance at each other, and for a second, I wonder if they saw us kissing at the bottom of the stairs this morning. I blush slightly and respond, "Yes, actually, we did that this morning before Mass."

She smiles and says, "Quite lovely, isn't it?" Did I see Natasha and Sidor quickly glance at each-other too? I believe I did!

Dinner is a delicious array of tastes different from Greek food, although reminiscent of my mother's cooking. I bask in the warmth of this table and this house and these beautiful people, who have brought me back home with their ways. Natasha refuses my help and insists that Diocles and I sit, while Sidor helps her serve our meal.

We start with klotski, potato dumplings in chicken broth, followed by a pot of roasted meat, which is so tender it falls apart with a touch of my fork. Also served are pelmeni, dumplings filled with minced beef, and mushrooms. On the table, there is a lovely salad of fresh tomatoes, cucumbers, and radishes, tossed in sour cream dressing. I eat everything and savor every bite and every memory.

I am allowed to help clear the table with Natasha, while the men discuss politics and Odessa's problems in recent years. I don't engage, but can't help but hear of the Jews' oppression in the city. Natasha tastes a koulourakia as she places them on a serving plate. "This is a delicious cookie, Maria!" I feel ridiculously pleased since this is the first time I have shared something that I cooked in my kitchen with anyone other than Diocles. "I must learn to make it!"

I am overjoyed! "Of course, we can make them together next time."

Natasha takes out the briki pot, adds water and asks me to stir in the coffee with sugar while she reaches for the cups and arranges them on a small tray.

"Thank you, Natasha, for making us so welcome in your home and thank you for your friendship."

She smiles sweetly and says, "We are happy you came to Odessa. Sidor is very fond of Diocles."

When the coffee is ready and poured, I take the tray to the dining table and Natasha carries the plate with my cookies and another plate of pryaniki cookies that she made. She insisted I try one in the kitchen, and I still have the lovely ginger spicy taste in my mouth. When we sit, the men switch their intense discussion to include us. "Maria, Diocles tells me that you work at the hospital. How do you find it?"

I can be honest with these caring people. "I love the healthy babies, and it is easy to care for them. But, the ones that need attention are the ones that often don't survive. All I can offer them is comfort and love, although there is quite often a sad ending. Just yesterday, I was asked to help with a woman who was having a difficult delivery, and it was the most rewarding experience of my time at the hospital."

Natasha is very interested, "Did she bring a healthy baby?"

I am happy to tell her, "Yes, a perfect girl!"

When the conversation turns to children, Sidor tells us that they have not been blessed with children, although they have not given up hope and continue to pray that there is a child in their future. Like a flash in my mind's eye, I see Natasha sitting in a rocking chair singing a lullaby to a beautiful and healthy baby. The image is gone immediately, but there is no doubt that I felt it to my core. I take Natasha's hand and almost promise, "God will bless you! Speak to your future baby every day, she will hear you." I am as surprised as everyone else by my words in this tranquil room, but they are out there, lingering in the air. I see tears of hope in Natasha's eyes, and as my vision is reflected there, I know I am not wrong.

Diocles clears his throat as he overly compliments the meal, and I recognize it as an effort to soften the strain created by my statement and to relieve the palpable tension in the air. I support him by reaching for another pryaniki, moaning at the delicious flavor. Sidor takes a koulourakia and jokes, in good humor, "I might eat the whole plate, these are so good!"

Lost in her thoughts, Natasha is silent, and I suspect that she is speaking to her future child.

# LULA (ARGHIRULA) - Athens, Greece - 1943-44

I believe my father is trying his best, but he has not had a full conversation with me since he learned about Clorindo. When we go to my parents' house, he politely excuses himself saying he has work to do. My father was never one to show his feelings, but they are quite apparent now. I tell myself that he considers Clorindo just like other things that have never been allowed in our home. Alcohol, magazines, and playing cards are all the devil's work, so I'm sure an Italian sailor is on this list. He is cordial when they are in the same room, but certainly never friendly.

My mother, on the other hand, welcomes him with open arms and enjoys listening to him speak, and she giggles at his fractured Greek. "Arghiro', you look well!" she says as I embrace her. I think the same of her, as her beautiful skin has more color today than it has had in many months. She turns to Clorindo and gives him one of her precious hugs, and I can see this pleases him immensely. He hands her a large sack, as he does every time he visits.

She thanks him profusely, "Theos se esteile se emas!" *God sent you to us!*

I take his hand and, looking at his handsome face, say, "Nai, echei!" *Yes, He has!*

My mother touches my face and says softly, "Xero oti tha akolouthiseie tin kardia sou." *I know you will follow your heart.* I take her hand and kiss it. I love her so much for accepting and understanding, although we both know that my life will undoubtedly take some turns that will be painful for her.

Today is Sunday, and Clorindo has the entire day off. My brothers and sisters are all here, and my mother has cooked a wonderful meal, thanks to the sack of food that he brought her last week. He brings food every time he has the opportunity and, although we know he is stealing it, we pretend otherwise, except for my father, who has his own opinions, which he does not share with me. The sacks typically contain cornmeal, maccheroni, canned meats and vegetables, olive oil, and vinegar. He also brought fresh fish one time, which Mamma cooked that day. Today, there is more of the same and rice, chocolates, bread, and smoked fish, which pleases my mother to no end. In a separate bag, Clorindo brings my brothers a bottle of wine and one of Cognac. Tolis pats him on the back, and I feel the tears in my eyes because my brother has made it possible for me to be open about my love for this man, the enemy. Tolis takes the bottles and hides them under his jacket so that he does not forget to take them home and also so my father doesn't see them.

"Efcharisto'," *Thank you,* Tolis says and Christos repeats the thanks as he shakes Clorindo's hand.

Although everyone else is pleasant at dinner, my father does not engage in the conversation between my brothers or my attempt to translate to Clorindo. It is sometimes difficult to read my father's true feelings, but today I know exactly what makes him sullen. When my mother offers everyone coffee, my father excuses himself and returns to his paints and canvas.

I leave the table as Clorindo entertains the others with his broken Greek, and I walk across the room to the heavy drapes which serve as a wall to my father's private sanctuary. I stop and quietly call out, "Papa?" There is a small hesitation before he pulls the curtain aside so I can enter. In all my years growing up, I can count on one hand the number of times I have been on this side of the curtain. The same smell that permeates the house is just a little more pungent here. He stands straight and rigid and is surprised at my intrusion. I stand tall and try not to be intimidated by his height or stern demeanor. "I would like to speak with you," I say, and we stand for a few seconds, eyeing each other. He relents by pointing to the tall chair that his models occupy when he paints his saints. I exhale as I take the three steps to reach it, and I sit facing him directly.

Although he is not far, I can see the distance makes him comfortable, and he perches on the edge of the large table that holds his paints, oils, and canvases.

When he stretches out his legs, his feet almost touch the easel where his latest work faces him. I take a deep breath and say, "Eisai poly thymomenos me mena?" *Are you very angry with me?*

He responds immediately and without a second thought, "Nai!" *Yes.*

I feel the tears stinging my eyes, but I don't want to cry, so I choke them back. "Papa, I am very sorry if I hurt you, but I want you to know that I love this man deeply, and I will spend the rest of my life at his side, no matter where it leads us. I hope that you can forgive me." I might have only imagined that his demeanor softened, but I soon realize that he will not be responding. Pushing back the curtain, I return to the family, just as my mother pours coffee from the briki to the cups. Clorindo stands and smiles as he pulls out my chair, and I know that if I have to choose between him and my father, I will want him, even if there is a chance that I might be wrong.

I glance at my watch to be sure I will be home before curfew and Clorindo stands. "We have lots of time!" I tell him.

"Lo so!," *I know,* he says. "Ho bisogno di parlare con tuo padre!" *I need to speak to your father.* If this entire situation weren't so disagreeable, I would have laughed out loud. But, he is not asking my permission, and, without hesitation, he walks to the curtain and softly says, "Boro na se do?" *Can I see you?* The wait feels very long, but I eventually see my father's hand as he pulls back the curtain to allow Clorindo to enter.

We are all stunned and look in the direction of my father's domain and then at each other. Elena says, "Einai gennaios anthropos!" *He is a brave man.*

Christos immediately responds, "I enais trelos anthropos!" *Or a crazy man.* We all laugh nervously, but my mother nods her head and smiles her angelic smile in full approval.

I try my best to listen and half expect to be summoned to help translate. But I am neither beckoned nor can I hear them. So I keep my eyes on the curtain, and eventually, Clorindo steps out with a neutral expression on his face, and I can't establish if the conversation went well. I look at him anxiously as he approaches and raise one eyebrow in question. He doesn't speak, but he winks, so the others can't see. I am flooded with relief and turn my attention back to the discussion about the conditions in Athens.

When Clorindo gets my attention, he points to his watch, reminding me that it is now time to leave. As we are saying our good-byes at the door, my father joins us. I wait for him to lecture me on the mistake I am making; instead, without a word, he walks to me and places a kiss on my forehead, like a blessing. I hug him with all my might, and I know that I have never loved him more. When I look at Mamma, she has the same angelic, knowing smile, and I am amazed, once more, at her secure emotional connection to my father.

"Ci sposiamo!" Clorindo says, the second we close the door behind us. Did he just say "We will get married?"

"Clorindo, o pateras mou tha prepei na enkrinei!" *My father will never approve!* And at this moment, I am full of doubt that it will ever happen.

Clorindo puts both his hands around my waist and pulls me close, saying, "He already has!"

My head spins with a myriad of emotions ranging from

extreme joy to absolute misery at the reality that I may need to follow him to his country and leave my family. But, in these trying times we can only plan one day at a time, and with extreme joy, we plan a wedding day based on his work schedule. August 22$^{nd}$ is the first available Sunday, and it is only three weeks away. My father has reserved time at his church for the ceremony, and cousin Maria has offered her home to have a simple celebration. We are all fully aware of the shortage of everything, but gathering the family in joy is enough for us.

The Pierakos house is far more spacious than my mother's and is on Orfeos Street. Maria is my father's first cousin and the daughter of his older brother, who was also a priest but died a few years ago. Maria and her husband Takis Pierakos have lived in Athens for ten years with their son Giannis, who is almost the same age as me. They are the sweetest people, and I will always be grateful for their kindness and understanding.

"Theia Maria, I can't thank you enough for your generosity!"

She stops me mid-sentence. "Arghirula, we are family. Family supports each other. Besides, I am a hopeless romantic, and I see you are truly in love." She has been speaking to my mother, which warms my heart.

The day is hot and sunny with a beautiful blue sky. My sisters, Elena and Aphrodite, help me dress in my best shirtwaist dress, which is light blue, and I tie a wide white belt around my waist. My shoes match the belt, and they have platform heels. They are from Effie and are the prettiest ones I own. As usual, my hair is a mass of curls, which my sisters try to help me tame. I miss Effie so much, and today I miss her even more and wish she could be here to share my happiness. I wrote her several letters in the last few months, telling her about Clorindo and how much I know she would love him. "I hope that you will meet him someday. He fills my heart with indescribable joy!" I tell her in my latest letter, in which I also let her know that we will marry. "I hope that someday we will all be together," I tell her, although I know how unlikely it is that this dream will ever come true.

There is not too much religious difference between Catholic and Greek Orthodox. We celebrate both. We have a service in the Orthodox church to satisfy my father and one in the Catholic church to fulfill the Italian Navy requirement. The celebration at cousin Maria's home is simple, and all the people I love are present. Clorindo does not seem sad that there is no one to represent his family, and we are happy as we pretend that all things are ordinary, and I do not think beyond this day and the happiness I feel in my heart at the moment.

I don't know where Tolis has been staying for the last three days, but we have not seen him. Of course, we have not left the house since Sunday. And we have only gotten out of bed to eat and drink. We can't keep our hands to ourselves, and we explore each other the way that only two people who fear separation might do. "No matter what happens, I will always thank God that he brought me here to find you."

I feel tears in my throat. "S'agapo toso poly." *I love you so much.*

Clorindo and I steal hours and days together and I am happy deep in my soul and beyond mere words. But my joy turns to fear and sadness when the days pass, and I do not see him for a week and have no direct word from him. I only know what my brothers tell me, "Italy is about to exit from the war!"

In early September, the news is devastating. Italy surrendered, reinforcements were sent to the German troops in Kefalonia, and they have taken control of the island, which was once controlled by the Italians. Word has it that thousands of Italian soldiers were killed, and by the end of September, the Wehrmacht are shooting Italians on the streets. They have already surrendered, with no trials and with no mercy. Greek families hide Italian soldiers when they begin to understand how cold-bloodedly the Germans slaughter the Italians. The inhabitants of this island only now start to realize what has been happening on the mainland.

Adolf Hitler asked the Bulgarian government to extend its occupation zone to encompass additional territory. As would be expected, the Greeks are infuriated, and they protest. Yesterday, a strike was organized by EAM, and it rallied hundreds of thousands in central Athens. A massive crowd attempted to march from Omonoia Square towards Syntagma Square along Panepistimiou Street, but came across a barricade put up by the German army forces, Italian Cavalry, and Greek collaborationist police. The protesters were fired upon during their attempt to breach the barrier and were forced to withdraw, but many died and were wounded.

All my information comes from Tolis, who is directly involved, but he has no news of Clorindo. "Please see what you can find out? I have not seen him in weeks, and I'm afraid of what might have happened to him!"

He seems frustrated, "I have been doing nothing else, Arghiro'! The situation is out of control, and the shift between the Germans and Italians is confusing at best." He softens because of my tears, puts his arm around me and promises, "Basilis and I are working on it. Please be patient. We are worried too."

There are more weeks of painful waiting, but eventually, Tolis brings me news of Clorindo. He has been confined to the base since Benito Mussolini fell from power, and his successor Marshal Badoglio surrendered Italy unconditionally to the Allied forces. I cannot control my anguish, and Tolis is helpless. "I'm trying to figure out what to do to help him, Arghiro', but I will tell you that we need to do something because the Allied forces will not go easy on Axis soldiers, I can guarantee it!" I am inconsolable! "I will continue to ask around," Tolis says, and I have no alternative but to wait and cry with pain and crippling fear.

The BBC reports, "We have just learned that the Island of Cephalonia has suffered a significant loss of lives. Thousands of men of the Acqui Division were massacred after running out of ammunition and surrendering." We gather around the radio at the Taverna intent on listening to the transmission that reports the code word "Achse" to all subordinate commands. It is the German forces' signal to attack Italian forces in all the war theatres of the Mediterranean.

My heart turns to stone. "Tolis, you promised!!" and I start to walk home in a fuzzy haze.

Tolis catches up and takes my arm to steady me, saying, "I have turned to everyone that I know. We just have to wait. But, as I already told you, he is still in Piraeus." His words do not console me, and I turn my anger towards my brother, my faithful ally, as I feel myself crumble.

The weeks turn to months, and Christmas comes and passes with no celebration other than attending Mass with my family. The church has become a haven for me, and I sometimes sit alone in the first pew for hours, lost in my thoughts, and I cry until I am exhausted.

It is the end of January, and Tolis is away more often than he is home, but tonight he storms into the house, telling me that someone will help us. "Who?" I can't believe my ears! Although I have not given up hope, it feels as though my life is frozen in this horrific time.

The idea that there is someone to help is beyond my grasp at the moment. "It doesn't matter who, Arghiro', and I can't name, for everyone's safety," he tells me as he gathers clothes, underwear, and socks, throwing it all into a bag.

"Where are you going?" Is he leaving now?

He takes my shoulders and stops my violent shaking. "Calm yourself, please!" he says quietly. "I will be gone for just a day or two."

He is gone two nights, and during this time, I only move from the chair to the bed and otherwise pace the floor of the small apartment. "God! Did you bring him to me only to take him away so soon?" I scream at the walls. Then I pray, "Please, dear Lord...please!" and, inevitably, I cry myself to sleep.

Tolis, true to his word, returns after endless hours gathering information from whatever sources are available to him. The Italian sailors have been confined to their base in Piraeus and are on lockdown for their safety. He tells me, "If we can safely get Clorindo off his base, we have someone willing to hide him here in Athens until things are resolved.

"Oh, dear God, you have answered my prayers!" I say out loud.

Tolis continues, "Italian servicemen are being shot down on the streets everywhere in the city!" He is visibly shaken.

"What should I do?" I ask.

He doesn't hesitate. "You can go with me to speak to the person who has made the arrangements." We turn towards the door.

"Of course!" I am so grateful that someone is willing to help us. "To whom do we speak? Where do we go?"

As he opens the door, he says something, which I ask him to please repeat because I can't believe my ears. "We are going home to see Papa."

Papa is, as usual, behind the curtain. I run in and pull the curtain back without announcing myself, but as surprised as he is by the intrusion, he calmly stops his work and accepts my hug. "Efcharisto, Papa!" *Thank you!* I say through uncontrollable tears. He holds me and lets me cry, and this makes me feel incredibly protected and grateful.

Tolis waits for me to calm myself and tells my father, "Basilis and I are going to the base today, and we have a truck at our disposal, which should safely get us through the streets."

My father nods and says, "Cousin Maria is expecting you. She asked that you enter through a door in the back of the house." The woman is a saint! The repercussions for hiding an Italian soldier these days are significant, but this woman, these people, are ready to help us.

"Thea, pos boroume na sas epistrepsoume?" *How can we repay her?*

His look softens, and he says, "We can only pray that God continues to keep us in his care, my dear."

Tolis asks, "Do you want to come with us?" There is only one obvious response.

"S'agapo, adelfos!" *I love you, brother.* I say from the bottom of my heart.

Basilis waits for us right outside the house. "The truck is ready!" he tells us and Tolis seems relieved. We need to walk to Kifissia, which is quite far, but, on arrival, I realize the brilliance of the plan. The owner of Varsos Bakery, Michail Varsos, is a portly man and has a friendly way. Without hesitation, he walks us to the shop's side.

"The back of the truck is closed, so I would recommend that your 'guest' sit there." Michail is a man my brothers know from their group, and it is also evident that this is not the first time that his bakery truck has been used for this purpose.

"Se efcharisto', file mou," *Thank you, my friend*, Basilis says, patting him on the back. They open the back door and direct me to sit behind the seat. The product typically goes here, and there are a few boxes and some freshly baked bread. I sit with my back to the front seat, and I am thankful that we are not going too far because I know this ride will make me feel nauseous for many reasons. My brothers each jump into a front seat and put on white caps. Basilis drives slowly and deliberately, so as not to call undue attention.

We soon stop, and Tolis turns to me as he steps out of the truck. "You do not move! And hand me that box." I pick up the box he points to, and I hand it to him over the front seat. I am surprised that it is so light, but quickly realize it is empty.

I hope with all my heart that we can get him to safety, and I don't allow myself to think that he will most probably have to go back to his home in Italy.

"Dear God, I put myself entirely in your hands." I pray silently.

Tolis and Basilis are gone a long time, but when I look at my watch, it has only been barely ten minutes when the truck doors open, and Clorindo climbs into the back next to me. He is dressed in civilian clothes and civilian shoes, but he still smells the same. I am choked up with emotion at seeing him and break down in his arms as he holds me tight and kisses my hair, my face, and my lips. Tears are all over my face, and I can't tell if they are all mine or mingled with his. "I tuoi fratelli sono santi." *Your brothers are saints.* He whispers in my ear.

"Xero!" *I Know!* I respond.

The ride to Orfeos Street feels longer than before, but now I am resting comfortably in Clorindo's arms and I could stay like this for eternity. Tolis and Basilis only speak to each other, not betraying that there are people in the back of their truck. "What is happening?" I ask sincerely.

He holds me even closer and speaks in a shallow voice, "It has gotten completely out of control, and the number of Italian soldiers killed is climbing into the thousands. All we can do now is hide and wait until things shift." We sit quietly for a while, trying to absorb the reality. "I am so grateful to your family for saving my life...." he can barely finish the sentence.

When we arrive at cousin Maria's home, it is quiet, and it seems deserted. Basilis pulls the truck next to the house, and Tolis jumps out to check the street and stand guard. When he gives us the signal, Clorindo and I jump out quickly and run to the back of the house, where we have to walk through a small maze of bushes to a door that can't be seen until you reach it. Maria and Takis are holding open the door as they hurry us in. I hug my cousin. "Theos na se evlogei!" *God Bless you!* I say from my very soul. I will be forever grateful for the risk this family is taking to help a fellow human being and one that means the entire world to me.

Tolis walks casually to the back of the house, holding a bakery box and gives it to Clorindo. "Edo einai ta pragmata sas." Here are your things. Clorindo puts the box down and takes Tolis into a bear hug.

"Tha eimai gia panta sto chreos sas." *I will be forever in your debt.*

334

My brother responds, "To kaname afto gia tin adelfi mas, etsi kalytera na tin antimetopizete Kala!" *We did this for our sister, so you'd better treat her well!*

Clorindo is emotional, "Te lo prometto!" *I promise you!*

The room is small but arranged neatly with a bed, a dresser, a bookcase, and a straight-backed chair. In a corner, there is a small propane burner. The very tiny cabinet holds a briki, two small pots, two dishes, two bowls, two cups, and utensils. There is a little table pushed against the wall. There is a toilet, a sink in the small bathroom, and a sizeable makeshift basin on the floor under a water hose. Not luxurious but incredibly practical. It is more than Clorindo expected, and we can't contain our gratitude to this family. "Arghiro', you should come and go cautiously, making sure that no one is watching you enter and leave. Also, the street is tranquil and residential, so you should be safe enough coming out after dark, but don't wander far from the house in case you need to identify yourself"

I glance at the door that connects this space to the house. Takis explains, "The other side of that door is blocked by a large piece of furniture, which is too large to move easily, but can be moved if need be." There is a place in heaven for these people, of that I am sure!

When we are settled, my brothers say good-bye and leave to return the truck to the baker. I hug them and promise to be careful. Cousin Maria and Takis give us a key and remind us, "Let us know if there is anything you need from us, but consider this your home for as long as you need it."

When they leave, I collapse on the chair in a torrent of

tears, which I am sure are part of gratitude and part fear. Clorindo puts his arms around me and says, "Please don't cry. It hurts my heart that I am the reason for your sadness." I look at him, surprised at what he thinks, and turn into his embrace.

"You are the reason for all of my joy!"

As days turn into weeks, we find a rhythm in our daily lives. Other than to step out of the door where the bushes are tall, Clorindo does not leave this room. Once food and tobacco were available to him, but now we must rely on others' generosity to keep us fed. Cousin Maria has a small garden behind the house, but it does not produce much since there is limited access to seeds of any kind and certainly not now that it is February and quite cold. She shares, but there is barely enough for her small family. Today, in front of our door, she left a piece of bread and an onion. I know what a great sacrifice this is, and I so much appreciate her kind heart. "Are you leaving?" He looks disappointed. "How long will you be gone?" I sit back on the bed and kiss him.

"Not long," I promise.

Although money is inflated and devalued and we have very little of it, I have some in the purse. Because of our desperate times, the black market has become common even for the average person. It is a system of interacting supply and demand, uncontrolled by a state authority or any kind of intervention, so it is a "free market" of prices. My real treasure is a pair of shoes and two sweaters, in perfect condition, which Effie left behind. I pull my coat tighter, and I walk towards Asurmatos, where my brothers told me to check first. There are crowds of people walking and moving around in the same space. I meld in, as I was told to do, and before long, and as expected, someone whispers, "I have oil." I cannot afford to pay for the oil, but the person is very interested in the shoes I have to offer. Soon, I can swap the sweaters, and I eventually come away with oil, soap, bread, beans, coffee, cornflour, and a small supply of tobacco. With everything loaded in my pouch, I start my walk to my parents' house.

My mother is pleased to see me. "Arghiro', my dear, how are you? How is Clorindo?"

I hug her and say, "I am well, Mamma. Clorindo is well, but the hours in the day are extremely long for him. Basilis brought him Italian books, so he occupies most of his time reading." She helps me unload my treasures, and we take our time dividing all except the tobacco, which is very specifically for my husband. I keep a small portion of the coffee, bread, and soap for myself and a part of the beans and flour for cousin Maria. "How is Papa?" I ask, noticing that he is not home.

"He went to church this morning," she replies, and I know he prays for all of us. I notice that my mother uses the coffee I brought, which makes it clear that she has run out. I discreetly add some of the coffee I planned on taking home to her supply. It saddens me to know that my parents are doing without so much.

My mother's sadness over her Jewish friends' condition is the topic of conversation and practically an obsession. She commiserates for over an hour and, although I am helpless to console her, I realize she needs to talk about it. The conversation eventually becomes about my marriage when, out of the blue, she asks me, "Are you happy, Arghirula?" I laugh at her sudden shift and the question.

"Mamma, I don't think any of us are happy right now."

She gives me her wise, beautiful smile and repeats, "Are you happy?"

I answer her honestly, "Mamma, I never thought that I could be as happy as I am now!"

She is not surprised at my response and just nods her sweet head. "Arghiro', I think you know that some significant changes will undoubtedly come. I also want you to know that we will support any decisions that you will be forced to make." How is this woman so wise? I am rewarded with a jar of fasolada to take home, and I feel better for having visited my mother, more because of how she makes me feel than anything else, and I hope to be a mother like this someday.

When I get back to my cousin Maria's house, I knock on her front door and am welcomed with a big smile and a warm hug. I give her my small offering, and she is so grateful that it embarrasses me. "Cousin Maria, there is not enough coffee on the earth to repay you for saving my husband's life!"

She looks at me earnestly and responds, "We are family, my dear. I am certain your parents would do the same for my son." I believe that they would.

Clorindo has straightened up the room and made the bed. He is fully dressed as if he has somewhere to go, and is sitting in the chair reading when I let myself in with the key. I put the things I brought on the little cabinet near the burner. He takes me in his arms and kisses me as if I have been gone for weeks. "Hai fame?" I ask him.

"Si!" he responds as he inspects the bounty. I take the soup from my mother and pour some of it into the little pot. Clorindo lights the burner and inhales the delicious scent of the fasolada. "Your Mamma is a saint!" I smile in agreement.

"Cousin Maria gave us the bread and cucumber." The kindness and generosity touch him, and I know he is holding back tears. "Let's eat!" I say, and he pulls the tiny table to the bed, where he sits.

The meal of bean soup and bread, accompanied by fresh cucumber, feels like a real feast, and we are so incredibly happy. We have a cup of coffee, which tastes weak but good enough, and I give him the tobacco. You would think the pouch was filled with gold, looking at his joyful face! "You are incredible!" He says this with so much love on his face that I feel he means it.

"I love you!" I say in response. He kisses me, and as I inhale his scent, I am once again convinced that I am where I should be.

This month has been painfully sad for the Greeks. The awful sound of the air raid siren brings chills along with the warnings, and we spend the better part of two days cowering in the corner of the bathroom, praying that our house will not be in the line of the falling bombs. Every hit feels as if it is right outside, and the house shakes more than once. When the bombing starts in Piraeus, Clorindo hears it before me. "Le senti?" he asks. I listen. "Ci mandano le caramelle!" I struggle to translate but soon realize he is making a joke to lighten the mood. "They are sending us candy!" I hug him tightly and pray out loud that we are spared and that my family is safe.

I have not had a period for three months. My mixed emotional feelings are my secret, but my physical changes are bound to be noticed before long, if not by Clorindo, certainly by my mother. "There is something I have to tell you!" I say as Clorindo puts his arm around me in bed. We are not facing each other, which makes it a little easier. I can feel his body tense behind me.

"Dimmi!" he says. *Tell me!*

I hesitate, but respond, "Sono incinta!"

I can feel his body relax, which makes it easier to have this conversation. He turns me to face him and kisses me tenderly, then sits up and rakes his fingers through his hair. "What are we going to do?" I don't understand the question.

"We are going to have a baby!" This is no time for a language barrier.

He smiles and says, "I know what it means to be incita!"

I put my arms around him and say, "This baby is sent from God. Because, no matter what happens, we will always have a part of each other."

His eyes fill with tears. "We have no future to offer this innocent child," he says.

"All we can offer is our perfect love for each other." Even as I say this, I realize how uncertain the future will be, but I also know how much this baby will be loved.

"I am already in love with him!" he whispers.

"Maybe it will be a girl!" I say.

"No, it is a boy...I know it!" We cry tears of joy and fear until we fall asleep.

He has taken to calling me Lula. I don't mind that he changed my name and understand why, and, actually, for the same reason, I find it easier to refer to him as Clory. War has strange effects on time. Our names don't matter, our heritage does not matter, and the fact that any day can be our last also does not matter. We are here, two people from different countries, thrown together because of some horrific event, and yet the love we have for each other has no space and no time. It just is, and I thank God every day.

The summer is sweltering, and my unavoidable extra weight only makes me more uncomfortable. I spend many long days in our tiny room's coolness and sometimes need to force myself to exercise. Tolis brought me a bike, and I ride at least an hour a day. I ride in the more hilly neighborhood streets, where I hardly ever see anyone and can avoid an enemy soldier's possible encounter. If there has been turmoil the day before, I do not venture out. I love the sun, so I offer to help cousin Maria with her small patch of garden. I help her remove the weeds and prepare the ground for any future planting of seeds that we might be able to find and swap. Often, she does not come out and lets me enjoy the chore alone.

Clorindo reads and writes long letters to his family. He has beautiful handwriting, and his emotions are honest and straightforward. "Read the letter to me, please." I often ask him because I know I am usually the main subject of his flowery prose, and it confirms, once again, his love for me.

Today, he teases me by reading, "My wife has gotten

extremely fat!!" Once I realize he is joking, I hit him with the book on the end table. We both laugh, and he reads the right lines he has written. "We are healthy, although food is still scarce. Lula is feeling well, and we are anxiously counting the days until our child's birth. No matter what destiny has in store for us, today, we feel blessed." There are many sweet sentiments about how much he misses everyone and how he looks forward to the day when we can all be together. We both know that this letter, like so many others, may not reach them, but he writes often and sometimes asks me to practice my Italian by writing to my new family.

Every day I practice speaking Italian. I learned the alphabet and, since the language is phonetic, I am doing very well with both reading and writing. Clory is a very calm instructor and patiently repeats words and sounds until I get them right. So, when he asks me to write notes at the bottom of his letters, it seems like a natural thing.

In the second week of September, I gather some belongings and move into my parents' house to await our child's birth. "I can't think of better hands in which to put my care. And, to be honest, I am a little afraid!" I tell Clory, and he agrees wholeheartedly. I am only with my mother for two days, when my brothers ask Papa if they can bring Clorindo to see me. My father doesn't hesitate in giving his approval but questions, "Is it safe to move him and let him walk the streets?"

Tolis explains, "The streets are no longer protected and guarded like before. There is a shift in control, and we are gaining momentum. Winston Churchill has every intention to return the Greek King to power." My father looks doubtful as he turns to me.

"I am certain Clorindo will want to be near for the birth of his child," he says.

Greece has been devastated by occupation and famine for over three years. There is a significant shift as British troops are welcomed, and German troops' evacuation is expected soon. My brothers scramble to get word as to what is likely to happen to the many soldiers hiding all over Athens and in the countryside, but there is confusion and not many clear answers.

Our son makes his noisy entrance into the world on Monday, September 25th, 1944. He is a beautiful, perfect baby boy. As Clory and I have already discussed, we will name him Michele after his paternal grandfather. Clory arrives during the night, as soon as he gets word that the baby is born. He cradles the baby and marvels at the miracle, not only of the birth, but the fact that we are here with a roof over our heads and love in our hearts. He unwraps the baby to count his toes, "Uno, due, tre...." We laugh, and he kisses me before my mother chases him out.

"She needs to rest! The baby has eaten so you can take him with you."

I fall into a warm and exhausted sleep even before the bedroom door closes. I dream of beautiful blue skies with golden sunshine and children, my children, running in the park without a care in the world. I feel tears on my face in my twilight sleep as I realize that my son is not born free.

Although there is not enough food to feed us, my milk flows well, and "Michelino" is fed and happy. I spend as much time outdoors as possible, even if it is just sitting at my mother's front door. He is a happy baby and smiles often, and he melts my heart. Clorindo is moving around more freely, and the overall energy of the city seems to have shifted.

On Thursday, October 12th, Athens is liberated! The Germans lower the Swastika flag on the Acropolis, and the Nazi forces begin vacating the city. After these long years of their occupation, there is joy and celebration. Blue and white Greek flags fly, and bells ring joyously. It is over!

Tolis has spent endless hours in search of information and instructions for Clorindo. Although Greeks are celebrating the city's liberation, Tolis explains, "The Germans are withdrawing north to avoid being cut off by the Red Army of the Soviets. We are not done yet! There will be an uprising in our country!"

We have a six day window between the liberation of Greece and the arrival of British forces. Clorindo, along with other Italian soldiers in Greece, will be taken as a prisoner of war. I am inconsolable as he tries to explain why this will be for the best. "I have to report back to base on November 4th." He is holding me as I collapse.

"Are you in trouble for hiding?" I want to know.

He responds, "No, not at all. And so that my service is not interrupted, I need to follow orders and surrender to British troops."

"Where will they take you? For how long?"

He is not yet sure. "We won't know until we report. There are British camps all over the world."

I can barely speak, "Will I ever see you again? What about our son?"

He paces around the room and tries to gather his thoughts. "Lula, listen, please. I need you to consider our choices calmly." I am sobbing. "You can stay here and, hopefully, someday I will come back. But, you know things are not going to get better in Greece, and they might very well get worse. I want you and the baby to go to my family, where they will take care of you and keep you safe." I have a mental image of a small Italian village with nothing but sheep and goats. But, the seriousness of what he is suggesting keeps me from joking. I look into his eyes and see that he is dead serious.

"How do we get there?" I ask.

# MARIA - Odessa, Russia - 1906

Diocles and I are both exhausted when we return home after work; however, we typically discuss our day as we share our evening meal. Tonight I tell Diocles about the very young woman who gave birth to a healthy baby three days ago. "The mother's condition is slipping, and the doctors predict that she will die by the end of the week."

Diocles asks, "Is her husband at her side?"

I respond sadly, "There is no one at her side. She walked into the hospital alone when she was in labor. She was almost delirious from the pain, and they immediately brought her to the birthing room. She struggled through the delivery, and she needed to be aided for many hours because her body was too weak to do the job."

Diocles is sadly shaking his head. "No mother, no father...no one?"

I also shake my head and repeat, "No one! We do not know her name or anything about her at all.

"And, the baby, is it ill?"

I can see the sweet tiny face before my eyes. "Not at all! She is a beautiful and perfectly healthy girl of good weight and glowing skin. She makes you feel that her mother

346

might have been beautiful before her troubles." The last few days have been bittersweet. Caring for the perfect child is so rewarding because she is doing so well. On the other hand, knowing we are losing the young mother is difficult and heart-wrenching.

"What will happen to the baby if the mother dies?" Diocles is curious.

"There is a baby house connected to the hospital."

Diocles seems relieved that there is a place to care for her. But, I know all too well that the children placed there do not develop because they do not get adequate care, as they are left unattended for hours and barely have human contact. It pains me to think that she will be there.

The young mother is still holding on to her life, although she is in a coma. Nearly two weeks have passed since the baby was born. I spend as much time as possible with the baby, and I hold her almost always. I love the way she feels and the way she smells. They will not move the baby as long as her mother is alive, and I find myself saying extra prayers for the poor woman to hang on.

On Friday, they called me to the Director's office. "Maria, I know you have become quite attached to the baby." We both know to which baby he is referring. "We are removing life support from the mother later today and do not expect her to survive the night." Although expected, it is painful to know what is about to happen.

"I understand," I say simply. And, of course, I do understand. I return to the baby immediately after being excused. I take my time feeding her milk from a bottle, and I rock her to sleep, watching her angel face and feeling her peace. It is difficult to leave the hospital, although the night nurse is already fussing over the sweet child.

I am trying to prepare dinner through tears of anguish, when I hear a soft knock at the door. Assuming that Diocles left his key at home, I wipe my tears as I walk across the room to open the door for him. But, instead of seeing my husband, I see Natasha. "I thought you might be tired," she says, extending the aromatic clay crock of lamb stew and loaf of homemade bread. I look up at her face to thank her from my heart, and she rewards me with her beautiful smile and angelic aura. In that instant, in that split second, I know that God answers prayers in many different ways.

I open the door further and step aside. "Natasha, please come in! I have to speak to you about something so very, very important!"

The process of adoption and the paperwork that accompanies it seems far less complicated than I would have expected when you consider that it is such a tremendous life-altering experience for everyone involved. Natasha and Sidor are thrilled at becoming the parents of this beautiful, healthy child. The baby has no idea how blessed she is to now belong to this perfect family. Diocles and I are to be krestnyye, *godparents*, and we could not be more pleased.

They baptized her Maria and call her Masha. Natasha is in love with her and spends all her waking moments doting on her. There is nothing but absolute joy in their home, and I feel the warmth of my childhood years whenever I am in the presence of these extraordinary people.

"Maria, you have not eaten anything! Do you not like it?" I have eaten Natasha's stroganoff many times before, but today the smell alone is disturbing.

"I'm so sorry, Natasha, I'm not hungry," I respond as she scrambles to remove the plate.

"I will make you some tea with jam!"

The men are in deep conversation, and Masha is sound asleep in the other room. I stand to help clear the table, but I feel dizzy and immediately sit back down. Natasha takes my elbow, helps me up, and leads me to the kitchen. "How far along are you?" she asks. I have to figure out what she means, but it only takes a second. I cover my mouth to avoid screaming out loud, but I dance around the kitchen.

"Yes, Natasha! You are probably right! How could I not know?"

As she makes tea, she asks, "When was your last menstruation?" I have to think because I do not get it regularly and have never kept track. Although it is a common subject with my patients, I never applied it to myself for some reason. I bask in the knowledge that a baby is growing inside me, and the joy is like no other I have ever felt.

I turn to Natasha. "Do you think Diocles will be pleased?" I have a sudden apprehension, and, although I try to shake it, it is at the forefront of my happiness.

Natasha, my dear friend, quickly serves coffee to the men and puts lots of jam in my tea. She hurries us through dessert and practically pushes us out the door. "Good night, we will talk tomorrow," she says.

When we walk into our apartment, Diocles remarks, "There was no offer of a second cup of coffee!" he says, laughing as he takes my hand and guides me towards the bedroom. I hesitate, and he looks at me with concern.

"Let's talk for a moment!" I say. He turns towards the divan, still holding my hand, and we sit next to each other. He leans with his elbows on his knees and turns to look at me.

"Are you not well?" he asks. I guess he was watching me at dinner, after all.

"I take a deep breath and hold it for a second. "I am quite well!" I respond. "I think we are going to have a baby."

The room is filled with utter silence as he absorbs the words, and I fear that he is unhappy with the news. I lean down to look at him, hoping for a response, and see the tear on his cheek. He coughs to clear the emotion and without a sound, takes me in his arms. My world is perfect at this moment, and I lose myself in his love. But, as much as I try to imagine our child, I do not get a vision like the one for Natasha. I do not see myself nursing a baby or rocking one or singing a lullaby.

# LULA - Athens, Greece - 1944

Our good-byes are long and sad, faced with the uncertainty of everything before us. "They promise me that arrangements will be made for transport to Italy for you and Michelino." The thought of leaving Athens is incredibly frightening, and I fear that the baby is too young to travel, although he is as healthy as he can be under the circumstances. There is very little food available, so I feel fortunate that, so far, I have plenty of milk to nurse him. "In Italy, he can drink milk right from our cow and eat vegetables directly from our garden." Clory paints such a beautiful picture of calm and good health that I can almost see the crops and a barn full of gentle animals, like a nativity scene.

They take him at the end of October, just a few weeks before his 27th birthday. The only information he shares is that he will be in a POW camp in Egypt and that there will be orders for me to join him in Italy. "What do you mean... orders?" I use all my strength to keep myself together as I feel my world collapse.

"The Navy will notify you when arrangements are in place for your transport to Italy." They have all the information they need." He gives me an envelope, saying, "In here are written the names of my family, now your family too, in Chianchetelle." I look at the short list: Michele, Attilio, Vittoria, Giovanna.

"Is there a street address?" I ask.

"No need, he says laughing. Everyone knows my father." I am prepared, but frightened, and I tell him so. He smiles, but his eyes are so sad as he leans his face down to kiss the top of Michelino's head. Simultaneously, we both lose our composure and shed a torrent of tears on our innocent son.


I easily fit into my role as a mother because I am in my parents' home, where my blessed Mamma teaches me to handle the day-to-day responsibilities that come with a baby. Of course, the fact that she often takes on the role when the baby needs soothing also keeps me sane. I miss my husband to the core of my being and often find myself falling into a dark place where I have difficulty seeing any brightness, except for my son.

I expect to receive a notice from the Italian Navy with instructions, but the weeks pass, and there is none. There are a million questions in my mind, and, if it were not for the fact that there is a real human baby in my arms, there are times that I wonder if I imagined my time with Clory.

The EAM and freedom fighters want to restore our country so that it is ruled by the people and for the people, but last month the British set about building a new National Guard to disarm ELAS. Last Sunday, there was a demonstration and several processions of Greek republicans, anti-monarchists, socialists, and communists who made their way towards Syntagma Square. Police tried to stop them, but several thousand broke through. There was a cry to "shoot the bastards!" followed by a lethal fusillade from Greek police, which, they say, lasted about a half hour with dozens of casualties. By mid-day, the square was jammed with tens of thousands of people, but they were cleared after several hours by a British paratroopers column. We heard this morning that my brothers were among the men in the square. We have not heard from them in a month. We have no idea where they are since we are locked in our own home! The British have heavy armaments at their disposal and are burning and bombing houses and carving city segments. It is just as frightening to me as when the Germans were here and, in some ways, maybe more so since I am a different person in many ways.

It is Christmas day, and our greatest gift is that my brothers are safe! They arrive in the morning, and they are both exhausted but exhilarated. We spend hours discussing Greece's current conditions and the horrors that they witnessed while I marvel at their bravery. "Have you heard from Clorindo?" Tolis asks me as he takes the baby from my mother.

"Yes, I have received two letters from him since he left!"

Basilis smiles and teases, "Can you share any part of the letters?"

Both letters tucked away, I feel his loving warmth in his words and am protective of his written thoughts. I read them repeatedly, and I have them memorized, "He is safe and lonely." I tell them. They respond by nodding their heads, relieved.

"Do you know where he is?" Tolis asks. Now I need

to retrieve the letter so I can show my brother the return address. "The middle of nowhere!" my brother says when he looks at the return address "Tel El Kebir, Egypt." I have no idea where this is, but I know it is far from here and probably also from Italy. They do not ask to read the letter, and I appreciate their respect for my privacy.

"At the bottom of his letters is stamped 'censored,'" I tell them.

"Have you written to him?"

I want to cry. "I write to him every day, but I could only mail two letters, and I have no way of knowing if they reach him.

"Did you mention the turmoil in Greece?"

I make a face at my brother, "Do you think I'm stupid? They read everything! I only talk about the baby and how much I miss him." They look relieved.

The boys are only home for the day, and we understand, based on their stories, that Greece is in the middle of civil war, and they may have to hide.

Although months pass with no word about transport to Italy, finally, a letter is addressed to me that is not from Clorindo. I am not surprised to read the return address, "Ministero Della Difesa Marina, Republica Italiana." I am momentarily frozen on the spot just as I hear the baby give out a loud, hungry cry. I calmly fold up the letter, put it in my sweater pocket, and pick up my son to nurse him.

# JOAN - Weehawken, New Jersey - 1969

I awaken to the sound of my family's voices in the kitchen, but I recall my entire vivid dream in the moments between sleep and wakefulness. I am an old woman with gray strands through my hair. My lined face shows my years, but it is mostly the look of my hands that shows my advanced age. The swollen knuckles and tops of my hands are wrinkled. My nails are short but manicured and polished a pleasant shade of pink. I am wearing a wedding band, but no engagement ring. My hands are resting on my lap, my eyes are closed, and I lean back in a big green chair, listening to music that makes me happy. I somehow sense that the room is not empty, although it is incredibly quiet, except for the soft music. I want to see my old woman's eyes, but they remain closed throughout the dream. Although I do not move, I can see a small smile on my dream face and feel the explosion of joy and gratitude that fills my dream heart.

I sit up in bed and recall the dream before standing and bringing myself back to the present. How strange!! I cannot interpret it in any way. Is it a prediction of some future event that makes no sense right now? Or just a reflection of total and extreme happiness on this day when I will vow undying devotion to Sheldon, my best friend, and the love of my life?

Today, August 2, is my wedding day! I rush out since I have to take the bus into New York City and make my way uptown to Henri Bendel for my nine o'clock hair appointment! Happy because the weather looks good so far, I barely fuss, put on a sundress and sandals, and don't bother with makeup.

I cheerfully step out the front door and see Sheldon's car parked right in front of my house. It seems strange that it is here instead of two blocks over on Oak Street where his apartment is, but I know there is a parking problem. However, I also know that against my better judgment, the guys had Sheldon's bachelor party last night. When I get closer to the car, I notice, with horror, that it is sitting on three rims and four mangled tires. I am beside myself! We need this car to drive to The Motel On The Mountain tonight after our reception! Is he kidding me??? My mood has soured, and the sky starts to get cloudy as I stomp back up the stairs. The phone rings eight times before he finally picks up with a groggy "hello." I have no friendly greeting to offer.

"GET THE CAR FIXED!"

His response, "Who's this?"

The pampering at the beauty salon relaxes me, and I am in a much better mood when I get home and see that the car is gone. I have time to eat a sandwich of leftover meatballs my mother made yesterday, and I lie down before the girls show up. The house is miraculously empty and quiet, so I enjoy the last few hours at home before moving out and starting my new life as a married woman.

# MARIA - Odessa, Russia - 1906

Diocles is almost finished with his work here, so we prepare for our voyage back to Athens. It is relatively easy to get our physical belongings in order, but I feel sad at the thought of leaving Natasha, Sidor, and Masha. They have become my family, and I will miss them intensely. I am always weepy and do not help the situation. "Maria, I will also miss our friends, but there will often be times like this in doing my work." I know he is right.

"Let's go to the steps!" I jump up from the table where we have been having our Sunday mid-day meal. He puts down the newspaper and laughs."

Are you sure you want to walk that far in your condition?"

I know I want to be outside! "We can turn around if I get tired," I suggest.

We walk in the warm sunshine at a leisurely pace, holding hands and enjoying the soft breeze. Diocles looks pensive as he says, "Someday, when we return, we will go to the ballet!" I laugh.

"I don't think I own the proper attire," I tell him.

"You would be the prettiest woman there, no matter

your clothing." I look up at him laughing, although I want so much to kiss him, and I would if only the street was not so crowded with families and couples strolling. He smiles back and says, "I wish you could see you through my eyes."

We eventually reach the steps, and he hesitantly asks, "Do you want to walk down?" Even though I genuinely want to, I respond, "I have a little discomfort in my lower back today, so I probably shouldn't." Diocles seems relieved by my decision and looks around for an empty bench. "There!" he points, "let's sit!" I hesitate, but realize that I feel the need to rest, although the beautiful steps are calling me! Who knows if I will ever see them again?

We spend the afternoon outside and come back home just as the sun is setting. We are tired and hungry, so I go about preparing something light to eat as Diocles finishes his evening prayers. Just as he enters the room and I am stirring the stew, the first sharp pain strikes. I drop the spoon, and gravy splatters on the stove as I double over in pain. Diocles is at my side in a second, but there is nothing he can do to help me. He is confused and looking for me to tell him what to do. I know that there is nothing he can do to stop this or change its direction. I know for sure that we are losing our baby.

Diocles is very attentive and loses some precious work time to stay home to care for me. Natasha tells him, "Diocles, you know I am here for her." He is worried because I was bleeding for two days after the miscarriage. I insisted on leaving the hospital after three days because I felt better physically. I would rather be in my own home to deal with my many emotions. I'm sad and feel somewhat guilty. Should I have gone to a doctor when I first felt pain in my back? Should I have rested more? What did I do wrong?

Diocles insists, "Maria, the doctors say you could not have avoided this outcome!" I cry. "And you are perfectly healthy, so there is no reason that you cannot have as many children as you want." He holds me tenderly and lets me cry until I fall asleep.

Although we had to delay our trip, today, we are halfway to Athens on a ship that looks very similar to the one that brought us to Odessa six months ago. This journey, however, is quite different, since Diocles and I have changed in many ways. We do not feel the same sexual tension that drew us back to our cabin only a few months ago, and although I have a spark of delicious memory, it does nothing to take away my sadness.

"Maria, are you asleep?" he asks softly in my ear.

"No, Diocles, I am not," I respond as I wipe the tears with the back of my hand. We are spooned together in the tiny bunk and, although it is very late, neither of us can sleep.

"We will have another baby, I promise you," he says so sincerely that I believe him.

"I feel that I have let you down!" Now I cry openly, and the damn is open. He hugs me tightly until I am all cried out.

"Why do you say that?" he asks earnestly. "We have no control over what God chooses for us. It is all predestined!" His words have a calming effect on my spirit, and I turn my sadness into hope. I am determined that, in God's grace, I will bear a healthy child for this man that I love so much. I will talk to my child, just as I told Natasha to speak to her future baby! I can see him, my son. I can see him! Tomorrow, I will write him a letter and tell him about his parents and how much we already love him. I feel liberated and hopeful as I turn to my husband with a renewed passion.

Athens' port is a beautiful sight, and I feel that I am home, probably more than I have ever felt before. Diocles holds me close as we stand on the deck. "I love you," he whispers. I look directly into his eyes and know the words are coming from his heart.

"I also love you." I realize I have to wait to be sure, but I already know, with my entire being, that his son is in my womb. And as I thank Jesus for our miracle, I know that I will call him Christos.

# LULA - Athens, Greece/ Chianchetelle, Italy - 1945

I t is hot for the beginning of August, and today I have to say good-bye to my mother, father, and sisters, and I fear that I will never see them again. Conditions in Greece are worse than ever. My family encourages me to take the opportunity that will bring my son and me to a possibly better place and, hopefully, a safer future. My parents' attachment to Michelino is inevitable since they have been with him since the day he came into this world and because he is the sweetest child. So, today we hold each other, and we cry, and Michelino, undoubtedly confused, cries too, as I pry his arms from my mother's neck.

I have packed our meager belongings in a large duffle bag that Tolis got for just this purpose. I have some clothes for both Michelino and me, and my brothers have brought me cheese and dried sausage, which my mother wrapped carefully and added to the bag. We have an assigned date and time to report to an address in Piraeus, and my brothers arrange to take us. I struggle with the baby, and my brother carries my bag, which will be my responsibility once we reach our destination.

We arrive at a building which is not far from where Clory's unit was, although his barracks are now empty. My good-bye to my brothers is one of the most painful things I have ever had to do, and I crumble in Tolis' arms. "After this mess is over, you will come back with your family." He can barely finish the sentence because he chokes with emotion. When Michelino starts to cry, I pick him up and put the bag's strap on my shoulder. We are going to be okay, I tell myself.

I hug my son tightly and promise him, "We are going to be fine!"

I check in at a desk right inside the main door and a young Italian sailor, who is cordial but not very friendly, asks my name. He checks a long list and asks me to move to the side to wait until someone comes to us. I wait for a painfully long time, and, eventually, I sit on my suitcase so I can cuddle Michelino, whose eyes are already closing.

More than an hour passes before another sailor retrieves us and leads us to a large room with instructions to find a spot at one of the many beds around the perimeter. Each cot has a small table next to it, and each table has a basin and a pitcher of water. The linen is clean, although the bed is small. I drop my suitcase on the floor and put Michelino down carefully. He continues to sleep soundly, and I take the time to remove the food from the bag, organize the clothes, and push it all under the bed. I place the wrapped food on the end table and sit next to the baby. I look around the room and see that the cots are filling up, and before long, there are dozens of women. A few have children, but most are alone. I have never felt so lonely and afraid in my entire life. I promised myself that I would not cry, so I close my eyes and pretend that I am with Effie having a cigarette in the park.

Most of the other women are near my age, and most are congenial since we are all confined and have a similar story and a strong desire to move on with our lives. The conversations are full of joy, sadness, hope, and fear. Michelino is everyone's favorite, and the ladies fight over playing with him, so he is mostly occupied and happy.

I use some of my free time to write letters to Clory, although they will probably never reach him. There is a fenced-in area behind the building and, although it is sometimes sweltering, we are outside for a good part of the day. The food they give us is tasteless, and it is limited. I try to provide Michelino with the more significant piece of the meat we get, but he doesn't like the taste of most of the things they offer, so he eats very little and looks relatively thin.

We've had no news about our departure for over a week, but today we are told that we sail on Friday. There is nothing to prepare, so we just count the days and hours until they tell us we are to board the small transport ship, SS Lavia, that will take us to Italy. The vessel's prior use was to carry troops to and from Italy, but today it brings 558 women and 16 children, including Michelino, who is the youngest. The women, almost exclusively war brides, come from all over Greece. They pour into the ship and look for their spots. Because I have a baby, someone suggests that I take a little private corner, and I am grateful to have it.

For the most part, it is just a matter of claiming a bed by dropping your belongings on it. The cots are less than a meter apart. I try to get my bearings, especially to a water supply, since I have to wash dirty diapers. A few of the girls help me find what I need, and, before long, we have created a clothesline where the diapers can dry.

We have barely pulled out of the port of Piraeus when I already begin to feel nauseated. The first day of the journey to Italy is full of many failed attempts to eat, walking around or taking care of my child. I can only lay on my cot and fight constant nausea. "Thank you!" I say to Caterina as she takes Michelino and feeds him dinner, which he spits out. Caterina and I have been together through this whole process, and we established early on that our husbands are in the same prisoner of war camp in Egypt.

"Apla koimaste," *Just sleep*, she whispers. I am so grateful to her for being my savior. I feel somewhat better the second day so that I can take care of my son.

We arrive at Bari's port in Puglia, Italy late at night on the third day. "I can't wait to get off this boat!" I tell Caterina.

She rolls her eyes. "I have so many more miles to go! But, at least this part is over!" She shows me her destination on the map, while Michelino tries to grab it. He has been such a good boy, except that he barely eats anything. He is skinny and pallid, and I know that I don't look much better. Caterina teases him with the map as he laughs and tries to take it from her. His laugh brightens the mood, and soon we are all discussing our hopes for the future.

"Do you think our husbands' families will welcome us into their homes?" one of the girls asks. Oddly, I never thought that they would not! But, now, I wonder if this is something I should worry over? Tonight, we will sleep on the docked ship and be assigned our transport tomorrow, depending on our final destination.

A crew member inspects our papers and, holding my note from Clory, says, "We don't go here." I ask him to repeat what he said. "We don't go to this town. Have you made arrangements for someone to pick you up in Caserta?" All the exhaustion and fear that I have been suppressing rises to my throat.

"NO!" I have no way of reaching them. All I have are names. Clory said, "Show this to anyone on the street, and they will take you to my father's house." So simple. "How far is Caserta from Chianchetelle?"

The young sailor responds honestly, "I have no idea where Chianchetelle is!" I know I promised myself I would not cry, so I don't, but I feel as if I am about to faint.

I sit on the bed, and Michelino climbs up on my lap, knowing that things are not right. "What will I do?" I ask no one in particular. Caterina steps up and takes my paper with the names and walks up to the young sailor checking another woman's documents. She gets his attention and taps her fingers on the list.

"She has to get to her family!" she asserts herself. He has no answer and just shrugs his shoulders. "Please, ask your captain if he can help us! This woman and her child must get to this town," she points to the name, "and to these people! You cannot abandon her in a strange place in a country foreign to her!" She hands the paper back to him and says, "What if she were your sister?" The sailor takes the form, clips it to his board, and responds, "I will speak to the captain" as he walks away.

I take Caterina's hand and kiss it. "Thank you, my friend."

There is no sleep tonight. Michelino vomited in the evening, and I am giving him water continuously, but he doesn't drink as much as I would like. When I touch his forehead with my lips, I feel that his body temperature is higher, although he is not burning up. I soak a towel in cold water and place it on his head and cuddle him. I put a little sugar in his water, and he drinks since it is tasty. My mother put sugar in a small pouch with the things my brother gave me. How is she so perceptive? Michelino is finally sleeping comfortably in my arms, but I still cannot summon sleep. Instead, I pray, "Dear God, thank you for my son. There are not enough ways to tell you how much I love him. If you are testing me with everything else, I will take the challenge and only ask that you keep him safe and stand by me while I do the rest!" Am I crying? I am not supposed to do that!

Morning finally arrives, and although he is very pale, Michelino seems a little better, and his head has cooled down. He eats a piece of stale bread and the end of the cheese that I have been carrying, and I give him some more sugar water. "Thank you, Lord," I whisper.

There is a line of vehicles meeting the ship: Carriages, carts, pullmans, and cars. There is some confusion as the women try to establish where they need to go. But, many women immediately unite with their new families, and the receptions vary from calm and reserved to loud, warm, and loving. Caterina and I say good-bye, with some emotion. "I promise to write and hope that someday we'll see each other again," she says. She hugs and kisses Michelino, and we both cry because the future is so uncertain.

My son and I, and the note with DiGiovanni written across it in my hand, walk towards the pullman that says Caserta. The bus's front looks like a big truck, like the Germans used when they entered Greece. There are two large wheels in the front and two smaller wheels on each side in the back. The bus is light gray, and there is an Italian flag painted on the side, although it looks like it is over whatever was there originally, and I can't read what that might be. There are seven windows on each side, and some of them look like they open. "Nome?" someone asks as I approach.

I tell him, "Lula DiGiovanni." They look at a list, find my name, check it off, and ask me to board. I look for a seat at a window that opens, and I am happy to find one on the left side. I sit Michelino in the center while I stow my satchel underneath. Once done, I take him in my arms and sit with him on my lap. He is still tired from our early wake up and not yet feeling well, so he cuddles up and falls asleep, while many of the women, and some young children, are still settling into their seats. It doesn't take long for me to fall asleep with the rocking motion of the bus.

The heat of the bus's interior and the heat of the baby on my chest keeps me asleep for a long time, and I eventually wake up sweating. I look at my watch and see that we have been traveling for three hours, although I have no idea exactly how long it will take to get to Caserta, and I also have no idea what I will do when I get there.

Michelino and I drank from the fountain before we got on the bus, and I also filled a bottle that I have in the bag. Michelino is still sleeping, but he is stirring. His stomach seems better, and he has not been sick since the middle of the night. Miraculously, no one has taken the seat next to me, so when Michelino wakes up, he sits and plays without bothering anyone. I brought some picture books that Basilis gave him, so he entertains himself.

I can't help but marvel at the beauty on these roads. My recent past was in stale rooms and destroyed buildings, polluted by ashes of bones. Although hot, the air is clean, and the sky is perfectly blue. I breathe deeply to cleanse my lungs. No matter what happens, I am grateful that I am here with my son. The ride is so long that, at dusk, the driver tells us that we have to stop so he can sleep. We all get out of the bus to stretch, and I find a bench to change Michelino's diaper. Although he is so good about going to the bathroom, come un ometto, *like a little man*, I put a diaper on him for the bus ride. I see that the diaper is very wet when I remove it, and I am so glad that he is not too dehydrated. I have no place to wash it, so I throw it out and only put another diaper on him when we return to the bus.

The driver offers a bag full of bread and a smaller bag with pieces of cheese and some dried meat slices that I don't recognize. The women, especially the ones with children, practically knock each other over to get some. I am towards the front of the line and have no problem using my shoulders to block anyone who will not wait for their turn. I take a small amount of everything and hope that Michelino will eat, and I am glad that he takes a nibble of cheese and a piece of bread.

We arrive in Caserta just as the sun is coming up. Michelino seems exhausted, and I feel the same. Caserta is a pretty town, as far as I can see driving through it. We pass a castle that is so beautiful that I feel like a princess just looking at it. The driver says this is the Reggio di Caserta, *The Royal Palace*. I point it out to Michelino, and I see his eyes get wide as he takes in the spectacle. "Someday, we will go see it!" I promise him, and I would like to believe that we will.

When we get off the bus, I look around for some instructions, and when I turn back towards the bus, I see that the driver has disappeared. There are many carriages and carts and one car picking up women and children, but I would have no way of knowing whom to ask. We stand for a long time, holding our suitcase filled with our meager worldly belongings, but no one approaches us. There is hardly anyone left, and most of the carriages are gone. I see a man and go to him, holding my paper. "Lo sai chi e'?" *Do you know who this is?* I ask him.

He looks at the paper with the name Michele DiGiovanni written in Clory's large script and lifts his shoulders as he says, "Non lo conosco, ma, aspetta!" He takes the paper and walks to every person waiting to pick up. I can see him showing it to them, and see everyone saying, "no" in one way or another.

I place the suitcase on the ground against a pole and

sit on it with Michelino on my lap, and I talk to God. "Are You still testing me? Because I don't know what to do, I will sit here and wait for a sign from you." My eyes are briefly closed for my prayer, but open when I hear the sound of horses and a carriage as it pulls up to the curb. I jump up to look into two men's faces, one younger and one older, but both bearing a strong resemblance to Clorindo. They hop off the carriage and run to us with open arms, saying, "Lula!" I take a second to thank God before I gratefully let them take charge of our lives.

The ride is long, although the horses are moving at a steady trot. But my father-in-law and brother-in-law are so warm and entertaining that the time does not matter. Their Italian is different from Clory's, and I often need to ask them to repeat what they said. They laugh, "Si, parliamo dialetto molte volte, scusa." Attilio explains that they sometimes slip into dialect and that, yes, it is different. They tell me to sit in the carriage's front seat, and my father-in-law, who already told me to call him Papa, sits in the back with Michelino.

"Grazie per l'onore del nome." He says this warmly, and I am sure that he is emotional for a few reasons. He misses his son, and it pleases him that he respected him enough that his first grandchild carries his name, in the Italian tradition. Michelino looks frail and weak as he sits on Papanonno's lap. But, it seems as if he has known him since the day he was born, and, as I see, the connection is already there. I remind myself that this family has had to adjust their thinking to accept me into their lives. They know practically nothing about me! But hopefully, they understand that only deep love would make a person give up their family and their country. They do not, for one instant, make me feel that I don't belong. Maybe some good things come out of dreadful wars, after all.

The sun is suspended in the sky as if it is hesitating before it sets when we ride into the little hamlet that is Chianchetelle. The quaintness, peaceful quiet and unpretentious people, are evident in the small streets and the friendly greetings from neighbors as we move past their humble homes. "Piu' capre e pecore delle persone," I can hear Clory say, and I think I am beginning to understand that he was not exaggerating when he said there are more goats and sheep than people here, although I have not yet seen any.

The carriage pulls up to a large house, and because I have a specific vision in my mind of what the house will look like, I hesitate. Attilio runs around to my side and extends a hand to me and takes Michelino in his other arm. The large front door opens, and I see a group of young people near my age looking out as Clory's mother greets me. She takes me into a warm embrace and says, "Benvenuta, mia cara!" *Welcome, my dear.*

They are all here, and I can name each one from Clory's descriptions. Much entertained, they laugh as we all talk at once.

"Sei stanca?" *Are you tired?* my mother-in-law asks.

"Si, sono molto stanca!" *Yes, I am exhausted!* I respond honestly. But, we both understand that my weariness is far more profound than just from my travels.

"Vieni." She takes my hand and leads me up a beautiful staircase to the upper floor and the bedrooms. I did not notice until now that she is carrying my suitcase. She takes me to a bedroom that is detached from the others and says, "Questa e la tua stanza!" It is beautiful, and I feel blessed.

There is a large bed on one side and a small bed in the corner, with large dressers, lamps, and chairs filling the rest of the space. To me, it looks like a room that I would imagine in that beautiful castle we passed this morning. The only thing missing is my loving husband, but the time will pass, and I pray for his safe return soon. "Grazie, Mamma!" I say from my heart.

"Prima che dormi, devi mangiare!" *Before you sleep, you must eat!* I have a feeling she has expressed this once or twice before!

We return to the kitchen, where everyone is fussing over Michelino. I look at my baby and realize how thin and pale he has gotten, and I pray that I have done the right thing by bringing him here. "Ma, questo non mangia niente!" *This one doesn't eat anything!* Attilio says as the baby spits out a morsel of food. My mother-in-law and Vittoria quickly spring into action.

"Fammi fare!" Vittoria offers as she cuts small pieces of bread and some fresh strawberries into a bowl and pours milk over it until the bread floats. As I watch her, I remember Clory's words, "He will drink milk from our cow and eat vegetables from our garden." She takes a large spoonful of sugar and sprinkles it over the soaked bread. Michelino is delighted at the first bite and proceeds to finish the entire bowl. Bless her! He looks better already!

The table has a white tablecloth and platters of delicious-looking food covering it. There are plates of cheese and dried meats and the most beautiful tomato salad I have ever seen, with onions and fresh basil mixed right into it. The whole scene looks like a painting and is almost magical to my mentally fatigued mind. "Mangia, Lula!" Mamma says, "Sei troppo magra!" *You are too thin!*

I know I ate, but my exhaustion is so profound that dinner is a blur. I am barely conscious as I put my already sleeping baby into the soft, crisp sheets of his new bed, and I kiss his freshly washed hair. I am in my bed and sound asleep before I can even formulate a single thought.

I awaken to the sound of a rooster crowing, and as my eyes slowly open, I realize that last night, I slept more soundly than I have in years. I glance at Michelino to see if the rooster woke him too, but he is still sound asleep and drooling on his pillow. I quietly go to the window and carefully open the shutter, hoping to catch a glimpse of the rooster, but the most breathtaking view instead rewards me! There are grape plants, each on a stake, and in perfect rows as far as I can see. There is a morning mist hovering just above the hills, and the sky is golden with the early sunrise. The magnificent beauty of my new home and my new family's warmth are more than I could have ever dreamed, and I am overwhelmed with gratitude. Through happy tears, I visualize Clory's smiling face, and I understand that he was the road to my destiny. I am where I need to be.

When Clorindo comes home in the Spring, he does not speak often of his time in the prisoner of war camp. When

I press him, he tells me that it could have been worse and he would rather not discuss it.

In June, when we move to our apartment in Naples, Michelino clings to Mammanonna and is inconsolable. I try to explain that we are less than 100 kilometers away and we will visit often, but he is a smart boy and understands that things are changing drastically. He has no idea how much they are about to change! Today I will tell Clory that I did not menstruate this month. I am overjoyed at the thought of a baby sister for Michelino. I am certain it will be a girl!

# JOAN - Westport, Connecticut/ New Haven, Connecticut - 2011

Incredibly, my days are bearable, probably because I am hardly ever alone. The girls take me to the hospital and bring me home, but I opt to sleep in the pull-out chair most of the time. Even though they tell me he will not be waking up, I know his heart is still beating, and I will be at his side until his very last breath, assisted or not. "Did you sleep here again last night?" Jen looks at me sympathetically. I know the question is hypothetical, and they all know I hardly ever leave. It is emotionally more manageable for me to go home every few days to shower than to sleep alone. How will I ever get used to it?

I put on my shoes and give Sheldon his morning kisses. I kiss his cheek, close to his ear because of the mask, and then his head and his hand. And then I give in to my morning cry. I appreciate that the nurses give me privacy when I need it, and I lose all sense of time as I drown in my excruciating pain. I am eventually aware that I should not sit here all day, so I take my sweater and walk to the elevator and down to the lobby. I feel sluggish as if I'm underwater, but I crave coffee. The two-block walk to Dunkin' Donuts exhausts me, but the extra large coffee, light with cream, makes a slight difference in my mood. When I get back to room 220, I check my emails and flag those from friends who are checking in. I skim through the remainder and delete, delete, delete. I forward the flagged ones to Cassie, so she can send an update on her dad's condition to those few who don't yet know the current status. There are texts from my brothers and sisters and the girls. I respond, "I'm okay" to my siblings and a few "okays" to the girls. I don't fully register what they are instructing me to do because there are too many words. Time has a very different meaning, and if it weren't for my daughters and grandkids, I would curl up in a ball on the floor.

There is a stream of visitors all day, and I smile, chat, and cry, depending on who is with me. The girls come up together, and before long, Rachel and I are comforting each other. "I'm okay, baby. I'm not sure why God is choosing to take him now." Mica and Cassie will not buy into it.

"They are still administering high doses of steroids, Mom." Cassie says.

"Maybe it will reverse..." Mica says hesitantly.

Because we four are alone, our emotions are open and raw. We are way beyond trying to console each other. "Girls, at some point, we have to let him go. If he can hear us, he has to know that we release him. He may not be able to stay, but we know him. He will do anything we ask. We have to let him go; please say you understand." Our joint pain has removed all the air from the small room where we each find ourselves blanketed in our agony.

"You don't have to finish it, but please eat some, Mom!" I promise them that I will have the salad, encouraging them to leave to get home before the kids' bedtime. When they leave, I close the door, putting the salad in the trash without even opening the container. Instead, I unwrap the buttered roll that somebody ordered but didn't eat and tear it into small pieces and slowly eat it.

I watch an episode of Modern Family, but instead of making me laugh as it usually does, it depresses me. I turn off the TV and turn up the volume on the iPod next to Sheldon's head. I have been sitting for two hours on the chair next to the bed holding his hand. The love songs soon depress me, so I shut off the music, put my head on the back of the uncomfortable straight chair, close my eyes, and talk to God. "WHY?" I cry. "You know he has not finished living this life!" The tears sting my eyes. "We have so much more to do, and we have to watch the babies grow !" I stop, half expecting the voice of God to respond!

I physically feel my heart explode as I lean forward to kiss him, and I place both my hands on his forearm, just below the hospital gown's sleeve. I close my eyes and, knowingly and intentionally, pass all my emotional energy to him. I can't explain it, but it is physical! At the peak of my misery and torrential tears, I feel an electric current transfer from my body to his. It doesn't last more than seconds, but it is strong enough for me to believe that it would wake him. Of course, it doesn't wake him, and I collapse, wholly spent and heartbroken.

I am alone Sunday, exactly 48 hours after my last emotional breakdown, when Dr. Takyar comes into

Sheldon's room with a grin on his face that stretches from ear to ear. I never realized how handsome he is since it might be the first time I have seen him smile. "His lungs are reversing!" he beams. "I don't know how or why, but he is going to make it!" I crumple into the chair, and I know that our family's energy and extended family's love, prayers, and positivity are going to keep him here.

I joyfully make the call. "Cas, listen..." The girls are with me within the hour, and we are in a whole other place today since it will now be just a waiting game until they take him out of the coma. His lungs soften a little more every day, and we celebrate in the knowledge that the universe has chosen to let us keep him.

I sit in the big green chair and bask in the happiness of observing my healing husband. I push back my neglected hair, which is turning gray, and remind myself to make an appointment with Raymond. Since the girls insisted, I got a manicure this week so, although they are a little shorter than usual, they are a pretty shade of pink. I notice that the wrinkles on my hands are deepening, and my knuckles look swollen with arthritis. I had to stop wearing my engagement ring, but as soon as things settle, I will have it sized to put it back on my finger, where it belongs.

The lights are dim, and the doo-wops are soothing. I close my eyes, and as I lose myself to the music of our youth, my heart is filled with boundless gratitude as I look forward to going home with my husband.

## The End

# Epilogue

The most important lesson we learned eight years ago in 2011, is that we need each other, emotionally and physically, and that the strength of the earth's positive vibration comes from our combined energies. We proved that with our faith in God and each other and in family.

During his months of recovery and rehabilitation, Sheldon told us detailed stories of things he did while in his coma. He doesn't remember being asleep, but clearly remembers where he has been.

"We danced in Paris, do you remember?" ..."The temperature of the earth was cooled by one degree!" He proudly recounts how he was instrumental in "the temperature of the earth cooling by one degree!" and how he worked directly with gorillas. "Remember the Indian Trading Post? The stacks of woolen blankets were high, and they were so hot! But we sat on them because we had no options, and the girls were late in meeting us!" No one had the heart to tell him he was dreaming.

"My favorite day," he told me with a smile, "was the one I spent with AJ at Brighton Beach." Just then our five-year old grandson climbed on the bed and said, "Poppy, I remember. That was fun!"

That's when I had an epiphany! I recalled that the prior week, while his grandfather was asleep, AJ told me, "Nana, last night I had a dream that Pop and I were running in the sand." Every time I think about that moment, I visualize God's giant footsteps next to AJ's tiny ones.

My husband and I have been fortunate to satisfy our love of food and travel. We have visited some of the world's most wondrous places: London, Rome, Paris, Venice, Athens, Madrid, and the list goes on. We've seen the Taj Mahal both at sunrise and sunset. We've climbed pyramids, ridden camels, and slept in a tent in the desert under the blanket of a million stars. We've driven the Amalfi coast, prayed to our Lady of Fatima, knelt at the spot where Jesus was born, and cried at the Western Wall.

Every minute with Sheldon has been a blessing. But perhaps an even bigger blessing was the loving way my parents modeled to me and my four siblings what love and family looks like. Growing up, life in our home was loving and harmonious, and my parents never fought. They held hands, sang together, cooked together, and my father peeled oranges for my mother and rubbed her feet.

We were raised good people with great love and bond of family. In turn, our children grew up with the same respect and values we were taught, and we five siblings are still ridiculously close.

When we take our Christmas Eve family photo, we fill up every step of a massive staircase from top to bottom. And as our family continues to grow, we continue to love and care for one another the way Clorindo and Lula, and Diocles and Maria did, and I believe, still do.